EVERYMAN,
I WILL GO WITH THEE,
AND BE THY GUIDE,
IN THY MOST NEED
TO GO BY THY SIDE

EDITH
WHARTON

ETHAN FROME
SUMMER
BUNNER SISTERS

WITH AN INTRODUCTION
BY HERMIONE LEE

EVERYMAN'S LIBRARY
Alfred A. Knopf NewYork London Toronto

312

THIS IS A BORZOI BOOK
PUBLISHED BY ALFRED A. KNOPF

First included in Everyman's Library, 2008
Introduction Copyright © 2008 by Hermione Lee
Bibliography and Chronology Copyright © 2008
by Everyman's Library
Typography by Peter B. Willberg

US website: www.randomhouse.com/everymans

ISBN: 978-0-307-26825-9(US)
978-1-85159-312-8 (UK)

A CIP catalogue reference for this book is available from the
British Library

Book design by Barbara de Wilde and Carol Devine Carson

Typeset in the UK by AccComputing, North Barrow, Somerset

Printed and bound in Germany by GGP Media GmbH, Pössneck

E D I T H   W H A R T O N

———

CONTENTS

———

INTRODUCTION

'Bunner Sisters' is the name of a shop, and it is the only thing written by Edith Wharton to have such a title. It is not what you expect if you associate her mainly with class, wealth, and snobbery. But the underside of society interests her, too, more than she has been given credit for. Because she made her name as an analyst of rich, leisured Americans in Old New York, Wharton's strong strand of compassionate realism has tended to be undervalued. She is no Dreiser or Zola, but her writing life overlaps with theirs, and she is well aware of the economic and social inequities which underly the world she specializes in. She gives more thought than many of her fictional characters do to the lives of people who have to get up and go to work and struggle to make a living. In an early story called 'A Cup of Cold Water', a grim tale of urban struggle and despair, the central character looks out in the morning at the city going about its business: 'That obscure renewal of humble duties was more moving than the spectacle of an army with banners.' And he quotes one of Wharton's favourite lines from *Hamlet*, 'For every man hath business and desire.' It is like Dorothea's knowledge, in George Eliot's *Middlemarch*, that she must rouse herself, after a night of personal anguish, to an involvement in 'the involuntary, palpitating' life of humanity. Wharton admired, and emulated, George Eliot's seriousness and responsibility. She said in a letter of 1905 that she did not want *The House of Mirth* to be a superficial study of trivial people. On the contrary, she wanted to bring out the 'tragic implication' of a society with no 'inherited obligations', by concentrating on 'what its frivolity destroys'.

The unemployed, the hard-up, the pauperized and the shabby-genteel, servants and workers, press in at the corners of her fictions. She makes you wonder what it would be like to see events from their point of view – as in 'The Lady's Maid's Bell' or 'After Holbein', where the servants have their say. How would Undine Spragg's story read, in *The Custom of the Country*, from the point of view of Mrs Heeny, the masseuse and manicurist who collects society clippings, part subservient social parasite, part malevolent gossip? What would Lily Bart's story be like as told by Mrs Haffen, the charwoman she is so curt with, and who comes back to blackmail her, whose desperation and resentment burn off the page on which she appears? Lily Bart, slipping down the cold social surface she has tried to grip on to, reduced in the end to an incompetent milliner's assistant and a supplicant to the working-girl Nettie Struther, shows us the underside of the social fabric, the place the despised Mrs Haffen comes from. Only very rarely does Wharton shift the vantage point altogether to that underside (other examples are 'Mrs Mansey's View', 'Friends', 'A Cup of Cold Water' and 'Bewitched'). But when she does, she gives the lie to critics who accuse her of not understanding the 'real' America.

Bunner Sisters is the earliest, and by far the least well-known of her three superb novellas of poverty and deprivation, and it deserves to be as famous as *Ethan Frome* or *Summer*. Wharton's editors at Scribner's, Edward Burlingame and Charles Scribner, were nervous of its unflinching grimness. Wharton tried to get Burlingame to run it in *Scribner's Magazine* in 1892 and again in 1893. It was early in her publishing career, when her confidence in her own work was not yet high – but she knew it was good. 'Though I am not a good judge of what I write,' she told him, 'it seems to me, after several careful readings, up to the average of my writings.' But *Bunner Sisters* would not be published until 1916 (the year that she was writing *Summer*), and Scribner did not want to publish it on its own because (he told her in July 1916) it was 'just a little small for the best results in separate form'. So this realist masterpiece of thwarted lives was included in her war-time volume of stories, *Xingu*, and never had the impact it would have had if published separately.

Bunner Sisters is a poignant and cruel story of two sisters who, at the start of the novella, are making ends meet with a bit of sewing and a shabby-genteel basement shop that sells hat-trimmings, artificial flowers and other knick-knacks, in a run-down side-street in New York. They are a fretful pair, the older one, Ann Eliza, self-martyring and anxious, the younger,

Evelina, spoilt and dissatisfied. Into these dismal lives comes a seedy German clock-mender, Mr Ramy, who makes up to them both. When Ann Eliza, who has always indulged her younger sister, begins to fall for Mr Ramy, the narrator tells us: 'She had at last recognized her right to set up some lost opportunities of her own.' But *Bunner Sisters* only allows a brief vision of hopes and possibilities before it settles, implacably, for renunciation, loneliness, and disappointment. Evelina, obtusely and permanently unaware of her sister's feelings, marries Mr Ramy and is taken away to a fate which turns out, on her eventual return, to be as bad as any of Ann Eliza's worst imaginings. A sympathetic upper-class lady, who has troubles of her own, makes occasional visits to the Bunner sisters' shop, but we never find out her story, or even her name, and like everyone else in the story, she cannot be of any help to the sisters. Ann Eliza comes to feel that there is no God, 'only a black abyss above the roof of Bunner Sisters'. Wharton tells the story with a painstaking, Balzacian exactness and a scrupulous interest in these compressed lives. She shines a light which is at once harsh and compassionate on every detail – the district, the neighbours (who provide some subdued humour), the sisters' home-life, a Sunday outing to Central Park, or a ferry-crossing to Hoboken to visit Mr Ramy's friend the German washerwoman Mrs Hochmüller (a soft, tender piece of urban pastoral, unlike anything else in Wharton). But there is nothing soft or tender in the dialogue between the sisters. Any hint that the older sister's love for the younger might sentimentalize the story is bleakly made away with:

'Don't you talk like that, Evelina! I guess you're on'y tired out – and disheartened.'

'Yes, I'm disheartened,' Evelina murmured.

A few months earlier Ann Eliza would have met the confession with a word of pious admonition; now she accepted it in silence.

'Maybe you'll brighten up when your cough gets better,' she suggested.

'Yes – or my cough'll get better when I brighten up,' Evelina retorted with a touch of her old tartness.

'Does your cough keep on hurting you jest as much?'

'I don't see's there's much difference.'

At the end, Ann Eliza, horribly alone, sets out on a spring morning into the great city, which 'seemed to throb with the stir of innumerable beginnings'. But not for her.

*

In all three of these stories, a window of hope and love is opened onto a narrow, thwarted life, only to be closed shut again. The most startling example of this is *Ethan Frome* (1911) which became the best-known of all Wharton's works, frequently reprinted and adapted for stage and screen. This famously American, provincial novella began life around 1907 – amazingly enough, as a formal exercise in improving her French, written in the grand Paris setting of the Faubourg St-Germain. She told her friend Bernard Berenson that it amused her to do 'Starkfield, Massachusetts' and 'Shadd's Fall' in the rue de Varenne. A few years later, at the darkest point of her own marital crisis, she returned to this French exercise and turned it into a great work of art.

For readers more familiar with *The House of Mirth* or *The Custom of the Country*, *Ethan Frome* comes as a shock, and this is not just because of the dramatic switch from her usual territory to the remote hills and poor farmers' lives of nineteenth-century New England. What is just as startling is its quietness, what Henry James admiringly called its '*kept-downness*'. *Ethan Frome* is a story of silence and speechlessness. Voices and feelings are all 'snowed under'. (The first French translation, which she oversaw, was titled *Sous la neige*.) The characters live inside 'dumb melancholy' and 'secretive silence', broken by sudden outbursts of long-repressed emotion. The gravestones by the farm gate seem more articulate than the living ('We never got away – how should you?' they say). Their deep quiet, in the end, may be preferable to any words.

Ethan was a frustrated figure long before the crash which dooms him to a slow lifetime of silent misery. The first sighting of him, a ruined giant, is of someone who seems to be dragged back persistently by 'the jerk of a chain'. As one neighbour puts it: 'You've had an awful mean time, Ethan Frome.' This grim figure of endurance once had potential and aspirations. A sensitive young man with intellectual curiosity, he had interests in physics, astronomy, and geology. Though 'grave and inarticulate', he had an appetite for 'friendly human intercourse'. He looks after other people; he is kind and honourable and has a sense of duty. (His box-room 'study', with its home-made bookshelves, its engraving of Abraham Lincoln, and its calendar with 'Thoughts from the Poets', suggests his qualities.) But his father's accident and breakdown, his mother's illness and his confinement on the farm have doomed him: he cannot escape 'the long misery of his baffled past'. 'The silence had deepened about him year by year.'

Ethan's disabled father is an almost invisible figure in the story, but his mother's life, just touched in, is desolating. A woman who once kept her home 'spruce' and shining has had to watch her husband go 'soft in the brain', their farm and saw-mill run down, and the road by the farm-house go quiet after the railway took the traffic away: 'And mother never could get it through her head what had happened, and it preyed on her right along till she died.' In illness and solitude she became more and more silent:

Sometimes, in the long winter evenings, when in desperation her son asked her why she didn't 'say something', she would lift a finger and answer: 'Because I'm listening'; and on stormy nights, when the loud wind was about the house, she would complain, if he spoke to her: They're talking so loud out there that I can't hear you.'

That loud silence is echoed in the wretched marriage Ethan makes to the older cousin, Zenobia, who comes to look after his mother and who, after her death, seems a preferable alternative to utter loneliness. ('He had often thought since that it would not have happened if his mother had died in spring instead of winter.') Over seven years, Zeena Frome turns from an efficient manager into a joyless hypochondriac, and she too falls silent; because, as she spoke 'only to complain', Ethan has developed a habit of never listening or replying. Under her 'taciturnity', 'suspicions and resentments' fester.

Into this hostile household, summed up by the word 'exanimate', Mattie Silver, Zeena's orphaned twenty-year old cousin (everything in these villages is a family matter) arrives to help keep house. Mattie is ardent, sensual, innocent, and fragile (it

is one of the novella's triumphs that she is touching and plau-
sible, too) and Ethan falls deeply and silently in love with
her. In the one year she spends with the Fromes, the tender,
inarticulate relationship that grows up between them is marked
by the rhythms of rural life, as in a novel by Hardy or Gaskell:
the village dance, church picnics, walks home in the starry
night. Ethan fantasizes a life with Mattie, and he finds himself
longing for his lawful spouse to die. But such visions of release
are instantly replaced by that of 'his wife lying in their bedroom
asleep, her mouth slightly open, her false teeth in a tumbler
by the bed.' The climax comes on the night that Zeena leaves
them in the house, and they spend the quiet evening as if they
were husband and wife, yet without touching each other. This
sweet 'illusion of long-established intimacy' is disrupted when
Zeena's special red-glass pickle-dish, which Mattie has got
down from its secret place to 'make the supper-table pretty' is
broken by the cat, Zeena's baleful familiar. So deep and sure
is the tone of the book that this little, homely accident seems
as great a tragedy to us as to the characters. Zeena returns,
discovers the breakage, and bitterly laments her loss:

'You waited till my back was turned, and took the thing I set most
store by of anything I've got ... You're a bad girl, Mattie Silver ...
I was warned of it when I took you, and I tried to keep my things
where you couldn't get at 'em – and now you've took from me the
one I cared for most of all –'

It is one of the places in the novel where the pressure of feeling
bursts through the silence. And though all our sympathies go
to Ethan and Mattie, Zeena's own suffering – sick, lonely,
unloved, betrayed – rushes onto the page.

Zeena's 'inexorable' will and the force of circumstances
mean that there is no way out for the unconsummated lovers:
Mattie must go and Ethan must stay. Their passion finally
breaks through their shyness in intense, pared-down, simple
utterances, words 'like fragments torn from' the heart:

'Ethan, where'll I go if I leave you? I don't know how to get along
alone. You said so yourself just now. Nobody but you was ever good
to me. And there'll be that strange girl in the house ... and she'll sleep
in my bed, where I used to lay nights and listen to hear you come up
the stairs ...'

INTRODUCTION

Urged by Mattie (Ethan's role throughout is to be at the service of his women), they take what they hope will be a fatal sled-ride, a scene written with the utmost intensity. And because what is meant to be their farewell scene together is told with such concentrated lyricism, the coda to the novella, where we find out what has become of these three, nearly thirty years later, is one of the most quietly horrifying moments in all fiction, cruelly powerful and done with brilliant, ruthless economy. One of the village witnesses to Ethan's life-long incarceration concludes, grimly: 'The way they are now, I don't see's there's much difference between the Fromes up at the farm and the Fromes down in the graveyard; 'cept that down there they're all quiet, and the women have got to hold their tongues.'

In itself this story, with its grim final twist, is powerful enough. But (unlike in *Bunner Sisters* or *Summer*) we come at it through a frame narrator, who sets up the flashback into Ethan's story, signalled by several lines of dots. He acts as the conduit between the reticence of Starkfield and the eloquent piece of literature we are reading. Wharton's models for *Ethan Frome* were Emily Brontë's *Wuthering Heights* and – for their use of competing narrative versions – Browning's *The Ring and he Book* and Balzac's story 'La Grande Bretèche'. Ethan and Mattie owe something, too, to Hardy's Jude and Tess; Nietzsche, one of Wharton's most admired philosophers, lies behind Ethan's lost 'will to power'. Another acknowledged debt, as in all these novellas, was to Hawthorne. Ethan's name comes from Hawthorne's guilt-ridden, isolated hero Ethan Brand, and Zenobia's from the doomed feminist heroine of his satire on a New England utopia, *The Blithedale Romance*. That novel is told from the viewpoint of a cynical, semi-detached observer, Coverdale. Wharton's nameless narrator, like Coverdale or like Brontë's Mr Lockwood, seems to belong to another world. He is a man of progress, bringing electricity and communication with the outside world to Starkfield. But after a winter there, he begins to understand the isolation and deprivations of the natives a little better.

The narrator allows Wharton to be both outside of, and inward with, her subject. Like a biographer, he collects the evidence, listens to the different versions, and makes up his own story of the past. Like his author, he is as interested in the conditions of New England life as in the personal story. Wharton would say more than once, for instance in her introduction to a 1922 edition of *Ethan Frome*, that she wanted to present a truer picture of the 'snow-bound villages of Western Massachusetts', with their grim facts of 'insanity, incest and slow mental and moral starvation', than she had ever found in the 'rose-coloured' versions of earlier New England writers (she meant, rather unfairly, Mary Wilkins Freeman and Sarah Orne Jewett). She was always extremely irritated by critics who accused her of remoteness from or condescension towards this material. During her years at the Mount in Lenox, she was vividly aware of the bleakness of the surrounding landscape. The grimness of lives in remote New England farms and desolate little hill villages, particularly in winter, and the hard times of the industrial workers in the region, stirred Wharton's imagination as much as the life of the wealthy 'cottagers' in their opulent houses in Lenox or Stockbridge. There were violent contrasts in this environment between that wealth and the deprivation of the rural poor, between the romance of the landscape and the development of local industries. Lenox Dale, not far from the Mount, was an industrial centre. The Lenox Iron Works were founded in 1848. Clocks, carriages, china, and muskets were made in Pittsfield. Dalton, the industrial town on the banks of the Housatonic, had the thriving Crane Paper Mills, and there was a paper-making factory at Lee, near Lenox. Further north, in Adams and North Adams, there were shoe factories and cotton and wool mills. Technological advances like railway lines and tunnels and the influx of trolley cars and motors were changing the landscape. Wharton had written about these aspects of life in the Berkshires in *The Fruit of the Tree* (1907), which set 'the great glare of leisure' of the wealthy houses against the needs of the mill-workers. In *Ethan Frome* – and a few years later in *Summer* – she took the wealthy houses right out of the picture.

Her story had its specific factual origins in a terrible sledding-accident in Lenox in 1904, and in the lingering, fatal paralysis of a Lenox friend, Ethel Cram, after an injury in 1905. More broadly, it provides, by inference, a factual, sociological account of this bleak slice of American life. We learn, through the narrator, about the transactions between local farmers and builders, the effects of the railway, attitudes to debt and the status of doctors, the inadequate education of girls, and levels of rural unemployment. Occasionally her narrator uses a phrase which opens up the distance between 'us' and 'them': 'the hard compulsions of the poor', 'a community rich in pathological instances'. So, as she often does, Wharton uses a unique, pitiful story for a generalized, determinist account of environmental pressures, and holds romance and realism brilliantly in balance.

All the harsh matter-of-factness of life in Starkfield – dogged conversations about money and work, details of journeys, luggage, buildings, medicines, farming, the omnipresent but useless church, the ingrown, watchful community, the practical difficulties created by the weather – are mixed with suppressed romantic emotions, passionately invested in nature. What to the narrator seems a blank and desolate wilderness becomes, when we see it through Ethan and Mattie's eyes, a landscape full of detail and beauty. The emotions that are so 'kept down' come through in an intense sensual language straight out of Keats (one of Wharton's favourite poets). Ethan's awareness of huge cloudy meanings behind the daily face of things' calls up Huge cloudy symbols of a high romance' in Keats's anguished farewell to life and love, 'When I have fears that I may cease to be'. The wintry romance of Keats's 'The Eve of St Agnes' is touched in everywhere. The snow beats 'like hail against the loose-hinged windows', as, in Keats's poem, the 'frost-wind' blows the 'quick pattering' of the 'flaw-blown sleet' 'against the window-panes'. The warm little feast in the kitchen is a homely version of Porphyro's sensual banquet; the 'lustrous fleck' on Mattie's lip in the lamplight is like the 'lustrous' ight of Madeline and Porphyro's encounter, lit by moonlight. Mattie's erotic trance ('She looked up at him languidly, as though her lids were weighted with sleep and it cost her an effort to raise them') is like Madeline's tranced sleep. Ethan's ache' of cold weariness echoes Keats's knights in armour aching in their 'icy hoods and mails'. These lovers make a doomed attempt, like Keats's lovers, to flee away for ever into the storm; but the story, like the poem, ends with the crippled paralysis of an old 'beldame', who dies 'palsy-twitched, with meagre face deform'. In both there is the sense of it all having happened 'ages long ago'.

The 'high romance' in *Ethan Frome* speaks through nature:

Slowly the rim of the rainy vapours caught fire and burnt away, and a pure moon swung into the blue. Ethan, rising on his elbow, watched the landscape whiten and shape itself under the sculpture of the moon....He looked out at the slopes bathed in lustre, the silver-edged darkness of the woods, the spectral purple of the hills against the sky, and it seemed as though all the beauty of the night had been poured out to mock his wretchedness...

Wharton told Berenson that it gave her 'the greatest joy and fullest ease' to write this story. She knew that distance can create closeness, and that transforming painful materials can produce creative joy. *Ethan Frome* was an anguished elegy to love, and a description of being incarcerated in a terrible marriage. It was also a farewell to New England, written a long way away from it, and published as she would be leaving it for ever.

*

When Wharton returned to the landscape of *Ethan Frome*, five years later, she again used the word 'joy' to describe the process of writing about pain and loss. *Summer*, written in the summer of 1916 and published in 1917, was, she told Berenson in May 1917, written at 'a high pitch of creative joy'. It was her escape from the pressures and demands of her war-work in France, as much of an antidote as possible to refugees and hospitals. It is a high-coloured, full-blooded, sensual narrative with an intense appetite for life. But it is shadowed by violence and death and by dark emotions about nationhood, civilization, and savagery.

The idea for it suddenly came into focus, but she had had it in mind since *Ethan Frome*. She often mentioned them together, famously calling *Summer* the 'hot Ethan'. Like *Ethan Frome*, *Summer* is a novella set in the poorest and remotest part of New England, in which an inarticulate, untravelled character with an obscure sense that there might be some preferable life elsewhere has a brief moment of idyllic love and joy but is pulled back to the harsh realities of the place she lives in. *Summer*'s romance is fulfilled, not thwarted like Ethan's. It is one of the few Wharton fictions in which a love affair is acted out rather than denied. But, as elsewhere in her fiction, pain, loss, and grief rush up behind it.

The novel is brim-full of, and best known for, a sensual evocation of the New England countryside in heat, felt through the perceptions of a young woman close to nature: uneducated, speechless, throbbing with awakening eroticism. She feels and thinks through her blood, she lies on the ground like an animal, her face pressed to the earth and the warm currents of the grass running through her'. She feels earth and water, heat and light, sun and the colour of skies (*Summer* is full of fine sunsets) and the 'long wheeling fires' of stars on her pulses. She is all sap, growth and passive, sun-warmed earth-life, and Wharton piles this on with a Whitmanesque feel for minute, creaturely animalism. Heroine and author seem far apart, but Wharton gives her her own passionate feeling for nature and her nostalgia for her lost New England countryside, so remote from the war-bound rue de Varenne.

Pagan sensuality is at the heart of the novel's escapism, but the heroine is not a joyous figure, and the summery outdoors is not the novel's only landscape. Charity Royall is a discontented creature, more like a small-town Undine Spragg than like Mattie in *Ethan Frome*. (Conrad, who enjoyed *Summer*, praised her 'bewildered wilfulness' in a letter to Wharton in October 1917). She is trapped in a gossipy, puritanical, and philistine ittle town, which is almost all she has ever known. She lets out hot bursts of inarticulate resentment: 'How I hate everything!' Things don't change at North Dormer: people just get used to them.' The name of the town puns on the French for sleep, implying 'dormant' and 'dormitory'. North Dormer defines its level of civilization not against Boston or New York or the wider world but against 'the Mountain', a 'bad place' that looms over the town from fifteen miles away, where a squalid, degenerate community, 'a little colony of squatters', lives beyond the pale of the law or the church or any genteel 'household order'. (They are said to be descendants of the men who built the local railways fifty years before, who took to drink and 'disappeared into the woods'. Wharton derived them, she tells us in her memoir, *A Backward Glance*, from a real colony of 'drunken mountain outlaws' on Bear Mountain, near Lenox.) This is where Charity Royall was born, rescued as a little girl by Lawyer Royall from a convict and a bad mother, and brought up first by the lawyer and his wife, and then, after Mrs Royall's death, by him alone. Her name has been imposed on her, marking her out as a recipient of philanthropy, and a possession. She is made to feel 'poor and ignorant' and ashamed of her origins, protected only by the distinction of her guardian.

Mr Royall, though banked down for a great deal of *Summer* (because we mainly see him through Charity's eyes) is its most powerful and problematic character: Wharton always insisted that '*he's* the book'. A disappointed man who could have had a better career somewhere else, vigorous, intelligent, impressive, he is also gloomy, bitter, given to drink, and in need of female company. He once tries to break his way into Charity's room when she is seventeen; she holds him at bay by force of will, and never forgives him. When, after this, he asks to marry her, he seems to become 'a hideous parody of the fatherly old man she had always known'. She continues to live in his house, but on her own terms, which includes taking a pointless job at the moribund local library, where she sits furiously all day surrounded by books she has no idea how to read.

This is where she is at the start of the novella, which immediately introduces a blithe, handsome, cultured young visitor, Lucius Harney, an architect interested in old New England houses, with whom Charity falls in love. (Harney is thinly characterized, but he is meant to be lightweight.) Her secret love affair, 'a wondrous unfolding of her new self', which makes her even more conscious of her ignorance and provincialism, comes under the constant pressure of small-town surveillance. For all its romantic ardour, rhapsodically conveyed, it is increasingly felt to be a risky illusion, shadowed by menace and fear.

Large-scale realistic local set-pieces interrupt the idyll, which combine, as increasingly in Wharton's postwar American writing, nostalgia and distaste. There is a July Fourth celebration in Nettleton (based on Pittsfield), complete with omnibuses, shop displays of confectionery and fancy goods, a firemen's band and a picture show, trolley rides to the Lake and fireworks displaying 'Washington crossing the Delaware'. A romantic adventure for Charity, it ends humiliatingly in an encounter with a drunken, abusive Royall. That is followed by North Dormer's marking of Old Home Week with a banquet, a dance, a procession to the church, and speeches, for which the local girls are dressed – highly ironically in Charity's case – in vestal, sacrificial white. Wharton enjoys herself with these local American rituals, viewed through Charity's impressionable eyes. T. S. Eliot, reviewing *Summer* in the *Egoist* in January 1919, thought the whole thing was a satire on the New England novel, done by 'suppressing all evidence of European culture'. This is not quite true, as a touch of French culture is slipped into Nettleton when Lucius takes Charity to a little French restaurant. But these provincial festivals do display the American insularity and isolationism that Wharton had been complaining about in the early years of the war, before the United States involved itself in the struggle. She calls it, drily, sentimental decentralization', and makes fun of the genteel spinster, Miss Hatchard, who insists on the importance of reverting to the old ideals, the family and the homestead, and so on'.

The idea of 'home' in *Summer* goes beyond a satire on provincialism and insularity, though. It plays through the novella in subtle ways. Lucius is investigating the fine old eighteenth-century houses of rural New England, many of which have been left to decay: his architectural interests show up the local indifference, at the time, towards historical American homes. The lovers' secret trysting-place is a deserted, ghostly little house in an abandoned orchard, a fragile, pathetic, makeshift home. Lawyer Royall makes a speech at the ceremony, which shows him at his best, about 'home' as a site of potential, not of confinement. Those who have gone away from their old home may return 'for good': to make it a 'larger place' and 'to make the best of it'. Wharton was partly thinking, as she often did, about what it would have been like for her to go back to America and stay there, instead of living her life in France. But she was also implying that small-town America needed to look outward and could be improved by sending its sons off to war.

The grimmest 'home' in the novella is the savage place Charity comes from, a derelict shed on the mountain, described with as much brutality as Wharton can muster. This is where Charity goes when her lover leaves her for a girl of his own class and she becomes pregnant, and this is where she tells herself she belongs. There is no romance or decorum here to cover over the life of the body, displayed with shocking ruthlessness in the figure of Charity's dead mother:

A woman lay on it [a mattress on the floor] but she did not look like a dead woman; she seemed to have fallen across her squalid bed in a drunken sleep, and to have been left lying where she fell, in her ragged disordered clothes. One arm was flung above her head, one leg drawn up under a torn skirt that left the other bare to the knee: a swollen glistening leg with a ragged stocking rolled down about the ankle.... She looked at her mother's face, thin yet swollen, with lips parted in a frozen gasp above the broken teeth. There was no sign in it of anything human: she lay there like a dead dog in a ditch.

Charity's only consolation for this sight is the burial service, administered by the priest who is going to help her return to her guardian and her town, where she also belongs – and does not belong. The powerful burial scene on the mountain takes us back to the world of war in Europe from which *Summer* was meant to be an escape. All the ingredients of war that were at the forefront of Wharton's mind at this time – the slaughter, the corpses, the wretched women and children, the refugees with their homes destroyed, the balm of religious ritual, the efforts, however inadequate, of charity – cluster behind this scene. And Charity is a victim, like so many of the war survivors Wharton was dealing with at the time of writing *Summer*.

The choices she has, as a woman, are few and grim. This is one of Wharton's most outspoken and lacerating books about the limitations of women's lives – for all that she is not easily described as a feminist. Charity is at the mercy of a male double standard. Royall, himself prone to 'debauchery', is violently abusive about Charity's 'half human' mother and Charity's bad blood, and the person he talks to about this is the two-timing Lucius, as though both men are conspiring to judge and define the speechless, exploited girl. Charity's choices are to return to the 'animal' life of her mother or to have an abortion or to become a prostitute. These options are very clearly spelt out, much more openly than in any previous novel of Wharton's. There is even a visit to the abortionist: the sign reads 'Private Consultations . . . Lady Attendants', and the woman doctor seems to be Jewish. There are several uses of the word 'whore'. (As a result, *Summer* was banned in Pittsfield and much disapproved of by Wharton's Boston readers.) Charity is recognizably in the tradition of 'the woman who pays': pregnant Hetty Sorrel in *Adam Bede*, Tess abandoned by her lover in Hardy's novel. Wharton even has Charity encountering a preacher on the road, in a 'gospel tent', like Tess's encounter with a travelling evangelist. Most of all she invokes Hester Prynne in Hawthorne's *Scarlet Letter*, cast out by the Puritan community for adultery, more in tune with the natural wilderness than the town, and listening, as Charity listens, to the rhetoric of the preacher giving his great Election Day sermon on the values of America. Wharton plants the clue herself, comparing *Summer*'s realism with Hawthorne's in *A Backward Glance*. And there is a strong echo of Hawthorne's obsessional, spying old husband Chillingworth in Lawyer Royall.

The ending of *Summer* is extremely disturbing, and to some readers as harrowing as the ending of *Ethan Frome* and as bleak as *Bunner Sisters*. The window onto joy and romance closes down for ever, and Charity, in a state of passive horror and exhaustion, allows herself to be led off the mountain, and married, by her much-hated father figure. The ending can be read as a depressing immolation of youth and hope in a hypocritical and quasi-incestuous social compromise. Or it can be seen as a realist adjustment on both sides, since at this point Royall becomes grave, kindly, and forbearing, and Charity feels reassured and secure, as in a refuge. Royall's acceptance of Charity and her baby could be read not as exploitative but as bravely introducing into self-protective, small-town America a necessary new influx of 'strange blood'. Wharton's readers cannot agree about the ending, because the book pulls against itself. The loss of midsummer love is felt as unbearable but inevitable. Growing up (for countries as for people) is a process of 'tragic initiation', and it means moving from romance to 'ineluctable reality', adopting the stoicism that is the only virtue left in the face of great catastrophe, and 'making the best of it'.

Hermione Lee

HERMIONE LEE is Goldsmiths' Professor of English Literature and Fellow of New College, Oxford. Her books include biographies of Edith Wharton and Virginia Woolf, and critical studies of Elizabeth Bowen, Willa Cather and Philip Roth.

SELECT BIBLIOGRAPHY

BIBLIOGRAPHY AND EDITIONS
There is no complete, up-to-date bibliography of Edith Wharton, no complete edition of her letters (and none currently planned), and no complete edition of her novellas and short stories (the editions isted below all have omissions). This list provides the most useful current bibliographies and editions. The current state of Wharton studies and Wharton editions is well covered by Clare Colquitt in her 'Bibliographical Essay: Visions and Revisions of Wharton', in *A Historical Guide to Edith Wharton*, ed. Carol J. Singley, Oxford University Press, 2003.

STEPHEN GARRISON, *Edith Wharton: A Descriptive Bibliography*, University of Pittsburgh Press,1990.

KRISTIN O. LAUER and MARGARET P. MURRAY, *Edith Wharton: An Annotated Secondary Bibliography*, Garland, 1990.

PAUL LAUTER, *The Heath Anthology of American Literature*, 2002 (contains Edith Wharton's 1908 love diary, 'The Life Apart').

FREDERICK WEGENER, ed., *The Uncollected Critical Writings of Edith Wharton*, Princeton University Press, 1996.

Edith Wharton: The Collected Short Stories, ed. R. W. B. Lewis, Scribner's, 1968 (does not include *Bunner Sisters*).

Edith Wharton: Collected Stories 1891–1910, Collected Stories 1911–1937, ed. Maureen Howard, Library of America, 2001.

Edith Wharton: Ethan Frome, Norton Critical Edition, eds Kristin O. Lauer and Cynthia Griffin Wolff, Norton, 1995 (contains useful critical and background material including Wharton's own comments on *Ethan Frome*).

Edith Wharton's Library: A Catalogue, compiled by George Ramsden, introduction by Hermione Lee, Stone Trough Books, Settrington, 1999.

LIFE AND LETTERS
Since Wharton's death in 1937 biographical treatments have included a personal and catty memoir (Lubbock), copiously illustrated 'woman in her time' approaches (Auchincloss, Dwight), an authorized, pioneering, prize-winning life, with enormous amounts of new materials, for many years the 'standard' version (Lewis), feminist and revisionary treatments with significant new materials (Wolff, Benstock), and in

EDITH WHARTON

2007 my substantial new account of the life and works. New letters are still coming to light, as in Bratton. Wharton's own versions of her life are guardedly revealing.

LOUIS AUCHINCLOSS, *Edith Wharton: A Woman in Her Time*, Michael Joseph, 1971.

SHARI BENSTOCK, *No Gifts From Chance: A Biography of Edith Wharton*, Scribner's and Hamish Hamilton, 1994, Penguin Books, 1995.

DANIEL BRATTON, ed., *Yrs Ever Affectionately: The Correspondence of Edith Wharton and Louis Bromfield*, Michigan State University Press, 2000.

ELEANOR DWIGHT, *Edith Wharton: An Extraordinary Life*, Harry N. Abrams, 1994.

HERMIONE LEE, *Edith Wharton*, Alfred A. Knopf and Chatto & Windus, 2007.

R. W. B. LEWIS, *Edith Wharton: A Biography*, Harper & Row, 1975, Harper Colophon Books, 1977.

R. W. B. LEWIS and NANCY LEWIS, eds, *The Letters of Edith Wharton*, Simon & Schuster, 1988.

PERCY LUBBOCK, *Portrait of Edith Wharton*, Jonathan Cape, 1947.

LYALL H. POWERS, *Henry James and Edith Wharton: Letters, 1900–1915*, Scribner's, 1990.

EDITH WHARTON, *A Backward Glance*, Appleton-Century, 1934.

EDITH WHARTON, *Novellas and Other Writings* (includes *Ethan Frome*, *Summer*, 'Life and I'), ed. Cynthia Griffin Wolff, Library of America, 1990.

CYNTHIA GRIFFIN WOLFF, *A Feast of Words: The Triumph of Edith Wharton*, Oxford University Press, 1977.

SELECTED CRITICISM

Wharton criticism is a major academic industry in North America, less so in Europe. I list what I have found to be the most useful and interesting examples. References to, or accounts of, *Ethan Frome* and *Summer* will be found in almost all these books; *Bunner Sisters* is much less often mentioned.

ELIZABETH AMMONS, *Edith Wharton's Argument with America*, University of Georgia Press, 1980.

DALE BAUER, *Edith Wharton's Brave New Politics*, University of Wisconsin Press, 1994.

JANET BEER, *Edith Wharton, Writers and their Work*, Northcote House Publishers, 2002.

SELECT BIBLIOGRAPH

MILLICENT BELL, ed., *The Cambridge Companion to Edith Wharton*, Cambridge University Press, 1995.

ALFRED BENDIXEN and ANNETTE ZILVERSMIT, *Edith Wharton: New Critical Essays*, Garland, 1992.

NANCY BENTLEY, *The Ethnography of Manners: Hawthorne, James, Wharton*, Cambridge University Press, 1995.

CLARE COLQUITT, SUSAN GOODMAN and CANDACE WAID, eds, *A Forward Glance: New Essays on Edith Wharton*, University of Delaware Press, 1999.

JUDITH FRYER, *Felicitous Space: The Imaginative Structures of Edith Wharton and Willa Cather*, University of North Carolina Press, 1986.

KATHERINE JOSLIN and ALAN PRICE, eds, *Wretched Exotic: Essays on Edith Wharton in Europe*, Peter Lang, 1993.

MAUREEN E. MONTGOMERY, *Displaying Women: Spectacles of Leisure in Edith Wharton's New York*, Routledge, 1998.

BLAKE NEVIUS, *Edith Wharton: A Study of her Fiction*, University of California Press, 1953.

JULIE OLINE-AMMENTROP, *Edith Wharton's Writings from the Great War*, Florida University Press, 2004.

CLAUDIA ROTH PIERPONT, *Passionate Minds*, Random House, 2001.

CLAIRE PRESTON, *Edith Wharton's Social Register*, Macmillan, 2000.

ALAN PRICE, *The End of the Age of Innocence: Edith Wharton and the First World War*, Robert Hale, 1996.

CAROL J. SINGLEY, *Edith Wharton: Matters of Mind and Spirit*, Houghton Mifflin, 2000.

CAROL J. SINGLEY, ed., *A Historical Guide to Edith Wharton*, Oxford University Press, 2003.

ADELINE R. TINTNER, *Edith Wharton in Context*, University of Alabama Press, 1999.

JAMES W. TUTTLETON, KRISTIN O. LAUER and MARGARET P. MURRAY, eds, *Edith Wharton: The Contemporary Reviews*, Cambridge University Press, 1992.

CANDACE WAID, *Edith Wharton's Letters from the Underworld: Fictions of Women and Writing*, University of North Carolina, 1991.

EDMUND WILSON, 'Justice to Edith Wharton', *The Wound and the Bow*, W. H. Allen & Co., 1941.

BACKGROUND

These are useful introductions to Wharton's historical, cultural and intellectual context. Veblen provides an important parallel for her social analysis. Wharton's short book on other writers' fictional methods sheds a highly interesting light on her own work.

EDITH WHARTON

LOUIS AUCHINCLOSS, *The Vanderbilt Era*, Scribner's, 1989.

ERIC HOMBERGER, *Mrs Astor's New York*, Yale University Press, 2002.

SCOTT MARSHALL et al., *The Mount, Home of Edith Wharton*, Edith Wharton Restoration, 1997.

LLOYD MORRIS, *Incredible New York*, Syracuse, 1951.

JOHN TOMSICH, *A Genteel Endeavor: American Culture and Politics in the Gilded Age*, Stanford University Press, 1971.

ALAN TRACHTENBERG, *The Incorporation of America. Culture and Society in the Gilded Age*, Hill and Wang, 1982.

THORSTEIN VEBLEN, *The Theory of the Leisure Class*, Macmillan, 1899.

EDITH WHARTON, *The Writing of Fiction*, Scribner's, 1925.

CHRONOLOGY

DATE	AUTHOR'S LIFE	LITERARY CONTEXT
1861		George Eliot: *Silas Marner.*
		Dickens: *Great Expectations.*
		Rebecca Harding Davis: *Life in the Iron Mills.*
1862	Edith Newbold Jones born 24 January, in New York City.	Elizabeth Barrett Browning: *Last Poems.*
		Turgenev: *Fathers and Children.*
1863		Elizabeth Gaskell: *Sylvia's Lovers.*
		Longfellow: *Tales of a Wayside Inn.*
1864		Tennyson: *Enoch Arden.*
		Trollope: *Can You Forgive Her?*
		Death of Hawthorne (b. 1804).
1865		Whitman: *Drum-Taps.*
		Emerson: *English Traits.*
		Dickens: *Our Mutual Friend.*
		Gaskell: *Wives and Daughters.*
		Lewis Carroll: *Alice's Adventures in Wonderland.*
1866	Family moves to Europe to conserve income in postwar depression. Next six years spent in Italy, Spain, Paris and Germany.	Dostoevsky: *Crime and Punishment.*
		Gaskell: *Wives and Daughters.*
		Eliot: *Felix Holt.*
		Whittier: *Snow-Bound.*
1867		Arnold: *New Poems.*
		Turgenev: *Smoke.*
		Marx: *Das Kapital* (I).
1869		Mill: *The Subjection of Women.*
		Browning: *The Ring and the Book.*
		Harriet Beecher Stowe: *Old Town Folks.*
		Flaubert: *L'Education Sentimentale.*
		Tolstoy completes *War and Peace.*
1870		Death of Charles Dickens.
1871		Darwin: *The Descent of Man.*
		Birth of Proust.

Lincoln US president (to 1865). Ten states secede from Union on the slavery issue. American Civil War (to 1865). Battle of Bull Run: Union forces are completely routed. Britain declares itself neutral in the conflict. Victor Emmanuel II becomes king of a united Italy. Russia abolishes serfdom. Battle of Shiloh – Union forces successful. Battle of Antietam in which 23,000 are left dead on the field. Lincoln proposes that slaves in all states in rebellion against the government should be free on or after 1 January 1863. Greatest battle of the war fought at Gettysburg, Pennsylvania. Colonel Robert E. Lee, commanding the Confederate Army, is forced to retreat. Lincoln's Gettysburg Address. Bismarck gains power in Prussia.

Lincoln re-elected president. First Socialist International (to 1876).

Assassination of Lincoln. Andrew Johnson president (to 1869). Civil War ends. A general pardon is granted to the South. Negroes given full rights as citizens in the 14th Amendment. No state can come back into the Union unless it ratifies this amendment.

US Reconstruction under way. Petition requesting the franchise signed by 1500 women in Britain, and presented by John Stuart Mill to the House of Commons.

US purchases Alaska from Russia. Building of the first elevated railroad. Gladstone becomes leader of the Liberal Party in Britain and prime minister the following year (to 1874). Austro-Hungarian empire formed.
Ulysses S. Grant, ablest of Union generals, elected president.
Union Pacific railroad completed.
Rockefeller's Standard Oil Company begins to corner the market.
The West is opened up. There follows mass cultivation of land, an ever expanding frontier and population growth through immigration. These factors spell the end of the 'Wild West'.
Two national associations for American women's suffrage founded.
Suez Canal opens.
Franco-Prussian War (to 1871). Napoleon III defeated at Sedan, dethroned and exiled. Doctrine of papal infallibility.
French Third Republic suppresses Paris Commune. Wilhelm I first German emperor. Bismarck becomes German chancellor. Ku Klux Klan outlawed.

DATE	AUTHOR'S LIFE	LITERARY CONTEXT
1872	Family returns to United States. Edith works with governess and reads widely in father's library.	Eliot: *Middlemarch*. Turgenev: 'Spring Torrents'. Nietzsche: *The Birth of Tragedy*.
1874		
1876		James: *Roderick Hudson*. Twain: *Tom Sawyer*. Eliot: *Daniel Deronda*. Death of George Sand.
1877	Secretly completes manuscript of *Fast and Loose*, a short novel (30,000 words; unpublished).	Sarah Orne Jewett: *Deephaven*. James: *The American*. Tolstoy completes *Anna Karenina*. Birth of Gertrude Stein.
1878	Mother has twenty-nine of Edith's poems (*Verses*) privately printed.	Hardy: *The Return of the Native*. Stowe: *Poganuc People*.
1879	Longfellow shows Edith's poems to William Dean Howells. One poem published in *Atlantic Monthly*. Edith's social début in millionaire's private ballroom on Fifth Avenue.	James: *Daisy Miller*. Ibsen: *A Doll's House*.
1880	Two poems published in New York *World*. Travels with family to France.	Dostoevsky: *The Brothers Karamazov*. Death of George Eliot.
1881		James: *The Portrait of a Lady*; *Washington Square*. Death of Dostoevsky.
1882	Father dies in Cannes. Edith inherits over $20,000. Brief engagement to Harry Stevens (his mother opposes the marriage).	Twain: *The Prince and the Pauper*. Howells: *A Modern Instance*. Birth of Virginia Woolf and James Joyce.
1883	Returns to United States with her mother. Briefly becomes close to law student, Walter Berry. He considers marriage, but fails to propose. Edith meets Edward Wharton (Teddy), popular Bostonian and socialite.	Twain: *Life on the Mississippi*. James: *Portraits of Places* (travel sketches). Nietzsche: *Thus Spake Zarathustra* (to 1892). Death of Turgenev.

CHRONOLOGY

Grant wins office for a second time.

The Liberals are defeated in British elections. Disraeli becomes prime minister (to 1880). First Impressionist exhibition in Paris.
Alexander Graham Bell invents the telephone.
Death of Wild Bill Hickok (b.1837) – Western folk-hero.

Presidency of Rutherford B. Hayes (to 1881).
US Reconstruction collapses; southern states impose racist legislation.
Russia declares war on Turkey (to 1878).
Edison invents the phonograph.

Afghan War. Congress of Berlin.

Zulu War.

Standard Oil refines 95% of America's oil. Invention of the incandescent lamp. 1880s: growth of Women's Clubs in American cities; labour unrest – almost 10,000 strikes and lockouts; rise of magazines – *Cosmopolitan*, the *Ladies' Home Journal*, *McClure's*; electricity for private houses; rise of department stores. Taylor's 'time-study' experiments.
Gladstone becomes British prime minister for a second time (to 1885).
Presidency of James Garfield. Garfield assassinated. Presidency of Chester Arthur (to 1885). Founding of the American Federation of Labor.
Tsar Alexander II assassinated.
Jesse James shot and killed.
First central power plant in New York (Edison, backed by J. P. Morgan).
Married Women's Property Act in Britain.
Death of Garibaldi (b.1807) and Darwin (b.1809).

Death of Marx (b.1818) and Wagner (b.1813).
Russian Marxist Party founded.
Brooklyn Bridge opened.

DATE	AUTHOR'S LIFE	LITERARY CONTEXT
1884		Twain: *Huckleberry Finn.* Jewett: *A Country Doctor.* Maupassant: *Miss Harriet*; *Clair de Lune.*
1885	Marries Teddy Wharton.	Zola: *Germinal.* Marx: *Das Kapital* II. Howells: *The Rise of Silas Lapham.* Maupassant: *Bel-Ami.*
1886		James: *The Bostonians*; *The Princess Casamassima.* Death of Emily Dickinson. Stevenson: *Dr Jekyll and Mr Hyde.* Tolstoy: *The Death of Ivan Illych.* Nietzsche: *Beyond Good and Evil.*
1887		Mary Wilkins Freeman: *A Humble Romance.* Zola: *La Terre.*
1888	Edith and Teddy go on a four-month Aegean cruise. Edith inherits $120,000 from a cousin.	James: *The Aspern Papers.* Birth of Katherine Mansfield and T. S. Eliot.
1889		
1890	A story, 'Mrs Manstey's View', is accepted for publication by Scribner's.	James: *The Tragic Muse.* William James: *Principles of Psychology.* Ibsen: *Hedda Gabler.* Wilde: *The Picture of Dorian Gray.*
1891	Purchases 'narrow' house in Park Avenue.	Hardy: *Tess of the d'Urbervilles.* Gissing: *The Odd Women*; *New Grub Street.* Freeman: *A New England Nun.* Dewey: *Critical Theory of Ethics.* US International Copyright Bill improves authors' finances.
1892	Writes *Bunner Sisters* (published 1916).	Charlotte Perkins Gilman: 'The Yellow Wallpaper'. Death of Whitman (b. 1819).

CHRONOLOGY

Presidency of Grover Cleveland (to 1889).

The 'Great Upheaval': 700,000 on strike in the US. Demand for eight-hour day. Surrender of Geronimo.
Home Rule Bill for Ireland: Gladstone resigns, to be followed by Salisbury as prime minister (to 1892).

Wilhelm II becomes Kaiser.

Benjamin Harrison, Republican, elected president (to 1893).
Jane Addams establishes Hull Settlement House, Chicago.
Second Socialist International (to 1916).
Eiffel Tower built in Paris.
Census: US population 63 million. Enumerators instructed to distinguish between 'blacks', 'mulattoes', 'quadroons' and 'octoroons'. New constitution of the state of Mississippi prohibits inter-racial union (the prohibition stands for seventy-five years). Depression: drastic fall in agricultural prices.
Bismarck resigns.

Carnegie Hall opens in New York.

Financier Jay Gould dies worth $77 million.
Gladstone, now in his eighty-third year, becomes prime minister for a fourth time (to 1894).

DATE	AUTHOR'S LIFE	LITERARY CONTEXT
1893	Buys Land's End, on Atlantic front at Newport. Becomes friends with French novelist, Bourget.	Stephen Crane: *Maggie: A Girl of the Streets*. Sarah Grand: *The Heavenly Twins*. Death of Maupassant (b. 1850).
1894	Travels in Italy. Depression and illness interfere with writing.	George Moore: *Esther Waters*. Chopin: *Bayou Folk*. Twain: *Pudd'nhead Wilson*.
1895		Stephen Crane: *The Red Badge of Courage*. Grant Allen: *The Woman Who Did*. Wilde: *The Importance of Being Earnest*; *An Ideal Husband*.
1896	Eight-month trip to Europe.	Hardy: *Jude the Obscure*. Jewett: *The Country of the Pointed Firs*. Chekhov: *The Seagull*. Birth of Scott Fitzgerald.
1897	Publishes *The Decoration of Houses* with architect Ogden Codman.	Grand: *The Beth Book*. Chopin: *A Night in Acadie*. Wells: *The Invisible Man*. Robinson: *The Children of the Night*.
1898	Treated as outpatient in Dr S. Weir Mitchell's 'rest-cure' for nervous collapse.	James: *The Turn of the Screw*.
1899	Publishes first short story collection, *The Greater Inclination*. Travels in Europe.	Gilman: *Women and Economics*. Thorstein Veblen: *The Theory of the Leisure Class*. Chopin: *The Awakening*. James: *The Awkward Age*. Norris: *McTeague*. Chekhov: *The Lady with the Lap-dog*. Birth of Hemingway.
1900	Publishes *The Touchstone* (novella). Travels in Europe.	Conrad: *Lord Jim*. Dreiser: *Sister Carrie*. Freud: *The Interpretation of Dreams*.
1901	Buys 113-acre estate in Lenox, Massachusetts. Plans large house and gardens. *Crucial Instances* (stories) published. Mother dies. Edith inherits $90,000.	Mann: *Buddenbrooks*. Nietzsche: *The Will to Power*. First Nobel Prize for Literature.

CHRONOLOGY

DATE	AUTHOR'S LIFE	LITERARY CONTEXT
1902	Publishes first novel, *The Valley of Decision*, set in eighteenth-century Italy. Becomes friends with Theodore Roosevelt. Moves into 'The Mount', her new home in Lenox. Teddy has nervous illness.	James: *The Wings of the Dove*. Gide: *L'Immoraliste*. William James: *Varieties of Religious Experience*. Birth of Steinbeck.
1903	Travels in Europe with Teddy. Meets Henry James and art critic Bernard Berenson. Begins *The House of Mirth*.	James: *The Ambassadors*. Butler: *The Way of All Flesh*. G. E. Moore: *Principia Ethica*.
1904	Buys her first automobile. Travels in England and France. Works on *The House of Mirth* throughout busy summer at 'The Mount'. Guests include Henry James. Publishes *Italian Villas and Their Gardens*.	Chekhov: *The Cherry Orchard*. James: *The Golden Bowl*. Conrad: *Nostromo*. Death of Kate Chopin.
1905	Scribner's serialization of *The House of Mirth*, January–November. Published 14 October in book form, it becomes best-seller (140,000 copies by the end of the year). *Italian Backgrounds* published (first of several travel books).	Forster: *Where Angels Fear to Tread*. Shaw: *Major Barbara*.
1906	Travels in England and France. Stage adaptation of *The House of Mirth* (with Clyde Fitch). Play fails in New York.	Upton Sinclair: *The Jungle*. Death of Ibsen (b. 1828).
1907	Rents apartment in Paris. Publishes *The Fruit of the Tree*.	James: *The American Scene*. Henry Adams: *The Education of Henry Adams*.
1907–12	Divides time between homes in US and Paris. Travels in England and Italy. Has affair with journalist Morton Fullerton (1908–10); writes love sonnets and a diary to him.	
1908	*A Motor-Flight Through France*.	Forster: *A Room with a View*.
1909	It is revealed that Teddy has embezzled $50,000 of Edith's money.	Gertrude Stein: *Three Lives*. Gide: *La Porte étroite*. Wells: *Tono Bungay*; *Ann Veronica*.
1910	Moves to a new apartment in Paris and sells her New York houses.	Death of Mark Twain (b. 1835). Forster: *Howards End*.

CHRONOLOGY

HISTORICAL EVENTS

Women in Australia are granted the vote.

Women's Trade Union League founded in New York.
In Britain, Emmeline Pankhurst founds Women's Social and Political Union.
Wright brothers' first successful powered flight.
Death of Gauguin (b.1848).
Theodore Roosevelt re-elected US president.
Russo-Japanese War (to 1905).
Anglo-French Entente Cordiale. 'La belle époque' in France.

First Russian Revolution. Separation of church and state in France.
Series of mining disasters in US (to 1910); 2,494 killed.
Einstein's special theory of relativity.

San Francisco earthquake.
Clemenceau becomes French prime minister (to 1909).

Currency panic in US; run on banks; J. P. Morgan imports $100 million in gold from Europe to halt crisis.
Triple Entente of Britain, France and Russia.

Cubism begins in Paris. Asquith becomes prime minister in Britain (to 1916).
First Model T Ford car. Blériot flies across English Channel. Commercial manufacture of Bakelite means beginning of plastic age.
Diaghilev founds Ballets Russes. Marinetti's Futurist manifesto.
Death of King Edward VII (b.1841), who is succeeded by George V.

DATE	AUTHOR'S LIFE	LITERARY CONTEXT
1911	Drives through central Italy with Walter Berry. *Ethan Frome* (admired by reviewers).	Dreiser: *Jennie Gerhardt*.
1912	Worsening rifts with Teddy. Sells 'The Mount'. Visits England. *The Reef*.	Dreiser: *The Financier*. Mann: *Death in Venice*.
1913	*The Custom of the Country*. Divorced from Teddy. Travels with Berry in Sicily and Bernard Berenson in Germany. Last visit to US for ten years.	Proust: *A la Recherche du temps perdu* (to 1927). Alain-Fournier: *Le Grand Meaulnes*. Ellen Glasgow: *Virginia*. Lawrence: *Sons and Lovers*. Conrad: *Chance*.
1914		Joyce: *Dubliners*. Gides: *Les Caves du Vatican*.
1914–19	Based in Paris. Travels in North Africa and Spain. After outbreak of war, tireless fund-raising and other work for unemployed women, refugees, homeless children and tuberculosis convalescents. Visits front. Writes articles about life in the trenches for Scribner's. Publishes *Summer* (1917) and *The Marne* (1918) and rents château at Hyères on the Mediterranean (1919).	
1915	Continues with a series of visits to the front lines, delivering medical supplies. Organizes Children of Flanders Rescue Committee. Forms friendship with André Gide, fellow worker at the hostels.	Virginia Woolf: *The Voyage Out*. Ford: *The Good Soldier*. Lawrence: *The Rainbow*. Gilman: *Herland*. Roosevelt: *America and the World War*.
1916	Made a Chevalier of the Légion d'Honneur for her war work. Edits *The Book of the Homeless*, a fund-raising venture with contributions by distinguished writers, artists and musicians which raises $15,000. *Bunner Sisters* published in *Xingu and Other Stories*.	Joyce: *A Portrait of the Artist as a Young Man*. Death of Henry James (b.1843).

CHRONOLOGY

HISTORICAL EVENTS

Agadir crisis. Chinese Revolution.

Woodrow Wilson elected US president. Foundation of the 'Bull Moose'
Party by Theodore Roosevelt and his followers, splitting the Republican
Party completely. Poincaré becomes French prime minister, and is elected to
the presidency the following year (to 1920). First Balkan War.
Sinking of *Titanic*. Charlie Chaplin's first film.
Completion of new, even grander, Grand Central Station building.
Post-Impressionist exhibition in New York.
Stravinsky's *Rite of Spring* premiered in Paris, provoking riot.
Second Balkan War.

World War I (to 1918). President Wilson proclaims US neutrality. Ludlow
Massacre: striking miners killed in Colorado. Panama Canal opens.
Assassination of Jaurès, French socialist leader.

Sinking of the *Lusitania*.

Battle of the Somme – huge death tolls. Lloyd George British prime
minister. Rasputin assassinated. Dada begins in Zürich.

DATE	AUTHOR'S LIFE	LITERARY CONTEXT
1917		Yeats: *The Wild Swans at Coole.*
1918	Death of elder brother, Frederic Jones. Buys a villa in a village ten miles outside Paris.	Cather: *My Antonia.* Hopkins: *Poems.* Rebecca West: *The Return of the Soldier.*
1919	*French Ways and their Meanings* (to 1920).	Woolf: *Night and Day.* Anderson: *Winesburg, Ohio.* Dos Passos: *One Man's Initiation – 1917.*
1920	*The Age of Innocence.* (Wins Pulitzer Prize, 1921, first awarded to a woman.)	Katherine Mansfield: *Bliss.* Sinclair Lewis: *Main Street.* Lawrence: *Women in Love.* Pound: *Hugh Selwyn Mauberley.*
1921	*The Old Maid* (novella) turned down by several magazines because of its theme of illegitimate birth.	Huxley: *Crome Yellow.*
1922	*The Glimpses of the Moon* sells more than 100,000 copies in six months.	Lewis: *Babbitt.* Woolf: *Jacob's Room.* Mansfield: *The Garden Party.* Joyce: *Ulysses.* T. S. Eliot: *The Waste Land.* Death of Proust.
1922–31	Continues to travel, and buys her Hyères home. Reads and dislikes *Ulysses* and *The Waste Land.* Publishes *The Writing of Fiction*, several novels, collections of short stories and poems (including *A Son at the Front, Old New York, The Mother's Recompense.*)	
1923	Pays short visit to US to receive honorary Doctorate of Letters. Scott Fitzgerald works on film version of *The Glimpses of the Moon.*	Cather: *A Lost Lady.* Cummings: *Tulips and Chimneys.* Shaw: *Saint Joan.*
1924		Ford: *Parade's End* (to 1928). Mann: *The Magic Mountain.*

CHRONOLOGY

HISTORICAL EVENTS

Russian October Revolution. US enters war.

Wilson proposes 'Fourteen Points' for world peace. Armistice (11 November). Worldwide 'flu epidemic kills millions. Women over thirty gain vote in Britain. Irish rebel Con Markievicz elected first British woman MP but refuses her seat. Rutherford splits the atom. Nicholas II assassinated. Civil war in Russia (to 1921).
Versailles Peace Treaty (US refuses to ratify). Amendments 18 (Prohibition) and 19 (Women's Suffrage) to US constitution. Strikes and race riots throughout US; the 'Red Scare'.

League of Nations meets for first time. Huge majority to right-wing Bloc National in French general election. Warren G. Harding elected US president. Slump in US. First radio broadcasting station. The 'jazz rage'.

Quota laws restrict immigration to US. Irish Free State created.
Paris in the 1920s viewed as the cultural capital of the Western world, attracting artists and intellectuals of many nationalities. Famous expatriates there include Picasso, Man Ray, Miró, Chirico, Stravinsky, Prokofiev, Ford, Joyce, Beckett, Durrell, and the 'Lost Generation' of American writers, e.g. Hemingway, Pound, Williams, Stein, Dos Passos, Anderson and Fitzgerald. Mussolini gains power in Italy. Revival of the Ku Klux Klan. Russia becomes USSR: Stalin becomes general secretary of the Communist Party.

Talking pictures developed.

Repeated German defaults on war reparations lead Poincaré (French prime minister once again) to send troops into the Ruhr Valley (to 1925). Financial crisis in Germany. Hitler's Munich *putsch* fails. Calvin Coolidge elected US president after Harding's death. Birth control clinic opened in New York. Economic boom in US (to 1929).
Dawes Plan ends reparation crisis. Poincaré's Bloc National defeated by a coalition of the left, the Cartel des Gauches. French financial crisis which seven cabinets (to 1926) fail to resolve.

DATE	AUTHOR'S LIFE	LITERARY CONTEXT
1925	Meets Scott Fitzgerald and Sinclair Lewis.	Cather: *The Professor's House.* Fitzgerald: *The Great Gatsby.* Dreiser: *An American Tragedy.* Stein: *The Making of Americans.* Dos Passos: *Manhattan Transfer.* Woolf: *Mrs Dalloway*; *The Common Reader.* Gide: *Les Faux-monnayeurs.* Kafka: *The Trial.*
1926		Fitzgerald: *All the Sad Young Men.* Hemingway: *The Sun Also Rises.* Bromfield: *Early Autumn.*
1927	Death of Walter Berry. Attempts by literary figures in the US to promote Wharton for the Nobel Prize end in failure.	Woolf: *To the Lighthouse.* Hemingway: *Men without Women.* Cather: *Death Comes for the Archbishop.* Mauriac: *Thérèse Desqueyroux.*
1928	Death of Teddy Wharton.	Woolf: *Orlando.* Lawrence: *Lady Chatterley's Lover.* Waugh: *Decline and Fall.* Huxley: *Point Counter Point.* Yeats: *The Tower.*
1929	Awarded Gold Medal by American Academy of Arts and Letters. *Hudson River Bracketed.*	Woolf: *A Room of One's Own.* Faulkner: *The Sound and the Fury.* Hemingway: *A Farewell to Arms.*
1930	Aldous Huxley and Cyril Connolly visit Wharton at Hyères.	Dos Passos: *The 42nd Parallel.* Faulkner: *As I Lay Dying.* Hammett: *The Maltese Falcon.* Hart Crane: *The Bridge.* Freud: *Civilization and Its Discontents.* Death of Lawrence.
1932	*The Gods Arrive.* Writing autobiography, *A Backward Glance.* Visits Rome. Becomes increasingly interested in Roman Catholicism.	Glasgow: *The Sheltered Life.* Huxley: *Brave New World.*
1933	Begins work on *The Buccaneers* (published 1938).	Stein: *The Autobiography of Alice B. Toklas.* Ivy Compton Burnett: *More Women than Men.* Céline: *Voyage au bout de la nuit.*

CHRONOLOGY

HISTORICAL EVENTS

'Monkey Trial' (Scopes), Dayton, Tennessee.
Al Capone a powerful force in Chicago.
First public demonstration of television.
Period of Franco-German reconciliation under foreign minister Briand
(to 1930); Locarno Pact guarantees existing frontiers.
First Surrealist exhibition in Paris.
Adolf Hitler: *Mein Kampf*.

General Strike in UK. Germany joins the League of Nations. Poincaré
resumes premiership and succeeds in stabilizing French economy. Chanel
launches the 'little black dress'.

Lindbergh's solo Atlantic flight.

Kellog–Briand Pact outlaws war. First Five-Year Plan in USSR; Stalin is de
facto dictator. 26 million cars and 13 million radios in use in US. Herbert
Hoover elected US president. Amelia Earhart becomes first woman to fly the
Atlantic solo.

New York stock market crash. A worldwide depression follows. Mass
unemployment.

Museum of Modern Art in New York founded. Empire State Building
opened. Gandhi begins civil disobedience campaign in India.
The 1930s see increasingly unstable government in France, with 20 changes
of premier. Construction of Maginot line begins (to 1939).

Unemployment in US rises to 13 million. Franklin D. Roosevelt becomes
president. Lindbergh's son kidnapped. German war reparations suspended
indefinitely at Lausanne. President Doumer assassinated in France.

New Deal begins; Prohibition repealed. Hitler becomes chancellor of
Germany; Germany begins to re-arm. Growth of Fascist movement in
France.

DATE	AUTHOR'S LIFE	LITERARY CONTEXT
1934	*A Backward Glance* published.	Fitzgerald: *Tender is the Night*. Miller: *Tropic of Cancer*. Waugh: *A Handful of Dust*.
1935	Stage version of *The Old Maid* wins Pulitzer Prize for Drama.	Elizabeth Bowen: *The House in Paris*. Cather: *Lucy Gayheart*.
1936	Successful dramatization of *Ethan Frome*.	T. S. Eliot: *Collected Poems*. Dos Passos: *The Big Money*. Faulkner: *Absalom, Absalom!* Santayana: *The Last Puritan*. West: *The Thinking Reed*. Margaret Mitchell: *Gone with the Wind*.
1937	Completes final short story, 'All Souls'. Suffers a stroke in June. Dies 11 August. Buried at Versailles.	Woolf: *The Years*. Hemingway: *To Have and Have Not*. Wallace Stevens: *The Man with the Blue Guitar*.

CHRONOLOGY

ETHAN FROME

I had the story, bit by bit, from various people, and, as generally happens in such cases, each time it was a different story.

If you know Starkfield, Massachusetts, you know the post-
office. If you know the post-office you must have seen Ethan
Frome drive up to it, drop the reins on his hollow-backed
bay and drag himself across the brick pavement to the white
colonnade: and you must have asked who he was.

It was there that, several years ago, I saw him for the first
time; and the sight pulled me up sharp. Even then he was the
most striking figure in Starkfield, though he was but the ruin
of a man. It was not so much his great height that marked him,
for the 'natives' were easily singled out by their lank longitude
from the stockier foreign breed: it was the careless powerful
look he had, in spite of a lameness checking each step like the
jerk of a chain. There was something bleak and unapproachable in his face, and he was so stiffened and grizzled that I took
him for an old man and was surprised to hear that he was not
more than fifty-two. I had this from Harmon Gow, who had
driven the stage from Bettsbridge to Starkfield in pre-trolley
days and knew the chronicle of all the families on his line.

'He's looked that way ever since he had his smash-up; and
that's twenty-four years ago come next February,' Harmon
threw out between reminiscent pauses.

The 'smash-up' it was – I gathered from the same informant
– which, besides drawing the red gash across Ethan Frome's
forehead, had so shortened and warped his right side that it
cost him a visible effort to take the few steps from his buggy
to the post-office window. He used to drive in from his farm
every day at about noon, and as that was my own hour for
fetching my mail I often passed him in the porch or stood

beside him while we waited on the motions of the distributing hand behind the grating. I noticed that, although he came so punctually, he seldom received anything but a copy of the *Bettsbridge Eagle*, which he put without a glance into his sagging pocket. At intervals, however, the post-master would hand him an envelope addressed to Mrs Zenobia – or Mrs Zeena – Frome, and usually bearing conspicuously in the upper left-hand corner the address of some manufacturer of patent medicine and the name of his specific. These documents my neighbour would also pocket without a glance, as if too much used to them to wonder at their number and variety, and would then turn away with a silent nod to the post-master.

Every one in Starkfield knew him and gave him a greeting tempered to his own grave mien; but his taciturnity was respected and it was only on rare occasions that one of the older men of the place detained him for a word. When this happened he would listen quietly, his blue eyes on the speaker's face, and answer in so low a tone that his words never reached me; then he would climb stiffly into his buggy, gather up the reins in his left hand and drive slowly away in the direction of his farm.

'It was a pretty bad smash-up?' I questioned Harmon, looking after Frome's retreating figure, and thinking how gallantly his lean brown head, with its shock of light hair, must have sat on his shoulders before they were bent out of shape.

'Wust kind,' my informant assented. 'More'n enough to kill most men. But the Fromes are tough. Ethan'll likely touch a hundred.'

'Good God!' I exclaimed. At the moment Ethan Frome, after climbing to his seat, had leaned over to assure himself of the security of a wooden box – also with a druggist's label on it – which he had placed in the back of the buggy, and I saw his face as it probably looked when he thought himself alone. '*That* man touch a hundred? He looks as if he was dead and in hell now!'

Harmon drew a slab of tobacco from his pocket, cut off a wedge and pressed it into the leather pouch of his cheek.

'Guess he's been in Starkfield too many winters. Most of the smart ones get away.'

'Why didn't *he*?'

'Somebody had to stay and care for the folks. There warn't ever anybody but Ethan. First his father – then his mother – then his wife.'

'And then the smash-up?'

Harmon chuckled sardonically. 'That's so. He *had* to stay then.'

'I see. And since then they've had to care for him?'

Harmon thoughtfully passed his tobacco to the other cheek. 'Oh, as to that: I guess it's always Ethan done the caring.'

Though Harmon Gow developed the tale as far as his mental and moral reach permitted, there were perceptible gaps between his facts, and I had the sense that the deeper meaning of the story was in the gaps. But one phrase stuck in my memory and served as the nucleus about which I grouped my subsequent inferences: 'Guess he's been in Starkfield too many winters.'

Before my own time there was up I had learned to know what that meant. Yet I had come in the degenerate day of trolley, bicycle and rural delivery, when communication was easy between the scattered mountain villages, and the bigger towns in the valleys, such as Bettsbridge and Shadd's Falls, had libraries, theatres and Y.M.C.A. halls to which the youth of the hills could descend for recreation. But when winter shut down on Starkfield, and the village lay under a sheet of snow perpetually renewed from the pale skies, I began to see what life there – or rather its negation – must have been in Ethan Frome's young manhood.

I had been sent up by my employers on a job connected with the big power-house at Corbury Junction, and a long-drawn carpenters' strike had so delayed the work that I found myself anchored at Starkfield – the nearest habitable spot – for the best part of the winter. I chafed at first, and then, under the hypnotizing effect of routine, gradually began to find a grim satisfaction in the life. During the early part of my stay

I had been struck by the contrast between the vitality of the climate and the deadness of the community. Day by day, after the December snows were over, a blazing blue sky poured down torrents of light and air on the white landscape, which gave them back in an intenser glitter. One would have supposed that such an atmosphere must quicken the emotions as well as the blood; but it seemed to produce no change except that of retarding still more the sluggish pulse of Starkfield. When I had been there a little longer, and had seen this phase of crystal clearness followed by long stretches of sunless cold; when the storms of February had pitched their white tents about the devoted village, and the wild cavalry of March winds had charged down to their support; I began to understand why Starkfield emerged from its six months' siege like a starved garrison capitulating without quarter. Twenty years earlier the means of resistance must have been far fewer, and the enemy in command of almost all the lines of access between the beleaguered villages; and, considering these things, I felt the sinister force of Harmon's phrase: 'Most of the smart ones get away.' But if that were the case, how could any combination of obstacles have hindered the flight of a man like Ethan Frome?

During my stay at Starkfield I lodged with a middle-aged widow colloquially known as Mrs Ned Hale. Mrs Hale's father had been the village lawyer of the previous generation, and 'lawyer Varnum's house', where my landlady still lived with her mother, was the most considerable mansion in the village. It stood at one end of the main street, its classic portico and small-paned windows looking down a flagged path between Norway spruces to the slim white steeple of the Congregational church. It was clear that the Varnum fortunes were at the ebb, but the two women did what they could to preserve a decent dignity; and Mrs Hale, in particular, had a certain wan refinement not out of keeping with her pale old-fashioned house.

In the 'best parlour', with its black horse-hair and mahogany weakly illuminated by a gurgling Carcel lamp, I listened every evening to another and more delicately shaded version of the Starkfield chronicle. It was not that Mrs Ned Hale felt, or affected, any social superiority to the people about her; it was only that the accident of a finer sensibility and a little more education had put just enough distance between herself and her neighbours to enable her to judge them with detachment. She was not unwilling to exercise this faculty, and I had great hopes of getting from her the missing facts of Ethan Frome's story, or rather such a key to his character as should co-ordinate the facts I knew. Her mind was a storehouse of innocuous anecdote, and any question about her acquaintances brought forth a volume of detail; but on the subject of Ethan Frome I found her unexpectedly reticent. There was no hint of disapproval in her reserve; I merely felt in her an insurmountable reluctance to speak of him or his affairs, a low 'Yes, I knew them both . . . it was awful . . .' seeming to be the utmost concession that her distress could make to my curiosity.

So marked was the change in her manner, such depths of sad initiation did it imply, that, with some doubts as to my delicacy, I put the case anew to my village oracle, Harmon Gow; but got for my pains only an uncomprehending grunt.

'Ruth Varnum was always as nervous as a rat; and, come to think of it, she was the first one to see 'em after they was picked up. It happened right below lawyer Varnum's, down at the bend of the Corbury road, just round about the time that Ruth got engaged to Ned Hale. The young folks was all friends, and I guess she just can't bear to talk about it. She's had troubles enough of her own.'

All the dwellers in Starkfield, as in more notable communities, had had troubles enough of their own to make them comparatively indifferent to those of their neighbours; and though all conceded that Ethan Frome's had been beyond the common measure, no one gave me an explanation of the look in his face which, as I persisted in thinking, neither poverty nor physical suffering could have put there. Nevertheless, I might have contented myself with the story pieced together from these hints had it not been for the provocation of Mrs Hale's silence, and – a little later – for the accident of personal contact with the man.

On my arrival at Starkfield, Denis Eady, the rich Irish grocer, who was the proprietor of Starkfield's nearest approach to a livery stable, had entered into an agreement to send me over daily to Corbury Flats, where I had to pick up my train for the Junction. But about the middle of the winter Eady's horses fell ill of a local epidemic. The illness spread to the other Starkfield stables and for a day or two I was put to it to find a means of transport. Then Harmon Gow suggested that Ethan Frome's bay was still on his legs and that his owner might be glad to drive me over.

I stared at the suggestion. 'Ethan Frome? But I've never even spoken to him. Why on earth should he put himself out for me?'

Harmon's answer surprised me still more. 'I don't know as he would; but I know he wouldn't be sorry to earn a dollar.'

I had been told that Frome was poor, and that the saw-mill and the arid acres of his farm yielded scarcely enough to keep his household through the winter; but I had not supposed him to be in such want as Harmon's words implied, and I expressed my wonder.

'Well, matters ain't gone any too well with him,' Harmon said. 'When a man's been setting round like a hulk for twenty years or more, seeing things that want doing, it eats inter him, and he loses his grit. That Frome farm was always 'bout as bare's a milkpan when the cat's been round; and you know what one of them old water-mills is wuth nowadays. When Ethan could sweat over 'em both from sun-up to dark he kinder choked a living out of 'em; but his folks ate up most everything, even then, and I don't see how he makes out now. Fust his father got a kick, out haying, and went soft in the brain, and gave away money like Bible texts afore he died. Then his mother got queer and dragged along for years as weak as a baby; and his wife Zeena, she's always been the greatest hand at doctoring in the county. Sickness and trouble: that's what Ethan's had his plate full up with, ever since the very first helping.'

The next morning, when I looked out, I saw the hollow-backed bay between the Varnum spruces, and Ethan Frome, throwing back his worn bearskin, made room for me in the sleigh at his side. After that, for a week, he drove me over every morning to Corbury Flats, and on my return in the afternoon met me again and carried me back through the icy night to Starkfield. The distance each way was barely three miles, but the old bay's pace was slow, and even with firm snow under the runners we were nearly an hour on the way. Ethan Frome drove in silence, the reins loosely held in his left hand, his brown seamed profile, under the helmet-like peak of the cap, relieved against the banks of snow like the bronze image of a hero. He never turned his face to mine, or answered, except in monosyllables, the questions I put, or such slight pleasantries as I ventured. He seemed a part of the mute melancholy land-scape, an incarnation of its frozen woe, with all that was warm and sentient in him fast bound below the surface; but there was nothing unfriendly in his silence. I simply felt that he lived in a depth of moral isolation too remote for casual access, and I had the sense that his loneliness was not merely the result of his personal plight, tragic as I guessed that to be, but had in it, as Harmon Gow had hinted, the profound accumulated cold of many Starkfield winters.

Only once or twice was the distance between us bridged for a moment; and the glimpses thus gained confirmed my desire to know more. Once I happened to speak of an engi-neering job I had been on the previous year in Florida, and of the contrast between the winter landscape about us and that in which I had found myself the year before; and to my surprise Frome said suddenly: 'Yes: I was down there once, and for a good while afterward I could call up the sight of it in winter. But now it's all snowed under.'

He said no more, and I had to guess the rest from the inflection of his voice and his sharp relapse into silence.

Another day, on getting into my train at the Flats, I missed a volume of popular science – I think it was on some recent discoveries in bio-chemistry – which I had carried with me to read on the way. I thought no more about it till I got into the sleigh again that evening, and saw the book in Frome's hand.

'I found it after you were gone,' he said.

I put the volume into my pocket and we dropped back into our usual silence; but as we began to crawl up the long hill from Corbury Flats to the Starkfield ridge I became aware in the dusk that he had turned his face to mine.

'There are things in that book that I didn't know the first word about,' he said.

I wondered less at his words than at the queer note of resentment in his voice. He was evidently surprised and slightly aggrieved at his own ignorance.

'Does that sort of thing interest you?' I asked.

'It used to.'

'There are one or two rather new things in the book: there have been some big strides lately in that particular line of research.' I waited a moment for an answer that did not come; then I said: 'If you'd like to look the book through I'd be glad to leave it with you.'

He hesitated, and I had the impression that he felt himself about to yield to a stealing tide of inertia; then, 'Thank you – I'll take it,' he answered shortly.

I hoped that this incident might set up some more direct communication between us. Frome was so simple and straightforward that I was sure his curiosity about the book was based on a genuine interest in its subject. Such tastes and acquirements in a man of his condition made the contrast more poignant between his outer situation and his inner needs, and I hoped that the chance of giving expression to the latter might at least unseal his lips. But something in his past history, or in his present way of living, had apparently driven him too deeply into himself for any casual impulse to draw him back to his kind. At our next meeting he made no allusion to the book, and our intercourse seemed fated to remain as negative and one-sided as if there had been no break in his reserve.

Frome had been driving me over to the Flats for about a week when one morning I looked out of my window into a thick snow-fall. The height of the white waves massed against the garden-fence and along the wall of the church showed that the storm must have been going on all night, and that the drifts were likely to be heavy in the open. I thought it probable that my train would be delayed; but I had to be at the power-house for an hour or two that afternoon, and I decided, if Frome turned up, to push through to the Flats and wait there till my train came in. I don't know why I put it in the conditional, however, for I never doubted that Frome would appear. He was not the kind of man to be turned from his business by any commotion of the elements; and at the appointed hour his sleigh glided up through the snow like a stage-apparition behind thickening veils of gauze.

I was getting to know him too well to express either wonder or gratitude at his keeping his appointment; but I exclaimed in surprise as I saw him turn his horse in a direction opposite to that of the Corbury road.

'The railroad's blocked by a freight-train that got stuck in a drift below the Flats,' he explained, as we jogged off into the stinging whiteness.

'But look here – where are you taking me, then?'

'Straight to the Junction, by the shortest way,' he answered, pointing up School House Hill with his whip.

'To the Junction – in this storm? Why, it's a good ten miles!'

'The bay'll do it if you give him time. You said you had some business there this afternoon. I'll see you get there.'

He said it so quietly that I could only answer: 'You're doing me the biggest kind of a favour.'

'That's all right,' he rejoined.

Abreast of the schoolhouse the road forked, and we dipped down a lane to the left, between hemlock boughs bent inward to their trunks by the weight of the snow. I had often walked that way on Sundays, and knew that the solitary roof showing through bare branches near the bottom of the hill was that of Frome's saw-mill. It looked exanimate enough, with its idle wheel looming above the black stream dashed with yellow-white spume, and its cluster of sheds sagging under their white load. Frome did not even turn his head as we drove by, and still in silence we began to mount the next slope. About a mile farther, on a road I had never travelled, we came to an orchard of starved apple-trees writhing over a hillside among out-croppings of slate that nuzzled up through the snow like animals pushing out their noses to breathe. Beyond the orchard lay a field or two, their boundaries lost under drifts; and above the fields, huddled against the white immensities of land and sky, one of those lonely New England farm-houses that make the landscape lonelier.

'That's my place,' said Frome, with a sideway jerk of his lame elbow; and in the distress and oppression of the scene I did not know what to answer. The snow had ceased, and a flash of watery sunlight exposed the house on the slope above us in all its plaintive ugliness. The black wraith of a deciduous creeper flapped from the porch, and the thin wooden walls, under their worn coat of paint, seemed to shiver in the wind that had risen with the ceasing of the snow.

'The house was bigger in my father's time: I had to take down the "L", a while back,' Frome continued, checking with a twitch of the left rein the bay's evident intention of turning in through the broken-down gate.

I saw then that the unusually forlorn and stunted look of the house was partly due to the loss of what is known in New England as the 'L': that long deep-roofed adjunct usually built at right angles to the main house, and connecting it, by way of store-rooms and tool-house, with the wood-shed and cow-barn. Whether because of its symbolic sense, the image it presents of a life linked with the soil, and enclosing in itself the chief sources of warmth and nourishment, or whether merely because of the consolatory thought that it enables the dwellers in that harsh climate to get to their morning's work without facing the weather, it is certain that the 'L' rather than the house itself seems to be the centre, the actual hearthstone, of the New England farm. Perhaps this connection of ideas, which had often occurred to me in my rambles about Stark-field, caused me to hear a wistful note in Frome's words, and to see in the diminished dwelling the image of his own shrunken body.

'We're kinder side-tracked here now,' he added, 'but there was considerable passing before the railroad was carried through to the Flats.' He roused the lagging bay with another twitch; then, as if the mere sight of the house had let me too deeply into his confidence for any farther pretence of reserve, he went on slowly: 'I've always set down the worst of mother's trouble to that. When she got the rheumatism so bad she couldn't move around she used to sit up there and watch the road by the hour; and one year, when they was six months mending the Bettsbridge pike after the floods, and Harmon Gow had to bring his stage round this way, she picked up so that she used to get down to the gate most days to see him. But after the trains begun running nobody ever come by here to speak of, and mother never could get it through her head what had happened, and it preyed on her right along till she died.'

As we turned into the Corbury road the snow began to fall again, cutting off our last glimpse of the house; and Frome's silence fell with it, letting down between us the old veil of reticence. This time the wind did not cease with the return of the snow. Instead, it sprang up to a gale which now and then, from a tattered sky, flung pale sweeps of sunlight over a landscape chaotically tossed. But the bay was as good as Frome's word, and we pushed on to the Junction through the wild white scene.

In the afternoon the storm held off, and the clearness in the west seemed to my inexperienced eye the pledge of a fair evening. I finished my business as quickly as possible, and we set out for Starkfield with a good chance of getting there for supper. But at sunset the clouds gathered again, bringing an earlier night, and the snow began to fall straight and steadily from a sky without wind, in a soft universal diffusion more confusing than the gusts and eddies of the morning. It seemed to be a part of the thickening darkness, to be the winter night itself descending on us layer by layer.

The small ray of Frome's lantern was soon lost in this smothering medium, in which even his sense of direction, and the bay's homing instinct, finally ceased to serve us. Two or three times some ghostly landmark sprang up to warn us that we were astray, and then was sucked back into the mist; and when we finally regained our road the old horse began to show signs of exhaustion. I felt myself to blame for having accepted Frome's offer, and after a short discussion I persuaded him to let me get out of the sleigh and walk along through the snow at the bay's side. In this way we struggled on for another mile or two, and at last reached a point where Frome, peering into what seemed to me formless night, said: 'That's my gate down yonder.'

The last stretch had been the hardest part of the way. The bitter cold and the heavy going had nearly knocked the wind out of me, and I could feel the horse's side ticking like a clock under my hand.

'Look here, Frome,' I began, 'there's no earthly use in your going any farther –' but he interrupted me: 'Nor you neither. There's been about enough of this for anybody.'

I understood that he was offering me a night's shelter at the farm, and without answering I turned into the gate at his side, and followed him to the barn, where I helped him to unharness and bed down the tired horse. When this was done he un-hooked the lantern from the sleigh, stepped out again into the night, and called to me over his shoulder: 'This way.'

Far off above us a square of light trembled through the screen of snow. Staggering along in Frome's wake I floundered toward it, and in the darkness almost fell into one of the deep drifts against the front of the house. Frome scrambled up the slippery steps of the porch, digging a way through the snow with his heavily booted foot. Then he lifted his lantern, found the latch, and led the way into the house. I went after him into a low unlit passage, at the back of which a ladder-like staircase rose into obscurity. On our right a line of light marked the door of the room which had sent its ray across the night; and behind the door I heard a woman's voice droning querulously.

Frome stamped on the worn oil-cloth to shake the snow from his boots, and set down his lantern on a kitchen chair which was the only piece of furniture in the hall. Then he opened the door.

'Come in,' he said; and as he spoke the droning voice grew still.

It was that night that I found the clue to Ethan Frome, and began to put together this vision of his story. . . . . . .
. . . .
. . . .

I

The village lay under two feet of snow, with drifts at the windy corners. In a sky of iron the points of the Dipper hung like icicles and Orion flashed his cold fires. The moon had set, but the night was so transparent that the white house-fronts between the elms looked grey against the snow, clumps of bushes made black stains on it, and the basement windows of the church sent shafts of yellow light far across the endless undulations.

Young Ethan Frome walked at a quick pace along the deserted street, past the bank and Michael Eady's new brick store and Lawyer Varnum's house with the two black Norway spruces at the gate. Opposite the Varnum gate, where the road fell away toward the Corbury valley, the church reared its slim white steeple and narrow peristyle. As the young man walked toward it the upper windows drew a black arcade along the side wall of the building, but from the lower openings, on the side where the ground sloped steeply down to the Corbury road, the light shot its long bars, illuminating many fresh furrows in the track leading to the basement door, and show-ing, under an adjoining shed, a line of sleighs with heavily blanketed horses.

The night was perfectly still, and the air so dry and pure that it gave little sensation of cold. The effect produced on Frome was rather of a complete absence of atmosphere, as though nothing less tenuous than ether intervened between the white earth under his feet and the metallic dome overhead. 'It's like being in an exhausted receiver,' he thought. Four or five years earlier he had taken a year's course at a technological college at Worcester, and dabbled in the laboratory with a friendly

professor of physics; and the images supplied by that experience still cropped up, at unexpected moments, through the
totally different associations of thought in which he had since
been living. His father's death, and the misfortunes following
it, had put a premature end to Ethan's studies; but though they
had not gone far enough to be of much practical use they had
fed his fancy and made him aware of huge cloudy meanings
behind the daily face of things.

As he strode along through the snow the sense of such meanings glowed in his brain and mingled with the bodily flush
produced by his sharp tramp. At the end of the village he
paused before the darkened front of the church. He stood
there a moment, breathing quickly, and looking up and down
the street, in which not another figure moved. The pitch of
the Corbury road, below lawyer Varnum's spruces, was the
favourite coasting-ground of Starkfield, and on clear evenings
the church corner rang till late with the shouts of the coasters;
but to-night not a sled darkened the whiteness of the long
declivity. The hush of midnight lay on the village, and all its
wakening life was gathered behind the church windows, from
which strains of dance-music flowed with the broad bands of
yellow light.

The young man, skirting the side of the building, went down
the slope toward the basement door. To keep out of range of
the revealing rays from within he made a circuit through the
untrodden snow and gradually approached the farther angle of
the basement wall. Thence, still hugging the shadow, he edged
his way cautiously forward to the nearest window, holding back
his straight spare body and craning his neck till he got a glimpse
of the room.

Seen thus, from the pure and frosty darkness in which he
stood, it seemed to be seething in a mist of heat. The metal
reflectors of the gas-jets sent crude waves of light against the
whitewashed walls, and the iron flanks of the stove at the end
of the hall looked as though they were heaving with volcanic
fires. The floor was thronged with girls and young men. Down
the side wall facing the window stood a row of kitchen chairs

from which the older women had just risen. By this time the music had stopped, and the musicians – a fiddler, and the young lady who played the harmonium on Sundays – were hastily refreshing themselves at one corner of the supper-table which aligned its devastated pie-dishes and ice-cream saucers on the platform at the end of the hall. The guests were preparing to leave, and the tide had already set toward the passage where coats and wraps were hung, when a young man with a sprightly foot and a shock of black hair shot into the middle of the floor and clapped his hands. The signal took instant effect. The musicians hurried to their instruments, the dancers – some already half-muffled for departure – fell into line down each side of the room, the older spectators slipped back to their chairs, and the lively young man, after diving about here and there in the throng, drew forth a girl who had already wound a cherry-coloured 'fascinator' about her head, and, leading her up to the end of the floor, whirled her down its length to the bounding tune of a Virginia reel.

Frome's heart was beating fast. He had been straining for a glimpse of the dark head under the cherry-coloured scarf and it vexed him that another eye should have been quicker than his. The leader of the reel, who looked as if he had Irish blood in his veins, danced well, and his partner caught his fire. As she passed down the line, her light figure swinging from hand to hand in circles of increasing swiftness, the scarf flew off her head and stood out behind her shoulders, and Frome, at each turn, caught sight of her laughing panting lips, the cloud of dark hair about her forehead, and the dark eyes which seemed the only fixed points in a maze of flying lines.

The dancers were going faster and faster, and the musicians, to keep up with them, belaboured their instruments like jockeys lashing their mounts on the home-stretch; yet it seemed to the young man at the window that the reel would never end. Now and then he turned his eyes from the girl's face to that of her partner, which, in the exhilaration of the dance, had taken on a look of almost impudent ownership. Denis Eady was the son of Michael Eady, the ambitious Irish grocer, whose suppleness and effrontery had given Starkfield its first notion of 'smart' business methods, and whose new brick store testified to the success of the attempt. His son seemed likely to follow in his steps, and was meanwhile applying the same arts to the conquest of the Starkfield maidenhood. Hitherto Ethan Frome had been content to think him a mean fellow; but now he positively invited a horse-whipping. It was strange that the girl did not seem aware of it: that she could lift her rapt face to her dancer's, and drop her hands into his, without appearing to feel the offence of his look and touch.

Frome was in the habit of walking into Starkfield to fetch home his wife's cousin, Mattie Silver, on the rare evenings when some chance of amusement drew her to the village. It was his wife who had suggested, when the girl came to live with them, that such opportunities should be put in her way. Mattie Silver came from Stamford, and when she entered the Fromes' household to act as her cousin Zeena's aid it was thought best, as she came without pay, not to let her feel too sharp a contrast between the life she had left and the isolation of a Starkfield farm. But for this – as Frome sardonically reflected – it would hardly have occurred to Zeena to take any thought for the girl's amusement.

When his wife first proposed that they should give Mattie an occasional evening out he had inwardly demurred at having to do the extra two miles to the village and back after his hard day on the farm; but not long afterward he had reached the point of wishing that Starkfield might give all its nights to revelry.

Mattie Silver had lived under his roof for a year, and from early morning till they met at supper he had frequent chances of seeing her; but no moments in her company were comparable to those when, her arm in his, and her light step flying to keep time with his long stride, they walked back through the night to the farm. He had taken to the girl from the first day, when he had driven over to the Flats to meet her, and she had smiled and waved to him from the train, crying out 'You must be Ethan!' as she jumped down with her bundles, while he reflected, looking over her slight person: 'She don't look much on house-work, but she ain't a fretter, anyhow.' But it was not only that the coming to his house of a bit of hopeful young life was like the lighting of a fire on a cold hearth. The girl was more than the bright serviceable creature he had thought her. She had an eye to see and an ear to hear: he could show her things and tell her things, and taste the bliss of feeling that all he imparted left long reverberations and echoes he could wake at will.

It was during their night walks back to the farm that he felt most intensely the sweetness of this communion. He had always been more sensitive than the people about him to the appeal of natural beauty. His unfinished studies had given form to this sensibility and even in his unhappiest moments field and sky spoke to him with a deep and powerful persuasion. But hitherto the emotion had remained in him as a silent ache, veiling with sadness the beauty that evoked it. He did not even know whether any one else in the world felt as he did, or whether he was the sole victim of this mournful privilege. Then he learned that one other spirit had trembled with the same touch of wonder: that at his side, living under his roof and eating his bread, was a creature to whom he could say: 'That's Orion down yonder; the big fellow to the right is Aldebaran, and the bunch of little ones – like bees swarming – they're the Pleiades...' or whom he could hold entranced before a ledge of granite thrusting up through the fern while he unrolled the huge panorama of the ice age, and the long dim stretches of succeeding time. The fact that admiration for his learning mingled with Mattie's wonder at what he taught was not the least part of his pleasure. And there were other sensations, less definable but more exquisite, which drew them together with a shock of silent joy: the cold red of sunset behind winter hills, the flight of cloud-flocks over slopes of golden stubble, or the intensely blue shadows of hemlocks on sunlit snow. When she said to him once: 'It looks just as if it was painted!' it seemed to Ethan that the art of definition could go no farther, and that words had at last been found to utter his secret soul. . . .

As he stood in the darkness outside the church these memories came back with the poignancy of vanished things. Watching Mattie whirl down the floor from hand to hand, he wondered how he could ever have thought that his dull talk interested her. To him, who was never gay but in her presence, her gaiety seemed plain proof of indifference. The face she lifted to her dancers was the same which, when she saw him, always looked like a window that has caught the sunset. He even noticed two or three gestures which, in his fatuity, he had thought she kept for him: a way of throwing her head back when she was amused, as if to taste her laugh before she let it out, and a trick of sinking her lids slowly when anything charmed or moved her.

The sight made him unhappy, and his unhappiness roused his latent fears. His wife had never shown any jealousy of Mattie, but of late she had grumbled increasingly over the house-work and found oblique ways of attracting attention to the girl's inefficiency. Zeena had always been what Starkfield called 'sickly', and Frome had to admit that, if she were as ailing as she believed, she needed the help of a stronger arm than the one which lay so lightly in his during the night walks to the farm. Mattie had no natural turn for house-keeping, and her training had done nothing to remedy the defect. She was quick to learn, but forgetful and dreamy, and not disposed to take the matter seriously. Ethan had an idea that if she were to marry a man she was fond of the dormant instinct would wake, and her pies and biscuits become the pride of the county; but domest-icity in the abstract did not interest her. At first she was so awk-ward that he could not help laughing at her; but she laughed with him and that made them better friends. He did his best to supplement her unskilled efforts, getting up earlier than usual to light the kitchen fire, carrying in the wood overnight, and neglecting the mill for the farm that he might help her about the house during the day. He even crept down on Satur-day nights to scrub the kitchen floor after the women had gone to bed; and Zeena, one day, had surprised him at the churn and had turned away silently, with one of her queer looks.

Of late there had been other signs of his wife's disfavour, as intangible but more disquieting. One cold winter morning, as he dressed in the dark, his candle flickering in the draught of the ill-fitting window, he had heard her speak from the bed behind him.

'The doctor don't want I should be left without anybody to do for me,' she said in her flat whine.

He had supposed her to be asleep, and the sound of her voice had startled him, though she was given to abrupt explosions of speech after long intervals of secretive silence.

He turned and looked at her where she lay indistinctly outlined under the dark calico quilt, her high-boned face taking a greyish tinge from the whiteness of the pillow.

'Nobody to do for you?' he repeated.

'If you say you can't afford a hired girl when Mattie goes.'

Frome turned away again, and taking up his razor stooped to catch the reflection of his stretched cheek in the blotched looking-glass above the wash-stand.

'Why on earth should Mattie go?'

'Well, when she gets married, I mean,' his wife's drawl came from behind him.

'Oh, she'd never leave us as long as you needed her,' he returned, scraping hard at his chin.

'I wouldn't ever have it said that I stood in the way of a poor girl like Mattie marrying a smart fellow like Denis Eady,' Zeena answered in a tone of plaintive self-effacement.

Ethan, glaring at his face in the glass, threw his head back to draw the razor from ear to chin. His hand was steady, but the attitude was an excuse for not making an immediate reply.

'And the doctor don't want I should be left without anybody,' Zeena continued. 'He wanted I should speak to you about a girl he's heard about, that might come —'

Ethan laid down the razor and straightened himself with a laugh.

'Denis Eady! If that's all I guess there's no such hurry to look round for a girl.'

'Well, I'd like to talk to you about it,' said Zeena obstinately.

He was getting into his clothes in fumbling haste. 'All right. But I haven't got the time now; I'm late as it is,' he returned, holding his old silver turnip-watch to the candle.

Zeena, apparently accepting this as final, lay watching him in silence while he pulled his suspenders over his shoulders and jerked his arms into his coat; but as he went toward the door she said, suddenly and incisively: 'I guess you're always late, now you shave every morning.'

That thrust had frightened him more than any vague insinuations about Denis Eady. It was a fact that since Mattie Silver's coming he had taken to shaving every day; but his wife always seemed to be asleep when he left her side in the winter darkness, and he had stupidly assumed that she would not notice any change in his appearance. Once or twice in the past he had been faintly disquieted by Zenobia's way of letting things happen without seeming to remark them, and then, weeks afterward, in a casual phrase, revealing that she had all along taken her notes and drawn her inferences. Of late, however, there had been no room in his thoughts for such vague apprehensions. Zeena herself, from an oppressive reality, had faded into an insubstantial shade. All his life was lived in the sight and sound of Mattie Silver, and he could no longer conceive of its being otherwise. But now, as he stood outside the church, and saw Mattie spinning down the floor with Denis Eady, a throng of disregarded hints and menaces wove their cloud about his brain . . .

II

As the dancers poured out of the hall Frome, drawing back behind the projecting storm-door, watched the segregation of the grotesquely muffled groups, in which a moving lantern ray now and then lit up a face flushed with food and dancing. The villagers, being afoot, were the first to climb the slope to the main street, while the country neighbouts packed themselves more slowly into the sleighs under the shed.

'Ain't you riding, Mattie?' a woman's voice called back from the throng about the shed, and Ethan's heart gave a jump. From where he stood he could not see the persons coming out of the hall till they had advanced a few steps beyond the wooden sides of the storm-door; but through its cracks he heard a clear voice answer: 'Mercy no! Not on such a night.'

She was there, then, close to him, only a thin board between. In another moment she would step forth into the night, and his eyes, accustomed to the obscurity, would discern her as clearly as though she stood in daylight. A wave of shyness pulled him back into the dark angle of the wall, and he stood there in silence instead of making his presence known to her. It had been one of the wonders of their intercourse that from the first, she, the quicker, finer, more expressive, instead of crushing him by the contrast, had given him something of her own ease and freedom; but now he felt as heavy and loutish as in his student days, when he had tried to 'jolly' the Worcester girls at a picnic.

He hung back, and she came out alone and paused within a few yards of him. She was almost the last to leave the hall, and she stood looking uncertainly about her as if wondering why he did not show himself. Then a man's figure approached, coming so close to her that under their formless wrappings they seemed merged in one dim outline.

'Gentleman friend gone back on you? Say, Matt, that's tough! No, I wouldn't be mean enough to tell the other girls. I ain't as low-down as that.' (How Frome hated Denis's banter!) 'But look at here, ain't it lucky I got the old man's cutter down there waiting for us?'

Frome heard the girl's voice, gaily incredulous: 'What on earth's your father's cutter doin' down there?'

'Why, waiting for me to take a ride. I got the roan colt too. I kinder knew I'd want to take a ride to-night,' Eady, in his triumph, tried to put a sentimental note into his bragging voice.

The girl seemed to waver, and Frome saw her twirl the end of her scarf irresolutely about her fingers. Not for the world would he have made a sign to her, though it seemed to him that his life hung on her next gesture.

'Hold on a minute while I unhitch the colt,' Denis called to her, springing toward the shed.

She stood perfectly still, looking after him, in an attitude of tranquil expectancy torturing to the hidden watcher. Frome noticed that she no longer turned her head from side to side, as though peering through the night for another figure. She let Denis Eady lead out the horse, climb into the cutter and fling back the bearskin to make room for her at his side; then, with a swift motion of flight, she turned about and darted up the slope toward the front of the church.

'Good-bye! Hope you'll have a lovely ride!' she called back to him over her shoulder.

Denis laughed, and gave the horse a cut that brought him quickly abreast of her.

'Come along! Get in quick! It's as slippery as thunder on this turn,' he cried, leaning over to reach out a hand.

She laughed back at him: 'Good-night! I'm not getting in.'

By this time they had passed beyond Frome's earshot and he could only follow the shadowy pantomime of their silhouettes as they continued to move along the crest of the slope above him. He saw Eady, after a moment, jump from the cutter and go toward the girl with the reins over one arm. The other he tried to slip through hers; but she eluded him nimbly, and Frome's heart, which had swung out over a black void, trembled back to safety. A moment later he heard the jingle of departing sleigh bells and discerned a figure advancing alone toward the empty expanse of snow before the church.

In the black shade of the Varnum spruces he caught up with her and she turned with a quick 'Oh!'

'Think I'd forgotten you, Matt?' he asked with sheepish glee.

She answered seriously: 'I thought maybe you couldn't come back for me.'

'Couldn't? What on earth could stop me?'

'I knew Zeena wasn't feeling any too good to-day.'

'Oh, she's in bed long ago.' He paused, a question struggling in him. 'Then you meant to walk home all alone?'

'Oh, I ain't afraid!' she laughed.

They stood together in the gloom of the spruces, an empty world glimmering about them wide and grey under the stars. He brought his question out.

'If you thought I hadn't come, why didn't you ride back with Denis Eady?'

'Why, where *were* you? How did you know? I never saw you!'

Her wonder and his laughter ran together like spring rills in a thaw. Ethan had the sense of having done something arch and ingenious. To prolong the effect he groped for a dazzling phrase, and brought out, in a growl of rapture: 'Come along.'

He slipped an arm through hers, as Eady had done, and fancied it was faintly pressed against her side; but neither of them moved. It was so dark under the spruces that he could barely see the shape of her head beside his shoulder. He longed to stoop his cheek and rub it against her scarf. He would have liked to stand there with her all night in the blackness. She moved forward a step or two and then paused again above the dip of the Corbury road. Its icy slope, scored by innumerable runners, looked like a mirror scratched by travellers at an inn.

'There was a whole lot of them coasting before the moon set,' she said.

'Would you like to come in and coast with them some night?' he asked.

'Oh, *would* you, Ethan? It would be lovely!'

'We'll come to-morrow if there's a moon.'

She lingered, pressing closer to his side. 'Ned Hale and Ruth Varnum came just as *near* running into the big elm at the bottom. We were all sure they were killed.' Her shiver ran down his arm. 'Wouldn't it have been too awful? They're so happy!'

'Oh, Ned ain't much at steering. I guess I can take you down all right!' he said disdainfully.

He was aware that he was 'talking big', like Denis Eady; but his reaction of joy had unsteadied him, and the inflection with which she had said of the engaged couple 'They're so happy!' made the words sound as if she had been thinking of herself and him.

'The elm *is* dangerous, though. It ought to be cut down,' she insisted.

'Would you be afraid of it, with me?'

'I told you I ain't the kind to be afraid,' she tossed back, almost indifferently; and suddenly she began to walk on with a rapid step.

These alterations of mood were the despair and joy of Ethan Frome. The motions of her mind were as incalculable as the flit of a bird in the branches. The fact that he had no right to show his feelings, and thus provoke the expression of hers, made him attach a fantastic importance to every change in her look and tone. Now he thought she understood him, and feared; now he was sure she did not, and despaired. Tonight the pressure of accumulated misgivings sent the scale drooping toward despair, and her indifference was the more chilling after the flush of joy into which she had plunged him by dismissing Denis Eady. He mounted School House Hill at her side and walked on in silence till they reached the lane leading to the saw-mill; then the need of some definite assurance grew too strong for him.

'You'd have found me right off if you hadn't gone back to have that last reel with Denis,' he brought out awkwardly. He could not pronounce the name without a stiffening of the muscles of his throat.

'Why, Ethan, how could I tell you were there?'

'I suppose what folks say is true,' he jerked out at her, instead of answering.

She stopped short, and he felt, in the darkness, that her face was lifted quickly to his. 'Why, what do folks say?'

'It's natural enough you should be leaving us,' he floundered on, following his thought.

'Is that what they say?' she mocked back at him; then, with a sudden drop of her sweet treble: 'You mean that Zeena – ain't suited with me any more?' she faltered.

Their arms had slipped apart and they stood motionless, each seeking to distinguish the other's face.

'I know I ain't anything like as smart as I ought to be,' she went on, while he vainly struggled for expression. 'There's lots of things a hired girl could do that come awkward to me still – and I haven't got much strength in my arms. But if she'd only tell me I'd try. You know she hardly ever says anything, and sometimes I can see she ain't suited, and yet I don't know why.' She turned on him with a sudden flash of indignation. 'You'd ought to tell me, Ethan Frome – you'd ought to! Unless *you* want me to go too —'

Unless he wanted her to go too! The cry was balm to his raw wound. The iron heavens seemed to melt and rain down sweetness. Again he struggled for the all-expressive word, and again, his arm in hers, found only a deep 'Come along.'

They walked on in silence through the blackness of the hemlock-shaded lane, where Ethan's saw-mill gloomed through the night, and out again into the comparative clearness of the fields. On the farther side of the hemlock belt the open country rolled away before them grey and lonely under the stars. Sometimes their way led them under the shade of an overhanging bank or through the thin obscurity of a clump of leafless trees. Here and there a farmhouse stood far back among the fields, mute and cold as a grave-stone. The night was so still that they heard the frozen snow crackle under their feet. The crash of a loaded branch falling far off in the woods reverberated like a musket-shot, and once a fox barked, and Mattie shrank closer to Ethan, and quickened her steps.

At length they sighted the group of larches at Ethan's gate, and as they drew near it the sense that the walk was over brought back his words.

'Then you don't want to leave us, Matt?'

He had to stoop his head to catch her stifled whisper: 'Where'd I go, if I did?'

The answer sent a pang through him but the tone suffused him with joy. He forgot what else he had meant to say and pressed her against him so closely that he seemed to feel her warmth in his veins.

'You ain't crying are you, Matt?'

'No, of course I'm not,' she quavered.

They turned in at the gate and passed under the shaded knoll where, enclosed in a low fence, the Frome grave-stones slanted at crazy angles through the snow. Ethan looked at them curiously. For years that quiet company had mocked his restlessness, his desire for change and freedom. 'We never got away – how should you?' seemed to be written on every headstone; and whenever he went in or out of his gate he thought with a shiver: 'I shall just go on living here till I join them.' But now all desire for change had vanished, and the sight of the little enclosure gave him a warm sense of continuance and stability.

'I guess we'll never let you go, Matt,' he whispered, as though even the dead, lovers once, must conspire with him to keep her; and brushing by the graves, he thought: 'We'll always go on living here together, and some day she'll lie there beside me.'

He let the vision possess him as they climbed the hill to the house. He was never so happy with her as when he abandoned

himself to these dreams. Half-way up the slope Mattie
stumbled against some unseen obstruction and clutched his
sleeve to steady herself. The wave of warmth that went
through him was like the prolongation of his vision. For the
first time he stole his arm about her, and she did not resist.
They walked on as if they were floating on a summer stream.

Zeena always went to bed as soon as she had had her supper,
and the shutterless windows of the house were dark. A dead
cucumber-vine dangled from the porch like the crape streamer
tied to the door for a death, and the thought flashed through
Ethan's brain: 'If it was there for Zeena –' Then he had a
distinct sight of his wife lying in their bedroom asleep, her
mouth slightly open, her false teeth in a tumbler by the bed . . .

They walked around to the back of the house, between the
rigid gooseberry bushes. It was Zeena's habit, when they came
back late from the village, to leave the key of the kitchen door
under the mat. Ethan stood before the door, his head heavy
with dreams, his arm still about Mattie. 'Matt –' he began, not
knowing what he meant to say.

She slipped out of his hold without speaking, and he
stooped down and felt for the key.

'It's not there!' he said, straightening himself with a start.

They strained their eyes at each other through the icy darkness. Such a thing had never happened before.

'Maybe she's forgotten it,' Mattie said in a tremulous whisper; but both of them knew that it was not like Zeena to forget.

'It might have fallen off into the snow,' Mattie continued,
after a pause during which they had stood intently listening.

'It must have been pushed off, then,' he rejoined in the same
tone. Another wild thought tore through him. What if tramps
had been there – what if . . .

Again he listened, fancying he heard a distant sound in the
house; then he felt in his pocket for a match, and kneeling
down, passed its light slowly over the rough edges of snow
about the doorstep.

He was still kneeling when his eyes, on a level with the
lower panel of the door, caught a faint ray beneath it. Who

could be stirring in that silent house? He heard a step on the stairs, and again for an instant the thought of tramps tore through him. Then the door opened and he saw his wife.

Against the dark background of the kitchen she stood up tall and angular, one hand drawing a quilted counterpane to her flat breast, while the other held a lamp. The light, on a level with her chin, drew out of the darkness her puckered throat and the projecting wristbone of the hand that clutched the quilt, and deepened fantastically the hollows and prominences of her high-boned face under its ring of crimping-pins. To Ethan, still in the rosy haze of his hour with Mattie, the sight came with the intense precision of the last dream before waking. He felt as if he had never before known what his wife looked like.

She drew aside without speaking, and Mattie and Ethan passed into the kitchen, which had the deadly chill of a vault after the dry cold of the night.

'Guess you forgot about us, Zeena,' Ethan joked, stamping the snow from his boots.

'No. I just felt so mean I couldn't sleep.'

Mattie came forward, unwinding her wraps, the colour of the cherry scarf in her fresh lips and cheeks. 'I'm so sorry, Zeena! Isn't there anything I can do?'

'No; there's nothing.' Zeena turned away from her. 'You might 'a' shook off that snow outside,' she said to her husband.

She walked out of the kitchen ahead of them and pausing in the hall raised the lamp at arm's-length, as if to light them up the stairs.

Ethan paused also, affecting to fumble for the peg on which he hung his coat and cap. The doors of the two bedrooms faced each other across the narrow upper landing, and to-night it was peculiarly repugnant to him that Mattie should see him follow Zeena.

'I guess I won't come up yet awhile,' he said, turning as if to go back to the kitchen.

Zeena stopped short and looked at him. 'For the land's sake – what you going to do down here?'

'I've got the mill accounts to go over.'

She continued to stare at him, the flame of the unshaded lamp bringing out with microscopic cruelty the fretful lines of her face.

'At this time o' night? You'll ketch your death. The fire's out long ago.'

Without answering he moved away toward the kitchen. As he did so his glance crossed Mattie's and he fancied that a fugitive warning gleamed through her lashes. The next moment they sank to her flushed cheeks and she began to mount the stairs ahead of Zeena.

'That's so. It *is* powerful cold down here,' Ethan assented; and with lowered head he went up in his wife's wake, and followed her across the threshold of their room.

III

There was some hauling to be done at the lower end of the wood-lot, and Ethan was out early the next day.

The winter morning was as clear as crystal. The sunrise burned red in a pure sky, the shadows on the rim of the wood-lot were darkly blue, and beyond the white and scintillating fields patches of far-off forest hung like smoke.

It was in the early morning stillness, when his muscles were swinging to their familiar task and his lungs expanding with long draughts of mountain air, that Ethan did his clearest thinking. He and Zeena had not exchanged a word after the door of their room had closed on them. She had measured out some drops from a medicine-bottle on a chair by the bed and, after swallowing them, and wrapping her head in a piece of yellow flannel, had lain down with her face turned away. Ethan undressed hurriedly and blew out the light so that he should not see her when he took his place at her side. As he lay there he could hear Mattie moving about in her room, and her candle, sending its small ray across the landing, drew a scarcely perceptible line of light under his door. He kept his eyes fixed on the light till it vanished. Then the room grew perfectly black, and not a sound was audible but Zeena's asthmatic breathing. Ethan felt confusedly that there were many things he ought to think about, but through his tingling veins and tired brain only one sensation throbbed: the warmth of Mattie's shoulder against his. Why had he not kissed her when he held her there? A few hours earlier he would not have asked himself the question. Even a few minutes earlier, when they had stood alone outside the house, he would not have dared to think of kissing her. But since he had seen her lips in the lamplight he felt that they were his.

Now, in the bright morning air, her face was still before him. It was part of the sun's red and of the pure glitter on the snow. How the girl had changed since she had come to Starkfield! He remembered what a colourless slip of a thing she had looked the day he had met her at the station. And all the first winter, how she had shivered with cold when the northerly gales shook the thin clapboards and the snow beat like hail against the loose-hung windows!

He had been afraid that she would hate the hard life, the cold and loneliness; but not a sign of discontent escaped her. Zeena took the view that Mattie was bound to make the best of Starkfield since she hadn't any other place to go to; but this did not strike Ethan as conclusive. Zeena, at any rate, did not apply the principle in her own case.

He felt all the more sorry for the girl because misfortune had, in a sense, indentured her to them. Mattie Silver was the daughter of a cousin of Zenobia Frome's, who had inflamed his clan with mingled sentiments of envy and admiration by descending from the hills to Connecticut, where he had married a Stamford girl and succeeded to her father's thriving 'drug' business. Unhappily Orin Silver, a man of far-reaching aims, had died too soon to prove that the end justifies the means. His accounts revealed merely what the means had been; and these were such that it was fortunate for his wife and daughter that his books were examined only after his impressive funeral. His wife died of the disclosure, and Mattie, at twenty, was left alone to make her way on the fifty dollars obtained from the sale of her piano. For this purpose her equipment, though varied, was inadequate. She could trim a hat, make molasses candy, recite 'Curfew shall not ring to-night', and play 'The Lost Chord' and a pot-pourri from 'Carmen'. When she tried to extend the field of her activities in the direction of stenography and book-keeping her health broke down, and six months on her feet behind the counter of a department store did not tend to restore it. Her nearest relations had been induced to place their savings in her father's hands, and though, after his death, they ungrudgingly acquitted themselves of the

Christian duty of returning good for evil by giving his daughter all the advice at their disposal, they could hardly be expected to supplement it by material aid. But when Zenobia's doctor recommended her looking about for some one to help her with the house-work the clan instantly saw the chance of exacting a compensation from Mattie. Zenobia, though doubtful of the girl's efficiency, was tempted by the freedom to find fault without much risk of losing her; and so Mattie came to Starkfield.

Zenobia's fault-finding was of the silent kind, but not the less penetrating for that. During the first months Ethan alternately burned with the desire to see Mattie defy her and trembled with fear of the result. Then the situation grew less strained. The pure air, and the long summer hours in the open, gave back life and elasticity to Mattie, and Zeena, with more leisure to devote to her complex ailments, grew less watchful of the girl's omissions; so that Ethan, struggling on under the burden of his barren farm and failing saw-mill, could at least imagine that peace reigned in his house.

There was really, even now, no tangible evidence to the contrary; but since the previous night a vague dread had hung on his sky-line. It was formed of Zeena's obstinate silence, of Mattie's sudden look of warning, of the memory of just such fleeting imperceptible signs as those which told him, on certain stainless mornings, that before night there would be rain.

His dread was so strong that, man-like, he sought to postpone certainty. The hauling was not over till mid-day, and as the lumber was to be delivered to Andrew Hale, the Starkfield builder, it was really easier for Ethan to send Jotham Powell, the hired man, back to the farm on foot, and drive the load down to the village himself. He had scrambled up on the logs, and was sitting astride of them, close over his shaggy greys, when, coming between him and their steaming necks, he had a vision of the warning look that Mattie had given him the night before.

'If there's going to be any trouble I want to be there,' was his vague reflection, as he threw to Jotham the unexpected order to unhitch the team and lead them back to the barn.

It was a slow trudge home through the heavy fields, and when the two men entered the kitchen Mattie was lifting the coffee from the stove and Zeena was already at the table. Her husband stopped short at sight of her. Instead of her usual calico wrapper and knitted shawl she wore her best dress of brown merino, and above her thin strands of hair, which still preserved the tight undulations of the crimping-pins, rose a hard perpendicular bonnet, as to which Ethan's clearest notion was that he had had to pay five dollars for it at the Bettsbridge Emporium. On the floor beside her stood his old valise and a bandbox wrapped in newspapers.

'Why, where are you going, Zeena?' he exclaimed.

'I've got my shooting pains so bad that I'm going over to Bettsbridge to spend the night with Aunt Martha Pierce and see that new doctor,' she answered in a matter-of-fact tone, as if she had said she was going into the storeroom to take a look at the preserves, or up to the attic to go over the blankets.

In spite of her sedentary habits such abrupt decisions were not without precedent in Zeena's history. Twice or thrice before she had suddenly packed Ethan's valise and started off to Bettsbridge, or even Springfield, to seek the advice of some new doctor, and her husband had grown to dread these expeditions because of their cost. Zeena always came back laden with expensive remedies, and her last visit to Springfield had been commemorated by her paying twenty dollars for an electric battery of which she had never been able to learn the use. But for the moment his sense of relief was so great as to preclude all other feelings. He had now no doubt that Zeena had spoken the truth in saying, the night before, that she had sat up because she felt 'too mean' to sleep: her abrupt resolve to seek medical advice showed that, as usual, she was wholly absorbed in her health.

As if expecting a protest, she continued plaintively: 'If you're too busy with the hauling I presume you can let Jotham Powell drive me over with the sorrel in time to ketch the train at the Flats.'

Her husband hardly heard what she was saying. During

the winter months there was no stage between Starkfield and Bettsbridge, and the trains which stopped at Corbury Flats were slow and infrequent. A rapid calculation showed Ethan that Zeena could not be back at the farm before the following evening . . .

'If I'd supposed you'd 'a' made any objection to Jotham Powell's driving me over —' she began again, as though his silence had implied refusal. On the brink of departure she was always seized with a flux of words. 'All I know is,' she continued, 'I can't go on the way I am much longer. The pains are clear away down to my ankles now, or I'd 'a' walked in to Starkfield on my own feet, sooner 'n put you out, and asked Michael Eady to let me ride over on his wagon to the Flats, when he sends to meet the train that brings his groceries. I'd 'a' had two hours to wait in the station, but I'd sooner 'a' done it, even with this cold, than to have you say —'

'Of course Jotham'll drive you over,' Ethan roused himself to answer. He became suddenly conscious that he was looking at Mattie while Zeena talked to him, and with an effort he turned his eyes to his wife. She sat opposite the window, and the pale light reflected from the banks of snow made her face look more than usually drawn and bloodless, sharpened the three parallel creases between ear and cheek, and drew querulous lines from her thin nose to the corners of her mouth. Though she was but seven years her husband's senior, and he was only twenty-eight, she was already an old woman.

Ethan tried to say something befitting the occasion, but there was only one thought in his mind: the fact that, for the first time since Mattie had come to live with them, Zeena was to be away for a night. He wondered if the girl were thinking of it too. . . .

He knew that Zeena must be wondering why he did not offer to drive her to the Flats and let Jotham Powell take the lumber to Starkfield, and at first he could not think of a pretext for not doing so; then he said: 'I'd take you over myself, only I've got to collect the cash for the lumber.'

As soon as the words were spoken he regretted them, not

only because they were untrue – there being no prospect of his receiving cash payment from Hale – but also because he knew from experience the imprudence of letting Zeena think he was in funds on the eve of one of her therapeutic excursions. At the moment, however, his one desire was to avoid the long drive with her behind the ancient sorrel who never went out of a walk.

Zeena made no reply: she did not seem to hear what he had said. She had already pushed her plate aside, and was measuring out a draught from a large bottle at her elbow.

'It ain't done me a speck of good, but I guess I might as well use it up,' she remarked; adding, as she pushed the empty bottle toward Mattie: 'If you can get the taste out it'll do for pickles.'

IV

As soon as his wife had driven off Ethan took his coat and cap from the peg. Mattie was washing up the dishes, humming one of the dance tunes of the night before. He said 'So long, Matt,' and she answered gaily 'So long, Ethan'; and that was all.

It was warm and bright in the kitchen. The sun slanted through the south window on the girl's moving figure, on the cat dozing in a chair, and on the geraniums brought in from the door-way, where Ethan had planted them in the summer to 'make a garden' for Mattie. He would have liked to linger on, watching her tidy up and then settle down to her sewing; but he wanted still more to get the hauling done and be back at the farm before night.

All the way down to the village he continued to think of his return to Mattie. The kitchen was a poor place, not 'spruce' and shining as his mother had kept it in his boyhood; but it was surprising what a homelike look the mere fact of Zeena's absence gave it. And he pictured what it would be like that evening, when he and Mattie were there after supper. For the first time they would be alone together indoors, and they would sit there, one on each side of the stove, like a married couple, he in his stocking feet and smoking his pipe, she laughing and talking in that funny way she had, which was always as new to him as if he had never heard her before.

The sweetness of the picture, and the relief of knowing that his fears of 'trouble' with Zeena were unfounded, sent up his spirits with a rush, and he, who was usually so silent, whistled and sang aloud as he drove through the snowy fields. There was in him a slumbering spark of sociability which the long Starkfield winters had not yet extinguished. By nature grave

39

and inarticulate, he admired recklessness and gaiety in others
and was warmed to the marrow by friendly human intercourse. At Worcester, though he had the name of keeping to
himself and not being much of a hand at a good time, he had
secretly gloried in being clapped on the back and hailed as
'Old Ethe' or 'Old Stiff'; and the cessation of such familiarities
had increased the chill of his return to Starkfield.

There the silence had deepened about him year by year. Left
alone, after his father's accident, to carry the burden of farm
and mill, he had had no time for convivial loiterings in the
village; and when his mother fell ill the loneliness of the house
grew more oppressive than that of the fields. His mother had
been a talker in her day, but after her 'trouble' the sound of
her voice was seldom heard, though she had not lost the power
of speech. Sometimes, in the long winter evenings, when in
desperation her son asked her why she didn't 'say something',
she would lift a finger and answer: 'Because I'm listening'; and
on stormy nights, when the loud wind was about the house,
she would complain, if he spoke to her: 'They're talking so
out there that I can't hear you.'

It was only when she drew toward her last illness, and his
cousin Zenobia Pierce came over from the next valley to help
him nurse her, that human speech was heard again in the
house. After the mortal silence of his long imprisonment
Zeena's volubility was music in his ears. He felt that he might
have 'gone like his mother' if the sound of a new voice had
not come to steady him. Zeena seemed to understand his case
at a glance. She laughed at him for not knowing the simplest
sick-bed duties and told him to 'go right along out' and leave
her to see to things. The mere fact of obeying her orders, of
feeling free to go about his business again and talk with other
men, restored his shaken balance and magnified his sense of
what he owed her. Her efficiency shamed and dazzled him.
She seemed to possess by instinct all the household wisdom
that his long apprenticeship had not instilled in him. When
the end came it was she who had to tell him to hitch up and
go for the undertaker, and she thought it 'funny' that he had

not settled beforehand who was to have his mother's clothes and the sewing-machine. After the funeral, when he saw her preparing to go away, he was seized with an unreasoning dread of being left alone on the farm; and before he knew what he was doing he had asked her to stay there with him. He had often thought since that it would not have happened if his mother had died in spring instead of winter . . .

When they married it was agreed that, as soon as he could straighten out the difficulties resulting from Mrs Frome's long illness, they would sell the farm and saw-mill and try their luck in a large town. Ethan's love of nature did not take the form of a taste for agriculture. He had always wanted to be an engineer, and to live in towns, where there were lectures and big libraries and 'fellows doing things'. A slight engineering job in Florida, put in his way during his period of study at Worcester, increased his faith in his ability as well as his eagerness to see the world; and he felt sure that, with a 'smart' wife like Zeena, it would not be long before he had made himself a place in it.

Zeena's native village was slightly larger and nearer to the railway than Starkfield, and she had let her husband see from the first that life on an isolated farm was not what she had expected when she married. But purchasers were slow in coming, and while he waited for them Ethan learned the impossibility of transplanting her. She chose to look down on Starkfield, but she could not have lived in a place which looked down on her. Even Bettsbridge or Shadd's Falls would not have been sufficiently aware of her, and in the greater cities which attracted Ethan she would have suffered a complete loss of identity. And within a year of their marriage she developed the 'sickliness' which had since made her notable even in a community rich in pathological instances. When she came to take care of his mother she had seemed to Ethan like the very genius of health, but he soon saw that her skill as a nurse had been acquired by the absorbed observation of her own symptoms.

Then she too fell silent. Perhaps it was the inevitable effect of life on the farm, or perhaps, as she sometimes said, it was because Ethan 'never listened'. The charge was not wholly unfounded. When she spoke it was only to complain, and to complain of things not in his power to remedy; and to check a tendency to impatient retort he had first formed the habit of not answering her, and finally of thinking of other things while she talked. Of late, however, since he had had reasons for observing her more closely, her silence had begun to trouble him. He recalled his mother's growing taciturnity, and wondered if Zeena were also turning 'queer'. Women did, he knew. Zeena, who had at her fingers' ends the pathological chart of the whole region, had cited many cases of the kind while she was nursing his mother; and he himself knew of certain lonely farm-houses in the neighbourhood where stricken creatures pined, and of others where sudden tragedy had come of their presence. At times, looking at Zeena's shut face, he felt the chill of such forebodings. At other times her silence seemed deliberately assumed to conceal far-reaching intentions, mysterious conclusions drawn from suspicions and resentments impossible to guess. That supposition was even more disturbing than the other; and it was the one which had come to him the night before, when he had seen her standing in the kitchen door.

Now her departure for Bettsbridge had once more eased his mind, and all his thoughts were on the prospect of his evening with Mattie. Only one thing weighed on him, and that was his having told Zeena that he was to receive cash for the lumber. He foresaw so clearly the consequences of this imprudence that with considerable reluctance he decided to ask Andrew Hale for a small advance on his load.

When Ethan drove into Hale's yard the builder was just getting out of his sleigh.

'Hello, Ethe!' he said. 'This comes handy.'

Andrew Hale was a ruddy man with a big grey moustache and a stubbly double-chin unconstrained by a collar; but his scrupulously clean shirt was always fastened by a small diamond stud. This display of opulence was misleading, for though he did a fairly good business it was known that his easy-going habits and the demands of his large family frequently kept him what Starkfield called 'behind'. He was an old friend of Ethan's family, and his house one of the few to which Zeena occasionally went, drawn there by the fact that Mrs Hale, in her youth, had done more 'doctoring' than any other woman in Starkfield, and was still a recognized authority on symptoms and treatment.

Hale went up to the greys and patted their sweating flanks. 'Well, sir,' he said, 'you keep them two as if they was pets.'

Ethan set about unloading the logs and when he had finished his job he pushed open the glazed door of the shed which the builder used as his office. Hale sat with his feet up on the stove, his back propped against a battered desk strewn with papers: the place, like the man, was warm, genial and untidy.

'Sit right down and thaw out,' he greeted Ethan.

The latter did not know how to begin, but at length he managed to bring out his request for an advance of fifty dollars. The blood rushed to his thin skin under the sting of Hale's astonishment. It was the builder's custom to pay at the end of three months, and there was no precedent between the two men for a cash settlement.

Ethan felt that if he had pleaded an urgent need Hale might have made shift to pay him; but pride, and an instinctive prudence, kept him from resorting to this argument. After his father's death it had taken time to get his head above water, and he did not want Andrew Hale, or any one else in Starkfield, to think he was going under again. Besides, he hated lying; if he wanted the money he wanted it, and it was nobody's business to ask why. He therefore made his demand with the awkwardness of a proud man who will not admit to himself that he is stooping; and he was not much surprised at Hale's refusal.

The builder refused genially, as he did everything else: he treated the matter as something in the nature of a practical joke, and wanted to know if Ethan meditated buying a grand piano or adding a 'cupolo' to his house; offering, in the latter case, to give his services free of cost.

Ethan's arts were soon exhausted, and after an embarrassed pause he wished Hale good-day and opened the door of the

office. As he passed out the builder suddenly called after him:
'See here – you ain't in a tight place, are you?'

'Not a bit,' Ethan's pride retorted before his reason had time
to intervene.

'Well, that's good! Because I *am*, a shade. Fact is, I was going
to ask you to give me a little extra time on that payment.
Business is pretty slack, to begin with, and then I'm fixing up
a little house for Ned and Ruth when they're married. I'm
glad to do it for 'em, but it costs.' His look appealed to Ethan
for sympathy. 'The young people like things nice. You know
how it is yourself: it's not so long ago since you fixed up your
own place for Zeena.'

Ethan left the greys in Hale's stable and went about some other
business in the village. As he walked away the builder's last
phrase lingered in his ears, and he reflected grimly that his
seven years with Zeena seemed to Starkfield 'not so long'.

The afternoon was drawing to an end, and here and there a
lighted pane spangled the cold grey dusk and made the snow
look whiter. The bitter weather had driven every one indoors
and Ethan had the long rural street to himself. Suddenly he
heard the brisk play of sleigh-bells and a cutter passed him,
drawn by a free-going horse. Ethan recognized Michael Eady's
roan colt, and young Denis Eady, in a handsome new fur cap,
leaned forward and waved a greeting. 'Hello, Ethe!' he shouted
and spun on.

The cutter was going in the direction of the Frome farm,
and Ethan's heart contracted as he listened to the dwindling
bells. What more likely than that Denis Eady had heard of
Zeena's departure for Bettsbridge, and was profiting by the
opportunity to spend an hour with Mattie? Ethan was ashamed
of the storm of jealousy in his breast. It seemed unworthy of
the girl that his thoughts of her should be so violent.

He walked on to the church corner and entered the shade
of the Varnum spruces, where he had stood with her the night
before. As he passed into their gloom he saw an indistinct outline just ahead of him. At his approach it melted for an instant

into two separate shapes and then conjoined again, and he heard a kiss, and a half-laughing 'Oh!' provoked by the discovery of his presence. Again the outline hastily disunited and the Varnum gate slammed on one half while the other hurried on ahead of him. Ethan smiled at the discomfiture he had caused. What did it matter to Ned Hale and Ruth Varnum if they were caught kissing each other? Everybody in Starkfield knew they were engaged. It pleased Ethan to have surprised a pair of lovers on the spot where he and Mattie had stood with such a thirst for each other in their hearts; but he felt a pang at the thought that these two need not hide their happiness.

He fetched the greys from Hale's stable and started on his long climb back to the farm. The cold was less sharp than earlier in the day and a thick fleecy sky threatened snow for the morrow. Here and there a star pricked through, showing behind it a deep well of blue. In an hour or two the moon would push up over the ridge behind the farm, burn a gold-edged rent in the clouds, and then be swallowed by them. A mournful peace hung on the fields, as though they felt the relaxing grasp of the cold and stretched themselves in their long winter sleep.

Ethan's ears were alert for the jingle of sleigh-bells, but not a sound broke the silence of the lonely road. As he drew near the farm he saw, through the thin screen of larches at the gate, a light twinkling in the house above him. 'She's up in her room,' he said to himself, 'fixing herself up for supper'; and he remembered Zeena's sarcastic stare when Mattie, on the evening of her arrival, had come down to supper with smoothed hair and a ribbon at her neck.

He passed by the graves on the knoll and turned his head to glance at one of the older headstones, which had interested him deeply as a boy because it bore his name.

SACRED TO THE MEMORY OF
ETHAN FROME AND ENDURANCE HIS WIFE,
WHO DWELLED TOGETHER IN PEACE
FOR FIFTY YEARS.

He used to think that fifty years sounded like a long time to live together; but now it seemed to him that they might pass in a flash. Then, with a sudden dart of irony, he wondered if, when their turn came, the same epitaph would be written over him and Zeena.

He opened the barn-door and craned his head into the obscurity, half-fearing to discover Denis Eady's roan colt in the stall beside the sorrel. But the old horse was there alone, mumbling his crib with toothless jaws, and Ethan whistled cheerfully while he bedded down the greys and shook an extra measure of oats into their mangers. His was not a tuneful throat, but harsh melodies burst from it as he locked the barn and sprang up the hill to the house. He reached the kitchen-porch and turned the door-handle; but the door did not yield to his touch.

Startled at finding it locked he rattled the handle violently; then he reflected that Mattie was alone and that it was natural she should barricade herself at nightfall. He stood in the darkness expecting to hear her step. It did not come, and after vainly straining his ears he called out in a voice that shook with joy: 'Hello, Matt!'

Silence answered; but in a minute or two he caught a sound on the stairs and saw a line of light about the doorframe, as he had seen it the night before. So strange was the precision with which the incidents of the previous evening were repeating themselves that he half expected, when he heard the key turn, to see his wife before him on the threshold; but the door opened, and Mattie faced him.

She stood just as Zeena had stood, a lifted lamp in her hand, against the black background of the kitchen. She held the light at the same level, and it drew out with the same distinctness her slim young throat and the brown wrist no bigger than a child's. Then, striking upward, it threw a lustrous fleck on her lips, edged her eyes with velvet shade, and laid a milky whiteness above the black curve of her brows.

She wore her usual dress of darkish stuff, and there was no bow at her neck; but through her hair she had run a streak of crimson ribbon. This tribute to the unusual transformed and glorified her. She seemed to Ethan taller, fuller, more womanly in shape and motion. She stood aside, smiling silently, while he entered, and then moved away from him with something soft and flowing in her gait. She set the lamp on the table, and he saw that it was carefully laid for supper, with fresh dough-nuts, stewed blueberries and his favourite pickles in a dish of gay red glass. A bright fire glowed in the stove and the cat lay stretched before it, watching the table with a drowsy eye.

Ethan was suffocated with the sense of well-being. He went out into the passage to hang up his coat and pull off his wet boots. When he came back Mattie had set the teapot on the table and the cat was rubbing itself persuasively against her ankles.

'Why, Puss! I nearly tripped over you,' she cried, the laughter sparkling through her lashes.

Again Ethan felt a sudden twinge of jealousy. Could it be his coming that gave her such a kindled face?

'Well, Matt, any visitors?' he threw off, stooping down carelessly to examine the fastening of the stove.

She nodded and laughed 'Yes, one,' and he felt a blackness settling on his brows.

'Who was that?' he questioned, raising himself up to slant a glance at her beneath his scowl.

Her eyes danced with malice. 'Why, Jotham Powell. He came in after he got back, and asked for a drop of coffee before he went down home.'

The blackness lifted and light flooded Ethan's brain. 'That all? Well, I hope you made out to let him have it.' And after a pause he felt it right to add: 'I suppose he got Zeena over to the Flats all right?'

'Oh, yes; in plenty of time.'

The name threw a chill between them, and they stood a moment looking sideways at each other before Mattie said with a shy laugh: 'I guess it's about time for supper.'

They drew their seats up to the table, and the cat, unbidden, jumped between them into Zeena's empty chair. 'Oh, Puss!' said Mattie, and they laughed again.

Ethan, a moment earlier, had felt himself on the brink of eloquence; but the mention of Zeena had paralysed him. Mattie seemed to feel the contagion of his embarrassment, and sat with downcast lids, sipping her tea, while he feigned an insatiable appetite for dough-nuts and sweet pickles. At last, after casting about for an effective opening, he took a long gulp of tea, cleared his throat, and said: 'Looks as if there'd be more snow.'

She feigned great interest. 'Is that so? Do you suppose it'll interfere with Zeena's getting back?' She flushed red as the question escaped her, and hastily set down the cup she was lifting.

Ethan reached over for another helping of pickles.

'You never can tell, this time of year, it drifts so bad on the Flats.' The name had benumbed him again, and once more he felt as if Zeena were in the room between them.

'Oh, Puss, you're too greedy!' Mattie cried.

The cat, unnoticed, had crept up on muffled paws from Zeena's seat to the table, and was stealthily elongating its body in the direction of the milk-jug, which stood between Ethan and Mattie. The two leaned forward at the same moment and their hands met on the handle of the jug. Mattie's hand was underneath, and Ethan kept his clasped on it a moment longer than was necessary. The cat, profiting by his unusual demonstration, tried to effect an unnoticed retreat, and in doing so backed into the pickle-dish, which fell to the floor with a crash.

Mattie, in an instant, had sprung from her chair and was down on her knees by the fragments.

'Oh, Ethan, Ethan – it's all to pieces! What will Zeena say?'

But this time his courage was up. 'Well, she'll have to say it to the cat, any way!' he rejoined with a laugh, kneeling down at Mattie's side to scrape up the swimming pickles.

She lifted stricken eyes to him. 'Yes, but, you see, she never meant it should be used, not even when there was company; and I had to get up on the step-ladder to reach it down from the top shelf of the china-closet, where she keeps it with all her best things, and of course she'll want to know why I did it—'

The case was so serious that it called forth all of Ethan's latent resolution.

'She needn't know anything about it if you keep quiet. I'll get another just like it to-morrow. Where did it come from? I'll go to Shadd's Falls for it if I have to!'

'Oh, you'll never get another even there! It was a wedding present – don't you remember? It came all the way from Phila-delphia, from Zeena's aunt that married the minister. That's why she wouldn't ever use it. Oh, Ethan, Ethan, what in the world shall I do?'

She began to cry, and he felt as if every one of her tears were pouring over him like burning lead. 'Don't, Matt, don't – oh, *don't!*' he implored her.

She struggled to her feet, and he rose and followed her help-lessly while she spread out the pieces of glass on the kitchen dresser. It seemed to him as if the shattered fragments of their evening lay there.

'Here, give them to me,' he said in a voice of sudden authority.

She drew aside, instinctively obeying his tone. 'Oh, Ethan, what are you going to do?'

Without replying he gathered the pieces of glass into his broad palm and walked out of the kitchen to the passage. There he lit a candle-end, opened the china-closet, and, reaching his long arm up to the highest shelf, laid the pieces together with such accuracy of touch that a close inspection convinced him of the impossibility of detecting from below that the dish was broken. If he glued it together the next morning months might elapse before his wife noticed what had happened, and meanwhile he might after all be able to match the dish at Shadd's Falls or Bettsbridge. Having satisfied himself that there was no risk of immediate discovery he went back to the kitchen with a lighter step, and found Mattie disconsolately removing the last scraps of pickle from the floor.

'It's all right, Matt. Come back and finish supper,' he commanded her.

Completely reassured, she shone on him through tear-hung lashes, and his soul swelled with pride as he saw how his tone subdued her. She did not even ask what he had done. Except when he was steering a big log down the mountain to his mill he had never known such a thrilling sense of mastery.

V

They finished supper, and while Mattie cleared the table Ethan went to look at the cows and then took a last turn about the house. The earth lay dark under a muffled sky and the air was so still that now and then he heard a lump of snow come thumping down from a tree far off on the edge of the wood-lot.

When he returned to the kitchen Mattie had pushed up his chair to the stove and seated herself near the lamp with a bit of sewing. The scene was just as he had dreamed of it that morning. He sat down, drew his pipe from his pocket and stretched his feet to the glow. His hard day's work in the keen air made him feel at once lazy and light of mood, and he had a confused sense of being in another world, where all was warmth and harmony and time could bring no change. The only drawback to his complete well-being was the fact that he could not see Mattie from where he sat; but he was too indolent to move and after a moment he said: 'Come over here and sit by the stove.'

Zeena's empty rocking-chair stood facing him. Mattie rose obediently, and seated herself in it. As her young brown head detached itself against the patch-work cushion that habitually framed his wife's gaunt countenance, Ethan had a momentary shock. It was almost as if the other face, the face of the superseded woman, had obliterated that of the intruder. After a moment Mattie seemed to be affected by the same sense of constraint. She changed her position, leaning forward to bend her head above her work, so that he saw only the foreshortened tip of her nose and the streak of red in her hair; then she slipped to her feet, saying 'I can't see to sew,' and went back to her chair by the lamp.

Ethan made a pretext of getting up to replenish the stove, and

when he returned to his seat he pushed it sideways that he
might have a view of her profile and of the lamplight falling on
her hands. The cat, who had been a puzzled observer of these
unusual movements, jumped up into Zeena's chair, rolled itself
into a ball, and lay watching them with narrowed eyes.

Deep quiet sank on the room. The clock ticked above the
dresser, a piece of charred wood fell now and then in the stove,
and the faint sharp scent of the geraniums mingled with the
odour of Ethan's smoke, which began to throw a blue haze
about the lamp and to hang its greyish cobwebs in the shadowy
corners of the room.

All constraint had vanished between the two, and they began
to talk easily and simply. They spoke of every-day things, of
the prospect of snow, of the next church sociable, of the loves
and quarrels of Starkfield. The commonplace nature of what
they said produced in Ethan an illusion of long-established intimacy which no outburst of emotion could have given, and he
set his imagination adrift on the fiction that they had always
spent their evenings thus and would always go on doing so . . .

'This is the night we were to have gone coasting, Matt,' he
said at length, with the rich sense, as he spoke, that they could
go on any other night they chose, since they had all time before
them.

She smiled back at him. 'I guess you forgot!'

'No, I didn't forget; but it's as dark as Egypt outdoors. We
might go to-morrow if there's a moon.'

She laughed with pleasure, her head tilted back, the lamplight sparkling on her lips and teeth. 'That would be lovely,
Ethan!'

He kept his eyes fixed on her, marvelling at the way her face
changed with each turn of their talk, like a wheat-field under
a summer breeze. It was intoxicating to find such magic in his
clumsy words, and he longed to try new ways of using it.

'Would you be scared to go down the Corbury road with
me on a night like this?' he asked.

Her cheeks burned redder. 'I ain't any more scared than
you are!'

'Well, *I'd* be scared, then; I wouldn't do it. That's an ugly corner down by the big elm. If a fellow didn't keep his eyes open he'd go plumb into it.' He luxuriated in the sense of protection and authority which his words conveyed. To prolong and intensify the feeling he added: 'I guess we're well enough here.'

She let her lids sink slowly, in the way he loved. 'Yes, we're well enough here,' she sighed.

Her tone was so sweet that he took the pipe from his mouth and drew his chair up to the table. Leaning forward, he touched the farther end of the strip of brown stuff that she was hemming. 'Say, Matt,' he began with a smile, 'what do you think I saw under the Varnum spruces, coming along home just now? I saw a friend of yours getting kissed.'

The words had been on his tongue all the evening, but now that he had spoken them they struck him as inexpressibly vulgar and out of place.

Mattie blushed to the roots of her hair and pulled her needle rapidly twice or thrice through her work, insensibly drawing the end of it away from him. 'I suppose it was Ruth and Ned,' she said in a low voice, as though he had suddenly touched on something grave.

Ethan had imagined that his allusion might open the way to the accepted pleasantries, and these perhaps in turn to a harmless caress, if only a mere touch on her hand. But now he felt as if her blush had set a flaming guard about her. He supposed it was his natural awkwardness that made him feel so. He knew that most young men made nothing at all of giving a pretty girl a kiss, and he remembered that the night before, when he had put his arm about Mattie, she had not resisted. But that had been out-of-doors, under the open irresponsible night. Now, in the warm lamplit room, with all its ancient implications of conformity and order, she seemed infinitely farther away from him and more unapproachable.

To ease his constraint he said: 'I suppose they'll be setting a date before long.'

'Yes. I shouldn't wonder if they got married some time

along in the summer.' She pronounced the word *married* as if her voice caressed it. It seemed a rustling covert leading to enchanted glades. A pang shot through Ethan, and he said, twisting away from her in his chair: 'It'll be your turn next, I wouldn't wonder.'

She laughed a little uncertainly. 'Why do you keep on saying that?'

He echoed her laugh. 'I guess I do it to get used to the idea.'

He drew up to the table again and she sewed on in silence, with dropped lashes, while he sat in fascinated contemplation of the way in which her hands went up and down above the strip of stuff, just as he had seen a pair of birds make short perpendicular flights over a nest they were building. At length, without turning her head or lifting her lids, she said in a low tone: 'It's not because you think Zeena's got anything against me, is it?'

His former dread started up full-armed at the suggestion. 'Why, what do you mean?' he stammered.

She raised distressed eyes to his, her work dropping on the table between them. 'I don't know. I thought last night she seemed to have.'

'I'd like to know what,' he growled.

'Nobody can tell with Zeena.' It was the first time they had ever spoken so openly of her attitude toward Mattie, and the repetition of the name seemed to carry it to the farther corners of the room and send it back to them in long repercussions of sound. Mattie waited, as if to give the echo time to drop, and then went on: 'She hasn't said anything to *you?*'

He shook his head. 'No, not a word.'

She tossed the hair back from her forehead with a laugh. 'I guess I'm just nervous, then. I'm not going to think about it any more.'

'Oh, no – don't let's think about it, Matt!'

The sudden heat of his tone made her colour mount again, not with a rush, but gradually, delicately, like the reflection of a thought stealing slowly across her heart. She sat silent, her hands clasped on her work, and it seemed to him that a warm current flowed toward him along the strip of stuff that still lay unrolled between them. Cautiously he slid his hand palm-downward along the table till his finger-tips touched the end of the stuff. A faint vibration of her lashes seemed to show that she was aware of his gesture, and that it had sent a counter-current back to her; and she let her hands lie motionless on the other end of the strip.

As they sat thus he heard a sound behind him and turned his head. The cat had jumped from Zeena's chair to dart at a mouse in the wainscot, and as a result of the sudden movement the empty chair had set up a spectral rocking.

'She'll be rocking in it herself this time to-morrow,' Ethan thought. 'I've been in a dream, and this is the only evening we'll ever have together.' The return to reality was as painful as the return to consciousness after taking an anæsthetic. His body and brain ached with indescribable weariness, and he could think of nothing to say or to do that should arrest the mad flight of the moments.

His alteration of mood seemed to have communicated itself to Mattie. She looked up at him languidly, as though her lids were weighted with sleep and it cost her an effort to raise them. Her glance fell on his hand, which now completely covered the end of her work and grasped it as if it were a part of herself. He saw a scarcely perceptible tremor cross her face, and without knowing what he did he stooped his head and kissed the bit of stuff in his hold. As his lips rested on it he felt it glide slowly from beneath them, and saw that Mattie had risen and was silently rolling up her work. She fastened it with a pin, and then, finding her thimble and scissors, put them with the roll of stuff into the box covered with fancy paper which he had once brought to her from Bettsbridge.

He stood up also, looking vaguely about the room. The clock above the dresser struck eleven.

'Is the fire all right?' she asked in a low voice.

He opened the door of the stove and poked aimlessly at the embers. When he raised himself again he saw that she was dragging toward the stove the old soap-box lined with carpet in which the cat made its bed. Then she recrossed the floor and lifted two of the geranium pots in her arms, moving them away from the cold window. He followed her and brought the other geraniums, the hyacinth bulbs in a cracked custard bowl and the German ivy trained over an old croquet hoop.

When these nightly duties were performed there was nothing left to do but to bring in the tin candlestick from the passage, light the candle and blow out the lamp. Ethan put the candlestick in Mattie's hand and she went out of the kitchen ahead of him, the light that she carried before her making her dark hair look like a drift of mist on the moon.

'Good night, Matt,' he said as she put her foot on the first step of the stairs.

She turned and looked at him a moment. 'Good night, Ethan,' she answered, and went up.

When the door of her room had closed on her he remembered that he had not even touched her hand.

VI

The next morning at breakfast Jotham Powell was between them, and Ethan tried to hide his joy under an air of exaggerated indifference, lounging back in his chair to throw scraps to the cat, growling at the weather, and not so much as offering to help Mattie when she rose to clear away the dishes.

He did not know why he was so irrationally happy, for nothing was changed in his life or hers. He had not even touched the tip of her fingers or looked her full in the eyes. But their evening together had given him a vision of what life at her side might be, and he was glad now that he had done nothing to trouble the sweetness of the picture. He had a fancy that she knew what had restrained him . . .

There was a last load of lumber to be hauled to the village, and Jotham Powell – who did not work regularly for Ethan in winter – had 'come round' to help with the job. But a wet snow, melting to sleet, had fallen in the night and turned the roads to glass. There was more wet in the air and it seemed likely to both men that the weather would 'milden' toward afternoon and make the going safer. Ethan therefore proposed to his assistant that they should load the sledge at the wood-lot, as they had done on the previous morning, and put off the 'teaming' to Starkfield till later in the day. This plan had the advantage of enabling him to send Jotham to the Flats after dinner to meet Zenobia, while he himself took the lumber down to the village.

He told Jotham to go out and harness up the greys, and for a moment he and Mattie had the kitchen to themselves. She had plunged the breakfast dishes into a tin dish-pan and was bending above it with her slim arms bared to the elbow, the steam from the hot water beading her forehead and tightening her rough hair into little brown rings like the tendrils on the traveller's joy.

Ethan stood looking at her, his heart in his throat. He wanted to say: 'We shall never be alone again like this.' Instead, he reached down his tobacco-pouch from a shelf of the dresser, put it into his pocket and said: 'I guess I can make out to be home for dinner.'

She answered 'All right, Ethan,' and he heard her singing over the dishes as he went.

As soon as the sledge was loaded he meant to send Jotham back to the farm and hurry on foot into the village to buy the glue for the pickle-dish. With ordinary luck he should have had time to carry out this plan; but everything went wrong from the start. On the way over to the wood-lot one of the greys slipped on a glare of ice and cut his knee; and when they got him up again Jotham had to go back to the barn for a strip of rag to bind the cut. Then, when the loading finally began, a sleety rain was coming down once more, and the tree trunks were so slippery that it took twice as long as usual to lift them and get them in place on the sledge. It was what Jotham called a sour morning for work, and the horses, shivering and stamping under their wet blankets, seemed to like it as little as the men. It was long past the dinner-hour when the job was done, and Ethan had to give up going to the village because he wanted to lead the injured horse home and wash the cut himself.

He thought that by starting out again with the lumber as soon as he had finished his dinner he might get back to the farm with the glue before Jotham and the old sorrel had had time to fetch Zenobia from the Flats; but he knew the chance was a slight one. It turned on the state of the roads and on the possible lateness of the Bettsbridge train. He remembered afterward, with a grim flash of self-derision, what importance he had attached to the weighing of these probabilities . . .

As soon as dinner was over he set out again for the wood-lot, not daring to linger till Jotham Powell left. The hired man was still drying his wet feet at the stove, and Ethan could only give Mattie a quick look as he said beneath his breath: 'I'll be back early.'

He fancied that she nodded her comprehension; and with that scant solace he had to trudge off through the rain.

He had driven his load half-way to the village when Jotham Powell overtook him, urging the reluctant sorrel toward the Flats. 'I'll have to hurry up to do it,' Ethan mused, as the sleigh dropped down ahead of him over the dip of the school-house hill. He worked like ten at the unloading, and when it was over hastened on to Michael Eady's for the glue. Eady and his assistant were both 'down street', and young Denis, who seldom deigned to take their place, was lounging by the stove with a knot of the golden youth of Starkfield. They hailed Ethan with ironic compliment and offers of conviviality; but no one knew where to find the glue. Ethan, consumed with the longing for a last moment alone with Mattie, hung about impatiently while Denis made an ineffectual search in the obscurer corners of the store.

'Looks as if we were all sold out. But if you'll wait around till the old man comes along maybe he can put his hand on it.'

'I'm obliged to you, but I'll try if I can get it down at Mrs Homan's,' Ethan answered, burning to be gone.

Denis's commercial instinct compelled him to aver on oath that what Eady's store could nor produce would never be found at the widow Homan's; but Ethan, heedless of this boast, had already climbed to the sledge and was driving on to the rival establishment. Here, after considerable search, and sympathetic questions as to what he wanted it for, and whether ordinary flour paste wouldn't do as well if she couldn't find it, the widow Homan finally hunted down her solitary bottle of glue to its hiding-place in a medley of cough-lozenges and corset-laces.

'I hope Zeena ain't broken anything she sets store by,' she called after him as he turned the greys toward home.

The fitful bursts of sleet had changed into a steady rain and the horses had heavy work even without a load behind them. Once or twice, hearing sleigh-bells, Ethan turned his head, fancying that Zeena and Jotham might overtake him; but the old sorrel was not in sight, and he set his face against the rain and urged on his ponderous pair.

The barn was empty when the horses turned into it and, after giving them the most perfunctory ministrations they had ever received from him, he strode up to the house and pushed open the kitchen door.

Mattie was there alone, as he had pictured her. She was bending over a pan on the stove; but at the sound of his step she turned with a start and sprang to him.

'See, here, Matt, I've got some stuff to mend the dish with! Let me get at it quick,' he cried, waving the bottle in one hand while he put her lightly aside; but she did not seem to hear him.

'Oh, Ethan – Zeena's come,' she said in a whisper, clutching his sleeve.

They stood and stared at each other, pale as culprits.

'But the sorrel's not in the barn!' Ethan stammered.

'Jotham Powell brought some goods over from the Flats for his wife, and he drove right on home with them,' she explained.

He gazed blankly about the kitchen, which looked cold and squalid in the rainy winter twilight.

'How is she?' he asked, dropping his voice to Mattie's whisper.

She looked away from him uncertainly. 'I don't know. She went right up to her room.'

'She didn't say anything?'

'No.'

Ethan let out his doubts in a low whistle and thrust the bottle back into his pocket. 'Don't fret; I'll come down and mend it in the night,' he said. He pulled on his wet coat again and went back to the barn to feed the greys.

While he was there Jotham Powell drove up with the sleigh, and when the horses had been attended to Ethan said to him: 'You might as well come back up for a bite.' He was not sorry to assure himself of Jotham's neutralizing presence at the supper table, for Zeena was always 'nervous' after a journey.

But the hired man, though seldom loth to accept a meal not included in his wages, opened his stiff jaws to answer slowly: 'I'm obliged to you, but I guess I'll go along back.'

Ethan looked at him in surprise. 'Better come up and dry off. Looks as if there'd be something hot for supper.'

Jotham's facial muscles were unmoved by this appeal and, his vocabulary being limited, he merely repeated: 'I guess I'll go along back.'

To Ethan there was something vaguely ominous in this stolid rejection of free food and warmth, and he wondered what had happened on the drive to nerve Jotham to such stoicism. Perhaps Zeena had failed to see the new doctor or had not liked his counsels: Ethan knew that in such cases the first person she met was likely to be held responsible for her grievance.

When he re-entered the kitchen the lamp lit up the same scene of shining comfort as on the previous evening. The table had been as carefully laid, a clear fire glowed in the stove, the cat dozed in its warmth, and Mattie came forward carrying a plate of dough-nuts.

She and Ethan looked at each other in silence; then she said, as she had said the night before: 'I guess it's about time for supper.'

VII

Ethan went out into the passage to hang up his wet garments. He listened for Zeena's step and, not hearing it, called her name up the stairs. She did not answer, and after a moment's hesitation he went up and opened her door. The room was almost dark, but in the obscurity he saw her sitting by the window, bolt upright, and knew by the rigidity of the outline projected against the pane that she had not taken off her travelling dress.

'Well, Zeena,' he ventured from the threshold.

She did not move, and he continued: 'Supper's about ready. Ain't you coming?'

She replied: 'I don't feel as if I could touch a morsel.'

It was the consecrated formula, and he expected it to be followed, as usual, by her rising and going down to supper. But she remained seated, and he could think of nothing more felicitous than: 'I presume you're tired after the long ride.'

Turning her head at this, she answered solemnly: 'I'm a great deal sicker than you think.'

Her words fell on his ear with a strange shock of wonder. He had often heard her pronounce them before – what if at last they were true?

He advanced a step or two into the dim room. 'I hope that's not so, Zeena,' he said.

She continued to gaze at him through the twilight with a mien of wan authority, as of one consciously singled out for a great fate. 'I've got complications,' she said.

Ethan knew the word for one of exceptional import. Almost everybody in the neighbourhood had 'troubles', frankly localized and specified; but only the chosen had 'complications'. To have them was in itself a distinction, though it was also, in most cases, a death-warrant. People struggled on for years with 'troubles', but they almost always succumbed to 'complications'.

Ethan's heart was jerking to and fro between two extremities of feeling, but for the moment compassion prevailed. His wife looked so hard and lonely, sitting there in the darkness with such thoughts.

'Is that what the new doctor told you?' he asked, instinctively lowering his voice.

'Yes. He says any regular doctor would want me to have an operation.'

Ethan was aware that, in regard to the important question of surgical intervention, the female opinion of the neighbourhood was divided, some glorying in the prestige conferred by operations while others shunned them as indelicate. Ethan, from motives of economy, had always been glad that Zeena was of the latter faction.

In the agitation caused by the gravity of her announcement he sought a consolatory short cut. 'What do you know about this doctor anyway? Nobody ever told you that before.'

He saw his blunder before she could take it up: she wanted sympathy, not consolation.

'I didn't need to have anybody tell me I was losing ground every day. Everybody but you could see it. And everybody in Bettsbridge knows about Dr Buck. He has his office in Worcester, and comes over once a fortnight to Shadd's Falls and Bettsbridge for consultations. Eliza Spears was wasting away with kidney trouble before she went to him, and now she's up and around, and singing in the choir.'

'Well, I'm glad of that. You must do just what he tells you,' Ethan answered sympathetically.

She was still looking at him. 'I mean to,' she said. He was struck by a new note in her voice. It was neither whining nor reproachful, but drily resolute.

'What does he want you should do?' he asked, with a mounting vision of fresh expenses.

'He wants I should have a hired girl. He says I oughtn't to have to do a single thing around the house.'

'A hired girl?' Ethan stood transfixed.

'Yes. And Aunt Martha found me one right off. Everybody said I was lucky to get a girl to come away out here, and I agreed to give her a dollar extry to make sure. She'll be over to-morrow afternoon.'

Wrath and dismay contended in Ethan. He had foreseen an immediate demand for money, but not a permanent drain on his scant resources. He no longer believed what Zeena had told him of the supposed seriousness of her state: he saw in her expedition to Bettsbridge only a plot hatched between herself and her Pierce relations to foist on him the cost of a servant; and for the moment wrath predominated.

'If you meant to engage a girl you ought to have told me before you started,' he said.

'How could I tell you before I started? How did I know what Dr Buck would say?'

'Oh, Dr Buck —' Ethan's incredulity escaped in a short laugh. 'Did Dr Buck tell you how I was to pay her wages?'

Her voice rose furiously with his. 'No, he didn't. For I'd 'a' been ashamed to tell *him* that you grudged me the money to get back my health, when I lost it nursing your own mother!'

'*You* lost your health nursing mother?'

'Yes; and my folks all told me at the time you couldn't do no less than marry me after—'

'Zeena!'

Through the obscurity which hid their faces their thoughts seemed to dart at each other like serpents shooting venom. Ethan was seized with horror of the scene and shame at his own share in it. It was as senseless and savage as a physical fight between two enemies in the darkness.

He turned to the shelf above the chimney, groped for matches and lit the one candle in the room. At first its weak flame made no impression on the shadows; then Zeena's face stood grimly out against the uncurtained pane, which had turned from grey to black.

It was the first scene of open anger between the couple in their sad seven years together, and Ethan felt as if he had lost an irretrievable advantage in descending to the level of recrimination. But the practical problem was there and had to be dealt with.

'You know I haven't got the money to pay for a girl, Zeena. You'll have to send her back: I can't do it.'

'The doctor says it'll be my death if I go on slaving the way I've had to. He doesn't understand how I've stood it as long as I have.'

'Slaving! –' He checked himself again, 'You sha'n't lift a hand, if he says so. I'll do everything round the house myself—'

She broke in: 'You're neglecting the farm enough already,' and this being true, he found no answer, and left her time to add ironically: 'Better send me over to the almshouse and done with it . . . I guess there's been Fromes there afore now.'

The taunt burned into him, but he let it pass. 'I haven't got the money. That settles it.'

There was a moment's pause in the struggle, as though the combatants were testing their weapons. Then Zeena said in a level voice: 'I thought you were to get fifty dollars from Andrew Hale for that lumber.'

'Andrew Hale never pays under three months.' He had hardly spoken when he remembered the excuse he had made for not accompanying his wife to the station the day before; and the blood rose to his frowning brows.

'Why, you told me yesterday you'd fixed it up with him to pay cash down. You said that was why you couldn't drive me over to the Flats.'

Ethan had no suppleness in deceiving. He had never before been convicted of a lie, and all the resources of evasion failed him. 'I guess that was a misunderstanding,' he stammered.

'You ain't got the money?'

'No.'

'And you ain't going to get it?'

'No.'

'Well, I couldn't know that when I engaged the girl, could I?'

'No.' He paused to control his voice. 'But you know it now. I'm sorry, but it can't be helped. You're a poor man's wife, Zeena; but I'll do the best I can for you.'

For a while she sat motionless, as if reflecting, her arms stretched along the arms of her chair, her eyes fixed on vacancy. 'Oh, I guess we'll make out,' she said mildly.

The change in her tone reassured him. 'Of course we will! There's a whole lot more I can do for you, and Mattie —'

Zeena, while he spoke, seemed to be following out some elaborate mental calculation. She emerged from it to say: 'There'll be Mattie's board less, anyhow —'

Ethan, supposing the discussion to be over, had turned to go down to supper. He stopped short, not grasping what he heard. 'Mattie's board less – ?' he began.

Zeena laughed. It was an odd unfamiliar sound – he did not remember ever having heard her laugh before. 'You didn't suppose I was going to keep two girls, did you? No wonder you were scared at the expense!'

He still had but a confused sense of what she was saying. From the beginning of the discussion he had instinctively avoided the mention of Mattie's name, fearing he hardly knew what: criticism, complaints, or vague allusions to the imminent probability of her marrying. But the thought of a definite rupture had never come to him, and even now could not lodge itself in his mind.

'I don't know what you mean,' he said. 'Mattie Silver's not a hired girl. She's your relation.'

'She's a pauper that's hung onto us all after her father'd done his best to ruin us. I've kep' her here a whole year: it's somebody else's turn now.'

As the shrill words shot out Ethan heard a tap on the door, which he had drawn shut when he turned back from the threshold.

'Ethan – Zeena!' Mattie's voice sounded gaily from the landing, 'do you know what time it is? Supper's been ready half an hour.'

Inside the room there was a moment's silence; then Zeena called out from her seat: 'I'm not coming down to supper.'

'Oh, I'm sorry! Aren't you well? Sha'n't I bring you up a bite of something?'

Ethan roused himself with an effort and opened the door. 'Go along down, Matt. Zeena's just a little tired. I'm coming.'

He heard her 'All right!' and her quick step on the stairs; then he shut the door and turned back into the room. His wife's attitude was unchanged, her face inexorable, and he was seized with the despairing sense of his helplessness.

'You ain't going to do it, Zeena?'

'Do what?' she emitted between flattened lips.

'Send Mattie away – like this?'

'I never bargained to take her for life!'

He continued with rising vehemence: 'You can't put her out of the house like a thief – a poor girl without friends or money. She's done her best for you and she's got no place to go to. You may forget she's your kin but everybody else'll remember it. If you do a thing like that what do you suppose folks'll say of you?'

Zeena waited a moment, as if giving him time to feel the full force of the contrast between his own excitement and her composure. Then she replied in the same smooth voice: 'I know well enough what they say of my having kep' her here as long as I have.'

Ethan's hand dropped from the door-knob, which he had held clenched since he had drawn the door shut on Mattie. His wife's retort was like a knife-cut across the sinews and he felt suddenly weak and powerless. He had meant to humble himself, to argue that Mattie's keep didn't cost much, after all, that he could make out to buy a stove and fix up a place in the attic for the hired girl – but Zeena's words revealed the peril of such pleadings.

'You mean to tell her she's got to go – at once?' he faltered out, in terror of letting his wife complete her sentence.

As if trying to make him see reason she replied impartially:

'The girl will be over from Bettsbridge to-morrow, and I presume she's got to have somewheres to sleep.'

Ethan looked at her with loathing. She was no longer the listless creature who had lived at his side in a state of sullen self-absorption, but a mysterious alien presence, an evil energy secreted from the long years of silent brooding. It was the sense of his helplessness that sharpened his antipathy. There had never been anything in her that one could appeal to; but as long as he could ignore and command he had remained indifferent. Now she had mastered him and he abhorred her. Mattie was her relation, not his: there were no means by which he could compel her to keep the girl under her roof. All the long misery of his baffled past, of his youth of failure, hardship and vain effort, rose up in his soul in bitterness and seemed to take shape before him in the woman who at every turn had barred his way. She had taken everything else from him; and now she meant to take the one thing that made up for all the others. For a moment such a flame of hate rose in him that it ran down his arm and clenched his fist against her. He took a wild step forward and then stopped.

'You're – you're not coming down?' he said in a bewildered voice.

'No. I guess I'll lay down on the bed a little while,' she answered mildly; and he turned and walked out of the room.

In the kitchen Mattie was sitting by the stove, the cat curled up on her knees. She sprang to her feet as Ethan entered and carried the covered dish of meat-pie to the table.

'I hope Zeena isn't sick?' she asked.

'No.'

She shone at him across the table. 'Well, sit right down then. You must be starving.' She uncovered the pie and pushed it over to him. So they were to have one more evening together, her happy eyes seemed to say!

He helped himself mechanically and began to eat; then disgust took him by the throat and he laid down his fork.

Mattie's tender gaze was on him and she marked the gesture.

'Why, Ethan, what's the matter? Don't it taste right?'

'Yes – it's first-rate. Only I –' He pushed his plate away, rose from his chair, and walked around the table to her side. She started up with frightened eyes.

'Ethan, there's something wrong! I *knew* there was!'

She seemed to melt against him in her terror, and he caught her in his arms, held her fast there, felt her lashes beat his cheek like netted butterflies.

'What is it – what is it?' she stammered; but he had found her lips at last and was drinking unconsciousness of everything but the joy they gave him.

She lingered a moment, caught in the same strong current; then she slipped from him and drew back a step or two, pale and troubled. Her look smote him with compunction, and he cried out, as if he saw her drowning in a dream: 'You can't go, Matt! I'll never let you!'

'Go – go?' she stammered. 'Must I go?'

The words went on sounding between them as though a torch of warning flew from hand to hand through a black landscape.

Ethan was overcome with shame at his lack of self-control in flinging the news at her so brutally. His head reeled and he had to support himself against the table. All the while he felt as if he were still kissing her, and yet dying of thirst for her lips.

'Ethan what has happened? Is Zeena mad with me?'

Her cry steadied him, though it deepened his wrath and pity. 'No, no,' he assured her, 'it's not that. But this new doctor has scared her about herself. You know she believes all they say the first time she sees them. And this one's told her she won't get well unless she lays up and don't do a thing about the house – not for months —'

He paused, his eyes wandering from her miserably. She stood silent a moment, drooping before him like a broken branch. She was so small and weak-looking that it wrung his heart; but suddenly she lifted her head and looked straight at him. 'And she wants somebody handier in my place? Is that it?'

'That's what she says to-night.'

'If she says it to-night she'll say it to-morrow.'

Both bowed to the inexorable truth: they knew that Zeena never changed her mind, and that in her case a resolve once taken was equivalent to an act performed.

There was a long silence between them; then Mattie said in a low voice: 'Don't be too sorry, Ethan.'

'Oh, God – oh, God,' he groaned. The glow of passion he had felt for her had melted to an aching tenderness. He saw her quick lids beating back the tears, and longed to take her in his arms and soothe her.

'You're letting your supper get cold,' she admonished him with a pale gleam of gaiety.

'Oh, Matt – Matt – where'll you go to?'

Her lids sank and a tremor crossed her face. He saw that for the first time the thought of the future came to her distinctly. 'I might get something to do over at Stamford,' she faltered, as if knowing that he knew she had no hope.

He dropped back into his seat and hid his face in his hands. Despair seized him at the thought of her setting out alone to renew the weary quest for work. In the only place where she was known she was surrounded by indifference or animosity; and what chance had she, inexperienced and untrained, among the million bread-seekers of the cities? There came back to him miserable tales he had heard at Worcester, and the faces of girls whose lives had begun as hopefully as Mattie's. . . . It was not possible to think of such things without a revolt of his whole being. He sprang up suddenly.

'You can't go, Matt! I won't let you! She's always had her way, but I mean to have mine now —'

Mattie lifted her hand with a quick gesture, and he heard his wife's step behind him.

Zeena came into the room with her dragging down-at-the-heel step, and quietly took her accustomed seat between them.

'I felt a little mite better, and Dr Buck says I ought to eat all I can to keep my stren'th up, even if I ain't got any appetite,' she said in her flat whine, reaching across Mattie for the teapot. Her 'good' dress had been replaced by the black calico and brown knitted shawl which formed her daily wear, and with them she had put on her usual face and manner. She poured out her tea, added a great deal of milk to it, helped herself largely to pie and pickles, and made the familiar gesture of adjusting her false teeth before she began to eat. The cat rubbed itself ingratiatingly against her and she said 'Good Pussy', stooped to stroke it and gave it a scrap of meat from her plate.

Ethan sat speechless, not pretending to eat, but Mattie nibbled valiantly at her food and asked Zeena one or two questions about her visit to Bettsbridge. Zeena answered in her every-day tone and, warming to the theme, regaled them with several vivid descriptions of intestinal disturbances among her friends and relatives. She looked straight at Mattie as she spoke, a faint smile deepening the vertical lines between her nose and chin.

When supper was over she rose from her seat and pressed her hand to the flat surface over the region of her heart. 'That pie of yours always sets a mite heavy, Matt,' she said, not ill-naturedly. She seldom abbreviated the girl's name, and when she did so it was always a sign of affability.

'I've a good mind to go and hunt up those stomach powders I got last year over in Springfield,' she continued. 'I ain't tried them for quite a while, and maybe they'll help the heartburn.'

Mattie lifted her eyes. 'Can't I get them for you, Zeena?' she ventured.

'No. They're in a place you don't know about,' Zeena answered darkly, with one of her secret looks.

She went out of the kitchen and Mattie, rising, began to clear the dishes from the table. As she passed Ethan's chair their eyes met and clung together desolately. The warm still kitchen looked as peaceful as the night before. The cat had sprung to Zeena's rocking-chair, and the heat of the fire was beginning to draw out the faint sharp scent of the geraniums. Ethan dragged himself wearily to his feet.

'I'll go out and take a look round,' he said, going toward the passage to get his lantern.

As he reached the door he met Zeena coming back into the

room, her lips twitching with anger, a flush of excitement on her sallow face. The shawl had slipped from her shoulders and was dragging at her down-trodden heels, and in her hands she carried the fragments of the red glass pickle-dish.

'I'd like to know who done this,' she said, looking sternly from Ethan to Mattie.

There was no answer, and she continued in a trembling voice: 'I went to get those powders I'd put away in father's old spectacle-case, top of the china-closet, where I keep the things I set store by, so's folks sha'n't meddle with them —' Her voice broke, and two small tears hung on her lashless lids and ran slowly down her cheeks. 'It takes the step-ladder to get at the top shelf, and I put Aunt Philura Maple's pickle-dish up there o' purpose when we was married, and it's never been down since, 'cept for the spring cleaning, and then I always lifted it with my own hands, so's 't it shouldn't get broke.' She laid the fragments reverently on the table. 'I want to know who done this,' she quavered.

At the challenge Ethan turned back into the room and faced her. 'I can tell you, then. The cat done it.'

'The *cat*?'

'That's what I said.'

She looked at him hard, and then turned her eyes to Mattie, who was carrying the dish-pan to the table.

'I'd like to know how the cat got into my china-closet,' she said.

'Chasin' mice, I guess,' Ethan rejoined. 'There was a mouse round the kitchen all last evening.'

Zeena continued to look from one to the other; then she emitted her small strange laugh. 'I knew the cat was a smart cat,' she said in a high voice, 'but I didn't know he was smart enough to pick up the pieces of my pickle-dish and lay 'em edge to edge on the very shelf he knocked 'em off of.'

Mattie suddenly drew her arms out of the steaming water. 'It wasn't Ethan's fault, Zeena! The cat *did* break the dish; but I got it down from the china-closet, and I'm the one to blame for its getting broken.'

Zeena stood beside the ruin of her treasure, stiffening into a stony image of resentment. '*You* got down my pickle-dish – what for?'

A bright flush flew to Mattie's cheeks. 'I wanted to make the supper-table pretty,' she said.

'You wanted to make the supper-table pretty; and you waited till my back was turned, and took the thing I set most store by of anything I've got, and wouldn't never use it, not even when the minister come to dinner, or Aunt Martha Pierce come over from Bettsbridge –' Zeena paused with a gasp, as if terrified by her own evocation of the sacrilege. 'You're a bad girl, Mattie Silver, and I always known it. It's the way your father begun, and I was warned of it when I took you, and I tried to keep my things where you couldn't get at 'em – and now you've took from me the one I cared for most of all –' She broke off in a short spasm of sobs that passed and left her more than ever like a shape of stone.

'If I'd 'a' listened to folks, you'd 'a' gone before now, and this wouldn't 'a' happened,' she said; and gathering up the bits of broken glass she went out of the room as if she carried a dead body . . .

VIII

When Ethan was called back to the farm by his father's illness his mother gave him, for his own use, a small room behind the untenanted 'best parlour'. Here he had nailed up shelves for his books, built himself a box-sofa out of boards and a mattress, laid out his papers on a kitchen-table, hung on the rough plaster wall an engraving of Abraham Lincoln and a calendar with 'Thoughts from the Poets', and tried, with these meagre properties, to produce some likeness to the study of a 'minister' who had been kind to him and lent him books when he was at Worcester. He still took refuge there in summer, but when Mattie came to live at the farm he had had to give her his stove, and consequently the room was uninhabitable for several months of the year.

To this retreat he descended as soon as the house was quiet, and Zeena's steady breathing from the bed had assured him that there was to be no sequel to the scene in the kitchen. After Zeena's departure he and Mattie had stood speechless, neither seeking to approach the other. Then the girl had returned to her task of clearing up the kitchen for the night and he had taken his lantern and gone on his usual round outside the house. The kitchen was empty when he came back to it; but his tobacco-pouch and pipe had been laid on the table, and under them was a scrap of paper torn from the back of a seedsman's catalogue, on which three words were written: 'Don't trouble, Ethan'.

Going into his cold dark 'study' he placed the lantern on the table and, stooping to its light, read the message again and again. It was the first time that Mattie had ever written to him, and the possession of the paper gave him a strange new sense of her nearness; yet it deepened his anguish by reminding him

74

that henceforth they would have no other way of communi-
cating with each other. For the life of her smile, the warmth
of her voice, only cold paper and dead words!

Confused motions of rebellion stormed in him. He was too
young, too strong, too full of the sap of living, to submit so
easily to the destruction of his hopes. Must he wear out all his
years at the side of a bitter querulous woman? Other possibilities had been in him, possibilities sacrificed, one by one, to
Zeena's narrow-mindedness and ignorance. And what good
had come of it? She was a hundred times bitterer and more
discontented than when he had married her: the one pleasure
left her was to inflict pain on him. All the healthy instincts of
self-defence rose up in him against such waste . . .

He bundled himself into his old coon-skin coat and lay
down on the box-sofa to think. Under his cheek he felt a
hard object with strange protuberances. It was a cushion which
Zeena had made for him when they were engaged – the only
piece of needlework he had ever seen her do. He flung it across
the floor and propped his head against the wall . . .

He knew a case of a man over the mountain – a young fellow
of about his own age – who had escaped from just such a life
of misery by going West with the girl he cared for. His wife
had divorced him, and he had married the girl and prospered.
Ethan had seen the couple the summer before at Shadd's Falls,
where they had come to visit relatives. They had a little girl
with fair curls, who wore a gold locket and was dressed like a
princess. The deserted wife had not done badly either. Her
husband had given her the farm and she had managed to sell
it, and with that and the alimony she had started a lunch-room
at Bettsbridge and bloomed into activity and importance.
Ethan was fired by the thought. Why should he not leave with
Mattie the next day, instead of letting her go alone? He would
hide his valise under the seat of the sleigh, and Zeena would
suspect nothing till she went upstairs for her afternoon nap and
found a letter on the bed . . .

His impulses were still near the surface, and he sprang up,
re-lit the lantern, and sat down at the table. He rummaged

in the drawer for a sheet of paper, found one, and began to write.

'Zeena, I've done all I could for you, and I don't see as it's been any use. I don't blame you, nor I don't blame myself. Maybe both of us will do better separate. I'm going to try my luck West, and you can sell the farm and mill, and keep the money—'

His pen paused on the word, which brought home to him the relentless conditions of his lot. If he gave the farm and mill to Zeena what would be left him to start his own life with? Once in the West he was sure of picking up work – he would not have feared to try his chance alone. But with Mattie depending on him the case was different. And what of Zeena's fate? Farm and mill were mortgaged to the limit of their value, and even if she found a purchaser – in itself an unlikely chance – it was doubtful if she could clear a thousand dollars on the sale. Meanwhile, how could she keep the farm going? It was only by incessant labour and personal supervision that Ethan drew a meagre living from his land, and his wife, even if she were in better health than she imagined, could never carry such a burden alone.

Well, she could go back to her people, then, and see what they would do for her. It was the fate she was forcing on Mattie – why not let her try it herself? By the time she had discovered his whereabouts, and brought suit for divorce, he would prob-ably – wherever he was – be earning enough to pay her a sufficient alimony. And the alternative was to let Mattie go forth alone, with far less hope of ultimate provision . . .

He had scattered the contents of the table-drawer in his search for a sheet of paper, and as he took up his pen his eye fell on an old copy of the *Bettsbridge Eagle*. The advertising sheet was folded uppermost, and he read the seductive words: 'Trips to the West: Reduced Rates'.

He drew the lantern nearer and eagerly scanned the fares; then the paper fell from his hand and he pushed aside his un-finished letter. A moment ago he had wondered what he and Mattie were to live on when they reached the West; now he saw that he had not even the money to take her there. Borrowing was out of the question: six months before he had given his only security to raise funds for necessary repairs to the mill, and he knew that without security no one at Starkfield would lend him ten dollars. The inexorable facts closed in on him like prison-warders hand-cuffing a convict. There was no way out – none. He was a prisoner for life, and now his one ray of light was to be extinguished.

He crept back heavily to the sofa, stretching himself out with limbs so leaden that he felt as if they would never move again. Tears rose in his throat and slowly burned their way to his lids.

As he lay there, the window-pane that faced him, growing gradually lighter, inlaid upon the darkness a square of moon-suffused sky. A crooked tree-branch crossed it, a branch of the apple-tree under which, on summer evenings, he had sometimes found Mattie sitting when he came up from the mill. Slowly the rim of the rainy vapours caught fire and burnt away, and a pure moon swung into the blue. Ethan, rising on his elbow, watched the landscape whiten and shape itself under the sculpture of the moon. This was the night on which he was to have taken Mattie coasting, and there hung the lamp to light them! He looked out at the slopes bathed in lustre, the silver-edged darkness of the woods, the spectral purple of the hills against the sky, and it seemed as though all the beauty of the night had been poured out to mock his wretchedness . . .

He fell asleep, and when he woke the chill of the winter dawn was in the room. He felt cold and stiff and hungry, and ashamed of being hungry. He rubbed his eyes and went to the window. A red sun stood over the grey rim of the fields, behind trees that looked black and brittle. He said to himself: 'This is Matt's last day,' and tried to think what the place would be without her.

As he stood there he heard a step behind him and she entered.

'Oh, Ethan – were you here all night?'

She looked so small and pinched, in her poor dress, with

the red scarf wound about her, and the cold light turning her paleness sallow, that Ethan stood before her without speaking.

'You must be frozen,' she went on, fixing lustreless eyes on him.

He drew a step nearer. 'How did you know I was here?'

'Because I heard you go down stairs again after I went to bed, and I listened all night, and you didn't come up.'

All his tenderness rushed to his lips. He looked at her and said: 'I'll come right along and make up the kitchen fire.'

They went back to the kitchen, and he fetched the coal and kindlings and cleared out the stove for her, while she brought in the milk and the cold remains of the meat-pie. When warmth began to radiate from the stove, and the first ray of sunlight lay on the kitchen floor, Ethan's dark thoughts melted in the mellower air. The sight of Mattie going about her work as he had seen her on so many mornings made it seem impossible that she should ever cease to be a part of the scene. He said to himself that he had doubtless exaggerated the significance of Zeena's threats, and that she too, with the return of daylight, would come to a saner mood.

He went up to Mattie as she bent above the stove, and laid his hand on her arm. 'I don't want you should trouble either,' he said, looking down into her eyes with a smile.

She flushed up warmly and whispered back: 'No, Ethan, I ain't going to trouble.'

'I guess things'll straighten out,' he added.

There was no answer but a quick throb of her lids, and he went on: 'She ain't said anything this morning?'

'No. I haven't seen her yet.'

'Don't you take any notice when you do.'

With this injunction he left her and went out to the cow-barn. He saw Jotham Powell walking up the hill through the morning mist, and the familiar sight added to his growing conviction of security.

As the two men were clearing out the stalls Jotham rested on his pitch-fork to say: 'Dan'l Byrne's goin' over to the Flats to-day noon, an' he c'd take Mattie's trunk along, and make it easier ridin' when I take her over in the sleigh.'

Ethan looked at him blankly, and he continued: 'Mis' Frome said the new girl'd be at the Flats at five, and I was to take Mattie then, so's 't she could ketch the six o'clock train for Stamford.'

Ethan felt the blood drumming in his temples. He had to wait a moment before he could find voice to say: 'Oh, it ain't so sure about Mattie's going—'

'That so?' said Jotham indifferently; and they went on with their work.

When they returned to the kitchen the two women were already at breakfast. Zeena had an air of unusual alertness and activity. She drank two cups of coffee and fed the cat with the scraps left in the pie-dish; then she rose from her seat and, walking over to the window, snipped two or three yellow leaves from the geraniums. 'Aunt Martha's ain't got a faded leaf on 'em; but they pine away when they ain't cared for,' she said reflectively. Then she turned to Jotham and asked: 'What time'd you say Dan'l Byrne'd be along?'

The hired man threw a hesitating glance at Ethan. 'Round about noon,' he said.

Zeena turned to Mattie. 'That trunk of yours is too heavy for the sleigh, and Dan'l Byrne'll be round to take it over to the Flats,' she said.

'I'm much obliged to you, Zeena,' said Mattie.

'I'd like to go over things with you first,' Zeena continued in an unperturbed voice. 'I know there's a huckaback towel missing; and I can't make out what you done with that match-safe 't used to stand behind the stuffed owl in the parlour.'

She went out, followed by Mattie, and when the men were alone Jotham said to his employer: 'I guess I better let Dan'l come round, then.'

Ethan finished his usual morning tasks about the house and barn; then he said to Jotham: 'I'm going down to Starkfield. Tell them not to wait dinner.'

The passion of rebellion had broken out in him again. That which had seemed incredible in the sober light of day had really come to pass, and he was to assist as a helpless spectator at Mattie's banishment. His manhood was humbled by the part he was compelled to play and by the thought of what Mattie must think of him. Confused impulses struggled in him as he strode along to the village. He had made up his mind to do something, but he did not know what it would be.

The early mist had vanished and the fields lay like a silver shield under the sun. It was one of the days when the glitter of winter shines through a pale haze of spring. Every yard of the road was alive with Mattie's presence, and there was hardly a branch against the sky or a tangle of brambles on the bank in which some bright shred of memory was not caught. Once, in the stillness, the call of a bird in a mountain ash was so like her laughter that his heart tightened and then grew large; and all these things made him see that something must be done at once.

Suddenly it occurred to him that Andrew Hale, who was a kind-hearted man, might be induced to reconsider his refusal and advance a small sum on the lumber if he were told that Zeena's ill-health made it necessary to hire a servant. Hale, after all, knew enough of Ethan's situation to make it possible for the latter to renew his appeal without too much loss of pride; and, moreover, how much did pride count in the ebullition of passions in his breast?

The more he considered his plan the more hopeful it seemed. If he could get Mrs Hale's ear he felt certain of success, and with fifty dollars in his pocket nothing could keep him from Mattie . . .

His first object was to reach Starkfield before Hale had started for his work; he knew the carpenter had a job down the Corbury road and was likely to leave his house early. Ethan's long strides grew more rapid with the accelerated beat of his thoughts, and as he reached the foot of School House Hill he caught sight of Hale's sleigh in the distance. He hurried forward to meet it, but as it drew nearer he saw that it was driven by the carpenter's youngest boy and that the figure at his side, looking like a large upright cocoon in spectacles, was that of Mrs Andrew Hale. Ethan signed to them to stop, and Mrs Hale leaned forward, her pink wrinkles twinkling with benevolence.

'Mr Hale? Why, yes, you'll find him down home now. He ain't going to his work this forenoon. He woke up with a touch o' lumbago, and I just made him put on one of old Dr Kidder's plasters and set right up into the fire.'

Beaming maternally on Ethan, she bent over to add: 'I on'y just heard from Mr Hale 'bout Zeena's going over to Betts-bridge to see that new doctor. I'm real sorry she's feeling so bad again! I hope he thinks he can do something for her? I don't know anybody round here's had more sickness than Zeena. I always tell Mr Hale I don't know what she'd 'a' done if she hadn't 'a' had you to look after her; and I used to say the same thing 'bout your mother. You've had an awful mean time, Ethan Frome.'

She gave him a last nod of sympathy while her son chirped to the horse; and Ethan, as she drove off, stood in the middle of the road and stared after the retreating sleigh.

It was a long time since any one had spoken to him as kindly as Mrs Hale. Most people were either indifferent to his troubles, or disposed to think it natural that a young fellow of his age should have carried without repining the burden of three crippled lives. But Mrs Hale had said 'You've had an awful mean time, Ethan Frome,' and he felt less alone with his misery. If the Hales were sorry for him they would surely respond to his appeal . . .

He started down the road toward their house, but at the end of a few yards he pulled up sharply, the blood in his face. For the first time, in the light of the words he had just heard, he saw what he was about to do. He was planning to take advantage of the Hales' sympathy to obtain money from them on false pretences. That was a plain statement of the cloudy purpose which had driven him in headlong to Starkfield.

With the sudden perception of the point to which his

madness had carried him, the madness fell and he saw his life before him as it was. He was a poor man, the husband of a sickly woman, whom his desertion would leave alone and destitute; and even if he had had the heart to desert her he could have done so only by deceiving two kindly people who had pitied him.

He turned and walked slowly back to the farm.

IX

At the kitchen door Daniel Byrne sat in his sleigh behind a big-boned grey who pawed the snow and swung his long head restlessly from side to side.

Ethan went into the kitchen and found his wife by the stove. Her head was wrapped in her shawl, and she was reading a book called 'Kidney Troubles and Their Cure' on which he had had to pay extra postage only a few days before.

Zeena did not move or look up when he entered, and after a moment he asked: 'Where's Mattie?'

Without lifting her eyes from the page she replied: 'I presume she's getting down her trunk.'

The blood rushed to his face. 'Getting down her trunk – alone?'

'Jotham Powell's down in the wood-lot, and Dan'l Byrne says he darsn't leave that horse,' she returned.

Her husband, without stopping to hear the end of the phrase, had left the kitchen and sprung up the stairs. The door of Mattie's room was shut, and he wavered a moment on the landing. 'Matt,' he said in a low voice; but there was no answer, and he put his hand on the door-knob.

He had never been in her room except once, in the early summer, when he had gone there to plaster up a leak in the eaves, but he remembered exactly how everything had looked: the red and white quilt on her narrow bed, the pretty pin-cushion on the chest of drawers, and over it the enlarged photograph of her mother, in an oxydized frame, with a bunch of dyed grasses at the back. Now all these and other tokens of her presence had vanished, and the room looked as bare and comfortless as when Zeena had shown her into it on the day of her arrival. In the middle of the floor stood her trunk, and

83

on the trunk she sat in her Sunday dress, her back turned to the door and her face in her hands. She had not heard Ethan's call because she was sobbing; and she did not hear his step till he stood close behind her and laid his hands on her shoulders.

'Matt – oh, don't – oh, *Matt!*'

She started up, lifting her wet face to his. 'Ethan – I thought I wasn't ever going to see you again!'

He took her in his arms, pressing her close, and with a trembling hand smoothed away the hair from her forehead.

'Not see me again? What do you mean?'

She sobbed out: 'Jotham said you told him we wasn't to wait dinner for you, and I thought —'

'You thought I meant to cut it?' he finished for her grimly.

She clung to him without answering, and he laid his lips on her hair, which was soft yet springy, like certain mosses on warm slopes, and had the faint woody fragrance of fresh sawdust in the sun.

Through the door they heard Zeena's voice calling out from below: 'Dan'l Byrne says you better hurry up if you want him to take that trunk.'

They drew apart with stricken faces. Words of resistance rushed to Ethan's lips and died there. Mattie found her handkerchief and dried her eyes; then, bending down, she took hold of a handle of the trunk.

Ethan put her aside. 'You let go, Matt,' he ordered her.

She answered: 'It takes two to coax it round the corner'; and submitting to this argument he grasped the other handle, and together they manœuvred the heavy trunk out to the landing.

'Now let go,' he repeated; then he shouldered the trunk and carried it down the stairs and across the passage to the kitchen. Zeena, who had gone back to her seat by the stove, did not lift her head from her book as he passed. Mattie followed him out of the door and helped him to lift the trunk into the back of the sleigh. When it was in place they stood side by side on the door-step, watching Daniel Byrne plunge off behind his fidgety horse.

It seemed to Ethan that his heart was bound with cords which an unseen hand was tightening with every tick of the clock. Twice he opened his lips to speak to Mattie and found no breath. At length, as she turned to re-enter the house, he laid a detaining hand on her.

'I'm going to drive you over, Matt,' he whispered.

She murmured back: 'I think Zeena wants I should go with Jotham.'

'I'm going to drive you over,' he repeated; and she went into the kitchen without answering.

At dinner Ethan could not eat. If he lifted his eyes they rested on Zeena's pinched face, and the corners of her straight lips seemed to quiver away into a smile. She ate well, declaring that the mild weather made her feel better, and pressed a second helping of beans on Jotham Powell, whose wants she generally ignored.

Mattie, when the meal was over, went about her usual task of clearing the table and washing up the dishes. Zeena, after feeding the cat, had returned to her rocking-chair by the stove, and Jotham Powell, who always lingered last, reluctantly pushed back his chair and moved toward the door.

On the threshold he turned back to say to Ethan: 'What time'll I come round for Mattie?'

Ethan was standing near the window, mechanically filling his pipe while he watched Mattie move to and fro. He answered: 'You needn't come round; I'm going to drive her over myself.'

He saw the rise of the colour in Mattie's averted cheek, and the quick lifting of Zeena's head.

'I want you should stay here this afternoon, Ethan,' his wife said. 'Jotham can drive Mattie over.'

Mattie flung an imploring glance at him, but he repeated curtly: 'I'm going to drive her over myself.'

Zeena continued in the same even tone: 'I wanted you should stay and fix up that stove in Mattie's room afore the girl gets here. It ain't been drawing right for nigh on a month now.'

Ethan's voice rose indignantly. 'If it was good enough for Mattie I guess it's good enough for a hired girl.'

'That girl that's coming told me she was used to a house where they had a furnace,' Zeena persisted with the same monotonous mildness.

'She'd better ha' stayed there then,' he flung back at her; and turning to Mattie he added in a hard voice: 'You be ready by three, Matt; I've got business at Corbury.'

Jotham Powell had started for the barn, and Ethan strode down after him aflame with anger. The pulses in his temples throbbed and a fog was in his eyes. He went about his task without knowing what force directed him, or whose hands and feet were fulfilling its orders. It was not till he led out the sorrel and backed him between the shafts of the sleigh that he once more became conscious of what he was doing. As he passed the bridle over the horse's head, and wound the traces around the shafts, he remembered the day when he had made the same preparations in order to drive over and meet his wife's cousin at the Flats. It was little more than a year ago, on just such a soft afternoon, with a 'feel' of spring in the air. The sorrel, turning the same big ringed eye on him, nuzzled the palm of his hand in the same way; and one by one all the days between rose up and stood before him . . .

He flung the bearskin into the sleigh, climbed to the seat, and drove up to the house. When he entered the kitchen it was empty, but Mattie's bag and shawl lay ready by the door. He went to the foot of the stairs and listened. No sound reached him from above, but presently he thought he heard some one moving about in his deserted study, and pushing open the door he saw Mattie, in her hat and jacket, standing with her back to him near the table.

She started at his approach and turning quickly, said: 'Is it time?'

'What are you doing here, Matt?' he asked her.

She looked at him timidly. 'I was just taking a look round – that's all,' she answered, with a wavering smile.

They went back into the kitchen without speaking, and Ethan picked up her bag and shawl.

'Where's Zeena?' he asked.

'She went upstairs right after dinner. She said she had those shooting pains again, and didn't want to be disturbed.'

'Didn't she say good-bye to you?'

'No. That was all she said.'

Ethan, looking slowly about the kitchen, said to himself with a shudder that in a few hours he would be returning to it alone. Then the sense of unreality overcame him once more, and he could not bring himself to believe that Mattie stood there for the last time before him.

'Come on,' he said almost gaily, opening the door and putting her bag into the sleigh. He sprang to his seat and bent over to tuck the rug about her as she slipped into the place at his side. 'Now then, go 'long,' he said, with a shake of the reins that sent the sorrel placidly jogging down the hill.

'We got lots of time for a good ride, Matt!' he cried, seeking her hand beneath the fur and pressing it in his. His face tingled and he felt dizzy, as if he had stopped in at the Starkfield saloon on a zero day for a drink.

At the gate, instead of making for Starkfield, he turned the sorrel to the right, up the Bettsbridge road. Mattie sat silent, giving no sign of surprise; but after a moment she said: 'Are you going round by Shadow Pond?'

He laughed and answered: 'I knew you'd know!'

She drew closer under the bearskin, so that, looking sideways around his coat-sleeve, he could just catch the tip of her nose and a blown brown wave of hair. They drove slowly up the road between fields glistening under the pale sun, and then bent to the right down a lane edged with spruce and larch. Ahead of them, a long way off, a range of hills stained by mottlings of black forest flowed away in round white curves against the sky. The lane passed into a pine-wood with boles reddening in the afternoon sun and delicate blue shadows on the snow. As they entered it the breeze fell and a warm stillness seemed to drop from the branches with the dropping

needles. Here the snow was so pure that the tiny tracks of
wood-animals had left on it intricate lace-like patterns, and
the bluish cones caught in its surface stood out like ornaments
of bronze.

Ethan drove on in silence till they reached a part of the
wood where the pines were more widely spaced; then he drew
up and helped Mattie to get out of the sleigh. They passed
between the aromatic trunks, the snow breaking crisply under
their feet, till they came to a small sheet of water with steep
wooded sides. Across its frozen surface, from the farther bank,
a single hill rising against the western sun threw the long con-
ical shadow which gave the lake its name. It was a shy secret
spot, full of the same dumb melancholy that Ethan felt in his
heart.

He looked up and down the little pebbly beach till his eye
lit on a fallen tree-trunk half submerged in snow.

'There's where we sat at the picnic,' he reminded her.

The entertainment of which he spoke was one of the few
that they had taken part in together: a 'church picnic' which,
on a long afternoon of the preceding summer, had filled the
retired place with merry-making. Mattie had begged him to
go with her but he had refused. Then, toward sunset, coming
down from the mountain where he had been felling timber,
he had been caught by some strayed revellers and drawn into
the group by the lake, where Mattie, encircled by facetious
youths, and bright as a blackberry under her spreading hat, was
brewing coffee over a gipsy fire. He remembered the shyness
he had felt at approaching her in his uncouth clothes, and
then the lighting up of her face, and the way she had broken
through the group to come to him with a cup in her hand.
They had sat for a few minutes on the fallen log by the pond,
and she had missed her gold locket, and set the young men
searching for it; and it was Ethan who had spied it in the
moss . . . That was all; but all their intercourse had been made
up of just such inarticulate flashes, when they seemed to come
suddenly upon happiness as if they had surprised a butterfly in
the winter woods . . .

'It was right there I found your locket,' he said, pushing his foot into a dense tuft of blueberry bushes.

'I never saw anybody with such sharp eyes!' she answered. She sat down on the tree-trunk in the sun and he sat down beside her.

'You were as pretty as a picture in that pink hat,' he said.

She laughed with pleasure. 'Oh, I guess it was the hat!' she rejoined.

They had never before avowed their inclination so openly, and Ethan, for a moment, had the illusion that he was a free man, wooing the girl he meant to marry. He looked at her hair and longed to touch it again, and to tell her that it smelt of the woods; but he had never learned to say such things.

Suddenly she rose to her feet and said: 'We mustn't stay here any longer.'

He continued to gaze at her vaguely, only half-roused from his dream. 'There's plenty of time,' he answered.

They stood looking at each other as if the eyes of each were straining to absorb and hold fast the other's image. There were things he had to say to her before they parted, but he could not say them in that place of summer memories, and he turned and followed her in silence to the sleigh. As they drove away the sun sank behind the hill and the pine-boles turned from red to grey.

By a devious track between the fields they wound back to the Starkfield road. Under the open sky the light was still clear, with a reflection of cold red on the eastern hills. The clumps of trees in the snow seemed to draw together in ruffled lumps, like birds with their heads under their wings; and the sky, as it paled, rose higher, leaving the earth more alone.

As they turned into the Starkfield road Ethan said: 'Matt, what do you mean to do?'

She did not answer at once, but at length she said: 'I'll try to get a place in a store.'

'You know you can't do it. The bad air and the standing all day nearly killed you before.'

'I'm a lot stronger than I was before I came to Starkfield.'

'And now you're going to throw away all the good it's done you!'

There seemed to be no answer to this, and again they drove on for a while without speaking. With every yard of the way some spot where they had stood, and laughed together or been silent, clutched at Ethan and dragged him back.

'Isn't there any of your father's folks could help you?'

'There isn't any of 'em I'd ask.'

He lowered his voice to say: 'You know there's nothing I wouldn't do for you if I could.'

'I know there isn't.'

'But I can't —'

She was silent, but he felt a slight tremor in the shoulder against his.

'Oh, Matt,' he broke out, 'if I could ha' gone with you now, I'd ha' done it —'

She turned to him, pulling a scrap of paper from her breast. 'Ethan – I found this,' she stammered. Even in the failing light he saw it was the letter to his wife that he had begun the night before and forgotten to destroy. Through his astonishment there ran a fierce thrill of joy. 'Matt –' he cried; 'if I could ha' done it, would you?'

'Oh, Ethan, Ethan – what's the use?' With a sudden movement she tore the letter in shreds and sent them fluttering off into the snow.

'Tell me, Matt! Tell me!' he adjured her.

She was silent for a moment; then she said, in such a low tone that he had to stoop his head to hear her: 'I used to think of it sometimes, summer nights, when the moon was so bright I couldn't sleep.'

His heart reeled with the sweetness of it. 'As long ago as that?'

She answered, as if the date had long been fixed for her: 'The first time was at Shadow Pond.'

'Was that why you gave me my coffee before the others?'

'I don't know. Did I? I was dreadfully put out when you

wouldn't go to the picnic with me; and then, when I saw you coming down the road, I thought maybe you'd gone home that way o' purpose; and that made me glad.'

They were silent again. They had reached the point where the road dipped to the hollow by Ethan's mill and as they descended the darkness descended with them, dropping down like a black veil from the heavy hemlock boughs.

'I'm tied hand and foot, Matt. There isn't a thing I can do,' he began again.

'You must write to me sometimes, Ethan.'

'Oh, what good'll writing do? I want to put my hand out and touch you. I want to do for you and care for you. I want to be there when you're sick and when you're lonesome.'

'You mustn't think but what I'll do all right.'

'You won't need me, you mean? I suppose you'll marry!'

'Oh, Ethan!' she cried.

'I don't know how it is you make me feel, Matt. I'd a'most rather have you dead than that!'

'Oh, I wish I was, I wish I was!' she sobbed.

The sound of her weeping shook him out of his dark anger, and he felt ashamed.

'Don't let's talk that way,' he whispered.

'Why shouldn't we, when it's true? I've been wishing it every minute of the day.'

'Matt! You be quiet! Don't you say it.'

'There's never anybody been good to me but you.'

'Don't say that either, when I can't lift a hand for you!'

'Yes; but it's true just the same.'

They had reached the top of School House Hill and Stark-field lay below them in the twilight. A cutter, mounting the road from the village, passed them by in a joyous flutter of bells, and they straightened themselves and looked ahead with rigid faces. Along the main street lights had begun to shine from the house-fronts and stray figures were turning in here and there at the gates. Ethan, with a touch of his whip, roused the sorrel to a languid trot.

As they drew near the end of the village the cries of children reached them, and they saw a knot of boys, with sleds behind them, scattering across the open space before the church.

'I guess this'll be their last coast for a day or two,' Ethan said, looking up at the mild sky.

Mattie was silent, and he added: 'We were to have gone down last night.'

Still she did not speak and, prompted by an obscure desire to help himself and her through their miserable last hour, he went on discursively: 'Ain't it funny we haven't been down together but just that once last winter?'

She answered: 'It wasn't often I got down to the village.'

'That's so,' he said.

They had reached the crest of the Corbury road, and between the indistinct white glimmer of the church and the black curtain of the Varnum spruces the slope stretched away below them without a sled on its length. Some erratic impulse prompted Ethan to say: 'How'd you like me to take you down now?'

She forced a laugh. 'Why, there isn't time!'

'There's all the time we want. Come along!' His one desire now was to postpone the moment of turning the sorrel toward the Flats.

'But the girl,' she faltered. 'The girl'll be waiting at the station.'

'Well, let her wait. You'd have to if she didn't. Come!'

The note of authority in his voice seemed to subdue her, and when he had jumped from the sleigh she let him help her out, saying only, with a vague feint of reluctance: 'But there isn't a sled round anywheres.'

'Yes, there is! Right over there under the spruces.

He threw the bearskin over the sorrel, who stood passively by the roadside, hanging a meditative head. Then he caught Mattie's hand and drew her after him toward the sled.

She seated herself obediently and he took his place behind her, so close that her hair brushed his face. 'All right, Matt?' he called out, as if the width of the road had been between them.

She turned her head to say: 'It's dreadfully dark. Are you sure you can see?'

He laughed contemptuously: 'I could go down this coast with my eyes tied!' and she laughed with him, as if she liked his audacity. Nevertheless he sat still a moment, straining his eyes down the long hill, for it was the most confusing hour of the evening, the hour when the last clearness from the upper sky is merged with the rising night in a blur that disguises landmarks and falsifies distances.

'Now!' he cried.

The sled started with a bound, and they flew on through the dusk, gathering smoothness and speed as they went, with the hollow night opening out below them and the air singing by like an organ. Mattie sat perfectly still, but as they reached the bend at the foot of the hill, where the big elm thrust out a deadly elbow, he fancied that she shrank a little closer.

'Don't be scared, Matt!' he cried exultantly, as they spun safely past it and flew down the second slope; and when they reached the level ground beyond, and the speed of the sled began to slacken, he heard her give a little laugh of glee.

They sprang off and started to walk back up the hill. Ethan dragged the sled with one hand and passed the other through Mattie's arm.

'Were you scared I'd run you into the elm?' he asked with a boyish laugh.

'I told you I was never scared with you,' she answered.

The strange exultation of his mood had brought on one of his rare fits of boastfulness. 'It *is* a tricky place, though. The least swerve, and we'd never ha' come up again. But I can measure distances to a hair's-breadth – always could.'

She murmured: 'I always say you've got the surest eye . . .'

Deep silence had fallen with the starless dusk, and they leaned on each other without speaking; but at every step of their climb Ethan said to himself: 'It's the last time we'll ever walk together.'

They mounted slowly to the top of the hill. When they were abreast of the church he stooped his head to her to ask:

'Are you tired?' and she answered, breathing quickly: 'It was splendid!'

With a pressure of his arm he guided her toward the Norway spruces. 'I guess this sled must be Ned Hale's. Anyhow I'll leave it where I found it.' He drew the sled up to the Varnum gate and rested it against the fence. As he raised himself he suddenly felt Mattie close to him among the shadows.

'Is this where Ned and Ruth kissed each other?' she whispered breathlessly, and flung her arms about him. Her lips, groping for his, swept over his face, and he held her fast in a rapture of surprise.

'Good-bye – good-bye,' she stammered, and kissed him again.

'Oh, Matt, I can't let you go!' broke from him in the same old cry.

She freed herself from his hold and he heard her sobbing. 'Oh, I can't go either!' she wailed.

'Matt! What'll we do? What'll we do?'

They clung to each other's hands like children, and her body shook with desperate sobs.

Through the stillness they heard the church clock striking five.

'Oh, Ethan, it's time!' she cried.

He drew her back to him. 'Time for what? You don't suppose I'm going to leave you now?'

'If I missed my train where'd I go?'

'Where are you going if you catch it?'

She stood silent, her hands lying cold and relaxed in his.

'What's the good of either of us going anywheres without the other one now?' he said.

She remained motionless, as if she had not heard him. Then she snatched her hands from his, threw her arms about his neck, and pressed a sudden drenched cheek against his face. 'Ethan! Ethan! I want you to take me down again!'

'Down where?'

'The coast. Right off,' she panted. 'So 't we'll never come up any more.'

'Matt! What on earth do you mean?'

She put her lips close against his ear to say: 'Right into the big elm. You said you could. So 't we'd never have to leave each other any more.'

'Why, what are you talking of? You're crazy!'

'I'm not crazy; but I will be if I leave you.'

'Oh, Matt, Matt –' he groaned.

She tightened her fierce hold about his neck. Her face lay close to his face.

'Ethan, where'll I go if I leave you? I don't know how to get along alone. You said so yourself just now. Nobody but you was ever good to me. And there'll be that strange girl in the house . . . and she'll sleep in my bed, where I used to lay nights and listen to hear you come up the stairs . . .'

The words were like fragments torn from his heart. With them came the hated vision of the house he was going back to – of the stairs he would have to go up every night, of the woman who would wait for him there. And the sweetness of Mattie's avowal, the wild wonder of knowing at last that all that had happened to him had happened to her too, made the other vision more abhorrent, the other life more intolerable to return to . . .

Her pleadings still came to him between short sobs, but he no longer heard what she was saying. Her hat had slipped back and he was stroking her hair. He wanted to get the feeling of it into his hand, so that it would sleep there like a seed in winter. Once he found her mouth again, and they seemed to be by the pond together in the burning August sun. But his cheek touched hers, and it was cold and full of weeping, and he saw the road to the Flats under the night and heard the whistle of the train up the line.

The spruces swathed them in blackness and silence. They might have been in their coffins underground. He said to himself: 'Perhaps it'll feel like this . . .' and then again: 'After this I sha'n't feel anything . . .'

Suddenly he heard the old sorrel whinny across the road, and thought: 'He's wondering why he doesn't get his supper . . .'

'Come,' Mattie whispered, tugging at his hand.

Her sombre violence constrained him: she seemed the embodied instrument of fate. He pulled the sled out, blinking like a night-bird as he passed from the shade of the spruces into the transparent dusk of the open. The slope below them was deserted. All Starkfield was at supper, and not a figure crossed the open space before the church. The sky, swollen with the clouds that announce a thaw, hung as low as before a summer storm. He strained his eyes through the dimness, and they seemed less keen, less capable than usual.

He took his seat on the sled and Mattie instantly placed herself in front of him. Her hat had fallen into the snow and his lips were in her hair. He stretched out his legs, drove his heels into the road to keep the sled from slipping forward, and bent her head back between his hands. Then suddenly he sprang up again.

'Get up,' he ordered her.

It was the tone she always heeded, but she cowered down in her seat, repeating vehemently: 'No, no, no!'

'Get up!'

'Why?'

'I want to sit in front.'

'No, no! How can you steer in front?'

'I don't have to. We'll follow the track.'

They spoke in smothered whispers, as though the night were listening.

'Get up! Get up!' he urged her; but she kept on repeating: 'Why do you want to sit in front?'

'Because I – because I want to feel you holding me,' he stammered, and dragged her to her feet.

The answer seemed to satisfy her, or else she yielded to the power of his voice. He bent down, feeling in the obscurity for the glassy slide worn by preceding coasters, and placed the runners carefully between its edges. She waited while he seated himself with crossed legs in the front of the sled; then she crouched quickly down at his back and clasped her arms about him. Her breath in his neck set him shuddering again, and he almost sprang from his seat. But in a flash he remembered the alternative. She was right: this was better than parting. He leaned back and drew her mouth to his . . .

Just as they started he heard the sorrel's whinny again, and the familiar wistful call, and all the confused images it brought with it, went with him down the first reach of the road. Half-way down there was a sudden drop, then a rise, and after that another long delirious descent. As they took wing for this it seemed to him that they were flying indeed, flying far up into the cloudy night, with Starkfield immeasurably below them, falling away like a speck in space . . . Then the big elm shot up ahead, lying in wait for them at the bend of the road, and he said between his teeth: 'We can fetch it; I know we can fetch it —'

As they flew toward the tree Mattie pressed her arms tighter, and her blood seemed to be in his veins. Once or twice the sled swerved a little under them. He slanted his body to keep it headed for the elm, repeating to himself again and again: 'I know we can fetch it'; and little phrases she had spoken ran through his head and danced before him on the air. The big tree loomed bigger and closer, and as they bore down on it he thought: 'It's waiting for us: it seems to know.' But suddenly his wife's face, with twisted monstrous lineaments, thrust itself between him and his goal, and he made an instinctive move-ment to brush it aside. The sled swerved in response, but he righted it again, kept it straight, and drove down on the black projecting mass. There was a last instant when the air shot past him like millions of fiery wires; and then the elm . . .

The sky was still thick, but looking straight up he saw a single star, and tried vaguely to reckon whether it were Sirius, or — or — The effort tired him too much, and he closed his heavy lids and thought that he would sleep . . . The stillness was so profound that he heard a little animal twittering somewhere near by under the snow. It made a small frightened *cheep* like a field mouse, and he wondered languidly if it were hurt. Then he understood that it must be in pain: pain so excruciating that he seemed, mysteriously, to feel it shooting through his own body. He tried in vain to roll over in the direction of the sound, and stretched his left arm out across the snow. And now it was as though he felt rather than heard the twittering; it seemed to be under his palm, which rested on something soft and springy. The thought of the animal's suffering was intolerable to him and he struggled to raise himself, and could not because a rock, or some huge mass, seemed to be lying on him. But he continued to finger about cautiously with his left hand, thinking he might get hold of the little creature and help it; and all at once he knew that the soft thing he had touched was Mattie's hair and that his hand was on her face.

He dragged himself to his knees, the monstrous load on him moving with him as he moved, and his hand went over and over her face, and he felt that the twittering came from her lips.

He got his face down close to hers, with his ear to her mouth, and in the darkness he saw her eyes open and heard her say his name.

'Oh, Matt, I thought we'd fetched it,' he moaned; and far off, up the hill, he heard the sorrel whinny, and thought: 'I ought to be getting him his feed . . .'

. . . .
. . . .
. . . .

The querulous drone ceased as I entered Frome's kitchen, and of the two women sitting there I could not tell which had been the speaker.

One of them, on my appearing, raised her tall bony figure from her seat, not as if to welcome me – for she threw me no more than a brief glance of surprise – but simply to set about preparing the meal which Frome's absence had delayed. A slatternly calico wrapper hung from her shoulders and the wisps of her thin grey hair were drawn away from a high forehead and fastened at the back by a broken comb. She had pale opaque eyes which revealed nothing and reflected nothing, and her narrow lips were of the same sallow colour as her face.

The other woman was much smaller and slighter. She sat huddled in an arm-chair near the stove, and when I came in she turned her head quickly toward me, without the least corresponding movement of her body. Her hair was as grey as her companion's, her face as bloodless and shrivelled, but amber-tinted, with swarthy shadows sharpening the nose and hollowing the temples. Under her shapeless dress her body kept its limp immobility, and her dark eyes had the bright witch-like stare that disease of the spine sometimes gives.

Even for that part of the country the kitchen was a poor-looking place. With the exception of the dark-eyed woman's chair, which looked like a soiled relic of luxury bought at a country auction, the furniture was of the roughest kind. Three coarse china plates and a broken-nosed milk-jug had been set on a greasy table scored with knife-cuts, and a couple of straw-bottomed chairs and a kitchen dresser of unpainted pine stood meagrely against the plaster walls.

'My, it's cold here! The fire must be 'most out,' Frome said, glancing about him apologetically as he followed me in.

The tall woman, who had moved away from us toward the dresser, took no notice; but the other, from her cushioned niche, answered complainingly, in a high thin voice: 'It's on'y just been made up this very minute. Zeena fell asleep and slep' ever so long, and I thought I'd be frozen stiff before I could wake her up and get her to 'tend to it.'

I knew then that it was she who had been speaking when we entered.

Her companion, who was just coming back to the table with the remains of a cold mince-pie in a battered pie-dish, set down her unappetizing burden without appearing to hear the accusation brought against her.

Frome stood hesitatingly before her as she advanced; then he looked at me and said: 'This is my wife, Mis' Frome.' After another interval he added, turning toward the figure in the arm-chair: 'And this is Miss Mattie Silver . . .'

. . . .

Mrs Ned Hale, tender soul, had pictured me as lost in the Flats and buried under a snow-drift; and her satisfaction on seeing me safely restored to her the next morning made me feel that my peril had caused me to advance several degrees in her favour.

Great was her amazement, and that of old Mrs Varnum, on learning that Ethan Frome's old horse had carried me to and from Corbury Junction through the worst blizzard of the winter; greater still their surprise when they heard that his master had taken me in for the night.

Beneath their exclamations of wonder I felt a secret curiosity to know what impressions I had received from my night in the Frome household, and divined that the best way of breaking down their reserve was to let them try to penetrate mine. I therefore confined myself to saying, in a matter-of-fact tone, that I had been received with great kindness, and that Frome had made a bed for me in a room on the ground-floor which seemed in happier days to have been fitted up as a kind of writing-room or study.

'Well,' Mrs Hale mused, 'in such a storm I suppose he felt

he couldn't do less than take you in – but I guess it went hard with Ethan. I don't believe but what you're the only stranger has set foot in that house for over twenty years. He's that proud he don't even like his oldest friends to go there; and I don't know as any do, any more, except myself and the doctor...'

'You still go there, Mrs Hale?' I ventured.

'I used to go a good deal after the accident, when I was first married; but after a while I got to think it made 'em feel worse to see us. And then one thing and another came, and my own troubles... But I generally make out to drive over there round about New Year's, and once in the summer. Only I always try to pick a day when Ethan's off somewheres. It's bad enough to see the two women sitting there – but *his* face, when he looks round that bare place, just kills me... You see, I can look back and call it up in his mother's day, before their troubles.'

Old Mrs Varnum, by this time, had gone up to bed, and her daughter and I were sitting alone, after supper, in the austere seclusion of the horse-hair parlour. Mrs Hale glanced at me tentatively, as though trying to see how much footing my con-jectures gave her; and I guessed that if she had kept silence till now it was because she had been waiting, through all the years, for some one who should see what she alone had seen.

I waited to let her trust in me gather strength before I said: 'Yes, it's pretty bad, seeing all three of them there together.'

She drew her mild brows into a frown of pain. 'It was just awful from the beginning. I was here in the house when they were carried up – they laid Mattie Silver in the room you're in. She and I were great friends, and she was to have been my brides-maid in the spring... When she came to I went up to her and stayed all night. They gave her things to quiet her, and she didn't know much till to'rd morning, and then all of a sudden she woke up just like herself, and looked straight at me out of her big eyes, and said... Oh, I don't know why I'm telling you all this,' Mrs Hale broke off, crying.

She took off her spectacles, wiped the moisture from them, and put them on again with an unsteady hand. 'It got about

the next day,' she went on, 'that Zeena Frome had sent Mattie
off in a hurry because she had a hired girl coming, and the
folks here could never rightly tell what she and Ethan were
doing that night coasting, when they'd ought to have been on
their way to the Flats to ketch the train . . . I never knew myself
what Zeena thought – I don't to this day. Nobody knows
Zeena's thoughts. Anyhow, when she heard o' the accident
she came right in and stayed with Ethan over to the minister's,
where they'd carried him. And as soon as the doctors said that
Mattie could be moved, Zeena sent for her and took her back
to the farm.'

'And there she's been ever since?'

Mrs Hale answered simply: 'There was nowhere else for
her to go;' and my heart tightened at the thought of the hard
compulsions of the poor.

'Yes, there she's been,' Mrs Hale continued, 'and Zeena's
done for her, and done for Ethan, as good as she could. It was
a miracle, considering how sick she was – but she seemed to
be raised right up just when the call came to her. Not as she's
ever given up doctoring, and she's had sick spells right along;
but she's had the strength given her to care for those two for
over twenty years, and before the accident came she thought
she couldn't even care for herself.'

Mrs Hale paused a moment, and I remained silent, plunged
in the vision of what her words evoked. 'It's horrible for them
all,' I murmured.

'Yes: it's pretty bad. And they ain't any of 'em easy people
either. Mattie *was*, before the accident; I never knew a sweeter
nature. But she's suffered too much – that's what I always say
when folks tell me how she's soured. And Zeena, she was
always cranky. Not but what she bears with Mattie wonderful
– I've seen that myself. But sometimes the two of them get
going at each other, and then Ethan's face'd break your
heart . . . When I see that, I think it's *him* that suffers most . . .
anyhow it ain't Zeena, because she ain't got the time . . . It's a
pity, though,' Mrs Hale ended, sighing, 'that they're all shut
up there'n that one kitchen. In the summertime, on pleasant

days, they move Mattie into the parlour, or out in the door-
yard, and that makes it easier . . . but winters there's the fires
to be thought of, and there ain't a dime to spare up at the
Fromes'.'

Mrs Hale drew a deep breath, as though her memory were
eased of its long burden, and she had no more to say; but
suddenly an impulse of complete avowal seized her.

She took off her spectacles again, leaned toward me across
the bead-work table-cover, and went on with lowered voice:
'There was one day, about a week after the accident, when
they all thought Mattie couldn't live. Well, I say it's a pity she
did. I said it right out to our minister once, and he was shocked
at me. Only he wasn't with me that morning when she first
came to . . . And I say, if she'd ha' died, Ethan might ha' lived;
and the way they are now, I don't see's there's much difference
between the Fromes up at the farm and the Fromes down in
the graveyard; 'cept that down there they're all quiet, and the
women have got to hold their tongues.'

SUMMER

I

A girl came out of lawyer Royall's house, at the end of the one street of North Dormer, and stood on the doorstep.
It was the beginning of a June afternoon. The springlike transparent sky shed a rain of silver sunshine on the roofs of the village, and on the pastures and larchwoods surrounding it. A little wind moved among the round white clouds on the shoulders of the hills, driving their shadows across the fields and down the grassy road that takes the name of street when it passes through North Dormer. The place lies high and in the open, and lacks the lavish shade of the more protected New England villages. The clump of weeping-willows about the duck pond, and the Norway spruces in front of the Hatchard gate, cast almost the only roadside shadow between lawyer Royall's house and the point where, at the other end of the village, the road rises above the church and skirts the black hemlock wall enclosing the cemetery.

The little June wind, frisking down the street, shook the doleful fringes of the Hatchard spruces, caught the straw hat of a young man just passing under them, and spun it clean across the road into the duck-pond.

As he ran to fish it out the girl on lawyer Royall's doorstep noticed that he was a stranger, that he wore city clothes, and that he was laughing with all his teeth, as the young and careless laugh at such mishaps.

Her heart contracted a little, and the shrinking that sometimes came over her when she saw people with holiday faces made her draw back into the house and pretend to look for the key that she knew she had already put into her pocket. A narrow greenish mirror with a gilt eagle over it hung on the passage wall, and she looked critically at her reflection, wished

for the thousandth time that she had blue eyes like Annabel
Balch, the girl who sometimes came from Springfield to spend
a week with old Miss Hatchard, straightened the sunburnt
hat over her small swarthy face, and turned out again into the
sunshine.

'How I hate everything!' she murmured.

The young man had passed through the Hatchard gate, and
she had the street to herself. North Dormer is at all times an
empty place, and at three o'clock on a June afternoon its few
able-bodied men are off in the fields or woods, and the women
indoors, engaged in languid household drudgery.

The girl walked along, swinging her key on a finger, and
looking about her with the heightened attention produced
by the presence of a stranger in a familiar place. What, she
wondered, did North Dormer look like to people from other
parts of the world? She herself had lived there since the age of
five, and had long supposed it to be a place of some importance. But about a year before, Mr Miles, the new Episcopal
clergyman at Hepburn, who drove over every other Sunday –
when the roads were not ploughed up by hauling – to hold a
service in the North Dormer church, had proposed, in a fit of
missionary zeal, to take the young people down to Nettleton
to hear an illustrated lecture on the Holy Land; and the dozen
girls and boys who represented the future of North Dormer
had been piled into a farm-waggon, driven over the hills to
Hepburn, put into a way-train and carried to Nettleton. In
the course of that incredible day Charity Royall had, for the
first and only time, experienced railway-travel, looked into
shops with plate-glass fronts, tasted cocoanut pie, sat in a
theatre, and listened to a gentleman saying unintelligible things
before pictures that she would have enjoyed looking at if his
explanations had not prevented her from understanding them.
This initiation had shown her that North Dormer was a small
place, and developed in her a thirst for information that her
position as custodian of the village library had previously failed
to excite. For a month or two she dipped feverishly and discon-
nectedly into the dusty volumes of the Hatchard Memorial

Library; then the impression of Nettleton began to fade, and she found it easier to take North Dormer as the norm of the universe than to go on reading.

The sight of the stranger once more revived memories of Nettleton, and North Dormer shrank to its real size. As she looked up and down it, from lawyer Royall's faded red house at one end to the white church at the other, she pitilessly took its measure. There it lay, a weather-beaten sunburnt village of the hills, abandoned of men, left apart by railway, trolley, telegraph, and all the forces that link life to life in modern communities. It had no shops, no theatres, no lectures, no 'business block'; only a church that was opened every other Sunday if the state of the roads permitted, and a library for which no new books had been bought for twenty years, and where the old ones mouldered undisturbed on the damp shelves. Yet Charity Royall had always been told that she ought to consider it a privilege that her lot had been cast in North Dormer. She knew that, compared to the place she had come from, North Dormer represented all the blessings of the most refined civilization. Everyone in the village had told her so ever since she had been brought there as a child. Even old Miss Hatchard had said to her, on a terrible occasion in her life: 'My child, you must never cease to remember that it was Mr Royall who brought you down from the Mountain.'

She had been 'brought down from the Mountain'; from the scarred cliff that lifted its sullen wall above the lesser slopes of Eagle Range, making a perpetual background of gloom to the lonely valley. The Mountain was a good fifteen miles away, but it rose so abruptly from the lower hills that it seemed almost to cast its shadow over North Dormer. And it was like a great magnet drawing the clouds and scattering them in storm across the valley. If ever, in the purest summer sky, there trailed a thread of vapour over North Dormer, it drifted to the Mountain as a ship drifts to a whirlpool, and was caught among the rocks, torn up and multiplied, to sweep back over the village in rain and darkness.

Charity was not very clear about the Mountain; but she

knew it was a bad place, and a shame to have come from, and that, whatever befell her in North Dormer, she ought, as Miss Hatchard had once reminded her, to remember that she had been brought down from there, and hold her tongue and be thankful. She looked up at the Mountain, thinking of these things, and tried as usual to be thankful. But the sight of the young man turning in at Miss Hatchard's gate had brought back the vision of the glittering streets of Nettleton, and she felt ashamed of her old sun-hat, and sick of North Dormer, and jealously aware of Annabel Balch of Springfield, opening her blue eyes somewhere far off on glories greater than the glories of Nettleton.

'How I hate everything!' she said again.

Half way down the street she stopped at a weak-hinged gate. Passing through it, she walked down a brick path to a queer little brick temple with white wooden columns supporting a pediment on which was inscribed in tarnished gold letters: 'The Honorius Hatchard Memorial Library, 1832'.

Honorius Hatchard had been old Miss Hatchard's great-uncle; though she would undoubtedly have reversed the phrase, and put forward, as her only claim to distinction, the fact that she was his great-niece. For Honorius Hatchard, in the early years of the nineteenth century, had enjoyed a modest celebrity. As the marble tablet in the interior of the library informed its infrequent visitors, he had possessed marked literary gifts, written a series of papers called 'The Recluse of Eagle Range', enjoyed the acquaintance of Washington Irving and Fitz-Greene Halleck, and been cut off in his flower by a fever contracted in Italy. Such had been the sole link between North Dormer and literature, a link piously commemorated by the erection of the monument where Charity Royall, every Tuesday and Thursday afternoon, sat at her desk under a freckled steel engraving of the deceased author, and wondered if he felt any deader in his grave than she did in his library.

Entering her prison-house with a listless step she took off her hat, hung it on a plaster bust of Minerva, opened the shutters, leaned out to see if there were any eggs in the swallow's nest above one of the windows, and finally, seating herself behind the desk, drew out a roll of cotton lace and a steel crochet hook. She was not an expert workwoman, and it had taken her many weeks to make the half-yard of narrow lace which she kept wound about the buckram back of a disintegrated copy of 'The Lamplighter'. But there was no other way of getting any lace to trim her summer blouse, and since Ally Hawes, the poorest girl in the village, had shown herself in church with enviable transparencies about the shoulders, Charity's hook had travelled faster. She unrolled the lace, dug the hook into a loop, and bent to the task with furrowed brows.

Suddenly the door opened, and before she had raised her eyes she knew that the young man she had seen going in at the Hatchard gate had entered the library.

Without taking any notice of her he began to move slowly about the long vault-like room, his hands behind his back, his short-sighted eyes peering up and down the rows of rusty bindings. At length he reached the desk and stood before her.

'Have you a card-catalogue?' he asked in a pleasant abrupt voice; and the oddness of the question caused her to drop her work.

'A *what*?'

'Why, you know —' He broke off, and she became conscious that he was looking at her for the first time, having apparently, on his entrance, included her in his general short-sighted survey as part of the furniture of the library.

The fact that, in discovering her, he lost the thread of his remark, did not escape her attention, and she looked down and smiled. He smiled also.

'No, I don't suppose you *do* know,' he corrected himself. 'In fact, it would be almost a pity —'

She thought she detected a slight condescension in his tone, and asked sharply: 'Why?'

'Because it's so much pleasanter, in a small library like this, to poke about by one's self – with the help of the librarian.'

He added the last phrase so respectfully that she was mollified, and rejoined with a sigh: 'I'm afraid I can't help you much.'

'Why?' he questioned in his turn; and she replied that there weren't many books anyhow, and that she'd hardly read any of them. 'The worms are getting at them,' she added gloomily.

'Are they? That's a pity, for I see there are some good ones.' He seemed to have lost interest in their conversation, and strolled away again, apparently forgetting her. His indifference nettled her, and she picked up her work, resolved not to offer him the least assistance. Apparently he did not need it, for he spent a long time with his back to her, lifting down, one after another, the tall cobwebby volumes from a distant shelf.

'Oh, I say!' he exclaimed; and looking up she saw that he had drawn out his handkerchief and was carefully wiping the edges of the book in his hand. The action struck her as an unwarranted criticism on her care of the books, and she said irritably: 'It's not my fault if they're dirty.'

He turned around and looked at her with reviving interest. 'Ah – then you're not the librarian?'

'Of course I am; but I can't dust all these books. Besides, nobody ever looks at them, now Miss Hatchard's too lame to come round.'

'No, I suppose not.' He laid down the book he had been wiping, and stood considering her in silence. She wondered if Miss Hatchard had sent him round to pry into the way the library was looked after, and the suspicion increased her resentment. 'I saw you going into her house just now, didn't I?' she asked, with the New England avoidance of the proper name. She was determined to find out why he was poking about among her books.

'Miss Hatchard's house? Yes – she's my cousin and I'm staying there,' the young man answered; adding, as if to disarm a visible distrust: 'My name is Harney – Lucius Harney. She may have spoken of me.'

'No, she hasn't,' said Charity, wishing she could have said: 'Yes, she has.'

'Oh, well —' said Miss Hatchard's cousin with a laugh; and after another pause, during which it occurred to Charity that her answer had not been encouraging, he remarked: 'You don't seem strong on architecture.'

Her bewilderment was complete: the more she wished to appear to understand him the more unintelligible his remarks became. He reminded her of the gentleman who had 'explained' the pictures at Nettleton, and the weight of her ignorance settled down on her again like a pall.

'I mean, I can't see that you have any books on the old houses about here. I suppose, for that matter, this part of the country hasn't been much explored. They all go on doing Plymouth and Salem. So stupid. My cousin's house, now, is remarkable. This place must have had a past – it must have been more of a place once.' He stopped short, with the blush of a shy man who overhears himself, and fears he has been voluble. 'I'm an architect, you see, and I'm hunting up old houses in these parts.'

She stared. 'Old houses? Everything's old in North Dormer, isn't it? The folks are, anyhow.'

He laughed, and wandered away again.

'Haven't you any kind of a history of the place? I think there was one written about 1840: a book or pamphlet about its first settlement,' he presently said from the farther end of the room.

She pressed her crochet hook against her lip and pondered. There was such a work, she knew: 'North Dormer and the Early Townships of Eagle County'. She had a special grudge against it because it was a limp weakly book that was always either falling off the shelf or slipping back and disappearing if one squeezed it in between sustaining volumes. She remembered, the last time she had picked it up, wondering how anyone could have taken the trouble to write a book about North Dormer and its neighbours: Dormer, Hamblin, Creston and Creston River. She knew them all, mere lost clusters of houses in the folds of the desolate ridges: Dormer, where North Dormer went for its apples; Creston River, where there used to be a paper-mill, and its grey walls stood decaying by the stream; and Hamblin, where the first snow always fell. Such were their titles to fame.

She got up and began to move about vaguely before the shelves. But she had no idea where she had last put the book, and something told her that it was going to play her its usual trick and remain invisible. It was not one of her lucky days.

'I guess it's somewhere,' she said, to prove her zeal; but she spoke without conviction, and felt that her words conveyed none.

'Oh, well —' he said again. She knew he was going, and wished more than ever to find the book.

'It will be for next time,' he added; and picking up the volume he had laid on the desk he handed it to her. 'By the way, a little air and sun would do this good; it's rather valuable.'

He gave her a nod and smile, and passed out.

II

The hours of the Hatchard Memorial librarian were from three to five; and Charity Royall's sense of duty usually kept her at her desk until nearly half-past four.

But she had never perceived that any practical advantage thereby accrued either to North Dormer or to herself, and she had no scruple in decreeing, when it suited her, that the library should close an hour earlier. A few minutes after Mr Harney's departure she formed this decision, put away her lace, fastened the shutters, and turned the key in the door of the temple of knowledge.

The street upon which she emerged was still empty: and after glancing up and down it she began to walk toward her house. But instead of entering she passed on, turned into a field-path and mounted to a pasture on the hillside. She let down the bars of the gate, followed a trail along the crumbling wall of the pasture, and walked on till she reached a knoll where a clump of larches shook out their fresh tassels to the wind. There she lay down on the slope, tossed off her hat and hid her face in the grass.

She was blind and insensible to many things, and dimly knew it; but to all that was light and air, perfume and colour, every drop of blood in her responded. She loved the roughness of the dry mountain grass under her palms, the smell of the thyme into which she crushed her face, the fingering of the wind in her hair and through her cotton blouse, and the creak of the larches as they swayed to it.

She often climbed up the hill and lay there alone for the mere pleasure of feeling the wind and of rubbing her cheeks in the grass. Generally at such times she did not think of anything, but lay immersed in an inarticulate well-being. Today the sense of well-being was intensified by her joy at escaping from the library. She liked well enough to have a friend drop in and talk to her when she was on duty, but she hated to be bothered about books. How could she remember where they were, when they were so seldom asked for? Orma Fry occasionally took out a novel, and her brother Ben was fond of what he called 'jography', and of books relating to trade and book-keeping; but no one else asked for anything except, at intervals, 'Uncle Tom's Cabin', or 'Opening a Chestnut Burr', or Longfellow. She had these under her hand, and could have found them in the dark; but unexpected demands came so rarely that they exasperated her like an injustice. . . .

She had liked the young man's looks, and his short-sighted eyes, and his odd way of speaking, that was abrupt yet soft, just as his hands were sunburnt and sinewy, yet with smooth nails like a woman's. His hair was sunburnt-looking too, or rather the colour of bracken after frost; his eyes grey, with the appealing look of the shortsighted, his smile shy yet confident, as if he knew lots of things she had never dreamed of, and yet wouldn't for the world have had her feel his superiority. But she did feel it, and liked the feeling; for it was new to her. Poor and ignorant as she was, and knew herself to be – humblest of the humble even in North Dormer, where to come from the Mountain was the worst disgrace – yet in her narrow world she had always ruled. It was partly, of course, owing to the fact that lawyer Royall was 'the biggest man in North Dormer'; so much too big for it, in fact, that outsiders, who didn't know, always wondered how it held him. In spite of everything – and in spite even of Miss Hatchard – lawyer Royall ruled in North Dormer; and Charity ruled in lawyer Royall's house. She had never put it to herself in those terms; but she knew her power, knew what it was made of, and hated it. Confusedly, the young man in the library had made her feel for the first time what might be the sweetness of dependence.

She sat up, brushed the bits of grass from her hair, and

looked down on the house where she held sway. It stood just below her, cheerless and untended, its faded red front divided from the road by a 'yard' with a path bordered by gooseberry bushes, a stone well overgrown with traveller's joy, and a sickly Crimson Rambler tied to a fan-shaped support, which Mr Royall had once brought up from Hepburn to please her. Behind the house a bit of uneven ground with clothes-lines strung across it stretched up to a dry wall, and beyond the wall a patch of corn and a few rows of potatoes strayed vaguely into the adjoining wilderness of rock and fern.

Charity could not recall her first sight of the house. She had been told that she was ill of a fever when she was brought down from the Mountain; and she could only remember waking one day in a cot at the foot of Mrs Royall's bed, and opening her eyes on the cold neatness of the room that was afterward to be hers.

Mrs Royall died seven or eight years later; and by that time Charity had taken the measure of most things about her. She knew that Mrs Royall was sad and timid and weak; she knew that lawyer Royall was harsh and violent, and still weaker. She knew that she had been christened Charity (in the white church at the other end of the village) to commemorate Mr Royall's disinterestedness in 'bringing her down', and to keep alive in her a becoming sense of her dependence; she knew that Mr Royall was her guardian, but that he had not legally adopted her, though everybody spoke of her as Charity Royall; and she knew why he had come back to live at North Dormer, instead of practising at Nettleton, where he had begun his legal career.

After Mrs Royall's death there was some talk of sending her to a boarding-school. Miss Hatchard suggested it, and had a long conference with Mr Royall, who, in pursuance of her plan, departed one day for Starkfield to visit the institution she recommended. He came back the next night with a black face; worse, Charity observed, than she had ever seen him; and by that time she had had some experience.

When she asked him how soon she was to start he answered shortly, 'You ain't going,' and shut himself up in the room he called his office; and the next day the lady who kept the school at Starkfield wrote that 'under the circumstances' she was afraid she could not make room just then for another pupil.

Charity was disappointed; but she understood. It wasn't the temptations of Starkfield that had been Mr Royall's undoing; it was the thought of losing her. He was a dreadfully 'lonesome' man; she had made that out because she was so 'lonesome' herself. He and she, face to face in that sad house, had sounded the depths of isolation; and though she felt no particular affection for him, and not the slightest gratitude, she pitied him because she was conscious that he was superior to the people about him, and that she was the only being between him and solitude. Therefore, when Miss Hatchard sent for her a day or two later, to talk of a school at Nettleton, and to say that this time a friend of hers would 'make the necessary arrangements', Charity cut her short with the announcement that she had decided not to leave North Dormer.

Miss Hatchard reasoned with her kindly, but to no purpose; she simply repeated: 'I guess Mr Royall's too lonesome.'

Miss Hatchard blinked perplexedly behind her eye-glasses. Her long frail face was full of puzzled wrinkles, and she leant forward, resting her hands on the arms of her mahogany arm-chair, with the evident desire to say something that ought to be said.

'The feeling does you credit, my dear.'

She looked about the pale walls of her sitting-room, seeking counsel of ancestral daguerreotypes and didactic samplers; but they seemed to make utterance more difficult.

'The fact is, it's not only – not only because of the advantages. There are other reasons. You're too young to understand—'

'Oh, no, I ain't,' said Charity harshly; and Miss Hatchard blushed to the roots of her blonde cap. But she must have felt a vague relief at having her explanation cut short, for she concluded, again invoking the daguerreotypes: 'Of course I shall always do what I can for you; and in case . . . in case . . . you know you can always come to me. . . .'

Lawyer Royall was waiting for Charity in the porch when she returned from this visit. He had shaved, and brushed his black coat, and looked a magnificent monument of a man; at such moments she really admired him.

'Well,' he said, 'is it settled?'

'Yes, it's settled. I ain't going.'

'Not to the Nettleton school?'

'Not anywhere.'

He cleared his throat and asked sternly: 'Why?'

'I'd rather not,' she said, swinging past him on her way to her room. It was the following week that he brought her up the Crimson Rambler and its fan from Hepburn. He had never given her anything before.

The next outstanding incident of her life had happened two years later, when she was seventeen. Lawyer Royall, who hated to go to Nettleton, had been called there in connection with a case. He still exercised his profession, though litigation languished in North Dormer and its outlying hamlets; and for once he had had an opportunity that he could not afford to refuse. He spent three days in Nettleton, won his case, and came back in high good-humour. It was a rare mood with him, and manifested itself on this occasion by his talking impressively at the supper-table of the 'rousing welcome' his old friends had given him. He wound up confidentially: 'I was a damn fool ever to leave Nettleton. It was Mrs Royall that made me do it.'

Charity immediately perceived that something bitter had happened to him, and that he was trying to talk down the recollection. She went up to bed early, leaving him seated in moody thought, his elbows propped on the worn oilcloth of the supper table. On the way up she had extracted from his overcoat pocket the key of the cupboard where the bottle of whiskey was kept.

She was awakened by a rattling at her door and jumped out of bed. She heard Mr Royall's voice, low and peremptory, and opened the door, fearing an accident. No other thought had occurred to her; but when she saw him in the doorway, a ray from the autumn moon falling on his discomposed face, she understood.

For a moment they looked at each other in silence; then, as he put his foot across the threshold, she stretched out her arm and stopped him.

'You go right back from here,' she said, in a shrill voice that startled her; 'you ain't going to have that key tonight.'

'Charity, let me in. I don't want the key. I'm a lonesome man,' he began, in the deep voice that sometimes moved her.

Her heart gave a startled plunge, but she continued to hold him back contemptuously. 'Well, I guess you made a mistake, then. This ain't your wife's room any longer.'

She was not frightened, she simply felt a deep disgust; and perhaps he divined it or read it in her face, for after staring at her a moment he drew back and turned slowly away from the door. With her ear to her keyhole she heard him feel his way down the dark stairs, and toward the kitchen; and she listened for the crash of the cupboard panel. But instead she heard him, after an interval, unlock the door of the house, and his heavy steps came to her through the silence as he walked down the path. She crept to the window and saw his bent figure striding up the road in the moonlight. Then a belated sense of fear came to her with the consciousness of victory, and she slipped into bed, cold to the bone.

A day or two later poor Eudora Skeff, who for twenty years had been the custodian of the Hatchard library, died suddenly of pneumonia; and the day after the funeral Charity went to see Miss Hatchard, and asked to be appointed librarian. The request seemed to surprise Miss Hatchard: she evidently questioned the new candidate's qualifications.

'Why, I don't know, my dear. Aren't you rather too young?' she hesitated.

'I want to earn some money,' Charity merely answered.

'Doesn't Mr Royall give you all you require? No one is rich in North Dormer.'

'I want to earn money enough to get away.'

'To get away?' Miss Hatchard's puzzled wrinkles deepened, and there was a distressful pause. 'You want to leave Mr Royall?'

'Yes: or I want another woman in the house with me,' said Charity resolutely.

Miss Hatchard clasped her nervous hands about the arms of her chair. Her eyes invoked the faded countenances on the wall, and after a faint cough of indecision she brought out: 'The . . . the housework's too hard for you, I suppose?'

Charity's heart grew cold. She understood that Miss Hatchard had no help to give her and that she would have to fight her way out of her difficulty alone. A deeper sense of isolation overcame her; she felt incalculably old. 'She's got to be talked to like a baby,' she thought, with a feeling of compassion for Miss Hatchard's long immaturity. 'Yes, that's it,' she said aloud. 'The housework's too hard for me: I've been coughing a good deal this fall.'

She noted the immediate effect of this suggestion. Miss Hatchard paled at the memory of poor Eudora's taking-off, and promised to do what she could. But of course there were people she must consult: the clergyman, the selectmen of North Dormer, and a distant Hatchard relative at Springfield. 'If you'd only gone to school!' she sighed. She followed Charity to the door, and there, in the security of the threshold, said with a glance of evasive appeal: 'I know Mr Royall is . . . trying at times; but his wife bore with him; and you must always remember, Charity, that it was Mr Royall who brought you down from the Mountain.'

Charity went home and opened the door of Mr Royall's 'office'. He was sitting there by the stove reading Daniel Webster's speeches. They had met at meals during the five days that had elapsed since he had come to her door, and she had walked at his side at Eudora's funeral; but they had not spoken a word to each other.

He glanced up in surprise as she entered, and she noticed that he was unshaved, and that he looked unusually old; but as she had always thought of him as an old man the change in his appearance did not move her. She told him she had been to see Miss Hatchard, and with what object. She saw that he was astonished; but he made no comment.

'I told her the housework was too hard for me, and I wanted to earn the money to pay for a hired girl. But I ain't going to pay for her: you've got to. I want to have some money of my own.'

Mr Royall's bushy black eyebrows were drawn together in a frown, and he sat drumming with ink-stained nails on the edge of his desk.

'What do you want to earn money for?' he asked.

'So's to get away when I want to.'

'Why do you want to get away?'

Her contempt flashed out. 'Do you suppose anybody'd stay at North Dormer if they could help it? You wouldn't, folks say!'

With lowered head he asked: 'Where'd you go to?'

'Anywhere where I can earn my living. I'll try here first, and if I can't do it here I'll go somewhere else. I'll go up the Mountain if I have to.' She paused on this threat, and saw that it had taken effect. 'I want you should get Miss Hatchard and the selectmen to take me at the library: and I want a woman here in the house with me,' she repeated.

Mr Royall had grown exceedingly pale. When she ended he stood up ponderously, leaning against the desk; and for a second or two they looked at each other.

'See here,' he said at length, as though utterance were difficult, 'there's something I've been wanting to say to you; I'd ought to have said it before. I want you to marry me.'

The girl still stared at him without moving. 'I want you to marry me,' he repeated, clearing his throat. 'The minister'll be up here next Sunday and we can fix it up then. Or I'll drive you down to Hepburn to the Justice, and get it done there. I'll do whatever you say.' His eyes fell under the merciless stare she continued to fix on him, and he shifted his weight uneasily from one foot to the other. As he stood there before her, unwieldy, shabby, disordered, the purple veins distorting the hands he pressed against the desk, and his long orator's jaw trembling with the effort of his avowal, he seemed like a hideous parody of the fatherly old man she had always known.

'Marry you? Me?' she burst out with a scornful laugh. 'Was that what you came to ask me the other night? What's come over you, I wonder? How long is it since you've looked at yourself in the glass?' She straightened herself, insolently conscious of her youth and strength. 'I suppose you think it would be cheaper to marry me than to keep a hired girl. Everybody knows you're the closest man in Eagle County; but I guess you're not going to get your mending done for you that way twice.'

Mr Royall did not move while she spoke. His face was ash-coloured and his black eyebrows quivered as though the blaze of her scorn had blinded him. When she ceased he held up his hand.

'That'll do – that'll about do,' he said. He turned to the door and took his hat from the hat-peg. On the threshold he paused. 'People ain't been fair to me – from the first they ain't been fair to me,' he said. Then he went out.

A few days later North Dormer learned with surprise that Charity had been appointed librarian of the Hatchard Memorial at a salary of eight dollars a month, and that old Verena Marsh, from the Creston Almshouse, was coming to live at lawyer Royall's and do the cooking.

III

It was not in the room known at the red house as Mr Royall's 'office' that he received his infrequent clients. Professional dignity and masculine independence made it necessary that he should have a real office, under a different roof, and his standing as the only lawyer of North Dormer required that the roof should be the same as that which sheltered the Town Hall and the post-office.

It was his habit to walk to this office twice a day, morning and afternoon. It was on the ground floor of the building, with a separate entrance, and a weathered name-plate on the door. Before going in he stepped in to the post-office for his mail – usually an empty ceremony – said a word or two to the town-clerk, who sat across the passage in idle state, and then went over to the store on the opposite corner, where Carrick Fry, the storekeeper, always kept a chair for him, and where he was sure to find one or two selectmen leaning on the long counter, in an atmosphere of rope, leather, tar and coffee-beans. Mr Royall, though monosyllabic at home, was not averse, in certain moods, to imparting his views to his fellow-townsmen; perhaps, also, he was unwilling that his rare clients should surprise him sitting, clerkless and unoccupied, in his dusty office. At any rate, his hours there were not much longer or more regular than Charity's at the library; the rest of the time he spent either at the store or in driving about the country on business connected with the insurance companies that he represented, or in sitting at home reading Bancroft's History of the United States and the speeches of Daniel Webster.

Since the day when Charity had told him that she wished to succeed to Eudora Skeff's post their relations had undefinably but definitely changed. Lawyer Royall had kept his word.

He had obtained the place for her at the cost of considerable manœuvering, as she guessed from the number of rival candidates, and from the acerbity with which two of them, Orma Fry and the eldest Targatt girl, treated her for nearly a year afterward. And he had engaged Verena Marsh to come up from Creston and do the cooking. Verena was a poor old widow, doddering and shiftless: Charity suspected that she came for her keep. Mr Royall was too close a man to give a dollar a day to a smart girl when he could get a deaf pauper for nothing. But at any rate, Verena was there, in the attic just over Charity, and the fact that she was deaf did not greatly trouble the young girl.

Charity knew that what had happened on that hateful night would not happen again. She understood that, profoundly as she had despised Mr Royall ever since, he despised himself still more profoundly. If she had asked for a woman in the house it was far less for her own defense than for his humiliation. She needed no one to defend her: his humbled pride was her surest protection. He had never spoken a word of excuse or extenuation; the incident was as if it had never been. Yet its consequences were latent in every word that he and she exchanged, in every glance they instinctively turned from each other. Nothing now would ever shake her rule in the red house.

On the night of her meeting with Miss Hatchard's cousin Charity lay in bed, her bare arms clasped under her rough head, and continued to think of him. She supposed that he meant to spend some time in North Dormer. He had said he was looking up the old houses in the neighbourhood; and though she was not very clear as to his purpose, or as to why anyone should look for old houses, when they lay in wait for one on every roadside, she understood that he needed the help of books, and resolved to hunt up the next day the volume she had failed to find, and any others that seemed related to the subject.

Never had her ignorance of life and literature so weighed on her as in reliving the short scene of her discomfiture. 'It's no use trying to be anything in this place,' she muttered to her pillow; and she shrivelled at the vision of vague metropolises,

shining super-Nettletons, where girls in better clothes than
Belle Balch's talked fluently of architecture to young men with
hands like Lucius Harney's. Then she remembered his sudden
pause when he had come close to the desk and had his first
look at her. The sight had made him forget what he was going
to say; she recalled the change in his face, and jumping up she
ran over the bare boards to her washstand, found the matches,
lit a candle, and lifted it to the square of looking-glass on
the white-washed wall. Her small face, usually so darkly pale,
glowed like a rose in the faint orb of light, and under her
rumpled hair her eyes seemed deeper and larger than by day.
Perhaps after all it was a mistake to wish they were blue. A
clumsy band and button fastened her unbleached night-gown
about the throat. She undid it, freed her thin shoulders, and
saw herself a bride in low-necked satin, walking down an aisle
with Lucius Harney. He would kiss her as they left the
church. . . . She put down the candle and covered her face with
her hands as if to imprison the kiss. At that moment she heard
Mr Royall's step as he came up the stairs to bed, and a fierce
revulsion of feeling swept over her. Until then she had merely
despised him; now deep hatred of him filled her heart. He
became to her a horrible old man. . . .

The next day, when Mr Royall came back to dinner, they
faced each other in silence as usual. Verena's presence at the
table was an excuse for their not talking, though her deafness
would have permitted the freest interchange of confidences.
But when the meal was over, and Mr Royall rose from the
table, he looked back at Charity, who had stayed to help the
old woman clear away the dishes.

'I want to speak to you a minute,' he said; and she followed
him across the passage, wondering.

He seated himself in his black horse-hair armchair, and she
leaned against the window, indifferently. She was impatient to
be gone to the library, to hunt for the book on North Dormer.

'See here,' he said, 'why ain't you at the library the days
you're supposed to be there?'

The question, breaking in on her mood of blissful abstraction, deprived her of speech, and she stared at him for a moment without answering.

'Who says I ain't?'

'There's been some complaints made, it appears. Miss Hatchard sent for me this morning —'

Charity's smouldering resentment broke into a blaze. 'I know! Orma Fry, and that toad of a Targatt girl – and Ben Fry, like as not. He's going round with her. The low-down sneaks – I always knew they'd try to have me out! As if anybody ever came to the library, anyhow!'

'Somebody did yesterday, and you weren't there.'

'Yesterday?' she laughed at her happy recollection. 'At what time wasn't I there yesterday, I'd like to know?'

'Round about four o'clock.'

Charity was silent. She had been so steeped in the dreamy remembrance of young Harney's visit that she had forgotten having deserted her post as soon as he had left the library.

'Who came at four o'clock?'

'Miss Hatchard did.'

'Miss Hatchard? Why, she ain't ever been near the place since she's been lame. She couldn't get up the steps if she tried.'

'She can be helped up, I guess. She was yesterday, anyhow, by the young fellow that's staying with her. He found you there, I understand, earlier in the afternoon; and he went back and told Miss Hatchard the books were in bad shape and needed attending to. She got excited, and had herself wheeled straight round; and when she got there the place was locked. So she sent for me, and told me about that, and about the other complaints. She claims you've neglected things, and that she's going to get a trained librarian.'

Charity had not moved while he spoke. She stood with her head thrown back against the window-frame, her arms hanging against her sides, and her hands so tightly clenched that she felt, without knowing what hurt her, the sharp edge of her nails against her palms.

Of all Mr Royall had said she had retained only the phrase:

'He told Miss Hatchard the books were in bad shape.' What did she care for the other charges against her? Malice or truth, she despised them as she despised her detractors. But that the stranger to whom she had felt herself so mysteriously drawn should have betrayed her! That at the very moment when she had fled up the hillside to think of him more deliciously he should have been hastening home to denounce her short-comings! She remembered how, in the darkness of her room, she had covered her face to press his imagined kiss closer; and her heart raged against him for the liberty he had not taken.

'Well, I'll go,' she said suddenly. 'I'll go right off.'

'Go where?' She heard the startled note in Mr Royall's voice.

'Why, out of their old library: straight out, and never set foot in it again. They needn't think I'm going to wait round and let them say they've discharged me!'

'Charity – Charity Royall, you listen —' he began, getting heavily out of his chair; but she waved him aside, and walked out of the room.

Upstairs she took the library key from the place where she always hid it under her pincushion – who said she wasn't care-ful? – put on her hat, and swept down again and out into the street. If Mr Royall heard her go he made no motion to detain her: his sudden rages probably made him understand the use-lessness of reasoning with hers.

She reached the brick temple, unlocked the door and entered into the glacial twilight. 'I'm glad I'll never have to sit in this old vault again when other folks are out in the sun!' she said aloud as the familiar chill took her. She looked with abhorrence at the long dingy rows of books, the sheep-nosed Minerva on her black pedestal, and the mild-faced young man in a high stock whose effigy pined above her desk. She meant to take out of the drawer her roll of lace and the library register, and go straight to Miss Hatchard to announce her resignation. But suddenly a great desolation overcame her, and she sat down and laid her face against the desk. Her heart was ravaged by life's cruellest discovery: the first creature who had come toward her out of the wilderness had brought her anguish instead of joy. She did not cry; tears came hard to her, and the storms of her heart spent themselves inwardly. But as she sat there in her dumb woe she felt her life to be too desolate, too ugly and intolerable.

'What have I ever done to it, that it should hurt me so?' she groaned, and pressed her fists against her lids, which were beginning to swell with weeping.

'I won't – I won't go there looking like a horror!' she muttered, springing up and pushing back her hair as if it stifled her. She opened the drawer, dragged out the register, and turned toward the door. As she did so it opened, and the young man from Miss Hatchard's came in whistling.

IV

He stopped and lifted his hat with a shy smile. 'I beg your pardon,' he said. 'I thought there was no one here.'

Charity stood before him, barring his way. 'You can't come in. The library ain't open to the public Wednesdays.'

'I know it's not; but my cousin gave me her key.'

'Miss Hatchard's got no right to give her key to other folks, any more'n I have. I'm the librarian and I know the by-laws. This is my library.'

The young man looked profoundly surprised.

'Why, I know it is; I'm so sorry if you mind my coming.'

'I suppose you came to see what more you could say to set her against me? But you needn't trouble: it's my library today, but it won't be this time tomorrow. I'm on the way now to take her back the key and the register.'

Young Harney's face grew grave, but without betraying the consciousness of guilt she had looked for.

'I don't understand,' he said. 'There must be some mistake. Why should I say things against you to Miss Hatchard – or to anyone?'

The apparent evasiveness of the reply caused Charity's indignation to overflow. 'I don't know why you should. I could understand Orma Fry's doing it, because she's always wanted to get me out of here ever since the first day. I can't see why, when she's got her own home, and her father to work for her; nor Ida Targatt, neither, when she got a legacy from her step-brother on'y last year. But anyway we all live in the same place, and when it's a place like North Dormer it's enough to make people hate each other just to have to walk down the same street every day. But you don't live here, and you don't know

130

anything about any of us, so what did you have to meddle
for? Do you suppose the other girls'd have kept the books any
better'n I did? Why, Orma Fry don't hardly know a book from
a flat-iron! And what if I don't always sit round here doing
nothing till it strikes five up at the church? Who cares if the
library's open or shut? Do you suppose anybody ever comes
here for books? What they'd like to come for is to meet the
fellows they're going with – if I'd let 'em. But I wouldn't let
Bill Sollas from over the hill hang round here waiting for the
youngest Targatt girl, because I know him . . . that's all . . . even
if I don't know about books all I ought to. . . .'

She stopped with a choking in her throat. Tremors of rage
were running through her, and she steadied herself against the
edge of the desk lest he should see her weakness.

What he saw seemed to affect him deeply, for he grew red
under his sunburn, and stammered out: 'But, Miss Royall,
I assure you . . . I assure you . . .'

His distress inflamed her anger, and she regained her voice
to fling back: 'If I was you I'd have the nerve to stick to what
I said!'

The taunt seemed to restore his presence of mind. 'I hope
I should if I knew; but I don't. Apparently something dis-
agreeable has happened, for which you think I'm to blame.
But I don't know what it is, because I've been up on Eagle
Ridge ever since the early morning.'

'I don't know where you've been this morning, but I know
you were here in this library yesterday; and it was you that
went home and told your cousin the books were in bad shape,
and brought her round to see how I'd neglected them.'

Young Harney looked sincerely concerned. 'Was that what
you were told? I don't wonder you're angry. The books *are* in
bad shape, and as some are interesting it's a pity. I told Miss
Hatchard they were suffering from dampness and lack of air;
and I brought her here to show her how easily the place could
be ventilated. I also told her you ought to have some one to
help you do the dusting and airing. If you were given a wrong
version of what I said I'm sorry; but I'm so fond of old books

that I'd rather see them made into a bonfire than left to moulder away like these.'

Charity felt her sobs rising and tried to stifle them in words. 'I don't care what you say you told her. All I know is she thinks it's all my fault, and I'm going to lose my job, and I wanted it more'n anyone in the village, because I haven't got anybody belonging to me, the way other folks have. All I wanted was to put aside money enough to get away from here sometime. D'you suppose if it hadn't been for that I'd have kept on sitting day after day in this old vault?'

Of this appeal her hearer took up only the last question. 'It *is* an old vault; but need it be? That's the point. And it's my putting the question to my cousin that seems to have been the cause of the trouble.' His glance explored the melancholy penumbra of the long narrow room, resting on the blotched walls, the discoloured rows of books, and the stern rosewood desk surmounted by the portrait of the young Honorius. 'Of course it's a bad job to do anything with a building jammed against a hill like this ridiculous mausoleum: you couldn't get a good draught through it without blowing a hole in the mountain. But it can be ventilated after a fashion, and the sun can be let in: I'll show you how if you like.' The architect's passion for improvement had already made him lose sight of her grievance, and he lifted his stick instructively toward the cornice. But her silence seemed to tell him that she took no interest in the ventilation of the library, and turning back to her abruptly he held out both hands. 'Look here – you don't mean what you said? You don't really think I'd do anything to hurt you?'

A new note in his voice disarmed her: no one had ever spoken to her in that tone.

'Oh, what *did* you do it for then?' she wailed. He had her hands in his, and she was feeling the smooth touch that she had imagined the day before on the hillside.

He pressed her hands lightly and let them go. 'Why, to make things pleasanter for you here; and better for the books. I'm sorry if my cousin twisted around what I said. She's excitable, and she lives on trifles: I ought to have remembered that. Don't punish me by letting her think you take her seriously.'

It was wonderful to hear him speak of Miss Hatchard as if she were a querulous baby: in spite of his shyness he had the air of power that the experience of cities probably gave. It was the fact of having lived in Nettleton that made lawyer Royall, in spite of his infirmities, the strongest man in North Dormer; and Charity was sure that this young man had lived in bigger places than Nettleton.

She felt that if she kept up her denunciatory tone he would secretly class her with Miss Hatchard; and the thought made her suddenly simple.

'It don't matter to Miss Hatchard how I take her. Mr Royall says she's going to get a trained librarian; and I'd sooner resign than have the village say she sent me away.'

'Naturally you would. But I'm sure she doesn't mean to send you away. At any rate, won't you give me the chance to find out first and let you know? It will be time enough to resign if I'm mistaken.'

Her pride flamed into her cheeks at the suggestion of his intervening. 'I don't want anybody should coax her to keep me if I don't suit.'

He coloured too. 'I give you my word I won't do that. Only wait till tomorrow, will you?' He looked straight into her eyes with his shy grey glance. 'You can trust me, you know – you really can.'

All the old frozen woes seemed to melt in her, and she murmured awkwardly, looking away from him: 'Oh, I'll wait.'

V

There had never been such a June in Eagle County. Usually it was a month of moods, with abrupt alternations of belated frost and midsummer heat; this year, day followed day in a sequence of temperate beauty. Every morning a breeze blew steadily from the hills. Toward noon it built up great canopies of white cloud that threw a cool shadow over fields and woods; then before sunset the clouds dissolved again, and the western light rained its unobstructed brightness on the valley.

On such an afternoon Charity Royall lay on a ridge above a sunlit hollow, her face pressed to the earth and the warm currents of the grass running through her. Directly in her line of vision a blackberry branch laid its frail white flowers and blue-green leaves against the sky. Just beyond, a tuft of sweet-fern uncurled between the beaded shoots of the grass, and a small yellow butterfly vibrated over them like a fleck of sunshine. This was all she saw; but she felt, above her and about her, the strong growth of the beeches clothing the ridge, the rounding of pale green cones on countless spruce-branches, the push of myriads of sweet-fern fronds in the cracks of the stony slope below the wood, and the crowding shoots of meadowsweet and yellow flags in the pasture beyond. All this bubbling of sap and slipping of sheaths and bursting of calyxes was carried to her on mingled currents of fragrance. Every leaf and bud and blade seemed to contribute its exhalation to the pervading sweetness in which the pungency of pine-sap prevailed over the spice of thyme and the subtle perfume of fern, and all were merged in a moist earth-smell that was like the breath of some huge sun-warmed animal.

Charity had lain there a long time, passive and sun-warmed

as the slope on which she lay, when there came between her
eyes and the dancing butterfly the sight of a man's foot in a
large worn boot covered with red mud.

'Oh, don't!' she exclaimed, raising herself on her elbow and
stretching out a warning hand.

'Don't what?' a hoarse voice asked above her head.

'Don't stamp on those bramble flowers, you dolt!' she
retorted, springing to her knees. The foot paused and then
descended clumsily on the frail branch, and raising her eyes
she saw above her the bewildered face of a slouching man with
a thin sunburnt beard, and white arms showing through his
ragged shirt.

'Don't you ever *see* anything, Liff Hyatt?' she assailed him,
as he stood before her with the look of a man who has stirred
up a wasp's nest.

He grinned. 'I seen you! That's what I come down for.'

'Down from where?' she questioned, stooping to gather up
the petals his foot had scattered.

He jerked his thumb toward the heights. 'Been cutting
down trees for Dan Targatt.'

Charity sank back on her heels and looked at him musingly.
She was not in the least afraid of poor Liff Hyatt, though he
'came from the Mountain', and some of the girls ran when
they saw him. Among the more reasonable he passed for a
harmless creature, a sort of link between the mountain and
civilized folk, who occasionally came down and did a little
wood-cutting for a farmer when hands were short. Besides,
she knew the Mountain people would never hurt her: Liff
himself had told her so once when she was a little girl, and had
met him one day at the edge of lawyer Royall's pasture. 'They
won't any of 'em touch you up there, f'ever you was to come
up. . . . But I don't s'pose you will,' he had added philosophi-
cally, looking at her new shoes, and at the red ribbon that Mrs
Royall had tied in her hair.

Charity had, in truth, never felt any desire to visit her birth-
place. She did not care to have it known that she was of the
Mountain, and was shy of being seen in talk with Liff Hyatt.

But today she was not sorry to have him appear. A great many things had happened to her since the day when young Lucius Harney had entered the doors of the Hatchard Memorial, but none, perhaps, so unforeseen as the fact of her suddenly finding it a convenience to be on good terms with Liff Hyatt. She continued to look up curiously at his freckled weather-beaten face, with feverish hollows below the cheekbones and the pale yellow eyes of a harmless animal. 'I wonder if he's related to me?' she thought, with a shiver of disdain.

'Is there any folks living in the brown house by the swamp, up under Porcupine?' she presently asked in an indifferent tone.

Liff Hyatt, for a while, considered her with surprise; then he scratched his head and shifted his weight from one tattered sole to the other.

'There's always the same folks in the brown house,' he said with his vague grin.

'They're from up your way, ain't they?'

'Their name's the same as mine,' he rejoined uncertainly.

Charity still held him with resolute eyes. 'See here, I want to go there some day and take a gentleman with me that's boarding with us. He's up in these parts drawing pictures.'

She did not offer to explain this statement. It was too far beyond Liff Hyatt's limitations for the attempt to be worth making. 'He wants to see the brown house, and go all over it,' she pursued.

Liff was still running his fingers perplexedly through his shock of straw-coloured hair. 'Is it a fellow from the city?' he asked.

'Yes. He draws pictures of things. He's down there now drawing the Bonner house.' She pointed to a chimney just visible over the dip of the pasture below the wood.

'The Bonner house?' Liff echoed incredulously.

'Yes. You won't understand – and it don't matter. All I say is: he's going to the Hyatts' in a day or two.'

Liff looked more and more perplexed. 'Bash is ugly sometimes in the afternoons.'

'I know. But I guess he won't trouble me.' She threw her

head back, her eyes full on Hyatt's. 'I'm coming too: you tell him.'

'They won't none of them trouble you, the Hyatts won't. What d'you want a take a stranger with you, though?'

'I've told you, haven't I? You've got to tell Bash Hyatt.'

He looked away at the blue mountains on the horizon; then his gaze dropped to the chimney-top below the pasture.

'He's down there now?'

'Yes.'

He shifted his weight again, crossed his arms, and continued to survey the distant landscape. 'Well, so long,' he said at last, inconclusively; and turning away he shambled up the hillside. From the ledge above her, he paused to call down: 'I wouldn't go there a Sunday'; then he clambered on till the trees closed in on him. Presently, from high overhead, Charity heard the ring of his axe.

She lay on the warm ridge, thinking of many things that the woodsman's appearance had stirred up in her. She knew nothing of her early life, and had never felt any curiosity about it: only a sullen reluctance to explore the corner of her memory where certain blurred images lingered. But all that had happened to her within the last few weeks had stirred her to the sleeping depths. She had become absorbingly interesting to herself, and everything that had to do with her past was illuminated by this sudden curiosity.

She hated more than ever the fact of coming from the Mountain; but it was no longer indifferent to her. Everything that in any way affected her was alive and vivid: even the hateful things had grown interesting because they were a part of herself.

'I wonder if Liff Hyatt knows who my mother was?' she mused; and it filled her with a tremor of surprise to think that some woman who was once young and slight, with quick motions of the blood like hers, had carried her in her breast, and watched her sleeping. She had always thought of her mother as so long dead as to be no more than a nameless pinch of earth; but now it occurred to her that the once-young woman might be alive, and wrinkled and elf-locked like the woman she had sometimes seen in the door of the brown house that Lucius Harney wanted to draw.

The thought brought her back to the central point in her mind, and she strayed away from the conjectures roused by Liff Hyatt's presence. Speculations concerning the past could not hold her long when the present was so rich, the future so rosy, and when Lucius Harney, a stone's throw away, was bending over his sketch-book, frowning, calculating, measuring, and then throwing his head back with the sudden smile that had shed its brightness over everything.

She scrambled to her feet, but as she did so she saw him coming up the pasture and dropped down on the grass to wait. When he was drawing and measuring one of 'his houses', as she called them, she often strayed away by herself into the woods or up the hillside. It was partly from shyness that she did so: from a sense of inadequacy that came to her most painfully when her companion, absorbed in his job, forgot her ignorance and her inability to follow his least allusion, and plunged into a monologue on art and life. To avoid the awkwardness of listening with a blank face, and also to escape the surprised stare of the inhabitants of the houses before which he would abruptly pull up their horse and open his sketch-book, she slipped away to some spot from which, without being seen, she could watch him at work, or at least look down on the house he was drawing. She had not been displeased, at first, to have it known to North Dormer and the neighbourhood that she was driving Miss Hatchard's cousin about the country in the buggy he had hired of lawyer Royall. She had always kept to herself, contemptuously aloof from village love-making, without exactly knowing whether her fierce pride was due to the sense of her tainted origin, or whether she was reserving herself for a more brilliant fate. Sometimes she envied the other girls their sentimental preoccupations, their long hours of inarticulate philandering with one of the few youths who still lingered in the village; but when she

pictured herself curling her hair or puffing a new ribbon on
her hat for Ben Fry or one of the Sollas boys the fever dropped
and she relapsed into indifference.

Now she knew the meaning of her disdains and reluctances.
She had learned what she was worth when Lucius Harney,
looking at her for the first time, had lost the thread of his
speech, and leaned reddening on the edge of her desk. But
another kind of shyness had been born in her: a terror of
exposing to vulgar perils the sacred treasure of her happiness. She was not sorry to have the neighbours suspect her of
'going with' a young man from the city; but she did not want
it known to all the countryside how many hours of the long
June days she spent with him. What she most feared was that
the inevitable comments should reach Mr Royall. Charity was
instinctively aware that few things concerning her escaped the
eyes of the silent man under whose roof she lived; and in spite
of the latitude which North Dormer accorded to courting
couples she had always felt that, on the day when she showed
too open a preference, Mr Royall might, as she phrased it,
make her 'pay for it'. How, she did not know; and her fear
was the greater because it was undefinable. If she had been
accepting the attentions of one of the village youths she would
have been less apprehensive: Mr Royall could not prevent her
marrying when she chose to. But everybody knew that 'going
with a city fellow' was a different and less straightforward
affair: almost every village could show a victim of the perilous
venture. And her dread of Mr Royall's intervention gave a
sharpened joy to the hours she spent with young Harney, and
made her, at the same time, shy of being too generally seen
with him.

As he approached she rose to her knees, stretching her arms
above her head with the indolent gesture that was her way of
expressing a profound well-being.

'I'm going to take you to that house up under Porcupine,'
she announced.

'What house? Oh, yes; that ramshackle place near the
swamp, with the gipsy-looking people hanging about. It's

curious that a house with traces of real architecture should have
been built in such a place. But the people were a sulky-looking
lot – do you suppose they'll let us in?'

'They'll do whatever I tell them,' she said with assurance.

He threw himself down beside her. 'Will they?' he rejoined
with a smile. 'Well, I should like to see what's left inside the
house. And I should like to have a talk with the people. Who
was it who was telling me the other day that they had come
down from the Mountain?'

Charity shot a sideward look at him. It was the first time he
had spoken of the Mountain except as a feature of the landscape. What else did he know about it, and about her relation
to it? Her heart began to beat with the fierce impulse of resistance which she instinctively opposed to every imagined slight.

'The Mountain? I ain't afraid of the Mountain!'

Her tone of defiance seemed to escape him. He lay breast-
down on the grass, breaking off sprigs of thyme and pressing
them against his lips. Far off, above the folds of the nearer
hills, the Mountain thrust itself up menacingly against a yellow
sunset.

'I must go up there some day: I want to see it,' he continued.

Her heart-beats slackened and she turned again to examine
his profile. It was innocent of all unfriendly intention.

'What'd you want to go up the Mountain for?'

'Why, it must be rather a curious place. There's a queer
colony up there, you know: sort of outlaws, a little independ-
ent kingdom. Of course you've heard them spoken of, but I'm
told they have nothing to do with the people in the valleys –
rather look down on them, in fact. I suppose they're rough
customers; but they must have a good deal of character.'

She did not quite know what he meant by having a good deal
of character; but his tone was expressive of admiration, and
deepened her dawning curiosity. It struck her now as strange
that she knew so little about the Mountain. She had never
asked, and no one had ever offered to enlighten her. North
Dormer took the Mountain for granted, and implied its dispar-
agement by an intonation rather than by explicit criticism.

'It's queer, you know,' he continued, 'that, just over there, on top of that hill, there should be a handful of people who don't give a damn for anybody.'

The words thrilled her. They seemed the clue to her own revolts and defiances, and she longed to have him tell her more.

'I don't know much about them. Have they always been there?'

'Nobody seems to know exactly how long. Down at Creston they told me that the first colonists are supposed to have been men who worked on the railway that was built forty or fifty years ago between Springfield and Nettleton. Some of them took to drink, or got into trouble with the police, and went off – disappeared into the woods. A year or two later there was a report that they were living up on the Mountain. Then I suppose others joined them – and children were born. Now they say there are over a hundred people up there. They seem to be quite outside the jurisdiction of the valleys. No school, no church – and no sheriff ever goes up to see what they're about. But don't people ever talk of them at North Dormer?'

'I don't know. They say they're bad.'

He laughed. 'Do they? We'll go and see, shall we?'

She flushed at the suggestion, and turned her face to his. 'You never heard, I suppose – I come from there. They brought me down when I was little.'

'You?' He raised himself on his elbow, looking at her with sudden interest. 'You're from the Mountain? How curious! I suppose that's why you're so different. . . .'

Her happy blood bathed her to the forehead. He was praising her – and praising her because she came from the Mountain!

'Am I . . . different?' she triumphed, with affected wonder.

'Oh, awfully!' He picked up her hand and laid a kiss on the sunburnt knuckles.

'Come,' he said, 'let's be off.' He stood up and shook the grass from his loose grey clothes. 'What a good day! Where are you going to take me tomorrow?'

VI

That evening after supper Charity sat alone in the kitchen and listened to Mr Royall and young Harney talking in the porch.

She had remained indoors after the table had been cleared and old Verena had hobbled up to bed. The kitchen window was open, and Charity seated herself near it, her idle hands on her knee. The evening was cool and still. Beyond the black hills an amber west passed into pale green, and then to a deep blue in which a great star hung. The soft hoot of a little owl came through the dusk, and between its calls the men's voices rose and fell.

Mr Royall's was full of a sonorous satisfaction. It was a long time since he had had anyone of Lucius Harney's quality to talk to: Charity divined that the young man symbolized all his ruined and unforgotten past. When Miss Hatchard had been called to Springfield by the illness of a widowed sister, and young Harney, by that time seriously embarked on his task of drawing and measuring all the old houses between Nettleton and the New Hampshire border, had suggested the possibility of boarding at the red house in his cousin's absence, Charity had trembled lest Mr Royall should refuse. There had been no question of lodging the young man: there was no room for him. But it appeared that he could still live at Miss Hatchard's if Mr Royall would let him take his meals at the red house; and after a day's deliberation Mr Royall consented.

Charity suspected him of being glad of the chance to make a little money. He had the reputation of being an avaricious man; but she was beginning to think he was probably poorer than people knew. His practice had become little more than a

vague legend, revived only at lengthening intervals by a sum-
mons to Hepburn or Nettleton; and he appeared to depend
for his living mainly on the scant produce of his farm, and on
the commissions received from the few insurance agencies that
he represented in the neighbourhood. At any rate, he had been
prompt in accepting Harney's offer to hire the buggy at a dollar
and a half a day; and his satisfaction with the bargain had manifested itself, unexpectedly enough, at the end of the first week,
by his tossing a ten-dollar bill into Charity's lap as she sat one
day retrimming her old hat.

'Here – go get yourself a Sunday bonnet that'll make all the
other girls mad,' he said, looking at her with a sheepish twinkle
in his deep-set eyes; and she immediately guessed that the
unwonted present – the only gift of money she had ever
received from him – represented Harney's first payment.

But the young man's coming had brought Mr Royall other
than pecuniary benefit. It gave him, for the first time in years,
a man's companionship. Charity had only a dim understanding
of her guardian's needs; but she knew he felt himself above the
people among whom he lived, and she saw that Lucius Harney
thought him so. She was surprised to find how well he seemed
to talk now that he had a listener who understood him; and
she was equally struck by young Harney's friendly deference.

Their conversation was mostly about politics, and beyond
her range; but tonight it had a peculiar interest for her, for they
had begun to speak of the Mountain. She drew back a little,
lest they should see she was in hearing.

'The Mountain? The Mountain?' she heard Mr Royall say.
'Why, the Mountain's a blot – that's what it is, sir, a blot. That
scum up there ought to have been run in long ago – and would
have, if the people down here hadn't been clean scared of
them. The Mountain belongs to this township, and it's North
Dormer's fault if there's a gang of thieves and outlaws living
over there, in sight of us, defying the laws of their country.
Why, there ain't a sheriff or a tax-collector or a coroner'd durst
go up there. When they hear of trouble on the Mountain the
selectmen look the other way, and pass an appropriation to

beautify the town pump. The only man that ever goes up is the minister, and he goes because they send down and get him whenever there's any of them dies. They think a lot of Christian burial on the Mountain – but I never heard of their having the minister up to marry them. And they never trouble the Justice of the Peace either. They just herd together like the heathen.'

He went on, explaining in somewhat technical language how the little colony of squatters had contrived to keep the law at bay, and Charity, with burning eagerness, awaited young Harney's comment; but the young man seemed more concerned to hear Mr Royall's views than to express his own.

'I suppose you've never been up there yourself?' he presently asked.

'Yes, I have,' said Mr Royall with a contemptuous laugh. 'The wiseacres down here told me I'd be done for before I got back; but nobody lifted a finger to hurt me. And I'd just had one of their gang sent up for seven years too.'

'You went up after that?'

'Yes, sir: right after it. The fellow came down to Nettleton and ran amuck, the way they sometimes do. After they've done a wood-cutting job they come down and blow the money in; and this man ended up with manslaughter. I got him convicted, though they were scared of the Mountain even at Nettleton; and then a queer thing happened. The fellow sent for me to go and see him in gaol. I went, and this is what he says: "The fool that defended me is a chicken-livered son of a — and all the rest of it," he says. "I've got a job to be done for me up on the Mountain, and you're the only man I seen in court that looks as if he'd do it." He told me he had a child up there – or thought he had – a little girl; and he wanted her brought down and reared like a Christian. I was sorry for the fellow, so I went up and got the child.' He paused, and Charity listened with a throbbing heart. 'That's the only time I ever went up the Mountain,' he concluded.

There was a moment's silence; then Harney spoke. 'And the child – had she no mother?'

'Oh, yes: there was a mother. But she was glad enough to have her go. She'd have given her to anybody. They ain't half human up there. I guess the mother's dead by now, with the life she was leading. Anyhow, I've never heard of her from that day to this.'

'My God, how ghastly,' Harney murmured; and Charity, choking with humiliation, sprang to her feet and ran upstairs. She knew at last: knew that she was the child of a drunken convict and of a mother who wasn't 'half human', and was glad to have her go; and she had heard this history of her origin related to the one being in whose eyes she longed to appear superior to the people about her! She had noticed that Mr Royall had not named her, had even avoided any allusion that might identify her with the child he had brought down from the Mountain; and she knew it was out of regard for her that he had kept silent. But of what use was his discretion, since only that afternoon, misled by Harney's interest in the outlaw colony, she had boasted to him of coming from the Mountain? Now every word that had been spoken showed her how such an origin must widen the distance between them.

During his ten days' sojourn at North Dormer Lucius Harney had not spoken a word of love to her. He had intervened in her behalf with his cousin, and had convinced Miss Hatchard of her merits as a librarian; but that was a simple act of justice, since it was by his own fault that those merits had been questioned. He had asked her to drive him about the country when he hired lawyer Royall's buggy to go on his sketching expeditions; but that too was natural enough, since he was unfamiliar with the region. Lastly, when his cousin was called to Springfield, he had begged Mr Royall to receive him as a boarder; but where else in North Dormer could he have boarded? Not with Carrick Fry, whose wife was paralysed, and whose large family crowded his table to overflowing; not with the Targatts, who lived a mile up the road, nor with poor old Mrs Hawes, who, since her eldest daughter had deserted her, barely had the strength to cook her own meals while Ally picked up her living as a seamstress. Mr Royall's was the only house where the young man could have been offered a decent hospitality. There had been nothing, therefore, in the outward course of events to raise in Charity's breast the hopes with which it trembled. But beneath the visible incidents resulting from Lucius Harney's arrival there ran an undercurrent as mysterious and potent as the influence that makes the forest break into leaf before the ice is off the pools.

The business on which Harney had come was authentic; Charity had seen the letter from a New York publisher commissioning him to make a study of the eighteenth century houses in the less familiar districts of New England. But incomprehensible as the whole affair was to her, and hard as she found it to understand why he paused enchanted before certain neglected and paintless houses, while others, refurbished and 'improved' by the local builder, did not arrest a glance, she could not but suspect that Eagle County was less rich in architecture than he averred, and that the duration of his stay (which he had fixed at a month) was not unconnected with the look in his eyes when he had first paused before her in the library. Everything that had followed seemed to have grown out of that look: his way of speaking to her, his quickness in catching her meaning, his evident eagerness to prolong their excursions and to seize on every chance of being with her.

The signs of his liking were manifest enough; but it was hard to guess how much they meant, because his manner was so different from anything North Dormer had ever shown her. He was at once simpler and more deferential than any one she had known; and sometimes it was just when he was simplest that she most felt the distance between them. Education and opportunity had divided them by a width that no effort of hers could bridge, and even when his youth and his admiration brought him nearest, some chance word, some unconscious allusion, seemed to thrust her back across the gulf.

Never had it yawned so wide as when she fled up to her room carrying with her the echo of Mr Royall's tale. Her first confused thought was the prayer that she might never see young Harney again. It was too bitter to picture him as the detached impartial listener to such a story. 'I wish he'd go away: I wish he'd go tomorrow, and never come back!' she moaned to her pillow; and far into the night she lay there, in the disordered dress she had forgotten to take off, her whole soul a tossing misery on which her hopes and dreams spun about like drowning straws.

Of all this tumult only a vague heart-soreness was left when she opened her eyes the next morning. Her first thought was of the weather, for Harney had asked her to take him to the brown house under Porcupine, and then around by Hamblin; and as the trip was a long one they were to start at nine. The sun rose without a cloud, and earlier than usual she was in the kitchen, making cheese sandwiches, decanting buttermilk into a bottle, wrapping up slices of apple pie, and accusing Verena of having given away a basket she needed, which had always hung on a hook in the passage. When she came out into the porch, in her pink calico, which had run a little in the washing, but was still bright enough to set off her dark tints, she had such a triumphant sense of being a part of the sunlight and the morning that the last trace of her misery vanished. What did it matter where she came from, or whose child she was, when love was dancing in her veins, and down the road she saw young Harney coming toward her?

Mr Royall was in the porch too. He had said nothing at breakfast, but when she came out in her pink dress, the basket in her hand, he looked at her with surprise. 'Where you going to?' he asked.

'Why – Mr Harney's starting earlier than usual today,' she answered.

'Mr Harney, Mr Harney? Ain't Mr Harney learned how to drive a horse yet?'

She made no answer, and he sat tilted back in his chair, drumming on the rail of the porch. It was the first time he had ever spoken of the young man in that tone, and Charity felt a faint chill of apprehension. After a moment he stood up and walked away toward the bit of ground behind the house, where the hired man was hoeing.

The air was cool and clear, with the autumnal sparkle that a north wind brings to the hills in early summer, and the night had been so still that the dew hung on everything, not as a lingering moisture, but in separate beads that glittered like diamonds on the ferns and grasses. It was a long drive to the foot of Porcupine: first across the valley, with blue hills bounding the open slopes; then down into the beech-woods, following the course of the Creston, a brown brook leaping over velvet ledges; then out again onto the farm-lands about Creston Lake, and gradually up the ridges of the Eagle Range. At last they reached the yoke of the hills, and before them opened another valley, green and wild, and beyond it more blue heights eddying away to the sky like the waves of a receding tide.

Harney tied the horse to a tree-stump, and they unpacked their basket under an aged walnut with a riven trunk out of which bumblebees darted. The sun had grown hot, and behind them was the noonday murmur of the forest. Summer insects danced on the air, and a flock of white butterflies fanned the mobile tips of the crimson fireweed. In the valley below not a house was visible; it seemed as if Charity Royall and young Harney were the only living beings in the great hollow of earth and sky.

Charity's spirits flagged and disquieting thoughts stole back on her. Young Harney had grown silent, and as he lay beside her, his arms under his head, his eyes on the network of leaves above him, she wondered if he were musing on what Mr Royall had told him, and if it had really debased her in his thoughts. She wished he had not asked her to take him that day to the brown house; she did not want him to see the people she came from while the story of her birth was fresh in his mind. More than once she had been on the point of suggesting that they should follow the ridge and drive straight to Hamblin, where there was a little deserted house he wanted to see; but shyness and pride held her back. 'He'd better know what kind of folks I belong to,' she said to herself, with a somewhat forced defiance; for in reality it was shame that kept her silent.

Suddenly she lifted her hand and pointed to the sky. 'There's a storm coming up.'

He followed her glance and smiled. 'Is it that scrap of cloud among the pines that frightens you?'

'It's over the Mountain; and a cloud over the Mountain always means trouble.'

'Oh, I don't believe half the bad things you all say of the Mountain! But anyhow, we'll get down to the brown house before the rain comes.'

He was not far wrong, for only a few isolated drops had fallen when they turned into the road under the shaggy flank of Porcupine, and came upon the brown house. It stood alone beside a swamp bordered with alder thickets and tall bulrushes. Not another dwelling was in sight, and it was hard to guess what motive could have actuated the early settler who had made his home in so unfriendly a spot.

Charity had picked up enough of her companion's erudition to understand what had attracted him to the house. She noticed the fan-shaped tracery of the broken light above the door, the flutings of the paintless pilasters at the corners, and the round window set in the gable; and she knew that, for reasons that still escaped her, these were things to be admired and recorded. Still, they had seen other houses far more 'typical' (the word was Harney's); and as he threw the reins on the horse's neck he said with a slight shiver of repugnance: 'We won't stay long.'

Against the restless alders turning their white lining to the storm the house looked singularly desolate. The paint was almost gone from the clapboards, the window-panes were broken and patched with rags, and the garden was a poisonous tangle of nettles, burdocks and tall swamp-weeds over which big blue-bottles hummed.

At the sound of wheels a child with a tow-head and pale eyes like Liff Hyatt's peered over the fence and then slipped

away behind an out-house. Harney jumped down and helped
Charity out; and as he did so the rain broke on them. It came
slantwise, on a furious gale, laying shrubs and young trees
flat, tearing off their leaves like an autumn storm, turning the
road into a river, and making hissing pools of every hollow.
Thunder rolled incessantly through the roar of the rain, and
a strange glitter of light ran along the ground under the
increasing blackness.

'Lucky we're here after all,' Harney laughed. He fastened
the horse under a half-roofless shed, and wrapping Charity in
his coat ran with her to the house. The boy had not reappeared,
and as there was no response to their knocks Harney turned
the door-handle and they went in.

There were three people in the kitchen to which the door
admitted them. An old woman with a handkerchief over her
head was sitting by the window. She held a sickly-looking
kitten on her knees, and whenever it jumped down and tried
to limp away she stooped and lifted it back without any change
of her aged, unnoticing face. Another woman, the unkempt
creature that Charity had once noticed in driving by, stood
leaning against the window-frame and stared at them; and near
the stove an unshaved man in a tattered shirt sat on a barrel
asleep.

The place was bare and miserable and the air heavy with
the smell of dirt and stale tobacco. Charity's heart sank. Old
derided tales of the Mountain people came back to her, and
the woman's stare was so disconcerting, and the face of the
sleeping man so sodden and bestial, that her disgust was tinged
with a vague dread. She was not afraid for herself, she knew
the Hyatts would not be likely to trouble her; but she was not
sure how they would treat a 'city fellow'.

Lucius Harney would certainly have laughed at her fears.
He glanced about the room, uttered a general 'How are you?'
to which no one responded, and then asked the younger
woman if they might take shelter till the storm was over.

She turned her eyes away from him and looked at Charity.

'You're the girl from Royall's, ain't you?'

The colour rose in Charity's face. 'I'm Charity Royall,' she said, as if asserting her right to the name in the very place where it might have been most open to question.

The woman did not seem to notice. 'You kin stay,' she merely said; then she turned away and stooped over a dish in which she was stirring something.

Harney and Charity sat down on a bench made of a board resting on two starch boxes. They faced a door hanging on a broken hinge, and through the crack they saw the eyes of the tow-headed boy and of a pale little girl with a scar across her cheek. Charity smiled, and signed to the children to come in; but as soon as they saw they were discovered they slipped away on bare feet. It occurred to her that they were afraid of rousing the sleeping man; and probably the woman shared their fear, for she moved about as noiselessly and avoided going near the stove.

The rain continued to beat against the house, and in one or two places it sent a stream through the patched panes and ran into pools on the floor. Every now and then the kitten mewed and struggled down, and the old woman stooped and caught it, holding it tight in her bony hands; and once or twice the man on the barrel half woke, changed his position and dozed again, his head falling forward on his hairy breast. As the minutes passed, and the rain still streamed against the windows, a loathing of the place and the people came over Charity. The sight of the weak-minded old woman, of the cowed children, and the ragged man sleeping off his liquor, made the setting of her own life seem a vision of peace and plenty. She thought of the kitchen at Mr Royall's, with its scrubbed floor and dresser full of china, and the peculiar smell of yeast and coffee and soft-soap that she had always hated, but that now seemed the very symbol of household order. She saw Mr Royall's room, with the high-backed horsehair chair, the faded rag carpet, the row of books on a shelf, the engraving of 'The Surrender of Burgoyne' over the stove, and the mat with a brown and white spaniel in a moss-green border. And then her mind travelled to Miss Hatchard's house, where all was freshness, purity and fragrance, and compared to which the red house had always seemed so poor and plain.

'This is where I belong – this is where I belong,' she kept repeating to herself, but the words had no meaning for her. Every instinct and habit made her a stranger among these poor swamp-people living like vermin in their lair. With all her soul she wished she had not yielded to Harney's curiosity, and brought him there.

The rain had drenched her, and she began to shiver under the thin folds of her dress. The younger woman must have noticed it, for she went out of the room and came back with a broken teacup which she offered to Charity. It was half full of whiskey, and Charity shook her head; but Harney took the cup and put his lips to it. When he had set it down Charity saw him feel in his pocket and draw out a dollar; he hesitated a moment, and then put it back, and she guessed that he did not wish her to see him offering money to people she had spoken of as being her kin.

The sleeping man stirred, lifted his head and opened his eyes. They rested vacantly for a moment on Charity and Harney, and then closed again, and his head drooped; but a look of anxiety came into the woman's face. She glanced out of the window and then came up to Harney. 'I guess you better go along now,' she said. The young man understood and got to his feet. 'Thank you,' he said, holding out his hand. She seemed not to notice the gesture, and turned away as they opened the door.

The rain was still coming down, but they hardly noticed it: the pure air was like balm in their faces. The clouds were rising and breaking, and between their edges the light streamed down from remote blue hollows. Harney untied the horse, and they drove off through the diminishing rain, which was already beaded with sunlight.

For a while Charity was silent, and her companion did not speak. She looked timidly at his profile: it was graver than usual, as though he too were oppressed by what they had seen. Then she broke out abruptly: 'Those people back there are the kind of folks I come from. They may be my relations, for all I know.' She did not want him to think that she regretted having told him her story.

'Poor creatures,' he rejoined. 'I wonder why they came down to that fever-hole.'

She laughed ironically. 'To better themselves! It's worse up on the Mountain. Bash Hyatt married the daughter of the farmer that used to own the brown house. That was him by the stove, I suppose.'

Harney seemed to find nothing to say and she went on: 'I saw you take out a dollar to give to that poor woman. Why did you put it back?'

He reddened, and leaned forward to flick a swamp-fly from the horse's neck. 'I wasn't sure —'

'Was it because you knew they were my folks, and thought I'd be ashamed to see you give them money?'

He turned to her with eyes full of reproach. 'Oh, Charity —' It was the first time he had ever called her by her name. Her misery welled over.

'I ain't – I ain't ashamed. They're my people, and I ain't ashamed of them,' she sobbed.

'My dear...' he murmured, putting his arm about her; and she leaned against him and wept out her pain.

It was too late to go around to Hamblin, and all the stars were out in a clear sky when they reached the North Dormer valley and drove up to the red house.

VII

Since her reinstatement in Miss Hatchard's favour Charity had not dared to curtail by a moment her hours of attendance at the library. She even made a point of arriving before the time, and showed a laudable indignation when the youngest Targatt girl, who had been engaged to help in the cleaning and rearranging of the books, came trailing in late and neglected her task to peer through the window at the Sollas boy. Nevertheless, 'library days' seemed more than ever irksome to Charity after her vivid hours of liberty; and she would have found it hard to set a good example to her subordinate if Lucius Harney had not been commissioned, before Miss Hatchard's departure, to examine with the local carpenter the best means of ventilating the 'Memorial'.

He was careful to prosecute this inquiry on the days when the library was open to the public; and Charity was therefore sure of spending part of the afternoon in his company. The Targatt girl's presence, and the risk of being interrupted by some passer-by suddenly smitten with a thirst for letters, restricted their intercourse to the exchange of commonplaces; but there was a fascination to Charity in the contrast between these public civilities and their secret intimacy.

The day after their drive to the brown house was 'library day', and she sat at her desk working at the revised catalogue, while the Targatt girl, one eye on the window, chanted out the titles of a pile of books. Charity's thoughts were far away, in the dismal house by the swamp, and under the twilight sky during the long drive home, when Lucius Harney had consoled her with endearing words. That day, for the first time since he had been boarding with them, he had failed to appear as usual at the midday meal. No message had come to explain his absence, and Mr Royall, who was more than usually taciturn, had betrayed no surprise, and made no comment. In itself this indifference was not particularly significant, for Mr Royall, in common with most of his fellow-citizens, had a way of accepting events passively, as if he had long since come to the conclusion that no one who lived in North Dormer could hope to modify them. But to Charity, in the reaction from her mood of passionate exaltation, there was something disquieting in his silence. It was almost as if Lucius Harney had never had a part in their lives: Mr Royall's imperturbable indifference seemed to relegate him to the domain of unreality.

As she sat at work, she tried to shake off her disappointment at Harney's non-appearing. Some trifling incident had probably kept him from joining them at midday; but she was sure he must be eager to see her again, and that he would not want to wait till they met at supper, between Mr Royall and Verena. She was wondering what his first words would be, and trying to devise a way of getting rid of the Targatt girl before he came, when she heard steps outside, and he walked up the path with Mr Miles.

The clergyman from Hepburn seldom came to North Dormer except when he drove over to officiate at the old white church which, by an unusual chance, happened to belong to the Episcopal communion. He was a brisk affable man, eager to make the most of the fact that a little nucleus of 'church-people' had survived in the sectarian wilderness, and resolved to undermine the influence of the ginger-bread-coloured Baptist chapel at the other end of the village; but he was kept busy by parochial work at Hepburn, where there were paper-mills and saloons, and it was not often that he could spare time for North Dormer.

Charity, who went to the white church (like all the best people in North Dormer), admired Mr Miles, and had even, during the memorable trip to Nettleton, imagined herself married to a man who had such a straight nose and such a beautiful way of speaking, and who lived in a brown-stone rectory covered with Virginia creeper. It had been a shock to

discover that the privilege was already enjoyed by a lady with
crimped hair and a large baby; but the arrival of Lucius Harney
had long since banished Mr Miles from Charity's dreams, and
as he walked up the path at Harney's side she saw him as he
really was: a fat middle-aged man with a baldness showing
under his clerical hat, and spectacles on his Grecian nose. She
wondered what had called him to North Dormer on a week-
day, and felt a little hurt that Harney should have brought him
to the library.

It presently appeared that his presence there was due to Miss
Hatchard. He had been spending a few days at Springfield, to
fill a friend's pulpit, and had been consulted by Miss Hatchard
as to young Harney's plan for ventilating the 'Memorial'. To
lay hands on the Hatchard ark was a grave matter, and Miss
Hatchard, always full of scruples, and of scruples about her
scruples (it was Harney's phrase), wished to have Mr Miles's
opinion before deciding.

'I couldn't,' Mr Miles explained, 'quite make out from your
cousin what changes you wanted to make, and as the other
trustees did not understand either I thought I had better drive
over and take a look – though I'm sure,' he added, turning his
friendly spectacles on the young man, 'that no one could be
more competent – but of course this spot has its peculiar
sanctity!'

'I hope a little fresh air won't desecrate it,' Harney laugh-
ingly rejoined; and they walked to the other end of the library
while he set forth his idea to the Rector.

Mr Miles had greeted the two girls with his usual friendliness, but Charity saw that he was occupied with other things,
and she presently became aware, by the scraps of conversation
drifting over to her, that he was still under the charm of his visit
to Springfield, which appeared to have been full of agreeable
incidents.

'Ah, the Coopersons . . . yes, you know them, of course,'
she heard. 'That's a fine old house! And Ned Cooperson has
collected some really remarkable impressionist pictures. . . .'
The names he cited were unknown to Charity. 'Yes; yes; the

Schaefer quartette played at Lyric Hall on Saturday evening; and on Monday I had the privilege of hearing them again at the Towers. Beautifully done...Bach and Beethoven... a lawn-party first...I saw Miss Balch several times, by the way...looking extremely handsome....'

Charity dropped her pencil and forgot to listen to the Targatt girl's sing-song. Why had Mr Miles suddenly brought up Annabel Balch's name?

'Oh, really?' she heard Harney rejoin; and, raising his stick, he pursued: 'You see, my plan is to move these shelves away, and open a round window in this wall, on the axis of the one under the pediment.'

'I suppose she'll be coming up here later to stay with Miss Hatchard?' Mr Miles went on, following on his train of thought; then, spinning about and tilting his head back: 'Yes, yes, I see – I understand: that will give a draught without materially altering the look of things. I can see no objection.'

The discussion went on for some minutes, and gradually the two men moved back toward the desk. Mr Miles stopped again and looked thoughtfully at Charity. 'Aren't you a little pale, my dear? Not overworking? Mr Harney tells me you and Mamie are giving the library a thorough overhauling.' He was always careful to remember his parishioners' Christian names, and at the right moment he bent his benignant spectacles on the Targatt girl.

Then he turned to Charity. 'Don't take things hard, my dear; don't take things hard. Come down and see Mrs Miles and me some day at Hepburn,' he said, pressing her hand and waving a farewell to Mamie Targatt. He went out of the library, and Harney followed him.

Charity thought she detected a look of constraint in Harney's eyes. She fancied he did not want to be alone with her; and with a sudden pang she wondered if he repented the tender things he had said to her the night before. His words had been more fraternal than lover-like; but she had lost their exact sense in the caressing warmth of his voice. He had made her feel that the fact of her being a waif from the Mountain

was only another reason for holding her close and soothing
her with consolatory murmurs; and when the drive was over,
and she got out of the buggy, tired, cold, and aching with
emotion, she stepped as if the ground were a sunlit wave and
she the spray on its crest.

Why, then, had his manner suddenly changed, and why did
he leave the library with Mr Miles? Her restless imagination
fastened on the name of Annabel Balch: from the moment it
had been mentioned she fancied that Harney's expression had
altered. Annabel Balch at a garden-party at Springfield, looking 'extremely handsome' . . . perhaps Mr Miles had seen her
there at the very moment when Charity and Harney were
sitting in the Hyatts' hovel, between a drunkard and a half-
witted old woman! Charity did not know exactly what a
garden-party was, but her glimpse of the flower-edged lawns
of Nettleton helped her to visualize the scene, and envious
recollections of the 'old things' which Miss Balch avowedly
'wore out' when she came to North Dormer made it only
too easy to picture her in her splendour. Charity understood
what associations the name must have called up, and felt the
uselessness of struggling against the unseen influences in
Harney's life.

When she came down from her room for supper he was not
there; and while she waited in the porch she recalled the tone
in which Mr Royall had commented the day before on their
early start. Mr Royall sat at her side, his chair tilted back, his
broad black boots with side-elastics resting against the lower
bar of the railings. His rumpled grey hair stood up above his
forehead like the crest of an angry bird, and the leather-brown
of his veined cheeks was blotched with red. Charity knew that
those red spots were the signs of a coming explosion.

Suddenly he said: 'Where's supper? Has Verena Marsh
slipped up again on her soda-biscuits?'

Charity threw a startled glance at him. 'I presume she's
waiting for Mr Harney.'

'Mr Harney, is she? She'd better dish up, then. He ain't
coming.' He stood up, walked to the door, and called out, in

the pitch necessary to penetrate the old woman's tympanum: 'Get along with the supper, Verena.'

Charity was trembling with apprehension. Something had happened – she was sure of it now – and Mr Royall knew what it was. But not for the world would she have gratified him by showing her anxiety. She took her usual place, and he seated himself opposite, and poured out a strong cup of tea before passing her the tea-pot. Verena brought some scrambled eggs, and he piled his plate with them. 'Ain't you going to take any?' he asked. Charity roused herself and began to eat.

The tone with which Mr Royall had said 'He's not coming' seemed to her full of an ominous satisfaction. She saw that he had suddenly begun to hate Lucius Harney, and guessed herself to be the cause of this change of feeling. But she had no means of finding out whether some act of hostility on his part had made the young man stay away, or whether he simply wished to avoid seeing her again after their drive back from the brown house. She ate her supper with a studied show of indifference, but she knew that Mr Royall was watching her and that her agitation did not escape him.

After supper she went up to her room. She heard Mr Royall cross the passage, and presently the sounds below her window showed that he had returned to the porch. She seated herself on her bed and began to struggle against the desire to go down and ask him what had happened. 'I'd rather die than do it,' she muttered to herself. With a word he could have relieved her uncertainty: but never would she gratify him by saying it.

She rose and leaned out of the window. The twilight had deepened into night, and she watched the frail curve of the young moon dropping to the edge of the hills. Through the darkness she saw one or two figures moving down the road; but the evening was too cold for loitering, and presently the strollers disappeared. Lamps were beginning to show here and there in the windows. A bar of light brought out the whiteness of a clump of lilies in the Hawes's yard: and farther down the street Carrick Fry's Rochester lamp cast its bold illumination on the rustic flower-tub in the middle of his grass-plot.

For a long time she continued to lean in the window. But a
fever of unrest consumed her, and finally she went downstairs,
took her hat from its hook, and swung out of the house. Mr
Royall sat in the porch, Verena beside him, her old hands
crossed on her patched skirt. As Charity went down the steps
Mr Royall called after her: 'Where you going?' She could
easily have answered: 'To Orma's', or 'Down to the Targatts';
and either answer might have been true, for she had no purpose. But she swept on in silence, determined not to recognize
his right to question her.

At the gate she paused and looked up and down the road.
The darkness drew her, and she thought of climbing the hill
and plunging into the depths of the larch-wood above the
pasture. Then she glanced irresolutely along the street, and
as she did so a gleam appeared through the spruces at Miss
Hatchard's gate. Lucius Harney was there, then – he had not
gone down to Hepburn with Mr Miles, as she had at first
imagined. But where had he taken his evening meal, and what
had caused him to stay away from Mr Royall's? The light was
positive proof of his presence, for Miss Hatchard's servants
were away on a holiday, and her farmer's wife came only in
the mornings, to make the young man's bed and prepare his
coffee. Beside that lamp he was doubtless sitting at this
moment. To know the truth Charity had only to walk half the
length of the village, and knock at the lighted window. She
hesitated a minute or two longer, and then turned toward Miss
Hatchard's.

She walked quickly, straining her eyes to detect anyone who
might be coming along the street; and before reaching the
Frys' she crossed over to avoid the light from their window.
Whenever she was unhappy she felt herself at bay against a
pitiless world, and a kind of animal secretiveness possessed her.
But the street was empty, and she passed unnoticed through the
gate and up the path to the house. Its white front glimmered
indistinctly through the trees, showing only one oblong of
light on the lower floor. She had supposed that the lamp was
in Miss Hatchard's sitting-room; but she now saw that it shone

through a window at the farther corner of the house. She did not know the room to which this window belonged, and she paused under the trees, checked by a sense of strangeness. Then she moved on, treading softly on the short grass, and keeping so close to the house that whoever was in the room, even if roused by her approach, would not be able to see her.

The window opened on a narrow verandah with a trellised arch. She leaned close to the trellis, and parting the sprays of clematis that covered it looked into a corner of the room. She saw the foot of a mahogany bed, an engraving on the wall, a wash-stand on which a towel had been tossed, and one end of the green-covered table which held the lamp. Half of the lamp-shade projected into her field of vision, and just under it two smooth sunburnt hands, one holding a pencil and the other a ruler, were moving to and fro over a drawing-board.

Her heart jumped and then stood still. He was there, a few feet away; and while her soul was tossing on seas of woe he had been quietly sitting at his drawing-board. The sight of those two hands, moving with their usual skill and precision, woke her out of her dream. Her eyes were opened to the dispropor-tion between what she had felt and the cause of her agitation; and she was turning away from the window when one hand abruptly pushed aside the drawing-board and the other flung down the pencil.

Charity had often noticed Harney's loving care of his draw-ings, and the neatness and method with which he carried on and concluded each task. The impatient sweeping aside of the drawing-board seemed to reveal a new mood. The gesture suggested sudden discouragement, or distaste for his work, and she wondered if he too were agitated by secret perplexities. Her impulse of flight was checked; she stepped up on the verandah and looked into the room.

Harney had put his elbows on the table and was resting his chin on his locked hands. He had taken off his coat and waist-coat, and unbuttoned the low collar of his flannel shirt; she saw the vigorous lines of his young throat, and the root of the muscles where they joined the chest. He sat staring straight

ahead of him, a look of weariness and self-disgust on his face:
it was almost as if he had been gazing at a distorted reflection
of his own features. For a moment Charity looked at him with
a kind of terror, as if he had been a stranger under familiar
lineaments; then she glanced past him and saw on the floor an
open portmanteau half full of clothes. She understood that he
was preparing to leave, and that he had probably decided to go
without seeing her. She saw that the decision, from whatever
cause it was taken, had disturbed him deeply; and she immediately concluded that his change of plan was due to some surrep-
titious interference of Mr Royall's. All her old resentments and
rebellions flamed up, confusedly mingled with the yearning
roused by Harney's nearness. Only a few hours earlier she had
felt secure in his comprehending pity; now she was flung back
on herself, doubly alone after that moment of communion.

Harney was still unaware of her presence. He sat without
moving, moodily staring before him at the same spot in the
wall-paper. He had not even had the energy to finish his pack-
ing, and his clothes and papers lay on the floor about the portmanteau. Presently he unlocked his clasped hands and stood
up; and Charity, drawing back hastily, sank down on the step
of the verandah. The night was so dark that there was not much
chance of his seeing her unless he opened the window, and
before that she would have time to slip away and be lost in the
shadow of the trees. He stood for a minute or two looking
around the room with the same expression of self-disgust, as
if he hated himself and everything about him; then he sat down
again at the table, drew a few more strokes, and threw his
pencil aside. Finally he walked across the floor, kicking the
portmanteau out of his way, and lay down on the bed, folding
his arms under his head, and staring up morosely at the ceiling.
Just so, Charity had seen him at her side, on the grass or the
pine-needles, his eyes fixed on the sky, and pleasure flashing
over his face like the flickers of sun the branches shed on it.
But now the face was so changed that she hardly knew it; and
grief at his grief gathered in her throat, rose to her eyes and
ran over.

She continued to crouch on the steps, holding her breath and stiffening herself into complete immobility. One motion of her hand, one tap on the pane, and she could picture the sudden change in his face. In every pulse of her rigid body she was aware of the welcome his eyes and lips would give her; but something kept her from moving. It was not the fear of any sanction, human or heavenly; she had never in her life been afraid. It was simply that she had suddenly understood what would happen if she went in. It was the thing that *did* happen between young men and girls, and that North Dormer ignored in public and snickered over on the sly. It was what Miss Hatchard was still ignorant of, but every girl of Charity's class knew about before she left school. It was what had happened to Ally Hawes's sister Julia, and had ended in her going to Nettleton, and in people's never mentioning her name.

It did not, of course, always end so sensationally; nor, perhaps, on the whole, so untragically. Charity had always suspected that the shunned Julia's fate might have its compensations. There were other worse endings that the village knew of, mean, miserable, unconfessed; other lives that went on drearily, without visible change, in the same cramped setting of hypocrisy. But these were not the reasons that held her back. Since the day before, she had known exactly what she would feel if Harney should take her in his arms: the melting of palm into palm and mouth on mouth, and the long flame burning her from head to foot. But mixed with this feeling was another: the wondering pride in his liking for her, the startled softness that his sympathy had put into her heart. Sometimes, when her youth flushed up in her, she had imagined yielding like other girls to furtive caresses in the twilight; but she could not so cheapen herself to Harney. She did not know why he was going; but since he was going she felt she must do nothing to deface the image of her that he carried away. If he wanted her he must seek her: he must not be surprised into taking her as girls like Julia Hawes were taken. . . .

No sound came from the sleeping village, and in the deep darkness of the garden she heard now and then a secret rustle of branches, as though some night-bird brushed them. Once a footfall passed the gate, and she shrank back into her corner; but the steps died away and left a profounder quiet. Her eyes were still on Harney's tormented face: she felt she could not move till he moved. But she was beginning to grow numb from her constrained position, and at times her thoughts were so indistinct that she seemed to be held there only by a vague weight of weariness.

A long time passed in this strange vigil. Harney still lay on the bed, motionless and with fixed eyes, as though following his vision to its bitter end. At last he stirred and changed his attitude slightly, and Charity's heart began to tremble. But he only flung out his arms and sank back into his former position. With a deep sigh he tossed the hair from his forehead; then his whole body relaxed, his head turned sideways on the pillow, and she saw that he had fallen asleep. The sweet expression came back to his lips, and the haggardness faded from his face, leaving it as fresh as a boy's.

She rose and crept away.

VIII

She had lost the sense of time, and did not know how late it was till she came out into the street and saw that all the windows were dark between Miss Hatchard's and the Royall house.

As she passed from under the black pall of the Norway spruces she fancied she saw two figures in the shade about the duck-pond. She drew back and watched; but nothing moved, and she had stared so long into the lamp-lit room that the darkness confused her, and she thought she must have been mistaken.

She walked on, wondering whether Mr Royall was still in the porch. In her exalted mood she did not greatly care whether he was waiting for her or not: she seemed to be floating high over life, on a great cloud of misery beneath which everyday realities had dwindled to mere specks in space. But the porch was empty, Mr Royall's hat hung on its peg in the passage, and the kitchen lamp had been left to light her to bed. She took it and went up.

The morning hours of the next day dragged by without incident. Charity had imagined that, in some way or other, she would learn whether Harney had already left; but Verena's deafness prevented her being a source of news, and no one came to the house who could bring enlightenment.

Mr Royall went out early, and did not return till Verena had set the table for the midday meal. When he came in he went straight to the kitchen and shouted to the old woman: 'Ready for dinner—' then he turned into the dining-room, where Charity was already seated. Harney's plate was in its usual place, but Mr Royall offered no explanation of his absence, and Charity asked none. The feverish exaltation of the night before had dropped, and she said to herself that he had gone away, indifferently, almost callously, and that now her life would lapse again into the narrow rut out of which he had lifted it. For a moment she was inclined to sneer at herself for not having used the arts that might have kept him.

She sat at table till the meal was over, lest Mr Royall should remark on her leaving; but when he stood up she rose also, without waiting to help Verena. She had her foot on the stairs when he called to her to come back.

'I've got a headache. I'm going up to lie down.'

'I want you should come in here first; I've got something to say to you.'

She was sure from his tone that in a moment she would learn what every nerve in her ached to know; but as she turned back she made a last effort of indifference.

Mr Royall stood in the middle of the office, his thick eye-brows beetling, his lower jaw trembling a little. At first she thought he had been drinking; then she saw that he was sober, but stirred by a deep and stern emotion totally unlike his usual transient angers. And suddenly she understood that, until then, she had never really noticed him or thought about him. Except on the occasion of his one offense he had been to her merely the person who is always there, the unquestioned central fact of life, as inevitable but as uninteresting as North Dormer itself, or any of the other conditions fate had laid on her. Even then she had regarded him only in relation to her-self, and had never speculated as to his own feelings, beyond instinctively concluding that he would not trouble her again in the same way. But now she began to wonder what he was really like.

He had grasped the back of his chair with both hands, and stood looking hard at her. At length he said: 'Charity, for once let's you and me talk together like friends.'

Instantly she felt that something had happened, and that he held her in his hand.

'Where is Mr Harney? Why hasn't he come back? Have you

sent him away?' she broke out, without knowing what she was saying.

The change in Mr Royall frightened her. All the blood seemed to leave his veins and against his swarthy pallor the deep lines in his face looked black.

'Didn't he have time to answer some of those questions last night? You was with him long enough!' he said.

Charity stood speechless. The taunt was so unrelated to what had been happening in her soul that she hardly understood it. But the instinct of self-defense awoke in her.

'Who says I was with him last night?'

'The whole place is saying it by now.'

'Then it was you that put the lie into their mouths. – Oh, how I've always hated you!' she cried.

She had expected a retort in kind, and it startled her to hear her exclamation sounding on through silence.

'Yes, I know,' Mr Royall said slowly. 'But that ain't going to help us much now.'

'It helps me not to care a straw what lies you tell about me!'

'If they're lies, they're not my lies: my Bible oath on that, Charity. I didn't know where you were: I wasn't out of this house last night.'

She made no answer and he went on: 'Is it a lie that you were seen coming out of Miss Hatchard's nigh onto midnight?'

She straightened herself with a laugh, all her reckless insolence recovered. 'I didn't look to see what time it was.'

'You lost girl . . . you . . . you . . . Oh, my God, why did you tell me?' he broke out, dropping into his chair, his head bowed down like an old man's.

Charity's self-possession had returned with the sense of her danger. 'Do you suppose I'd take the trouble to lie to *you*? Who are you, anyhow, to ask me where I go to when I go out at night?'

Mr Royall lifted his head and looked at her. His face had grown quiet and almost gentle, as she remembered seeing it sometimes when she was a little girl, before Mrs Royall died.

'Don't let's go on like this, Charity. It can't do any good to

either of us. You were seen going into that fellow's house ...
you were seen coming out of it.... I've watched this thing
coming, and I've tried to stop it. As God sees me, I have....'

'Ah, it *was* you, then? I knew it was you that sent him away!'

He looked at her in surprise. 'Didn't he tell you so?
I thought he understood.' He spoke slowly, with difficult
pauses, 'I didn't name you to him: I'd have cut my hand off
sooner. I just told him I couldn't spare the horse any longer;
and that the cooking was getting too heavy for Verena. I guess
he's the kind that's heard the same thing before. Anyhow, he
took it quietly enough. He said his job here was about done,
anyhow; and there didn't another word pass between us....
If he told you otherwise he told you an untruth.'

Charity listened in a cold trance of anger. It was nothing to
her what the village said ... but all this fingering of her dreams!

'I've told you he didn't tell me anything. I didn't speak with
him last night.'

'You didn't speak with him?'

'No ... It's not that I care what any of you say ... but
you may as well know. Things ain't between us the way you
think ... and the other people in this place. He was kind to
me; he was my friend; and all of a sudden he stopped coming,
and I knew it was you that done it – *you!*' All her unreconciled
memory of the past flamed out at him. 'So I went there last
night to find out what you'd said to him: that's all.'

Mr Royall drew a heavy breath. 'But, then – if he wasn't
there, what were you doing there all that time? – Charity, for
pity's sake, tell me. I've got to know, to stop their talking.'

This pathetic abdication of all authority over her did not
move her: she could feel only the outrage of his interference.

'Can't you see that I don't care what anybody says? It's true
I went there to see him; and he was in his room, and I stood
outside for ever so long and watched him; but I dursn't go in
for fear he'd think I'd come after him.... ' She felt her voice
breaking, and gathered it up in a last defiance. 'As long as I live
I'll never forgive you!' she cried.

Mr Royall made no answer. He sat and pondered with

sunken head, his veined hands clasped about the arms of his chair. Age seemed to have come down on him as winter comes on the hills after a storm. At length he looked up.

'Charity, you say you don't care; but you're the proudest girl I know, and the last to want people to talk against you. You know there's always eyes watching you: you're handsomer and smarter than the rest, and that's enough. But till lately you've never given them a chance. Now they've got it, and they're going to use it. I believe what you say, but they won't. . . . It was Mrs Tom Fry seen you going in . . . and two or three of them watched for you to come out again. . . . You've been with the fellow all day long every day since he come here . . . and I'm a lawyer, and I know how hard slander dies.' He paused, but she stood motionless, without giving him any sign of acquiescence or even of attention. 'He's a pleasant fellow to talk to – I liked having him here myself. The young men up here ain't had his chances. But there's one thing as old as the hills and as plain as daylight: if he'd wanted you the right way he'd have said so.'

Charity did not speak. It seemed to her that nothing could exceed the bitterness of hearing such words from such lips.

Mr Royall rose from his seat. 'See here, Charity Royall: I had a shameful thought once, and you've made me pay for it. Isn't that score pretty near wiped out? . . . There's a streak in me I ain't always master of, but I've always acted straight to you but that once. And you've known I would – you've trusted me. For all your sneers and your mockery you've always known I loved you the way a man loves a decent woman. I'm a good many years older than you, but I'm head and shoulders above this place and everybody in it, and you know that too. I slipped up once, but that's no reason for not starting again. If you'll come with me I'll do it. If you'll marry me we'll leave here and settle in some big town, where there's men, and business, and things doing. It's not too late for me to find an opening. . . . I can see it by the way folks treat me when I go down to Hepburn or Nettleton. . . .'

Charity made no movement. Nothing in his appeal reached

her heart, and she thought only of words to wound and wither. But a growing lassitude restrained her. What did anything matter that he was saying? She saw the old life closing in on her, and hardly heeded his fanciful picture of renewal.

'Charity – Charity – say you'll do it,' she heard him urge, all his lost years and wasted passion in his voice.

'Oh, what's the use of all this? When I leave here it won't be with you.'

She moved toward the door as she spoke, and he stood up and placed himself between her and the threshold. He seemed suddenly tall and strong, as though the extremity of his humiliation had given him new vigour.

'That's all, is it? It's not much.' He leaned against the door, so towering and powerful that he seemed to fill the narrow room. 'Well, then – look here. . . . You're right: I've no claim on you – why should you look at a broken man like me? You want the other fellow . . . and I don't blame you. You picked out the best when you seen it . . . well, that was always my way.' He fixed his stern eyes on her, and she had the sense that the struggle within him was at its highest. 'Do you want him to marry you?' he asked.

They stood and looked at each other for a long moment, eye to eye, with the terrible equality of courage that sometimes made her feel as if she had his blood in her veins.

'Do you want him to – say? I'll have him here in an hour if you do. I ain't been in the law thirty years for nothing. He's hired Carrick Fry's team to take him to Hepburn, but he ain't going to start for another hour. And I can put things to him so he won't be long deciding. . . . He's soft: I could see that. I don't say you won't be sorry afterward – but, by God, I'll give you the chance to be, if you say so.'

She heard him out in silence, too remote from all he was feeling and saying for any sally of scorn to relieve her. As she listened, there flitted through her mind the vision of Liff Hyatt's muddy boot coming down on the white bramble-flowers. The same thing had happened now; something transient and exquisite had flowered in her, and she had stood by and seen it trampled to earth. While the thought passed through her she was aware of Mr Royall, still leaning against the door, but crestfallen, diminished, as though her silence were the answer he most dreaded.

'I don't want any chance you can give me: I'm glad he's going away,' she said.

He kept his place a moment longer, his hand on the door-knob. 'Charity!' he pleaded. She made no answer, and he turned the knob and went out. She heard him fumble with the latch of the front door, and saw him walk down the steps. He passed out of the gate, and his figure, stooping and heavy, receded slowly up the street.

For a while she remained where he had left her. She was still trembling with the humiliation of his last words, which rang so loud in her ears that it seemed as though they must echo through the village, proclaiming her a creature to lend herself to such vile suggestions. Her shame weighed on her like a physical oppression: the roof and walls seemed to be closing in on her, and she was seized by the impulse to get away, under the open sky, where there would be room to breathe. She went to the front door, and as she did so Lucius Harney opened it.

He looked graver and less confident than usual, and for a moment or two neither of them spoke. Then he held out his hand. 'Are you going out?' he asked. 'May I come in?'

Her heart was beating so violently that she was afraid to speak, and stood looking at him with tear-dilated eyes; then she became aware of what her silence must betray, and said quickly: 'Yes: come in.'

She led the way into the dining-room, and they sat down on opposite sides of the table, the cruet-stand and japanned bread-basket between them. Harney had laid his straw hat on the table, and as he sat there, in his easy-looking summer clothes, a brown tie knotted under his flannel collar, and his smooth brown hair brushed back from his forehead, she pictured him as she had seen him the night before, lying on his bed, with the tossed locks falling into his eyes, and his bare throat rising out of his unbuttoned shirt. He had never seemed so remote as at the moment when that vision flashed through her mind.

'I'm so sorry it's good-bye: I suppose you know I'm leaving,' he began, abruptly and awkwardly; she guessed that he was wondering how much she knew of his reasons for going.

'I presume you found your work was over quicker than what you expected,' she said.

'Well, yes – that is, no: there are plenty of things I should have liked to do. But my holiday's limited; and now that Mr Royall needs the horse for himself it's rather difficult to find means of getting about.'

'There ain't any too many teams for hire around here,' she acquiesced; and there was another silence.

'These days here have been – awfully pleasant: I wanted to thank you for making them so,' he continued, his colour rising.

She could not think of any reply, and he went on: 'You've been wonderfully kind to me, and I wanted to tell you. . . . I wish I could think of you as happier, less lonely. . . . Things are sure to change for you by and by. . . .'

'Things don't change at North Dormer: people just get used to them.'

The answer seemed to break up the order of his prearranged consolations, and he sat looking at her uncertainly. Then he said, with his sweet smile: 'That's not true of you. It can't be.'

The smile was like a knife-thrust through her heart: everything in her began to tremble and break loose. She felt her tears run over, and stood up.

'Well, good-bye,' she said.

She was aware of his taking her hand, and of feeling that his touch was lifeless.

'Good-bye.' He turned away, and stopped on the threshold. 'You'll say good-bye for me to Verena?'

She heard the closing of the outer door and the sound of his quick tread along the path. The latch of the gate clicked after him.

The next morning when she arose in the cold dawn and

opened her shutters she saw a freckled boy standing on the other side of the road and looking up at her. He was a boy from a farm three or four miles down the Creston road, and she wondered what he was doing there at that hour, and why he looked so hard at her window. When he saw her he crossed over and leaned against the gate unconcernedly. There was no one stirring in the house, and she threw a shawl over her night-gown and ran down and let herself out. By the time she reached the gate the boy was sauntering down the road, whistling carelessly; but she saw that a letter had been thrust between the slats and the crossbar of the gate. She took it out and hastened back to her room.

The envelope bore her name, and inside was a leaf torn from a pocket-diary.

Dear Charity:

I can't go away like this. I am staying for a few days at Creston River. Will you come down and meet me at Creston pool? I will wait for you till evening.

IX

Charity sat before the mirror trying on a hat which Ally Hawes, with much secrecy, had trimmed for her. It was of white straw, with a drooping brim and a cherry-coloured lining that made her face glow like the inside of the shell on the parlour mantelpiece.

She propped the square of looking-glass against Mr Royall's black leather Bible, steadying it in front with a white stone on which a view of the Brooklyn Bridge was painted; and she sat before her reflection, bending the brim this way and that, while Ally Hawes's pale face looked over her shoulder like the ghost of wasted opportunities.

'I look awful, don't I?' she said at last with a happy sigh.

Ally smiled and took back the hat. 'I'll stitch the roses on right here, so's you can put it away at once.'

Charity laughed, and ran her fingers through her rough dark hair. She knew that Harney liked to see its reddish edges ruffled about her forehead and breaking into little rings at the nape. She sat down on her bed and watched Ally stoop over the hat with a careful frown.

'Don't you ever feel like going down to Nettleton for a day?' she asked.

Ally shook her head without looking up. 'No, I always remember that awful time I went down with Julia – to that doctor's.'

'Oh, Ally —'

'I can't help it. The house is on the corner of Wing Street and Lake Avenue. The trolley from the station goes right by it, and the day the minister took us down to see those pictures I recognized it right off, and couldn't seem to see anything

174

else. There's a big black sign with gold letters all across the front – 'Private Consultations'. She came as near as anything to dying. . . .'

'Poor Julia!' Charity sighed from the height of her purity and her security. She had a friend whom she trusted and who respected her. She was going with him to spend the next day – the Fourth of July – at Nettleton. Whose business was it but hers, and what was the harm? The pity of it was that girls like Julia did not know how to choose, and to keep bad fellows at a distance. . . . Charity slipped down from the bed, and stretched out her hands.

'Is it sewed? Let me try it on again.' She put the hat on, and smiled at her image. The thought of Julia had vanished . . .

The next morning she was up before dawn, and saw the yellow sunrise broaden behind the hills, and the silvery lustre preceding a hot day tremble across the sleeping fields.

Her plans had been made with great care. She had announced that she was going down to the Band of Hope picnic at Hepburn, and as no one else from North Dormer intended to venture so far it was not likely that her absence from the festivity would be reported. Besides, if it were she would not greatly care. She was determined to assert her independence, and if she stooped to fib about the Hepburn picnic it was chiefly from the secretive instinct that made her dread the profanation of her happiness. Whenever she was with Lucius Harney she would have liked some impenetrable mountain mist to hide her.

It was arranged that she should walk to a point of the Creston road where Harney was to pick her up and drive her across the hills to Hepburn in time for the nine-thirty train to Nettleton. Harney at first had been rather lukewarm about the trip. He declared himself ready to take her to Nettleton, but urged her not to go on the Fourth of July, on account of the crowds, the probable lateness of the trains, the difficulty of her getting back before night; but her evident disappointment caused him to give way, and even to affect a faint enthusiasm for the adventure. She understood why he was not more eager: he must have seen sights beside which even a Fourth of July at Nettleton would seem tame. But she had never seen anything; and a great longing possessed her to walk the streets of a big town on a holiday, clinging to his arm and jostled by idle crowds in their best clothes. The only cloud on the prospect was the fact that the shops would be closed; but she hoped he would take her back another day, when they were open.

She started out unnoticed in the early sunlight, slipping through the kitchen while Verena bent above the stove. To avoid attracting notice, she carried her new hat carefully wrapped up, and had thrown a long grey veil of Mrs Royall's over the new white muslin dress which Ally's clever fingers had made for her. All of the ten dollars Mr Royall had given her, and a part of her own savings as well, had been spent on renewing her wardrobe; and when Harney jumped out of the buggy to meet her she read her reward in his eyes.

The freckled boy who had brought her the note two weeks earlier was to wait with the buggy at Hepburn till their return. He perched at Charity's feet, his legs dangling between the wheels, and they could not say much because of his presence. But it did not greatly matter, for their past was now rich enough to have given them a private language; and with the long day stretching before them like the blue distance beyond the hills there was a delicate pleasure in postponement.

When Charity, in response to Harney's message, had gone to meet him at the Creston pool her heart had been so full of mortification and anger that his first words might easily have estranged her. But it happened that he had found the right word, which was one of simple friendship. His tone had instantly justified her, and put her guardian in the wrong. He had made no allusion to what had passed between Mr Royall and himself, but had simply let it appear that he had left because means of conveyance were hard to find at North Dormer, and because Creston River was a more convenient centre. He told her that he had hired by the week the buggy of the freckled boy's father, who served as livery-stable keeper to one or two melancholy summer boarding-houses on Creston Lake, and had discovered, within driving distance, a number of houses worthy of his pencil; and he said that he could not, while he was in the neighbourhood, give up the pleasure of seeing her as often as possible.

When they took leave of each other she promised to continue to be his guide; and during the fortnight which followed they roamed the hills in happy comradeship. In most of the village friendships between youths and maidens lack of conversation was made up for by tentative fondling; but Harney, except when he had tried to comfort her in her trouble on their way back from the Hyatts', had never put his arm about her, or sought to betray her into any sudden caress. It seemed to be enough for him to breathe her nearness like a flower's; and since his pleasure at being with her, and his sense of her youth and her grace, perpetually shone in his eyes and softened the inflections of his voice, his reserve did not suggest coldness, but the deference due to a girl of his own class.

The buggy was drawn by an old trotter who whirled them along so briskly that the pace created a little breeze; but when they reached Hepburn the full heat of the airless morning descended on them. At the railway station the platform was packed with a sweltering throng, and they took refuge in the waiting-room, where there was another throng, already dejected by the heat and the long waiting for retarded trains. Pale mothers were struggling with fretful babies, or trying to keep their older offspring from the fascination of the track; girls and their 'fellows' were giggling and shoving, and passing about candy in sticky bags, and older men, collarless and perspiring, were shifting heavy children from one arm to the other, and keeping a haggard eye on the scattered members of their families.

At last the train rumbled in, and engulfed the waiting multitude. Harney swept Charity up on to the first car and they captured a bench for two, and sat in happy isolation while the train swayed and roared along through rich fields and languid tree-clumps. The haze of the morning had become a sort of clear tremor over everything, like the colourless vibration about a flame; and the opulent landscape seemed to droop under it. But to Charity the heat was a stimulant: it enveloped the whole world in the same glow that burned at her heart. Now and then a lurch of the train flung her against Harney, and through her thin muslin she felt the touch of his sleeve. She steadied herself, their eyes met, and the flaming breath of the day seemed to enclose them.

The train roared into the Nettleton station, the descending mob caught them on its tide, and they were swept out into a vague dusty square thronged with seedy 'hacks' and long curtained omnibuses drawn by horses with tasselled fly-nets over their withers, who stood swinging their depressed heads drearily from side to side.

A mob of 'bus and hack drivers were shouting 'To the Eagle House', 'To the Washington House', 'This way to the Lake', 'Just starting for Greytop'; and through their yells came the popping of fire-crackers, the explosion of torpedoes, the banging of toy-guns, and the crash of a firemen's band trying to play the Merry Widow while they were being packed into a waggonette streaming with bunting.

The ramshackle wooden hotels about the square were all hung with flags and paper lanterns, and as Harney and Charity turned into the main street, with its brick and granite business blocks crowding out the old low-storied shops, and its towering poles strung with innumerable wires that seemed to tremble and buzz in the heat, they saw the double line of flags and lanterns tapering away gaily to the park at the other end of the perspective. The noise and colour of this holiday vision seemed to transform Nettleton into a metropolis. Charity could not believe that Springfield or even Boston had anything grander to show, and she wondered if, at this very moment, Annabel Balch, on the arm of as brilliant a young man, were threading her way through scenes as resplendent.

'Where shall we go first?' Harney asked; but as she turned her happy eyes on him he guessed the answer and said: 'We'll take a look round, shall we?'

The street swarmed with their fellow-travellers, with other excursionists arriving from other directions, with Nettleton's own population, and with the mill-hands trooping in from the factories on the Creston. The shops were closed, but one would scarcely have noticed it, so numerous were the glass doors swinging open on saloons, on restaurants, on drug-stores gushing from every soda-water tap, on fruit and confectionery shops stacked with strawberry-cake, cocoanut drops, trays of glistening molasses candy, boxes of caramels and chewing-gum, baskets of sodden strawberries, and dangling branches of bananas. Outside of some of the doors were trestles with banked-up oranges and apples, spotted pears and dusty rasp-berries; and the air reeked with the smell of fruit and stale coffee, beer and sarsaparilla and fried potatoes.

Even the shops that were closed offered, through wide expanses of plate-glass, hints of hidden riches. In some, waves of silk and ribbon broke over shores of imitation moss from which ravishing hats rose like tropical orchids. In others, the pink throats of gramophones opened their giant convolutions in a soundless chorus; or bicycles shining in neat ranks seemed to await the signal of an invisible starter; or tiers of fancy-goods in leatherette and paste and celluloid dangled their insidious graces; and, in one vast bay that seemed to project them into exciting contact with the public, wax ladies in daring dresses chatted elegantly, or, with gestures intimate yet blameless, pointed to their pink corsets and transparent hosiery.

Presently Harney found that his watch had stopped, and turned in at a small jeweller's shop which chanced to be still open. While the watch was being examined Charity leaned over the glass counter where, on a background of dark blue velvet, pins, rings and brooches glittered like the moon and stars. She had never seen jewellery so near by, and she longed to lift the glass lid and plunge her hand among the shining treasures. But already Harney's watch was repaired, and he laid his hand on her arm and drew her from her dream.

'Which do you like best?' he asked leaning over the counter at her side.

'I don't know. . . .' She pointed to a gold lily-of-the-valley with white flowers.

'Don't you think the blue pin's better?' he suggested, and immediately she saw that the lily of the valley was mere trumpery compared to the small round stone, blue as a mountain lake, with little sparks of light all round it. She coloured at her want of discrimination.

'It's so lovely I guess I was afraid to look at it,' she said.

He laughed, and they went out of the shop; but a few steps away he exclaimed: 'Oh, by Jove, I forgot something,' and turned back and left her in the crowd. She stood staring down a row of pink gramophone throats till he rejoined her and slipped his arm through hers.

'You mustn't be afraid of looking at the blue pin any longer, because it belongs to you,' he said; and she felt a little box being pressed into her hand. Her heart gave a leap of joy, but it reached her lips only in a shy stammer. She remembered other girls whom she had heard planning to extract presents from their fellows, and was seized with a sudden dread lest Harney should have imagined that she had leaned over the pretty things in the glass case in the hope of having one given to her. . . .

A little farther down the street they turned in at a glass doorway opening on a shining hall with a mahogany staircase, and brass cages in its corners. 'We must have something to eat,' Harney said; and the next moment Charity found herself in a dressing-room all looking-glass and lustrous surfaces, where a party of showy-looking girls were dabbing on powder and straightening immense plumed hats. When they had gone she took courage to bathe her hot face in one of the marble basins, and to straighten her own hat-brim, which the parasols of the crowd had indented. The dresses in the shops had so impressed her that she scarcely dared look at her reflection; but when she did so, the glow of her face under her cherry-coloured hat, and the curve of her young shoulders through the transparent muslin, restored her courage; and when she had taken the blue brooch from its box and pinned it on her bosom she walked toward the restaurant with her head high, as if she had always strolled through tessellated halls beside young men in flannels.

Her spirit sank a little at the sight of the slim-waisted waitresses in black, with bewitching mob-caps on their haughty heads, who were moving disdainfully between the tables. 'Not f'r another hour,' one of them dropped to Harney in passing; and he stood doubtfully glancing about him.

'Oh, well, we can't stay sweltering here,' he decided; 'let's try somewhere else –' and with a sense of relief Charity followed him from that scene of inhospitable splendour.

The 'somewhere else' turned out – after more hot tramping, and several failures – to be, of all things, a little open-air place in a back street that called itself a French restaurant, and consisted in two or three rickety tables under a scarlet-runner, between a patch of zinnias and petunias and a big elm bending over from the next yard. Here they lunched on queerly flavoured things, while Harney, leaning back in a crippled rocking-chair, smoked cigarettes between the courses and poured into Charity's glass a pale yellow wine which he said was the very same one drank in just such jolly places in France.

Charity did not think the wine as good as sarsaparilla, but she sipped a mouthful for the pleasure of doing what he did, and of fancying herself alone with him in foreign countries. The illusion was increased by their being served by a deep-bosomed woman with smooth hair and a pleasant laugh, who talked to Harney in unintelligible words, and seemed amazed and overjoyed at his answering her in kind. At the other tables other people sat, mill-hands probably, homely but pleasant looking, who spoke the same shrill jargon, and looked at Harney and Charity with friendly eyes; and between the table-legs a poodle with bald patches and pink eyes nosed about for scraps, and sat up on his hind legs absurdly.

Harney showed no inclination to move, for hot as their corner was, it was at least shaded and quiet; and, from the main thoroughfares came the clanging of trolleys, the incessant popping of torpedoes, the jingle of street-organs, the bawling of megaphone men and the loud murmur of increasing crowds.

He leaned back, smoking his cigar, patting the dog, and stirring the coffee that steamed in their chipped cups. 'It's the real thing, you know,' he explained; and Charity hastily revised her previous conception of the beverage.

They had made no plans for the rest of the day, and when Harney asked her what she wanted to do next she was too bewildered by rich possibilities to find an answer. Finally she confessed that she longed to go to the Lake, where she had not been taken on her former visit, and when he answered, 'Oh, there's time for that – it will be pleasanter later,' she suggested seeing some pictures like the ones Mr Miles had taken her to. She thought Harney looked a little disconcerted; but he passed his fine handkerchief over his warm brow, said gaily 'Come along, then,' and rose with a last pat for the pink-eyed dog.

Mr Miles's pictures had been shown in an austere Y.M.C.A. hall, with white walls and an organ; but Harney led Charity to a glittering place – everything she saw seemed to glitter – where they passed, between immense pictures of yellow-haired beauties stabbing villains in evening dress, into a velvet-curtained auditorium packed with spectators to the last limit of compression. After that, for a while, everything was merged in her brain in swimming circles of heat and blinding alternations of light and darkness. All the world has to show seemed to pass before her in a chaos of palms and minarets, charging cavalry regiments, roaring lions, comic policemen and scowling murderers; and the crowd around her, the hundreds of hot sallow candy-munching faces, young, old, middle-aged, but all kindled with the same contagious excitement, became part of the spectacle, and danced on the screen with the rest.

Presently the thought of the cool trolley-run to the Lake grew irresistible, and they struggled out of the theatre. As they stood on the pavement, Harney pale with the heat, and even Charity a little confused by it, a young man drove by in an electric run-about with a calico band bearing the words: 'Ten dollars to take you round the Lake'. Before Charity knew what was happening, Harney had waved a hand, and they were climbing in. 'Say, for twenny-five I'll run you out first to see

the ball-game and back,' the driver proposed with an insinuat-
ing grin; but Charity said quickly: 'Oh, I'd rather go rowing
on the Lake.' The street was so thronged that progress was
slow; but the glory of sitting in the little carriage while it
wriggled its way between laden omnibuses and trolleys made
the moments seem too short. 'Next turn is Lake Avenue,' the
young man called out over his shoulder; and as they paused in
the wake of a big omnibus groaning with Knights of Pythias
in cocked hats and swords, Charity looked up and saw on the
corner a brick house with a conspicuous black and gold sign
across its front. 'Dr Merkle; Private Consultations at all hours.
Lady Attendants,' she read; and suddenly she remembered
Ally Hawes's words: 'The house was at the corner of Wing
Street and Lake Avenue . . . there's a big black sign across the
front. . . .' Through all the heat and the rapture a shiver of cold
ran over her.

X

The Lake at last – a sheet of shining metal brooded over by drooping trees. Charity and Harney had secured a boat and, getting away from the wharves and the refreshment-booths, they drifted idly along, hugging the shadow of the shore. Where the sun struck the water its shafts flamed back blindingly at the heat-veiled sky; and the least shade was black by contrast. The Lake was so smooth that the reflection of the trees on its edge seemed enamelled on a solid surface; but gradually, as the sun declined, the water grew transparent, and Charity, leaning over, plunged her fascinated gaze into depths so clear that she saw the inverted tree-tops interwoven with the green growths of the bottom.

They rounded a point at the farther end of the Lake, and entering an inlet pushed their bow against a protruding tree-trunk. A green veil of willows overhung them. Beyond the trees, wheat-fields sparkled in the sun; and all along the horizon the clear hills throbbed with light. Charity leaned back in the stern, and Harney unshipped the oars and lay in the bottom of the boat without speaking.

Ever since their meeting at the Creston pool he had been subject to these brooding silences, which were as different as possible from the pauses when they ceased to speak because words were needless. At such times his face wore the expression she had seen on it when she had looked in at him from the darkness, and again there came over her a sense of the mysterious distance between them; but usually his fits of abstraction were followed by bursts of gaiety that chased away the shadow before it chilled her.

She was still thinking of the ten dollars he had handed to

the driver of the run-about. It had given them twenty minutes of pleasure, and it seemed unimaginable that anyone should be able to buy amusement at that rate. With ten dollars he might have bought her an engagement ring; she knew that Mrs Tom Fry's, which came from Springfield, and had a diamond in it, had cost only eight seventy-five. But she did not know why the thought had occurred to her. Harney would never buy her an engagement ring: they were friends and comrades, but no more. He had been perfectly fair to her: he had never said a word to mislead her. She wondered what the girl was like whose hand was waiting for his ring. . . .

Boats were beginning to thicken on the Lake and the clang of incessantly arriving trolleys announced the return of the crowds from the ball-field. The shadows lengthened across the pearl-grey water and two white clouds near the sun were turning golden. On the opposite shore men were hammering hastily at a wooden scaffolding in a field. Charity asked what it was for.

'Why, the fireworks. I suppose there'll be a big show.' Harney looked at her and a smile crept into his moody eyes. 'Have you never seen any good fireworks?'

'Miss Hatchard always sends up lovely rockets on the Fourth,' she answered doubtfully.

'Oh —' his contempt was unbounded. 'I mean a big performance like this: illuminated boats, and all the rest.'

She flushed at the picture. 'Do they send them up from the Lake, too?'

'Rather. Didn't you notice that big raft we passed? It's wonderful to see the rockets completing their orbits down under one's feet.' She said nothing, and he put the oars into the rowlocks. 'If we stay we'd better go and pick up something to eat.'

'But how can we get back afterward?' she ventured, feeling it would break her heart if she missed it.

He consulted a time-table, found a ten o'clock train and reassured her. 'The moon rises so late that it will be dark by eight, and we'll have over an hour of it.'

Twilight fell, and lights began to show along the shore. The trolleys roaring out from Nettleton became great luminous serpents coiling in and out among the trees. The wooden eating-houses at the Lake's edge danced with lanterns, and the dusk echoed with laughter and shouts and the clumsy splashing of oars.

Harney and Charity had found a table in the corner of a balcony built over the Lake, and were patiently awaiting an unattainable chowder. Close under them the water lapped the piles, agitated by the evolutions of a little white steamboat trellised with coloured globes which was to run passengers up and down the Lake. It was already black with them as it sheered off on its first trip.

Suddenly Charity heard a woman's laugh behind her. The sound was familiar, and she turned to look. A band of showily dressed girls and dapper young men wearing badges of secret societies, with new straw hats tilted far back on their square-clipped hair, had invaded the balcony and were loudly clamouring for a table. The girl in the lead was the one who had laughed. She wore a large hat with a long white feather, and from under its brim her painted eyes looked at Charity with amused recognition.

'Say! if this ain't like Old Home Week,' she remarked to the girl at her elbow; and giggles and glances passed between them. Charity knew at once that the girl with the white feather was Julia Hawes. She had lost her freshness, and the paint under her eyes made her face seem thinner; but her lips had the same lovely curve, and the same cold mocking smile, as if there were some secret absurdity in the person she was looking at, and she had instantly detected it.

Charity flushed to the forehead and looked away. She felt herself humiliated by Julia's sneer, and vexed that the mockery of such a creature should affect her. She trembled lest Harney should notice that the noisy troop had recognized her; but they found no table free, and passed on tumultuously.

Presently there was a soft rush through the air and a shower of silver fell from the blue evening sky. In another direction, pale Roman candles shot up singly through the trees, and a fire-haired rocket swept the horizon like a portent. Between these intermittent flashes the velvet curtains of the darkness were descending, and in the intervals of eclipse the voices of the crowds seemed to sink to smothered murmurs.

Charity and Harney, dispossessed by newcomers, were at length obliged to give up their table and struggle through the throng about the boat-landings. For a while there seemed no escape from the tide of late arrivals; but finally Harney secured the last two places on the stand from which the more privileged were to see the fireworks. The seats were at the end of a row, one above the other. Charity had taken off her hat to have an uninterrupted view; and whenever she leaned back to follow the curve of some dishevelled rocket she could feel Harney's knees against her head.

After a while the scattered fireworks ceased. A longer interval of darkness followed, and then the whole night broke into flower. From every point of the horizon, gold and silver arches sprang up and crossed each other, sky-orchards broke into blossom, shed their flaming petals and hung their branches with golden fruit; and all the while the air was filled with a soft supernatural hum, as though great birds were building their nests in those invisible tree-tops.

Now and then there came a lull, and a wave of moonlight swept the Lake. In a flash it revealed hundreds of boats, steel-dark against lustrous ripples; then it withdrew as if with a furling of vast translucent wings. Charity's heart throbbed with delight. It was as if all the latent beauty of things had been unveiled to her. She could not imagine that the world held anything more wonderful; but near her she heard someone say, 'You wait till you see the set piece,' and instantly her hopes took a fresh flight. At last, just as it was beginning to seem as though the whole arch of the sky were one great lid pressed against her dazzled eye-balls, and striking out of them continuous jets of jewelled light, the velvet darkness settled down again, and a murmur of expectation ran through the crowd.

'Now – now!' the same voice said excitedly; and Charity, grasping the hat on her knee, crushed it tight in the effort to restrain her rapture.

For a moment the night seemed to grow more impenetrably black; then a great picture stood out against it like a constellation. It was surmounted by a golden scroll bearing the inscription, 'Washington crossing the Delaware,' and across a flood of motionless golden ripples the National Hero passed, erect, solemn and gigantic, standing with folded arms in the stern of a slowly moving golden boat.

A long 'Oh-h-h' burst from the spectators: the stand creaked and shook with their blissful trepidations. 'Oh-h-h,' Charity gasped: she had forgotten where she was, had at last forgotten even Harney's nearness. She seemed to have been caught up into the stars. . . .

The picture vanished and darkness came down. In the obscurity she felt her head clasped by two hands: her face was drawn backward, and Harney's lips were pressed on hers. With sudden vehemence he wound his arms about her, holding her head against his breast while she gave him back his kisses. An unknown Harney had revealed himself, a Harney who dominated her and yet over whom she felt herself possessed of a new mysterious power.

But the crowd was beginning to move, and he had to release her. 'Come,' he said in a confused voice. He scrambled over the side of the stand, and holding up his arm caught her as she sprang to the ground. He passed his arm about her waist, steadying her against the descending rush of people; and she clung to him, speechless, exultant, as if all the crowding and confusion about them were a mere vain stirring of the air.

'Come,' he repeated, 'we must try to make the trolley.' He drew her along, and she followed, still in her dream. They walked as if they were one, so isolated in ecstasy that the people jostling them on every side seemed impalpable. But when they reached the terminus the illuminated trolley was already clanging on its way, its platforms black with passengers. The cars waiting behind it were as thickly packed; and the throng about the terminus was so dense that it seemed hopeless to struggle for a place.

'Last trip up the Lake,' a megaphone bellowed from the wharf, and the lights of the little steamboat came dancing out of the darkness.

'No use waiting here; shall we run up the Lake?' Harney suggested.

They pushed their way back to the edge of the water just as the gang-plank was lowered from the white side of the boat. The electric light at the end of the wharf flashed full on the descendlng passengers, and among them Charity caught sight of Julia Hawes, her white feather askew, and the face under it flushed with coarse laughter. As she stepped from the gang-plank she stopped short, her dark-ringed eyes darting malice.

'Hullo, Charity Royall!' she called out; and then, looking back over her shoulder: 'Didn't I tell you it was a family party? Here's grandpa's little darling come to take him home!'

A snigger ran through the group; and then, towering above them, and steadying himself by the hand-rail in a desperate effort at erectness, Mr Royall stepped stiffly ashore. Like the young men of the party, he wore a secret society emblem in the buttonhole of his black frock-coat. His head was covered by a new Panama hat, and his narrow black tie, half undone, dangled down on his rumpled shirt-front. His face, a livid brown, with red blotches of anger and lips sunken in like an old man's, was a lamentable ruin in the searching glare.

He was just behind Julia Hawes, and had one hand on her arm; but as he left the gang-plank he freed himself, and moved a step or two away from his companions. He had seen Charity at once, and his glance passed slowly from her to Harney, whose arm was still about her. He stood staring at them, and trying to master the senile quiver of his lips; then he drew himself up with the tremulous majesty of drunkenness, and stretched out his arm.

'You whore – you damn – bare-headed whore, you!' he enunciated slowly.

There was a scream of tipsy laughter from the party, and

Charity involuntarily put her hands to her head. She remembered that her hat had fallen from her lap when she jumped
up to leave the stand; and suddenly she had a vision of herself,
hatless, dishevelled, with a man's arm about her, confronting
that drunken crew, headed by her guardian's pitiable figure.
The picture filled her with shame. She had known since childhood about Mr Royall's 'habits': had seen him, as she went
up to bed, sitting morosely in his office, a bottle at his elbow;
or coming home, heavy and quarrelsome, from his business
expeditions to Hepburn or Springfield; but the idea of his
associating himself publicly with a band of disreputable girls
and bar-room loafers was new and dreadful to her.

'Oh —' she said in a gasp of misery; and releasing herself
from Harney's arm she went straight up to Mr Royall.

'You come home with me — you come right home with
me,' she said in a low stern voice, as if she had not heard his
apostrophe; and one of the girls called out: 'Say, how many
fellers does she want?'

There was another laugh, followed by a pause of curiosity,
during which Mr Royall continued to glare at Charity. At
length his twitching lips parted. 'I said, "You — damn —
whore!" he repeated with precision, steadying himself on
Julia's shoulder.

Laughs and jeers were beginning to spring up from the circle
of people beyond their group; and a voice called out from
the gangway: 'Now, then, step lively there — all *aboard!*' The
pressure of approaching and departing passengers forced the
actors in the rapid scene apart, and pushed them back into
the throng. Charity found herself clinging to Harney's arm
and sobbing desperately. Mr Royall had disappeared, and in
the distance she heard the receding sound of Julia's laugh.

The boat, laden to the taffrail, was puffing away on her last
trip.

XI

At two o'clock in the morning the freckled boy from Creston stopped his sleepy horse at the door of the red house, and Charity got out. Harney had taken leave of her at Creston River, charging the boy to drive her home. Her mind was still in a fog of misery, and she did not remember very clearly what had happened, or what they had said to each other, during the interminable interval since their departure from Nettleton; but the secretive instinct of the animal in pain was so strong in her that she had a sense of relief when Harney got out and she drove on alone.

The full moon hung over North Dormer, whitening the mist that filled the hollows between the hills and floated transparently above the fields. Charity stood a moment at the gate, looking out into the waning night. She watched the boy drive off, his horse's head wagging heavily to and fro; then she went around to the kitchen door and felt under the mat for the key. She found it, unlocked the door and went in. The kitchen was dark, but she discovered a box of matches, lit a candle and went upstairs. Mr Royall's door, opposite hers, stood open on his unlit room; evidently he had not come back. She went into her room, bolted her door and began slowly to untie the ribbon about her waist, and to take off her dress. Under the bed she saw the paper bag in which she had hidden her new hat from inquisitive eyes....

She lay for a long time sleepless on her bed, staring up at the moonlight on the low ceiling; dawn was in the sky when she fell asleep, and when she woke the sun was on her face.

She dressed and went down to the kitchen. Verena was there

alone: she glanced at Charity tranquilly, with her old deaf-looking eyes. There was no sign of Mr Royall about the house and the hours passed without his reappearing. Charity had gone up to her room, and sat there listlessly, her hands on her lap. Puffs of sultry air fanned her dimity window curtains and flies buzzed stiflingly against the bluish panes.

At one o'clock Verena hobbled up to see if she were not coming down to dinner; but she shook her head, and the old woman went away, saying: 'I'll cover up, then.'

The sun turned and left her room, and Charity seated herself in the window, gazing down the village street through the half-opened shutters. Not a thought was in her mind; it was just a dark whirlpool of crowding images; and she watched the people passing along the street, Dan Targart's team hauling a load of pine-trunks down to Hepburn, the sexton's old white horse grazing on the bank across the way, as if she looked at these familiar sights from the other side of the grave.

She was roused from her apathy by seeing Ally Hawes come out of the Frys' gate and walk slowly toward the red house with her uneven limping step. At the sight Charity recovered her severed contact with reality. She divined that Ally was coming to hear about her day: no one else was in the secret of the trip to Nettleton, and it had flattered Ally profoundly to be allowed to know of it.

At the thought of having to see her, of having to meet her eyes and answer or evade her questions, the whole horror of the previous night's adventure rushed back upon Charity. What had been a feverish nightmare became a cold and un-escapable fact. Poor Ally, at that moment, represented North Dormer, with all its mean curiosities, its furtive malice, its sham unconsciousness of evil. Charity knew that, although all relations with Julia were supposed to be severed, the tender-hearted Ally still secretly communicated with her; and no doubt Julia would exult in the chance of retailing the scandal of the wharf. The story, exaggerated and distorted, was probably already on its way to North Dormer.

Ally's dragging pace had not carried her far from the Frys'

gate when she was stopped by old Mrs Sollas, who was a great talker, and spoke very slowly because she had never been able to get used to her new teeth from Hepburn. Still, even this respite would not last long; in another ten minutes Ally would be at the door, and Charity would hear her greeting Verena in the kitchen, and then calling up from the foot of the stairs.

Suddenly it became clear that flight, and instant flight, was the only thing conceivable. The longing to escape, to get away from familiar faces, from places where she was known, had always been strong in her in moments of distress. She had a childish belief in the miraculous power of strange scenes and new faces to transform her life and wipe out bitter memories. But such impulses were mere fleeting whims compared to the cold resolve which now possessed her. She felt she could not remain an hour longer under the roof of the man who had publicly dishonoured her, and face to face with the people who would presently be gloating over all the details of her humiliation.

Her passing pity for Mr Royall had been swallowed up in loathing: everything in her recoiled from the disgraceful spectacle of the drunken old man apostrophizing her in the presence of a band of loafers and street-walkers. Suddenly, vividly, she relived again the horrible moment when he had tried to force himself into her room, and what she had before supposed to be a mad aberration now appeared to her as a vulgar incident in a debauched and degraded life.

While these thoughts were hurrying through her she had dragged out her old canvas school-bag, and was thrusting into it a few articles of clothing and the little packet of letters she had received from Harney. From under her pincushion she took the library key, and laid it in full view; then she felt at the back of a drawer for the blue brooch that Harney had given her. She would not have dared to wear it openly at North Dormer, but now she fastened it on her bosom as if it were a talisman to protect her in her flight. These preparations had taken but a few minutes, and when they were finished Ally Hawes was still at the Frys' corner talking to old Mrs Sollas. . . .

* * *

She had said to herself, as she always said in moments of revolt: 'I'll go to the Mountain – I'll go back to my own folks.' She had never really meant it before; but now, as she considered her case, no other course seemed open. She had never learned any trade that would have given her independence in a strange place, and she knew no one in the big towns of the valley, where she might have hoped to find employment. Miss Hatchard was still away; but even had she been at North Dormer she was the last person to whom Charity would have turned, since one of the motives urging her to flight was the wish not to see Lucius Harney. Travelling back from Nettleton, in the crowded brightly-lit train, all exchange of confidence between them had been impossible; but during their drive from Hepburn to Creston River she had gathered from Harney's snatches of consolatory talk – again hampered by the freckled boy's presence – that he intended to see her the next day. At the moment she had found a vague comfort in the assurance; but in the desolate lucidity of the hours that followed she had come to see the impossibility of meeting him again. Her dream of comradeship was over; and the scene on the wharf – vile and disgraceful as it had been – had after all shed the light of truth on her minute of madness. It was as if her guardian's words had stripped her bare in the face of the grinning crowd and proclaimed to the world the secret admonitions of her conscience.

She did not think these things out clearly; she simply followed the blind propulsion of her wretchedness. She did not want, ever again, to see anyone she had known; above all, she did not want to see Harney. . . .

She climbed the hill-path behind the house and struck through the woods by a short-cut leading to the Creston road. A lead-coloured sky hung heavily over the fields, and in the forest the motionless air was stifling; but she pushed on, impatient to reach the road which was the shortest way to the Mountain.

To do so, she had to follow the Creston road for a mile or two, and go within half a mile of the village; and she walked quickly, fearing to meet Harney. But there was no sign of him, and she had almost reached the branch road when she saw the flanks of a large white tent projecting through the trees by the roadside. She supposed that it sheltered a travelling circus which had come there for the Fourth; but as she drew nearer she saw, over the folded-back flap, a large sign bearing the inscription, 'Gospel Tent'. The interior seemed to be empty; but a young man in a black alpaca coat, his lank hair parted over a round white face, stepped from under the flap and advanced toward her with a smile.

'Sister, your Saviour knows everything. Won't you come in and lay your guilt before Him?' he asked insinuatingly, putting his hand on her arm.

Charity started back and flushed. For a moment she thought the evangelist must have heard a report of the scene at Nettle-ton; then she saw the absurdity of the supposition.

'I on'y wish't I had any to lay!' she retorted, with one of her fierce flashes of self-derision; and the young man murmured, aghast: 'Oh, Sister, don't speak blasphemy. . . .'

But she had jerked her arm out of his hold, and was run-ning up the branch road, trembling with the fear of meeting a familiar face. Presently she was out of sight of the village, and climbing into the heart of the forest. She could not hope to do the fifteen miles to the Mountain that afternoon; but she knew of a place half-way to Hamblin where she could sleep, and where no one would think of looking for her. It was a little deserted house on a slope in one of the lonely rifts of the hills. She had seen it once, years before, when she had gone on a nutting expedition to the grove of walnuts below it. The party had taken refuge in the house from a sudden mountain storm, and she remembered that Ben Sollas, who liked fright-ening girls, had told them that it was said to be haunted.

She was growing faint and tired, for she had eaten nothing since morning, and was not used to walking so far. Her head felt light and she sat down for a moment by the roadside. As she sat there she heard the click of a bicycle-bell, and started up to plunge back into the forest; but before she could move

the bicycle had swept around the curve of the road, and
Harney, jumping off, was approaching her with outstretched
arms.

'Charity! What on earth are you doing here?'

She stared as if he were a vision, so startled by the unexpec-
tedness of his being there that no words came to her.

'Where were you going? Had you forgotten that I was
coming?' he continued, trying to draw her to him; but she
shrank from his embrace.

'I was going away – I don't want to see you – I want you
should leave me alone,' she broke out wildly.

He looked at her and his face grew grave, as though the
shadow of a premonition brushed it.

'Going away – from me, Charity?'

'From everybody. I want you should leave me.'

He stood glancing doubtfully up and down the lonely forest
road that stretched away into sun-flecked distances.

'Where were you going?'

'Home.'

'Home – this way?'

She threw her head back defiantly. 'To my home – up
yonder: to the Mountain.'

As she spoke she became aware of a change in his face. He
was no longer listening to her, he was only looking at her, with
the passionate absorbed expression she had seen in his eyes after
they had kissed on the stand at Nettleton. He was the new
Harney again, the Harney abruptly revealed in that embrace,
who seemed so penetrated with the joy of her presence that he
was utterly careless of what she was thinking or feeling.

He caught her hands with a laugh. 'How do you suppose
I found you?' he said gaily. He drew out the little packet of his
letters and flourished them before her bewildered eyes.

'You dropped them, you imprudent young person – dropped them in the middle of the road, not far from here; and the
young man who is running the Gospel tent picked them up
just as I was riding by.' He drew back, holding her at arm's

length, and scrutinizing her troubled face with the minute searching gaze of his short-sighted eyes.

'Did you really think you could run away from me? You see you weren't meant to,' he said; and before she could answer he had kissed her again, not vehemently, but tenderly, almost fraternally, as if he had guessed her confused pain, and wanted her to know he understood it. He wound his fingers through hers.

'Come – let's walk a little. I want to talk to you. There's so much to say.'

He spoke with a boy's gaiety, carelessly and confidently, as if nothing had happened that could shame or embarrass them; and for a moment, in the sudden relief of her release from lonely pain, she felt herself yielding to his mood. But he had turned, and was drawing her back along the road by which she had come. She stiffened herself and stopped short.

'I won't go back,' she said.

They looked at each other a moment in silence; then he answered gently: 'Very well: let's go the other way, then.'

She remained motionless, gazing silently at the ground, and he went on: 'Isn't there a house up here somewhere – a little abandoned house – you meant to show me some day?' Still she made no answer, and he continued, in the same tone of tender reassurance: 'Let us go there now and sit down and talk quietly.' He took one of the hands that hung by her side and pressed his lips to the palm. 'Do you suppose I'm going to let you send me away? Do you suppose I don't understand?'

The little old house – its wooden walls sun-bleached to a ghostly grey – stood in an orchard above the road. The garden palings had fallen, but the broken gate dangled between its posts, and the path to the house was marked by rosebushes run wild and hanging their small pale blossoms above the crowding grasses. Slender pilasters and an intricate fanlight framed the opening where the door had hung; and the door itself lay rotting in the grass, with an old apple-tree fallen across it.

Inside, also, wind and weather had blanched everything to the same wan silvery tint: the house was as dry and pure as the interior of a long-empty shell. But it must have been exceptionally well built, for the little rooms had kept something of their human aspect: the wooden mantels with their neat classic ornaments were in place, and the corners of one ceiling retained a light film of plaster tracery.

Harney had found an old bench at the back door and dragged it into the house. Charity sat on it, leaning her head against the wall in a state of drowsy lassitude. He had guessed that she was hungry and thirsty, and had brought her some tablets of chocolate from his bicycle-bag, and filled his drinking-cup from a spring in the orchard; and now he sat at her feet, smoking a cigarette, and looking up at her without speaking. Outside, the afternoon shadows were lengthening across the grass, and through the empty window-frame that faced her she saw the Mountain thrusting its dark mass against a sultry sunset. It was time to go.

She stood up, and he sprang to his feet also, and passed his arm through hers with an air of authority. 'Now, Charity, you're coming back with me.'

She looked at him and shook her head. 'I ain't ever going back. You don't know.'

'What don't I know?' She was silent, and he continued: 'What happened on the wharf was horrible – it's natural you should feel as you do. But it doesn't make any real difference: you can't be hurt by such things. You must try to forget. And you must try to understand that men . . . men sometimes . . .'

'I know about men. That's why.'

He coloured a little at the retort, as though it had touched him in a way she did not suspect.

'Well, then . . . you must know one has to make allowances. . . . He'd been drinking. . . .'

'I know all that, too. I've seen him so before. But he wouldn't have dared speak to me that way if he hadn't . . .'

'Hadn't what? What do you mean?'

'Hadn't wanted me to be like those other girls. . . .' She

lowered her voice and looked away from him. 'So's 't he wouldn't have to go out. . . .'

Harney stared at her. For a moment he did not seem to seize her meaning; then his face grew dark. 'The damned hound! The villainous low hound!' His wrath blazed up, crimsoning him to the temples. 'I never dreamed – good God, it's too vile,' he broke off, as if his thoughts recoiled from the discovery.

'I won't never go back there,' she repeated doggedly.

'No —' he assented.

There was a long interval of silence, during which she imagined that he was searching her face for more light on what she had revealed to him; and a flush of shame swept over her.

'I know the way you must feel about me,' she broke out, '. . . telling you such things. . . .'

But once more, as she spoke, she became aware that he was no longer listening. He came close and caught her to him as if he were snatching her from some imminent peril: his impetuous eyes were in hers, and she could feel the hard beat of his heart as he held her against it.

'Kiss me again – like last night,' he said, pushing her hair back as if to draw her whole face up into his kiss.

XII

One afternoon toward the end of August a group of girls sat in a room at Miss Hatchard's in a gay confusion of flags, turkey-red, blue and white paper muslin, harvest sheaves and illuminated scrolls.

North Dormer was preparing for its Old Home Week. That form of sentimental decentralization was still in its early stages, and, precedents being few, and the desire to set an example contagious, the matter had become a subject of prolonged and passionate discussion under Miss Hatchard's roof. The incentive to the celebration had come rather from those who had left North Dormer than from those who had been obliged to stay there, and there was some difficulty in rousing the village to the proper state of enthusiasm. But Miss Hatchard's pale prim drawing-room was the centre of constant comings and goings from Hepburn, Nettleton, Springfield and even more distant cities; and whenever a visitor arrived he was led across the hall, and treated to a glimpse of the group of girls deep in their pretty preparations.

'All the old names . . . all the old names. . . .' Miss Hatchard would be heard, tapping across the hall on her crutches. 'Targatt . . . Sollas . . . Fry: this is Miss Orma Fry sewing the stars on the drapery for the organ-loft. Don't move, girls . . . and this is Miss Ally Hawes, our cleverest needle-woman . . . and Miss Charity Royall making our garlands of evergreen. . . . I like the idea of its all being home-made, don't you? We haven't had to call in any foreign talent: my young cousin Lucius Harney, the architect – you know he's up here preparing a book on Colonial houses – he's taken the whole thing in hand so cleverly; but you must come and see his sketch for the stage we're going to put up in the Town Hall.'

One of the first results of the Old Home Week agitation had, in fact, been the reappearance of Lucius Harney in the village street. He had been vaguely spoken of as being not far off, but for some weeks past no one had seen him at North Dormer, and there was a recent report of his having left Creston River, where he was said to have been staying, and gone away from the neighbourhood for good. Soon after Miss Hatchard's return, however, he came back to his old quarters in her house, and began to take a leading part in the planning of the festivities. He threw himself into the idea with extraordinary good-humour, and was so prodigal of sketches, and so inexhaustible in devices, that he gave an immediate impetus to the rather languid movement, and infected the whole village with his enthusiasm.

'Lucius has such a feeling for the past that he has roused us all to a sense of our privileges,' Miss Hatchard would say, lingering on the last word, which was a favourite one. And before leading her visitor back to the drawing-room she would repeat, for the hundredth time, that she supposed he thought it very bold of little North Dormer to start up and have a Home Week of its own, when so many bigger places hadn't thought of it yet; but that, after all, Associations counted more than the size of the population, didn't they? And of course North Dormer was so full of Associations... historic, literary (here a filial sigh for Honorius) and ecclesiastical... he knew about the old pewter communion service imported from England in 1769, she supposed? And it was so important, in a wealthy materialistic age, to set the example of reverting to the old ideals, the family and the homestead, and so on. This peroration usually carried her half-way back across the hall, leaving the girls to return to their interrupted activities.

The day on which Charity Royall was weaving hemlock garlands for the procession was the last before the celebration. When Miss Hatchard called upon the North Dormer maidenhood to collaborate in the festal preparations Charity had at first held aloof, but it had been made clear to her that her non-appearance might excite conjecture, and, reluctantly, she had joined the other workers. The girls, at first shy and embarrassed, and puzzled as to the exact nature of the pro-jected commemoration, had soon become interested in the amusing details of their task, and excited by the notice they received. They would not for the world have missed their afternoons at Miss Hatchard's, and, while they cut out and sewed and draped and pasted, their tongues kept up such an accompaniment to the sewing-machine that Charity's silence sheltered itself unperceived under their chatter.

In spirit she was still almost unconscious of the pleasant stir about her. Since her return to the red house, on the evening of the day when Harney had overtaken her on her way to the Mountain, she had lived at North Dormer as if she were suspended in the void. She had come back there because Harney, after appearing to agree to the impossibility of her doing so, had ended by persuading her that any other course would be madness. She had nothing further to fear from Mr Royall. Of this she had declared herself sure, though she had failed to add, in his exoneration, that he had twice offered to make her his wife. Her hatred of him made it impossible, at the moment, for her to say anything that might partly excuse him in Harney's eyes.

Harney, however, once satisfied of her security, had found plenty of reasons for urging her to return. The first, and the most unanswerable, was that she had nowhere else to go. But the one on which he laid the greatest stress was that flight would be equivalent to avowal. If – as was almost inevitable – rumours of the scandalous scene at Nettleton should reach North Dormer, how else would her disappearance be inter-preted? Her guardian had publicly taken away her character, and she immediately vanished from his house. Seekers after motives could hardly fail to draw an unkind conclusion. But if she came back at once, and was seen leading her usual life, the incident was reduced to its true proportions, as the outbreak of a drunken old man furious at being surprised in disreputable company. People would say that Mr Royall had insulted his ward to justify himself, and the sordid tale would fall into its place in the chronicle of his obscure debaucheries.

Charity saw the force of the argument; but if she acquiesced it was not so much because of that as because it was Harney's wish. Since that evening in the deserted house she could imagine no reason for doing or not doing anything except the fact that Harney wished or did not wish it. All her tossing contradictory impulses were merged in a fatalistic acceptance of his will. It was not that she felt in him any ascendency of character – there were moments already when she knew she was the stronger – but that all the rest of life had become a mere cloudy rim about the central glory of their passion. Whenever she stopped thinking about that for a moment she felt as she sometimes did after lying on the grass and staring up too long at the sky; her eyes were so full of light that everything about her was a blur.

Each time that Miss Hatchard, in the course of her period-ical incursions into the work-room, dropped an allusion to her young cousin, the architect, the effect was the same on Charity. The hemlock garland she was weaving fell to her knees and she sat in a kind of trance. It was so manifestly absurd that Miss Hatchard should talk of Harney in that familiar possessive way, as if she had any claim on him, or knew anything about him. She, Charity Royall, was the only being on earth who really knew him, knew him from the soles of his feet to the rumpled crest of his hair, knew the shifting lights in his eyes, and the inflexions of his voice, and the things he liked and disliked, and everything there was to know about him, as minutely and yet unconsciously as a child knows the walls of the room it wakes up in every morning. It was this fact, which nobody about her guessed, or would have understood, that made her life something apart and inviolable, as if nothing had any power to hurt or disturb her as long as her secret was safe.

The room in which the girls sat was the one which had been Harney's bedroom. He had been sent upstairs, to make room for the Home Week workers; but the furniture had not been moved, and as Charity sat there she had perpetually before her the vision she had looked in on from the midnight garden. The table at which Harney had sat was the one about which the girls were gathered; and her own seat was near the bed on which she had seen him lying. Sometimes, when the others were not looking, she bent over as if to pick up something, and laid her cheek for a moment against the pillow.

Toward sunset the girls disbanded. Their work was done, and the next morning at daylight the draperies and garlands were to be nailed up, and the illuminated scrolls put in place in the Town Hall. The first guests were to drive over from Hepburn in time for the midday banquet under a tent in Miss Hatchard's field; and after that the ceremonies were to begin. Miss Hatchard, pale with fatigue and excitement, thanked her young assistants, and stood in the porch, leaning on her crutches and waving a farewell as she watched them troop away down the street.

Charity had slipped off among the first; but at the gate she heard Ally Hawes calling after her, and reluctantly turned.

'Will you come over now and try on your dress?' Ally asked, looking at her with wistful admiration. 'I want to be sure the sleeves don't ruck up the same as they did yesterday.'

Charity gazed at her with dazzled eyes. 'Oh, it's lovely,' she said, and hastened away without listening to Ally's protest. She wanted her dress to be as pretty as the other girls' – wanted it, in fact, to outshine the rest, since she was to take part in the 'exercises' – but she had no time just then to fix her mind on such matters. . . .

She sped up the street to the library, of which she had the key about her neck. From the passage at the back she dragged forth a bicycle, and guided it to the edge of the street. She looked about to see if any of the girls were approaching; but they had drifted away together toward the Town Hall, and she sprang into the saddle and turned toward the Creston road. There was an almost continual descent to Creston, and with her feet against the pedals she floated through the still evening air like one of the hawks she had often watched slanting downward on motionless wings. Twenty minutes from the time when she had left Miss Hatchard's door she was turning up the wood-road on which Harney had overtaken her on the day of her flight; and a few minutes afterward she had jumped from her bicycle at the gate of the deserted house.

In the gold-powdered sunset it looked more than ever like some frail shell dried and washed by many seasons; but at the back, whither Charity advanced, drawing her bicycle after her, there were signs of recent habitation. A rough door made of boards hung in the kitchen doorway, and pushing it open she entered a room furnished in primitive camping fashion. In the window was a table, also made of boards, with an earthenware jar holding a big bunch of wild asters. Two canvas chairs stood near by, and in one corner was a mattress with a Mexican blanket over it.

The room was empty, and leaning her bicycle against the house Charity clambered up the slope and sat down on a rock under an old apple-tree. The air was perfectly still, and from where she sat she would be able to hear the tinkle of a bicycle-bell a long way down the road. . . .

She was always glad when she got to the little house before Harney. She liked to have time to take in every detail of its secret sweetness – the shadows of the apple-trees swaying on the grass, the old walnuts rounding their domes below the road, the meadows sloping westward in the afternoon light – before his first kiss blotted it all out. Everything unrelated to the hours spent in that tranquil place was as faint as the remembrance of a dream. The only reality was the wondrous unfolding of her new self, the reaching out to the light of all her contracted tendrils. She had lived all her life among people whose sensibilities seemed to have withered for lack of use; and more wonderful, at first, than Harney's endearments were the words that were a part of them. She had always thought of love as something confused and furtive, and he made it as bright and open as the summer air.

On the morrow of the day when she had shown him the way to the deserted house he had packed up and left Creston River for Boston; but at the first station he had jumped off the train with a hand-bag and scrambled up into the hills. For two golden rainless August weeks he had camped in the house, getting eggs and milk from the solitary farm in the valley, where no one knew him, and doing his cooking over a spirit-lamp. He got up every day with the sun, took a plunge in a brown pool he knew of, and spent long hours lying in the scented hemlock-woods above the house, or wandering along the yoke of the Eagle Ridge, far above the misty blue valleys that swept away east and west between the endless hills. And in the afternoon Charity came to him.

With part of what was left of her savings she had hired a bicycle for a month, and every day after dinner, as soon as her guardian started to his office, she hurried to the library, got out her bicycle, and flew down the Creston road. She knew that Mr Royall, like everyone else in North Dormer, was per-fectly aware of her acquisition: possibly he, as well as the rest of the village, knew what use she made of it. She did not care: she felt him to be so powerless that if he had questioned her she would probably have told him the truth. But they had never spoken to each other since the night on the wharf at Nettleton. He had returned to North Dormer only on the third day after that encounter, arriving just as Charity and Verena were sitting down to supper. He had drawn up his chair, taken his napkin from the side-board drawer, pulled it out of its ring, and seated himself as unconcernedly as if he had come in from his usual afternoon session at Carrick Fry's; and the long habit of the household made it seem almost natural that Charity should not so much as raise her eyes when he entered. She had simply let him understand that her silence was not accidental by leaving the table while he was still eating, and going up without a word to shut herself into her room. After that he formed the habit of talking loudly and genially to Verena whenever Charity was in the room; but otherwise there was no apparent change in their relations.

She did not think connectedly of these things while she sat waiting for Harney, but they remained in her mind as a sullen background against which her short hours with him flamed out like forest fires. Nothing else mattered, neither the good nor the bad, or what might have seemed so before she knew him. He had caught her up and carried her away into a new world, from which, at stated hours, the ghost of her came back to perform certain customary acts, but all so thinly and insubstantially that she sometimes wondered that the people she went about among could see her. . . .

Behind the swarthy Mountain the sun had gone down in waveless gold. From a pasture up the slope a tinkle of cow-bells sounded; a puff of smoke hung over the farm in the valley, trailed on the pure air and was gone. For a few minutes, in the clear light that is all shadow, fields and woods were outlined with an unreal precision; then the twilight blotted them out, and the little house turned grey and spectral under its wizened apple-branches.

Charity's heart contracted. The first fall of night after a day of radiance often gave her a sense of hidden menace: it was like looking out over the world as it would be when love had gone from it. She wondered if some day she would sit in that same place and watch in vain for her lover. . . .

His bicycle-bell sounded down the lane, and in a minute she was at the gate and his eyes were laughing in hers. They walked back through the long grass, and pushed open the door behind the house. The room at first seemed quite dark and they had to grope their way in hand in hand. Through the window-frame the sky looked light by contrast, and above the black mass of asters in the earthern jar one white star glimmered like a moth.

'There was such a lot to do at the last minute,' Harney was explaining, 'and I had to drive down to Creston to meet some-one who has come to stay with my cousin for the show.'

He had his arms about her, and his kisses were in her hair and on her lips. Under his touch things deep down in her struggled to the light and sprang up like flowers in sunshine. She twisted her fingers into his, and they sat down side by side on the improvised couch. She hardly heard his excuses for being late: in his absence a thousand doubts tormented her, but as soon as he appeared she ceased to wonder where he had come from, what had delayed him, who had kept him from her. It seemed as if the places he had been in, and the people he had been with, must cease to exist when he left them, just as her own life was suspended in his absence.

He continued, now, to talk to her volubly and gaily, deploring his lateness, grumbling at the demands on his time, and good-humouredly mimicking Miss Hatchard's benevolent agitation. 'She hurried off Miles to ask Mr Royall to speak at the Town Hall tomorrow: I didn't know till it was done.' Charity was silent, and he added: 'After all, perhaps it's just as well. No one else could have done it.'

Charity made no answer: she did not care what part her guardian played in the morrow's ceremonies. Like all the other figures peopling her meagre world he had grown non-existent to her. She had even put off hating him.

'Tomorrow I shall only see you from far off,' Harney continued. 'But in the evening there'll be the dance in the Town Hall. Do you want me to promise not to dance with any other girl?'

Any other girl? Were there any others? She had forgotten even that peril, so enclosed did he and she seem in their secret world. Her heart gave a frightened jerk.

'Yes, promise.'

He laughed and took her in his arms. 'You goose – not even if they're hideous?'

He pushed the hair from her forehead, bending her face back, as his way was, and leaning over so that his head loomed black between her eyes and the paleness of the sky, in which the white star floated . . .

Side by side they sped back along the dark wood-road to the village. A late moon was rising, full orbed and fiery, turning the mountain ranges from fluid grey to a massive blackness, and making the upper sky so light that the stars looked as faint as their own reflections in water. At the edge of the wood, half a mile from North Dormer, Harney jumped from his bicycle,

took Charity in his arms for a last kiss, and then waited while
she went on alone.

They were later than usual, and instead of taking the bicycle
to the library she propped it against the back of the woodshed
and entered the kitchen of the red house. Verena sat there
alone; when Charity came in she looked at her with mild
impenetrable eyes and then took a plate and a glass of milk from
the shelf and set them silently on the table. Charity nodded her
thanks, and sitting down fell hungrily upon her piece of pie
and emptied the glass. Her face burned with her quick flight
through the night, and her eyes were dazzled by the twinkle
of the kitchen lamp. She felt like a night-bird suddenly caught
and caged.

'He ain't come back since supper,' Verena said. 'He's down
to the Hall.'

Charity took no notice. Her soul was still winging through
the forest. She washed her plate and tumbler, and then felt
her way up the dark stairs. When she opened her door a
wonder arrested her. Before going out she had closed her
shutters against the afternoon heat, but they had swung partly
open, and a bar of moonlight, crossing the room, rested on
her bed and showed a dress of China silk laid out on it in virgin
whiteness. Charity had spent more than she could afford on
the dress, which was to surpass those of all the other girls; she
had wanted to let North Dormer see that she was worthy of
Harney's admiration. Above the dress, folded on the pillow,
was the white veil which the young women who took part
in the exercises were to wear under a wreath of asters; and
beside the veil a pair of slim white satin shoes that Ally had
produced from an old trunk in which she stored mysterious
treasures.

Charity stood gazing at all the outspread whiteness. It
recalled a vision that had come to her in the night after her
first meeting with Harney. She no longer had such visions . . .
warmer splendours had displaced them . . . but it was stupid of
Ally to have paraded all those white things on her bed, exactly
as Hattie Targatt's wedding dress from Springfield had been

spread out for the neighbours to see when she married Tom
Fry. . . .

Charity took up the satin shoes and looked at them
curiously. By day, no doubt, they would appear a little worn,
but in the moonlight they seemed carved of ivory. She sat
down on the floor to try them on, and they fitted her perfectly,
though when she stood up she lurched a little on the high
heels. She looked down at her feet, which the graceful mould
of the slippers had marvelously arched and narrowed. She had
never seen such shoes before, even in the shop-windows at
Nettleton . . . never, except . . . yes, once, she had noticed a pair
of the same shape on Annabel Balch.

A blush of mortification swept over her. Ally sometimes
sewed for Miss Balch when that brilliant being descended on
North Dormer, and no doubt she picked up presents of cast-
off clothing: the treasures in the mysterious trunk all came
from the people she worked for. There could be no doubt that
the white slippers were Annabel Balch's. . . .

As she stood there, staring down moodily at her feet, she
heard the triple click-click-click of a bicycle-bell under her
window. It was Harney's secret signal as he passed on his way
home. She stumbled to the window on her high heels, flung
open the shutters and leaned out. He waved to her and sped
by, his black shadow dancing merrily ahead of him down the
empty moonlit road; and she leaned there watching him till he
vanished under the Hatchard spruces.

XIII

The Town Hall was crowded and exceedingly hot. As Charity marched into it, third in the white muslin file headed by Orma Fry, she was conscious mainly of the brilliant effect of the wreathed columns framing the green-carpeted stage toward which she was moving and of the unfamiliar faces turning from the front rows to watch the advance of the procession.

But it was all a bewildering blur of eyes and colours till she found herself standing at the back of the stage, her great bunch of asters and goldenrod held well in front of her, and answering the nervous glance of Lambert Sollas, the organist from Mr Miles's church, who had come up from Nettleton to play the harmonium, and sat behind it, running his conductor's eye over the fluttered girls.

A moment later Mr Miles, pink and twinkling, emerged from the background, as if buoyed up on his broad white gown, and briskly dominated the bowed heads in the front rows. He prayed energetically and briefly and then retired, and a fierce nod from Lambert Sollas warned the girls that they were to follow at once with 'Home, Sweet Home'. It was a joy to Charity to sing: it seemed as though, for the first time, her secret rapture might burst from her and flash its defiance at the world. All the glow in her blood, the breath of the summer earth, the rustle of the forest, the fresh call of birds at sunrise, and the brooding midday languors, seemed to pass into her untrained voice, lifted and led by the sustaining chorus.

And then suddenly the song was over, and after an uncertain pause, during which Miss Hatchard's pearl-grey gloves started a furtive signalling down the hall, Mr Royall, emerging in turn, ascended the steps of the stage and appeared behind the flower-wreathed desk. He passed close to Charity, and she noticed that his gravely set face wore the look of majesty that used to awe and fascinate her childhood. His frock-coat had been carefully brushed and ironed, and the ends of his narrow black tie were so nearly even that the tying must have cost him a protracted struggle. His appearance struck her all the more because it was the first time she had looked him full in the face since the night at Nettleton, and nothing in his grave and impressive demeanour revealed a trace of the lamentable figure on the wharf.

He stood a moment behind the desk, resting his finger-tips against it, and bending slightly toward his audience; then he straightened himself and began.

At first she paid no heed to what he was saying: only frag-ments of sentences, sonorous quotations, allusions to illustrious men, including the obligatory tribute to Honorius Hatchard, drifted past her inattentive ears. She was trying to discover Harney among the notable people in the front row; but he was nowhere near Miss Hatchard, who, crowned by a pearl-grey hat that matched her gloves, sat just below the desk, supported by Mrs Miles and an important-looking unknown lady. Charity was near one end of the stage, and from where she sat the other end of the first row of seats was cut off by the screen of foliage masking the harmonium. The effort to see Harney around the corner of the screen, or through its interstices, made her unconscious of everything else; but the effort was unsuccessful, and gradually she found her attention arrested by her guardian's discourse.

She had never heard him speak in public before, but she was familiar with the rolling music of his voice when he read aloud, or held forth to the selectmen about the stove at Carrick Fry's. Today his inflections were richer and graver than she had ever known them: he spoke slowly, with pauses that seemed to invite his hearers to silent participation in his thought; and Charity perceived a light of response in their faces.

He was nearing the end of his address . . . 'Most of you,' he said, 'most of you who have returned here today, to make contact with this little place for a brief hour, have come only on a pious pilgrimage, and will go back presently to busy cities and lives full of larger duties. But that is not the only way of coming back to North Dormer. Some of us, who went out from here in our youth . . . went out, like you, to busy cities and larger duties . . . have come back in another way – come back for good. I am one of those, as many of you know. . . .' He paused, and there was a sense of suspense in the listening hall. 'My history is without interest, but it has its lesson: not so much for those of you who have already made your lives in other places, as for the young men who are perhaps planning even now to leave these quiet hills and go down into the struggle. Things they cannot foresee may send some of those young men back some day to the little township and the old homestead: they may come back for good. . . .' He looked about him, and repeated gravely: 'For *good*. There's the point I want to make . . . North Dormer is a poor little place, almost lost in a mighty landscape: perhaps, by this time, it might have been a bigger place, and more in scale with the landscape, if those who had to come back had come with that feeling in their minds – that they wanted to come back for *good* . . . and not for bad . . . or just for indifference. . . .

'Gentlemen, let us look at things as they are. Some of us have come back to our native town because we'd failed to get on elsewhere. One way or other, things had gone wrong with us . . . what we'd dreamed of hadn't come true. But the fact that we had failed elsewhere is no reason why we should fail here. Our very experiments in larger places, even if they were unsuccessful, ought to have helped us to make North Dormer a larger place . . . and you young men who are preparing even now to follow the call of ambition, and turn your back on the old homes – well, let me say this to you, that if ever you do come back to them it's worth while to come back to them for their good. . . . And to do that, you must keep on loving them while you're away from them; and even if you come back against your will – and thinking it's all a bitter mistake of Fate or Providence – you must try to make the best of it, and to make the best of your old town; and after a while – well, ladies and gentlemen, I give you my recipe for what it's worth; after a while, I believe you'll be able to say, as I can say today: "I'm glad I'm here." Believe me, all of you, the best way to help the places we live in is to be glad we live there.'

He stopped, and a murmur of emotion and surprise ran through the audience. It was not in the least what they had expected, but it moved them more than what they had expected would have moved them. 'Hear, hear!' a voice cried out in the middle of the hall. An outburst of cheers caught up the cry, and as they subsided Charity heard Mr Miles saying to someone near him: 'That was a *man* talking—' He wiped his spectacles.

Mr Royall had stepped back from the desk, and taken his seat in the row of chairs in front of the harmonium. A dapper white-haired gentleman – a distant Hatchard – succeeded him behind the goldenrod, and began to say beautiful things about the old oaken bucket, patient white-haired mothers, and where the boys used to go nutting . . . and Charity began again to search for Harney. . . .

Suddenly Mr Royall pushed back his seat, and one of the maple branches in front of the harmonium collapsed with a crash. It uncovered the end of the first row and in one of the seats Charity saw Harney, and in the next a lady whose face was turned toward him, and almost hidden by the brim of her drooping hat. Charity did not need to see the face. She knew at a glance the slim figure, the fair hair heaped up under the hat-brim, the long pale wrinkled gloves with bracelets slipping over them. At the fall of the branch Miss Balch turned her head toward the stage, and in her pretty thin-lipped smile there lingered the reflection of something her neighbour had been whispering to her. . . .

Someone came forward to replace the fallen branch, and Miss Balch and Harney were once more hidden. But to Charity the vision of their two faces had blotted out every-thing. In a flash they had shown her the bare reality of her situation. Behind the frail screen of her lover's caresses was the whole inscrutable mystery of his life: his relations with other people – with other women – his opinions, his prejudices, his principles, the net of influences and interests and ambitions in which every man's life is entangled. Of all these she knew nothing, except what he had told her of his architectural aspirations. She had always dimly guessed him to be in touch with important people, involved in complicated relations – but she felt it all to be so far beyond her understanding that the whole subject hung like a luminous mist on the farthest verge of her thoughts. In the foreground, hiding all else, there was the glow of his presence, the light and shadow of his face, the way his short-sighted eyes, at her approach, widened and deepened as if to draw her down into them; and, above all, the flush of youth and tenderness in which his words enclosed her.

Now she saw him detached from her, drawn back into the unknown, and whispering to another girl things that provoked the same smile of mischievous complicity he had so often called to her own lips. The feeling possessing her was not one of jealousy: she was too sure of his love. It was rather a terror of the unknown, of all the mysterious attractions that must even now be dragging him away from her, and of her own powerlessness to contend with them.

She had given him all she had – but what was it compared to the other gifts life held for him? She understood now the case of girls like herself to whom this kind of thing happened. They gave all they had, but their all was not enough: it could not buy more than a few moments. . . .

The heat had grown suffocating – she felt it descend on her in smothering waves, and the faces in the crowded hall began to dance like the pictures flashed on the screen at Nettleton. For an instant Mr Royall's countenance detached itself from the general blur. He had resumed his place in front of the harmonium, and sat close to her, his eyes on her face; and his look seemed to pierce to the very centre of her confused sensations. . . . A feeling of physical sickness rushed over her –

and then deadly apprehension. The light of the fiery hours in the little house swept back on her in a glare of fear. . . .

She forced herself to look away from her guardian, and became aware that the oratory of the Hatchard cousin had ceased, and that Mr Miles was again flapping his wings. Fragments of his peroration floated through her bewildered brain. . . . 'A rich harvest of hallowed memories. . . . A sanctified hour to which, in moments of trial, your thoughts will prayerfully return. . . . And now, O Lord, let us humbly and fervently give thanks for this blessed day of reunion, here in the old home to which we have come back from so far. Preserve it to us, O Lord, in times to come, in all its homely sweetness – in the kindliness and wisdom of its old people, in the courage and industry of its young men, in the piety and purity of this group of innocent girls —' He flapped a white wing in their direction, and at the same moment Lambert Sollas, with his fierce nod, struck the opening bars of 'Auld Lang Syne'. . . . Charity stared straight ahead of her and then, dropping her flowers, fell face downward at Mr Royall's feet.

XIV

North Dormer's celebration naturally included the villages attached to its township, and the festivities were to radiate over the whole group, from Dormer and the two Crestons to Hamblin, the lonely hamlet on the north slope of the Mountain where the first snow always fell. On the third day there were speeches and ceremonies at Creston and Creston River; on the fourth the principal performers were to be driven in buck-boards to Dormer and Hamblin.

It was on the fourth day that Charity returned for the first time to the little house. She had not seen Harney alone since they had parted at the wood's edge the night before the celebrations began. In the interval she had passed through many moods, but for the moment the terror which had seized her in the Town Hall had faded to the edge of consciousness. She had fainted because the hall was stiflingly hot, and because the speakers had gone on and on. . . . Several other people had been affected by the heat, and had had to leave before the exercises were over. There had been thunder in the air all the afternoon, and everyone said afterward that something ought to have been done to ventilate the hall. . . .

At the dance that evening – where she had gone reluctantly, and only because she feared to stay away, she had sprung back into instant reassurance. As soon as she entered she had seen Harney waiting for her, and he had come up with kind gay eyes, and swept her off in a waltz. Her feet were full of music, and though her only training had been with the village youths she had no difficulty in tuning her steps to his. As they circled about the floor all her vain fears dropped from her, and she even forgot that she was probably dancing in Annabel Balch's slippers.

When the waltz was over Harney, with a last hand-clasp, left her to meet Miss Hatchard and Miss Balch, who were just entering. Charity had a moment of anguish as Miss Balch appeared; but it did not last. The triumphant fact of her own greater beauty, and of Harney's sense of it, swept her apprehensions aside. Miss Balch, in an unbecoming dress, looked sallow and pinched, and Charity fancied there was a worried expression in her pale-lashed eyes. She took a seat near Miss Hatchard and it was presently apparent that she did not mean to dance. Charity did not dance often either. Harney explained to her that Miss Hatchard had begged him to give each of the other girls a turn; but he went through the form of asking Charity's permission each time he led one out, and that gave her a sense of secret triumph even completer than when she was whirling about the room with him. . . .

She was thinking of all this as she waited for him in the deserted house. The late afternoon was sultry, and she had tossed aside her hat and stretched herself at full length on the Mexican blanket because it was cooler indoors than under the trees. She lay with her arms folded beneath her head, gazing out at the shaggy shoulder of the Mountain. The sky behind it was full of the splintered glories of the descending sun, and before long she expected to hear Harney's bicycle-bell in the lane. He had bicycled to Hamblin, instead of driving there with his cousin and her friends, so that he might be able to make his escape earlier and stop on the way back at the deserted house, which was on the road to Hamblin. They had smiled together at the joke of hearing the crowded buck-boards roll by on the return, while they lay close in their hiding above the road. Such childish triumphs still gave her a sense of reckless security.

Nevertheless she had not wholly forgotten the vision of fear that had opened before her in the Town Hall. The sense of lastingness was gone from her and every moment with Harney would now be ringed with doubt.

The Mountain was turning purple against a fiery sunset from which it seemed to be divided by a knife-edge of quivering light; and above this wall of flame the whole sky was a pure pale green, like some cold mountain lake in shadow. Charity lay gazing up at it, and watching for the first white star. . . .

Her eyes were still fixed on the upper reaches of the sky when she became aware that a shadow had flitted across the glory-flooded room: it must have been Harney passing the window against the sunset. . . . She half raised herself, and then dropped back on her folded arms. The combs had slipped from her hair, and it trailed in a rough dark rope across her breast. She lay quite still, a sleepy smile on her lips, her indolent lids half shut. There was a fumbling at the padlock and she called out: 'Have you slipped the chain?' The door opened, and Mr Royall walked into the room.

She started up, sitting back against the cushions, and they looked at each other without speaking. Then Mr Royall closed the door-latch and advanced a few steps.

Charity jumped to her feet. 'What have you come for?' she stammered.

The last glare of the sunset was on her guardian's face, which looked ash-coloured in the yellow radiance.

'Because I knew you were here,' he answered simply.

She had become conscious of the hair hanging loose across her breast, and it seemed as though she could not speak to him till she had set herself in order. She groped for her combs, and tried to fasten up the coil. Mr Royall silently watched her.

'Charity,' he said, 'he'll be here in a minute. Let me talk to you first.'

'You've got no right to talk to me. I can do what I please.'

'Yes. What is it you mean to do?'

'I needn't answer that, or anything else.'

He had glanced away, and stood looking curiously about the illuminated room. Purple asters and red maple-leaves filled the jar on the table; on a shelf against the wall stood a lamp, the kettle, a little pile of cups and saucers. The canvas chairs were grouped about the table.

'So this is where you meet,' he said.

His tone was quiet and controlled, and the fact disconcerted her. She had been ready to give him violence for violence, but this calm acceptance of things as they were left her without a weapon.

'See here, Charity – you're always telling me I've got no rights over you. There might be two ways of looking at that – but I ain't going to argue it. All I know is I raised you as good as I could, and meant fairly by you always – except once, for a bad half-hour. There's no justice in weighing that half-hour against the rest, and you know it. If you hadn't, you wouldn't have gone on living under my roof. Seems to me the fact of your doing that gives me some sort of a right; the right to try and keep you out of trouble. I'm not asking you to consider any other.'

She listened in silence, and then gave a slight laugh. 'Better wait till I'm in trouble,' she said.

He paused a moment, as if weighing her words. 'Is that all your answer?'

'Yes, that's all.'

'Well – I'll wait.'

He turned away slowly, but as he did so the thing she had been waiting for happened; the door opened again and Harney entered.

He stopped short with a face of astonishment, and then, quickly controlling himself, went up to Mr Royall with a frank look.

'Have you come to see me, sir?' he said coolly, throwing his cap on the table with an air of proprietorship.

Mr Royall again looked slowly about the room; then his eyes turned to the young man.

'Is this your house?' he inquired.

Harney laughed: 'Well – as much as it's anybody's. I come here to sketch occasionally.'

'And to receive Miss Royall's visits?'

'When she does me the honour—'

'Is this the home you propose to bring her to when you get married?'

There was an immense and oppressive silence. Charity,

quivering with anger, started forward, and then stood silent, too humbled for speech. Harney's eyes had dropped under the old man's gaze; but he raised them presently, and looking steadily at Mr Royall, said: 'Miss Royall is not a child. Isn't it rather absurd to talk of her as if she were? I believe she considers herself free to come and go as she pleases, without any questions from anyone.' He paused and added: 'I'm ready to answer any she wishes to ask me.'

Mr Royall turned to her. 'Ask him when he's going to marry you, then —' There was another silence, and he laughed in his turn – a broken laugh, with a scraping sound in it. 'You darsn't!' he shouted out with sudden passion. He went close up to Charity, his right arm lifted, not in menace but in tragic exhortation.

'You darsn't, and you know it – and you know why!' He swung back again upon the young man. 'And you know why you ain't asked her to marry you, and why you don't mean to. It's because you hadn't need to; nor any other man either. I'm the only one that was fool enough not to know that; and I guess nobody'll repeat my mistake – not in Eagle County, anyhow. They all know what she is, and what she came from. They all know her mother was a woman of the town from Nettleton, that followed one of those Mountain fellows up to his place and lived there with him like a heathen. I saw her there sixteen years ago, when I went to bring this child down. I went to save her from the kind of life her mother was leading – but I'd better have left her in the kennel she came from. . . .' He paused and stared darkly at the two young people, and out beyond them, at the menacing Mountain with its rim of fire; then he sat down beside the table on which they had so often spread their rustic supper, and covered his face with his hands. Harney leaned in the window, a frown on his face: he was twirling between his fingers a small package that dangled from a loop of string. . . . Charity heard Mr Royall draw a hard breath or two, and his shoulders shook a little. Presently he stood up and walked across the room. He did not look again at the young people: they saw him feel his way to the door and fumble for the latch; and then he went out into the darkness.

After he had gone there was a long silence. Charity waited for Harney to speak; but he seemed at first not to find anything to say. At length he broke out irrelevantly: 'I wonder how he found out?'

She made no answer and he tossed down the package he had been holding, and went up to her.

'I'm so sorry, dear . . . that this should have happened. . . .'

She threw her head back proudly. 'I ain't ever been sorry – not a minute!'

'No.'

She waited to be caught into his arms, but he turned away from her irresolutely. The last glow was gone from behind the Mountain. Everything in the room had turned grey and indistinct, and an autumnal dampness crept up from the hollow below the orchard, laying its cold touch on their flushed faces. Harney walked the length of the room, and then turned back and sat down at the table.

'Come,' he said imperiously.

She sat down beside him, and he untied the string about the package and spread out a pile of sandwiches.

'I stole them from the love-feast at Hamblin,' he said with a laugh, pushing them over to her. She laughed too, and took one, and began to eat.

'Didn't you make the tea?'

'No,' she said. 'I forgot—'

'Oh, well – it's too late to boil the water now.' He said nothing more, and sitting opposite to each other they went on silently eating the sandwiches. Darkness had descended in the little room, and Harney's face was a dim blur to Charity. Suddenly he leaned across the table and laid his hand on hers.

'I shall have to go off for a while – a month or two, perhaps – to arrange some things; and then I'll come back . . . and we'll get married.'

His voice seemed like a stranger's: nothing was left in it of the vibrations she knew. Her hand lay inertly under his, and she left it there, and raised her head, trying to answer him. But the words died in her throat. They sat motionless, in their attitude of confident endearment, as if some strange death had surprised them. At length Harney sprang to his feet with a slight shiver. 'God! it's damp – we couldn't have come here much longer.' He went to the shelf, took down a tin candle-stick and lit the candle; then he propped an unhinged shutter against the empty window-frame and put the candle on the table. It threw up a queer shadow on his frowning forehead, and made the smile on his lips a grimace.

'But it's been good, though, hasn't it, Charity? . . . What's the matter – why do you stand there staring at me? Haven't the days here been good?' He went up to her and caught her to his breast. 'And there'll be others – lots of others . . . jollier . . . even jollier . . . won't there, darling?'

He turned her head back, feeling for the curve of her throat below the ear, and kissing her there, and on the hair and eyes and lips. She clung to him desperately, and as he drew her to his knees on the couch she felt as if they were being sucked down together into some bottomless abyss.

XV

That night, as usual, they said good-bye at the wood's edge. Harney was to leave the next morning early. He asked Charity to say nothing of their plans till his return, and, strangely even to herself, she was glad of the postponement. A leaden weight of shame hung on her, benumbing every other sensation, and she bade him good-bye with hardly a sign of emotion. His reiterated promises to return seemed almost wounding. She had no doubt that he intended to come back; her doubts were far deeper and less definable.

Since the fanciful vision of the future that had flitted through her imagination at their first meeting she had hardly ever thought of his marrying her. She had not had to put the thought from her mind; it had not been there. If ever she looked ahead she felt instinctively that the gulf between them was too deep, and that the bridge their passion had flung across it was as insubstantial as a rainbow. But she seldom looked ahead; each day was so rich that it absorbed her. . . . Now her first feeling was that everything would be different, and that she herself would be a different being to Harney. Instead of remaining separate and absolute, she would be compared with other people, and unknown things would be expected of her. She was too proud to be afraid, but the freedom of her spirit drooped. . . .

Harney had not fixed any date for his return; he had said he would have to look about first, and settle things. He had promised to write as soon as there was anything definite to say, and had left her his address, and asked her to write also. But the address frightened her. It was in New York, at a club with a long name in Fifth Avenue: it seemed to raise an insurmountable barrier between them. Once or twice, in the first days, she got out a sheet of paper, and sat looking at it, and trying to think what to say; but she had the feeling that her letter would never reach its destination. She had never written to anyone farther away than Hepburn.

Harney's first letter came after he had been gone about ten days. It was tender but grave, and bore no resemblance to the gay little notes he had sent her by the freckled boy from Creston River. He spoke positively of his intention of coming back, but named no date, and reminded Charity of their agreement that their plans should not be divulged till he had had time to 'settle things'. When that would be he could not yet foresee; but she could count on his returning as soon as the way was clear.

She read the letter with a strange sense of its coming from immeasurable distances and having lost most of its meaning on the way; and in reply she sent him a coloured post-card of Creston Falls, on which she wrote: 'With love from Charity'. She felt the pitiful inadequacy of this, and understood, with a sense of despair, that in her inability to express herself she must give him an impression of coldness and reluctance; but she could not help it. She could not forget that he had never spoken to her of marriage till Mr Royall had forced the word from his lips; though she had not had the strength to shake off the spell that bound her to him she had lost all spontaneity of feeling, and seemed to herself to be passively awaiting a fate she could not avert.

She had not seen Mr Royall on her return to the red house. The morning after her parting from Harney, when she came down from her room, Verena told her that her guardian had gone off to Worcester and Portland. It was the time of year when he usually reported to the insurance agencies he represented, and there was nothing unusual in his departure except its suddenness. She thought little about him, except to be glad he was not there. . . .

She kept to herself for the first days, while North Dormer was recovering from its brief plunge into publicity, and the subsiding agitation left her unnoticed. But the faithful Ally could not be long avoided. For the first few days after the close of the Old Home Week festivities Charity escaped her by roaming the hills all day when she was not at her post in the library; but after that a period of rain set in, and one pouring afternoon Ally, sure that she would find her friend indoors, came around to the red house with her sewing.

The two girls sat upstairs in Charity's room. Charity, her idle hands in her lap, was sunk in a kind of leaden dream, through which she was only half-conscious of Ally, who sat opposite her in a low rush-bottomed chair, her work pinned to her knee, and her thin lips pursed up as she bent above it.

'It was my idea running a ribbon through the gauging,' she said proudly, drawing back to contemplate the blouse she was trimming. 'It's for Miss Balch: she was awfully pleased.' She paused and then added, with a queer tremor in her piping voice: 'I darsn't have told her I got the idea from one I saw on Julia.'

Charity raised her eyes listlessly. 'Do you still see Julia sometimes?'

Ally reddened, as if the allusion had escaped her unintentionally. 'Oh, it was a long time ago I seen her with those gaugings. . . .'

Silence fell again, and Ally presently continued: 'Miss Balch left me a whole lot of things to do over this time.'

'Why – has she gone?' Charity inquired with an inner start of apprehension.

'Didn't you know? She went off the morning after they had the celebration at Hamblin. I seen her drive by early with Mr Harney.'

There was another silence, measured by the steady tick of the rain against the window, and, at intervals, by the snipping sound of Ally's scissors.

Ally gave a meditative laugh. 'Do you know what she told me before she went away? She told me she was going to send for me to come over to Springfield and make some things for her wedding.'

Charity again lifted her heavy lids and stared at Ally's pale pointed face, which moved to and fro above her moving fingers.

'Is she going to get married?'

Ally let the blouse sink to her knee, and sat gazing at it. Her lips seemed suddenly dry, and she moistened them a little with her tongue.

'Why, I presume so . . . from what she said. . . . Didn't you know?'

'Why should I know?'

Ally did not answer. She bent above the blouse, and began picking out a basting thread with the point of the scissors.

'Why should I know?' Charity repeated harshly.

'I didn't know but what . . . folks here say she's engaged to Mr Harney.'

Charity stood up with a laugh, and stretched her arms lazily above her head.

'If all the people got married that folks say are going to you'd have your time full making wedding-dresses,' she said ironically.

'Why – don't you believe it?' Ally ventured.

'It wouldn't make it true if I did – nor prevent it if I didn't.'

'That's so. . . . I only know I seen her crying the night of the party because her dress didn't set right. That was why she wouldn't dance any. . . .'

Charity stood absently gazing down at the lacy garment on Ally's knee. Abruptly she stooped and snatched it up.

'Well, I guess she won't dance in this either,' she said with sudden violence; and grasping the blouse in her strong young hands she tore it in two and flung the tattered bits to the floor.

'Oh, Charity —' Ally cried, springing up. For a long interval the two girls faced each other across the ruined garment. Ally burst into tears.

'Oh, what'll I say to her? What'll I do? It was real lace!' she wailed between her piping sobs.

Charity glared at her unrelentingly. 'You'd oughtn't to have brought it here,' she said, breathing quickly. 'I hate other people's clothes – it's just as if they was there themselves.' The two stared at each other again over this avowal, till Charity brought out, in a gasp of anguish: 'Oh, go – go – go – or I'll hate you too. . . .'

When Ally left her, she fell sobbing across her bed.

The long storm was followed by a north-west gale, and when it was over the hills took on their first umber tints, the sky grew more densely blue, and the big white clouds lay against the hills like snow-banks. The first crisp maple-leaves began to spin across Miss Hatchard's lawn, and the Virginia creeper on the Memorial splashed the white porch with scarlet. It was a golden triumphant September. Day by day the flame of the Virginia creeper spread to the hillsides in wider waves of carmine and crimson, the larches glowed like the thin yellow halo about a fire, the maples blazed and smouldered, and the black hemlocks turned to indigo against the incandescence of the forest.

The nights were cold, with a dry glitter of stars so high up that they seemed smaller and more vivid. Sometimes, as Charity lay sleepless on her bed through the long hours, she felt as though she were bound to those wheeling fires and swinging with them around the great black vault. At night she planned many things . . . it was then she wrote to Harney. But the letters were never put on paper, for she did not know how to express what she wanted to tell him. So she waited. Since her talk with Ally she had felt sure that Harney was engaged to Annabel Balch, and that the process of 'settling things' would involve the breaking of this tie. Her first rage of jealousy over, she felt no fear on this score. She was still sure that Harney would come back, and she was equally sure that, for the moment at least, it was she whom he loved and not Miss Balch. Yet the girl, no less, remained a rival, since she represented all the things that Charity felt herself most incapable of understanding or achieving. Annabel Balch was, if not the girl Harney ought to marry, at least the kind of girl it would be natural for him to marry. Charity had never been able to picture herself as his wife; had never been able to arrest the vision and follow it out in its daily consequences;

but she could perfectly imagine Annabel Balch in that relation to him.

The more she thought of these things the more the sense of fatality weighed on her: she felt the uselessness of struggling against the circumstances. She had never known how to adapt herself, she could only break and tear and destroy. The scene with Ally had left her stricken with shame at her own childish savagery. What would Harney have thought if he had witnessed it? But when she turned the incident over in her puzzled mind she could not imagine what a civilized person would have done in her place. She felt herself too unequally pitted against unknown forces. . . .

At length this feeling moved her to sudden action. She took a sheet of letter paper from Mr Royall's office, and sitting by the kitchen lamp, one night after Verena had gone to bed, began her first letter to Harney. It was very short:

> I want you should marry Annabel Balch if you promised to. I think maybe you were afraid I'd feel too bad about it. I feel I'd rather you acted right.
>
> Your loving
> CHARITY.

She posted the letter early the next morning, and for a few days her heart felt strangely light. Then she began to wonder why she received no answer.

One day as she sat alone in the library pondering these things the walls of books began to spin around her, and the rosewood desk to rock under her elbows. The dizziness was followed by a wave of nausea like that she had felt on the day of the exercises in the Town Hall. But the Town Hall had been crowded and stiflingly hot, and the library was empty, and so chilly that she had kept on her jacket. Five minutes before she had felt perfectly well; and now it seemed as if she were going to die. The bit of lace at which she still languidly worked dropped from her fingers, and the steel crochet hook clattered to the floor. She pressed her temples hard between her damp hands, steadying herself against the desk while the wave of sickness swept over her. Little by little it subsided, and after a few minutes she stood up, shaken and terrified, groped for her hat, and stumbled out into the air. But the whole sunlit autumn world reeled and roared around her as she dragged herself along the interminable length of the road home.

As she approached the red house she saw a buggy standing at the door, and her heart gave a leap. But it was only Mr Royall who got out, his travelling-bag in hand. He saw her coming, and waited in the porch. She was conscious that he was looking at her intently, as if there was something strange in her appearance, and she threw back her head with a desperate effort at ease. Their eyes met, and she said: 'You back?' as if nothing had happened, and he answered: 'Yes, I'm back,' and walked in ahead of her, pushing open the door of his office. She climbed to her room, every step of the stairs holding her fast as if her feet were lined with glue.

Two days later, she descended from the train at Nettleton, and walked out of the station into the dusty square. The brief interval of cold weather was over, and the day was as soft, and almost as hot, as when she and Harney had emerged on the same scene on the Fourth of July. In the square the same broken-down hacks and carry-alls stood drawn up in a despondent line, and the lank horses with fly-nets over their withers swayed their heads drearily to and fro. She recognized the staring signs over the eating-houses and billiard saloons, and the long lines of wires on lofty poles tapering down the main street to the park at its other end. Taking the way the wires pointed, she went on hastily, with bent head, till she reached a wide transverse street with a brick building at the corner. She crossed this street and glanced furtively up at the front of the brick building; then she returned, and entered a door opening on a flight of steep brass-rimmed stairs. On the second landing she rang a bell, and a mulatto girl with a bushy head and a frilled apron let her into a hall where a stuffed fox on his hind legs proffered a brass card-tray to visitors. At the back of the hall was a glazed door marked: 'Office'. After waiting a

few minutes in a handsomely furnished room, with plush sofas
surmounted by large gold-framed photographs of showy
young women, Charity was shown into the office. . . .

When she came out of the glazed door Dr Merkle followed,
and led her into another room, smaller, and still more crowded
with plush and gold frames. Dr Merkle was a plump woman
with small bright eyes, an immense mass of black hair coming
down low on her forehead, and unnaturally white and even
teeth. She wore a rich black dress, with gold chains and charms
hanging from her bosom. Her hands were large and smooth,
and quick in all their movements; and she smelt of musk and
carbolic acid.

She smiled on Charity with all her faultless teeth. 'Sit
down, my dear. Wouldn't you like a little drop of something to
pick you up? . . . No. . . . Well, just lay back a minute then. . . .
There's nothing to be done just yet; but in about a month, if
you'll step round again . . . I could take you right into my own
house for two or three days, and there wouldn't be a mite of
trouble. Mercy me! The next time you'll know better'n to fret
like this. . . .'

Charity gazed at her with widening eyes. This woman with
the false hair, the false teeth, the false murderous smile – what
was she offering her but immunity from some unthinkable
crime? Charity, till then, had been conscious only of a vague
self-disgust and a frightening physical distress; now, of a sudden, there came to her the grave surprise of motherhood. She
had come to this dreadful place because she knew of no other
way of making sure that she was not mistaken about her state;
and the woman had taken her for a miserable creature like
Julia. . . . The thought was so horrible that she sprang up, white
and shaking, one of her great rushes of anger sweeping over
her.

Dr Merkle, still smiling, also rose. 'Why do you run off in
such a hurry? You can stretch out right here on my sofa. . . .'
She paused, and her smile grew more motherly. 'Afterwards –
if there's been any talk at home, and you want to get away for

a while . . . I have a lady friend in Boston who's looking for a companion . . . you're the very one to suit her, my dear. . . .'

Charity had reached the door. 'I don't want to stay. I don't want to come back here,' she stammered, her hand on the knob; but with a swift movement Dr Merkle edged her from the threshold.

'Oh, very well. Five dollars, please.'

Charity looked helplessly at the doctor's tight lips and rigid face. Her last savings had gone in repaying Ally for the cost of Miss Balch's ruined blouse, and she had had to borrow four dollars from her friend to pay for her railway ticket and cover the doctor's fee. It had never occurred to her that medical advice could cost more than two dollars.

'I didn't know . . . I haven't got that much . . .' she faltered, bursting into tears.

Dr Merkle gave a short laugh which did not show her teeth, and inquired with concision if Charity supposed she ran the establishment for her own amusement? She leaned her firm shoulders against the door as she spoke, like a grim gaoler making terms with her captive.

'You say you'll come round and settle later? I've heard that pretty often too. Give me your address, and if you can't pay me I'll send the bill to your folks. . . . What? I can't understand what you say. . . . That don't suit you either? My, you're pretty particular for a girl that ain't got enough to settle her own bills. . . .' She paused, and fixed her eyes on the brooch with a blue stone that Charity had pinned to her blouse.

'Ain't you ashamed to talk that way to a lady that's got to earn her living, when you go about with jewellery like that on you? . . . It ain't in my line, and I do it only as a favour . . . but if you're a mind to leave that brooch as a pledge, I don't say no. . . . Yes, of course, you can get it back when you bring me my money. . . .'

On the way home, she felt an immense and unexpected quietude. It had been horrible to have to leave Harney's gift in the woman's hands, but even at that price the news she brought away had not been too dearly bought. She sat with half-closed eyes as the train rushed through the familiar landscape; and now the memories of her former journey, instead of flying before her like dead leaves, seemed to be ripening in her blood like sleeping grain. She would never again know what it was to feel herself alone. Everything seemed to have grown suddenly clear and simple. She no longer had any difficulty in picturing herself as Harney's wife now that she was the mother of his child; and compared to her sovereign right Annabel Balch's claim seemed no more than a girl's sentimental fancy.

That evening, at the gate of the red house, she found Ally waiting in the dusk. 'I was down at the post-office just as they were closing up, and Will Targatt said there was a letter for you, so I brought it.'

Ally held out the letter, looking at Charity with piercing sympathy. Since the scene of the torn blouse there had been a new and fearful admiration in the eyes she bent on her friend.

Charity snatched the letter with a laugh. 'Oh, thank you – good-night,' she called out over her shoulder as she ran up the path. If she had lingered a moment she knew she would have had Ally at her heels.

She hurried upstairs and felt her way into her dark room. Her hands trembled as she groped for the matches and lit her candle, and the flap of the envelope was so closely stuck that she had to find her scissors and slit it open. At length she read:

DEAR CHARITY:

I have your letter, and it touches me more than I can say. Won't you trust me, in return, to do my best? There are things it is hard to explain, much less to justify; but your generosity makes everything easier. All I can do now is to thank you from my soul for understanding. Your telling me that you wanted me to do right has helped me beyond expression. If ever there is a hope of realizing what we dreamed of you will see me back on the instant; and I haven't yet lost that hope.

She read the letter with a rush; then she went over and over it, each time more slowly and painstakingly. It was so beautifully expressed that she found it almost as difficult to understand as the gentleman's explanation of the Bible pictures at Nettleton; but gradually she became aware that the gist of its meaning lay in the last few words. 'If ever there is a hope of realizing what we dreamed of...'

But then he wasn't even sure of that? She understood now that every word and every reticence was an avowal of Annabel Balch's prior claim. It was true that he was engaged to her, and that he had not yet found a way of breaking his engagement.

As she read the letter over Charity understood what it must have cost him to write it. He was not trying to evade an importunate claim; he was honestly and contritely struggling between opposing duties. She did not even reproach him in her thoughts for having concealed from her that he was not free: she could not see anything more reprehensible in his conduct than in her own. From the first she had needed him more than he had wanted her, and the power that had swept them together had been as far beyond resistance as a great gale loosening the leaves of the forest.... Only, there stood between them, fixed and upright in the general upheaval, the indestructible figure of Annabel Balch....

Face to face with his admission of the fact, she sat staring at the letter. A cold tremor ran over her, and the hard sobs struggled up into her throat and shook her from head to foot. For a while she was caught and tossed on great waves of anguish that left her hardly conscious of anything but the blind struggle against their assaults. Then, little by little, she began to relive, with a dreadful poignancy, each separate stage of her poor romance. Foolish things she had said came back to her, gay answers Harney had made, his first kiss in the darkness between the fireworks, their choosing the blue brooch together, the way he had teased her about the letters she had dropped in her flight from the evangelist. All these memories, and a thousand others, hummed through her brain till his nearness grew so vivid that she felt his fingers in her hair, and his warm breath on her cheek as he bent her head back like a flower. These things were hers; they had passed into her blood, and become a part of her, they were building the child in her womb; it was impossible to tear asunder strands of life so interwoven.

The conviction gradually strengthened her, and she began to form in her mind the first words of the letter she meant to write to Harney. She wanted to write it at once, and with feverish hands she began to rummage in her drawer for a sheet of letter paper. But there was none left; she must go downstairs to get it. She had a superstitious feeling that the letter must be written on the instant, that setting down her secret in words would bring her reassurance and safety; and taking up her candle she went down to Mr Royall's office.

At that hour she was not likely to find him there: he had probably had his supper and walked over to Carrick Fry's. She pushed open the door of the unlit room, and the light of her lifted candle fell on his figure, seated in the darkness in his high-backed chair. His arms lay along the arms of the chair, and his head was bent a little; but he lifted it quickly as Charity entered. She started back as their eyes met, remembering that her own were red with weeping, and that her face was livid with the fatigue and emotion of her journey. But it was too late to escape, and she stood and looked at him in silence.

He had risen from his chair, and came toward her with outstretched hands. The gesture was so unexpected that she let him take her hands in his, and they stood thus, without speaking, till Mr Royall said gravely: 'Charity – was you looking for me?'

She freed herself abruptly and fell back. 'Me? No —' She set down the candle on his desk. 'I wanted some letter-paper, that's all.'

His face contracted, and the bushy brows jutted forward over his eyes. Without answering he opened the drawer of the desk, took out a sheet of paper and an envelope, and pushed them toward her. 'Do you want a stamp too?' he asked.

She nodded, and he gave her the stamp. As he did so she felt that he was looking at her intently, and she knew that the candle light flickering up on her white face must be distorting her swollen features and exaggerating the dark rings about her eyes. She snatched up the paper, her reassurance dissolving under his pitiless gaze, in which she seemed to read the grim perception of her state, and the ironic recollection of the day when, in that very room, he had offered to compel Harney to marry her. His look seemed to say that he knew she had taken the paper to write to her lover, who had left her as he had warned her she would be left. She remembered the scorn with which she had turned from him that day, and knew, if he guessed the truth, what a list of old scores it must settle. She turned and fled upstairs; but when she got back to her room all the words that had been waiting had vanished. . . .

If she could have gone to Harney it would have been different; she would only have had to show herself to let his memories speak for her. But she had no money left, and there was no one from whom she could have borrowed enough for such a journey. There was nothing to do but to write, and await his reply. For a long time she sat bent above the blank page; but she found nothing to say that really expressed what she was feeling. . . .

Harney had written that she had made it easier for him, and she was glad it was so; she did not want to make things hard. She knew she had it in her power to do that; she held his fate in her hands. All she had to do was to tell him the truth; but that was the very fact that held her back. . . . Her five minutes face to face with Mr Royall had stripped her of her last illusion, and brought her back to North Dormer's point of view. Distinctly and pitilessly there rose before her the fate of the girl who was married 'to make things right'. She had seen too many village love-stories end in that way. Poor Rose Coles's miserable marriage was of the number; and what good had come of it for her or for Halston Skeff? They had hated each other from the day the minister married them; and whenever old Mrs Skeff had a fancy to humiliate her daughter-in-law she had only to say: 'Who'd ever think the baby's only two? And for a seven months' child – ain't it a wonder what a size he is?' North Dormer had treasures of indulgence for brands in the burning, but only derision for those who succeeded in getting snatched from it; and Charity had always understood Julia Hawes's refusal to be snatched. . . .

Only – was there no alternative but Julia's? Her soul recoiled from the vision of the white-faced woman among the plush sofas and gilt frames. In the established order of things as she knew them she saw no place for her individual adventure. . . .

She sat in her chair without undressing till faint grey streaks began to divide the black slats of the shutters. Then she stood up and pushed them open, letting in the light. The coming of a new day brought a sharper consciousness of ineluctable reality, and with it a sense of the need of action. She looked at herself in the glass, and saw her face, white in the autumn dawn, with pinched cheeks and dark-ringed eyes, and all the marks of her state that she herself would never have noticed, but that Dr Merkle's diagnosis had made plain to her. She could not hope that those signs would escape the watchful village; even before her figure lost its shape she knew her face would betray her.

Leaning from her window she looked out on the dark and empty scene; the ashen houses with shuttered windows, the grey road climbing the slope to the hemlock belt above the cemetery, and the heavy mass of the Mountain black against a rainy sky. To the east a space of light was broadening above the forest; but over that also the clouds hung. Slowly her gaze travelled across the fields to the rugged curve of the hills. She had looked out so often on that lifeless circle, and wondered if anything could ever happen to anyone who was enclosed in it. . . .

Almost without conscious thought her decision had been reached; as her eyes had followed the circle of the hills her mind had also travelled the old round. She supposed it was something in her blood that made the Mountain the only answer to her questioning, the inevitable escape from all that hemmed her in and beset her. At any rate it began to loom in her now as it loomed against the rainy dawn; and the longer she looked at it the more clearly she understood that now at last she was really going there.

XVI

The rain held off, and an hour later, when she started, wild gleams of sunlight were blowing across the fields.

After Harney's departure she had returned her bicycle to its owner at Creston, and she was not sure of being able to walk all the way to the Mountain. The deserted house was on the road; but the idea of spending the night there was unendurable, and she meant to try to push on to Hamblin, where she could sleep under a wood-shed if her strength should fail her. Her preparations had been made with quiet forethought. Before starting she had forced herself to swallow a glass of milk and eat a piece of bread; and she had put in her canvas satchel a little packet of the chocolate that Harney always carried in his bicycle bag. She wanted above all to keep up her strength, and reach her destination without attracting notice....

Mile by mile she retraced the road over which she had so often flown to her lover. When she reached the turn where the wood-road branched off from the Creston highway she remembered the Gospel tent – long since folded up and transplanted – and her start of involuntary terror when the fat evangelist had said: 'Your Saviour knows everything. Come and confess your guilt.' There was no sense of guilt in her now, but only a desperate desire to defend her secret from irreverent eyes, and begin life again among people to whom the harsh code of the village was unknown. The impulse did not shape itself in thought: she only knew she must save her baby, and hide herself with it somewhere where no one would ever come to trouble them.

She walked on and on, growing more heavy-footed as the day advanced. It seemed a cruel chance that compelled her to retrace every step of the way to the deserted house; and when she came in sight of the orchard, and the silver-grey roof slanting crookedly through the laden branches, her strength failed her and she sat down by the roadside. She sat there a long time, trying to gather the courage to start again, and walk past the broken gate and the untrimmed rose-bushes strung with scarlet hips. A few drops of rain were falling, and she thought of the warm evenings when she and Harney had sat embraced in the shadowy room, and the noise of summer showers on the roof had rustled through their kisses. At length she understood that if she stayed any longer the rain might compel her to take shelter in the house overnight, and she got up and walked on, averting her eyes as she came abreast of the white gate and the tangled garden.

The hours wore on, and she walked more and more slowly, pausing now and then to rest, and to eat a little bread and an apple picked up from the roadside. Her body seemed to grow heavier with every yard of the way, and she wondered how she would be able to carry her child later, if already he laid such a burden on her. . . . A fresh wind had sprung up, scattering the rain and blowing down keenly from the mountain. Presently the clouds lowered again, and a few white darts struck her in the face: it was the first snow falling over Hamblin. The roofs of the lonely village were only half a mile ahead, and she was resolved to push beyond it, and try to reach the Mountain that night. She had no clear plan of action, except that, once in the settlement, she meant to look for Liff Hyatt, and get him to take her to her mother. She herself had been born as her own baby was going to be born; and whatever her mother's subsequent life had been, she could hardly help remembering the past, and receiving a daughter who was facing the trouble she had known.

Suddenly the deadly faintness came over her once more and she sat down on the bank and leaned her head against a tree-trunk. The long road and the cloudy landscape vanished from her eyes, and for a time she seemed to be circling about in some terrible wheeling darkness. Then that too faded.

She opened her eyes, and saw a buggy drawn up beside her,

and a man who had jumped down from it and was gazing at her with a puzzled face. Slowly consciousness came back, and she saw that the man was Liff Hyatt.

She was dimly aware that he was asking her something, and she looked at him in silence, trying to find strength to speak. At length her voice stirred in her throat, and she said in a whisper: 'I'm going up the Mountain.'

'Up the Mountain?' he repeated, drawing aside a little; and as he moved she saw behind him, in the buggy, a heavily coated figure with a familiar pink face and gold spectacles on the bridge of a Grecian nose.

'Charity! What on earth are you doing here?' Mr Miles exclaimed, throwing the reins on the horse's back and scrambling down from the buggy.

She lifted her heavy eyes to his. 'I'm going to see my mother.'

The two men glanced at each other, and for a moment neither of them spoke.

Then Mr Miles said: 'You look ill, my dear, and it's a long way. Do you think it's wise?'

Charity stood up. 'I've got to go to her.'

A vague mirthless grin contracted Liff Hyatt's face, and Mr Miles again spoke uncertainly. 'You know, then – you'd been told?'

She stared at him. 'I don't know what you mean. I want to go to her.'

Mr Miles was examining her thoughtfully. She fancied she saw a change in his expression, and the blood rushed to her forehead. 'I just want to go to her,' she repeated.

He laid his hand on her arm. 'My child, your mother is dying. Liff Hyatt came down to fetch me. . . . Get in and come with us.'

He helped her up to the seat at his side, Liff Hyatt clambered in at the back, and they drove off toward Hamblin. At first Charity had hardly grasped what Mr Miles was saying; the physical relief of finding herself seated in the buggy, and securely on her road to the Mountain, effaced the impression of his words. But as her head cleared she began to understand. She knew the Mountain had but the most infrequent intercourse with the valleys; she had often enough heard it said that no one ever went up there except the minister, when someone was dying. And now it was her mother who was dying... and she would find herself as much alone on the Mountain as anywhere else in the world. The sense of unescapable isolation was all she could feel for the moment; then she began to wonder at the strangeness of its being Mr Miles who had undertaken to perform this grim errand. He did not seem in the least like the kind of man who would care to go up the Mountain. But here he was at her side, guiding the horse with a firm hand, and bending on her the kindly gleam of his spectacles, as if there were nothing unusual in their being together in such circumstances.

For a while she found it impossible to speak, and he seemed to understand this, and made no attempt to question her. But presently she felt her tears rise and flow down over her drawn cheeks; and he must have seen them too, for he laid his hand on hers, and said in a low voice: 'Won't you tell me what is troubling you?'

She shook her head, and he did not insist: but after a while he said, in the same low tone, so that they should not be overheard: 'Charity, what do you know of your childhood, before you came down to North Dormer?'

She controlled herself, and answered: 'Nothing, only what I heard Mr Royall say one day. He said he brought me down because my father went to prison.'

'And you've never been up there since?'

'Never.'

Mr Miles was silent again, then he said: 'I'm glad you're coming with me now. Perhaps we may find your mother alive, and she may know that you have come.'

They had reached Hamblin, where the snow-flurry had left white patches in the rough grass on the roadside, and in the angles of the roofs facing north. It was a poor bleak village under the granite flank of the Mountain, and as soon as they left it they began to climb. The road was steep and full of ruts, and the horse settled down to a walk while they mounted and mounted, the world dropping away below them in great mottled stretches of forest and field, and stormy dark blue distances.

Charity had often had visions of this ascent of the Mountain but she had not known it would reveal so wide a country, and the sight of those strange lands reaching away on every side gave her a new sense of Harney's remoteness. She knew he must be miles and miles beyond the last range of hills that seemed to be the outmost verge of things, and she wondered how she had ever dreamed of going to New York to find him. . . .

As the road mounted the country grew bleaker, and they drove across fields of faded mountain grass bleached by long months beneath the snow. In the hollows a few white birches trembled, or a mountain ash lit its scarlet clusters; but only a scant growth of pines darkened the granite ledges. The wind was blowing fiercely across the open slopes; the horse faced it with bent head and straining flanks, and now and then the buggy swayed so that Charity had to clutch its side.

Mr Miles had not spoken again; he seemed to understand that she wanted to be left alone. After a while the track they were following forked, and he pulled up the horse, as if un-certain of the way. Liff Hyatt craned his head around from the back, and shouted against the wind: 'Left—' and they turned into a stunted pine-wood and began to drive down the other side of the Mountain.

A mile or two farther on they came out on a clearing where two or three low houses lay in stony fields, crouching among the rocks as if to brace themselves against the wind. They were hardly more than sheds, built of logs and rough boards, with tin stove-pipes sticking out of their roofs. The sun was setting, and dusk had already fallen on the lower world, but a yellow glare still lay on the lonely hillside and the crouching houses. The next moment it faded and left the landscape in dark autumn twilight.

'Over there,' Liff called out, stretching his long arm over Mr Miles's shoulder. The clergyman turned to the left, across a bit of bare ground overgrown with docks and nettles, and stopped before the most ruinous of the sheds. A stove-pipe reached its crooked arm out of one window, and the broken panes of the other were stuffed with rags and paper. In contrast to such a dwelling the brown house in the swamp might have stood for the home of plenty.

As the buggy drew up two or three mongrel dogs jumped out of the twilight with a great barking, and a young man slouched to the door and stood there staring. In the twilight Charity saw that his face had the same sodden look as Bash Hyatt's, the day she had seen him sleeping by the stove. He made no effort to silence the dogs, but leaned in the door, as if roused from a drunken lethargy, while Mr Miles got out of the buggy.

'Is it here?' the clergyman asked Liff in a low voice; and Liff nodded.

Mr Miles turned to Charity. 'Just hold the horse a minute, my dear: I'll go in first,' he said, putting the reins in her hands. She took them passively, and sat staring straight ahead of her at the darkening scene while Mr Miles and Liff Hyatt went up to the house. They stood a few minutes talking with the man in the door, and then Mr Miles came back. As he came close, Charity saw that his smooth pink face wore a frightened solemn look.

'Your mother is dead, Charity; you'd better come with me,' he said.

She got down and followed him while Liff led the horse away. As she approached the door she said to herself: 'This is where I was born . . . this is where I belong. . . .' She had said it to herself often enough as she looked across the sunlit valleys at the Mountain; but it had meant nothing then, and now it had become a reality. Mr Miles took her gently by the arm, and they entered what appeared to be the only room in the house. It was so dark that she could just discern a group of a dozen people sitting or sprawling about a table made of boards laid across two barrels. They looked up listlessly as Mr Miles and Charity came in, and a woman's thick voice said: 'Here's the preacher.' But no one moved.

Mr Miles paused and looked about him; then he turned to the young man who had met them at the door.

'Is the body here?' he asked.

The young man, instead of answering, turned his head toward the group. 'Where's the candle? I tole yer to bring a candle,' he said with sudden harshness to a girl who was lolling against the table. She did not answer, but another man got up and took from some corner a candle stuck into a bottle.

'How'll I light it? The stove's out,' the girl grumbled.

Mr Miles fumbled under his heavy wrappings and drew out a match-box. He held a match to the candle, and in a moment or two a faint circle of light fell on the pale aguish heads that started out of the shadow like the heads of nocturnal animals.

'Mary's over there,' someone said; and Mr Miles, taking the bottle in his hand, passed behind the table. Charity followed him, and they stood before a mattress on the floor in a corner of the room. A woman lay on it, but she did not look like a dead woman; she seemed to have fallen across her squalid bed in a drunken sleep, and to have been left lying where she fell, in her ragged disordered clothes. One arm was flung above her head, one leg drawn up under a torn skirt that left the other bare to the knee: a swollen glistening leg with a ragged stocking rolled down about the ankle. The woman lay on her back, her eyes staring up unblinkingly at the candle that trembled in Mr Miles's hand.

'She jus' dropped off,' a woman said, over the shoulder of the others; and the young man added: 'I jus' come in and found her.'

An elderly man with lank hair and a feeble grin pushed between them. 'It was like this: I says to her on'y the night before: if you don't take and quit, I says to her . . .'

Someone pulled him back and sent him reeling against a bench along the wall, where he dropped down muttering his unheeded narrative.

There was a silence; then the young woman who had been lolling against the table suddenly parted the group, and stood in front of Charity. She was healthier and robuster looking than the others, and her weather-beaten face had a certain sullen beauty.

'Who's the girl? Who brought her here?' she said, fixing her eyes mistrustfully on the young man who had rebuked her for not having a candle ready.

Mr Miles spoke. 'I brought her; she is Mary Hyatt's daughter.'

'What? Her too?' the girl sneered; and the young man turned on her with an oath. 'Shut your mouth, damn you, or get out of here,' he said; then he relapsed into his former apathy, and dropped down on the bench, leaning his head against the wall.

Mr Miles had set the candle on the floor and taken off his heavy coat. He turned to Charity. 'Come and help me,' he said.

He knelt down by the mattress, and pressed the lids over the dead woman's eyes. Charity, trembling and sick, knelt beside him, and tried to compose her mother's body. She drew the stocking over the dreadful glistening leg, and pulled the skirt down to the battered upturned boots. As she did so, she looked at her mother's face, thin yet swollen, with lips parted in a frozen gasp above the broken teeth. There was no sign in it of anything human: she lay there like a dead dog in a ditch. Charity's hands grew cold as they touched her.

Mr Miles drew the woman's arms across her breast and laid his coat over her. Then he covered her face with his handkerchief, and placed the bottle with the candle in it at her head. Having done this he stood up.

'Is there no coffin?' he asked, turning to the group behind him.

There was a moment of bewildered silence; then the fierce girl spoke up. 'You'd oughter brought it with you. Where'd we get one here, I'd like ter know?'

Mr Miles, looking at the others, repeated: 'Is it possible you have no coffin ready?'

'That's what I say: them that has it sleeps better,' an old woman murmured. 'But then she never had no bed. . . .'

'And the stove warn't hers,' said the lank-haired man, on the defensive.

Mr Miles turned away from them and moved a few steps apart. He had drawn a book from his pocket, and after a pause he opened it and began to read, holding the book at arm's length and low down, so that the pages caught the feeble light. Charity had remained on her knees by the mattress: now that her mother's face was covered it was easier to stay near her, and avoid the sight of the living faces which too horribly showed by what stages hers had lapsed into death.

'I am the Resurrection and the Life,' Mr Miles began; 'he that believeth in me, though he were dead, yet shall he live. . . . Though after my skin worms destroy my body, yet in my flesh shall I see God. . . .'

In my flesh shall I see God! Charity thought of the gaping mouth and stony eyes under the handkerchief, and of the glistening leg over which she had drawn the stocking. . . .

'We brought nothing into this world and we shall take nothing out of it —'

There was a sudden muttering and a scuffle at the back of the group. 'I brought the stove,' said the elderly man with lank hair, pushing his way between the others. 'I wen' down to Creston'n bought it . . . n' I got a right to take it outer here . . . n' I'll lick any feller says I ain't. . . .'

'Sit down, damn you!' shouted the tall youth who had been drowsing on the bench against the wall.

'For man walketh in a vain shadow, and disquieteth himself in vain; he heapeth up riches and cannot tell who shall gather them . . .'

'Well, it *are* his,' a woman in the background interjected in a frightened whine.

The tall youth staggered to his feet. 'If you don't hold your mouths I'll turn you all out o' here, the whole lot of you,' he cried with many oaths. 'G'wan, minister . . . don't let 'em faze you. . . .'

'Now is Christ risen from the dead and become the first-fruits of them that slept. . . . Behold, I show you a mystery. We shall not all sleep, but we shall all be changed, in a moment, in the twinkling of an eye, at the last trump. . . . For this corruptible must put on incorruption and this mortal must put on immortality. So when this corruption shall have put on incorruption, and when this mortal shall have put on immortality, then shall be brought to pass the saying that is written, Death is swallowed up in Victory. . . .'

One by one the mighty words fell on Charity's bowed head, soothing the horror, subduing the tumult, mastering her as they mastered the drink-dazed creatures at her back. Mr Miles read to the last word, and then closed the book.

'Is the grave ready?' he asked.

Liff Hyatt, who had come in while he was reading, nodded a 'Yes', and pushed forward to the side of the mattress. The young man on the bench, who seemed to assert some sort of right of kinship with the dead woman, got to his feet again, and the proprietor of the stove joined him. Between them they raised up the mattress; but their movements were unsteady, and the coat slipped to the floor, revealing the poor body in its helpless misery. Charity, picking up the coat, covered her mother once more. Liff had brought a lantern, and the old woman who had already spoken took it up, and opened the door to let the little procession pass out. The wind had dropped, and the night was very dark and bitterly cold. The old woman walked ahead, the lantern shaking in her hand and spreading out before her a pale patch of dead grass and coarse-leaved weeds enclosed in an immensity of blackness.

Mr Miles took Charity by the arm, and side by side they walked behind the mattress. At length the old woman with the lantern stopped, and Charity saw the light fall on the stooping shoulders of the bearers and on a ridge of upheaved earth over which they were bending. Mr Miles released her arm and approached the hollow on the other side of the ridge; and while the men stooped down, lowering the mattress into the grave, he began to speak again.

'Man that is born of woman hath but a short time to live and is full of misery. . . . He cometh up and is cut down . . . he fleeth as it were a shadow. . . . Yet, O Lord God most holy, O Lord most mighty, O holy and merciful Saviour, deliver us not into the bitter pains of eternal death . . .'

'Easy there . . . is she down?' piped the claimant to the stove; and the young man called over his shoulder: 'Lift the light there, can't you?'

There was a pause, during which the light floated uncertainly over the open grave. Someone bent over and pulled out Mr Miles's coat— ('No, no — leave the handkerchief,' he interposed) — and then Liff Hyatt, coming forward with a spade, began to shovel in the earth.

'Forasmuch as it hath pleased Almighty God of His great mercy to take unto Himself the soul of our dear sister here departed, we therefore commit her body to the ground; earth to earth, ashes to ashes, dust to dust . . .' Liff's gaunt shoulders rose and bent in the lantern light as he dashed the clods of earth into the grave. 'God — it's froze a'ready,' he muttered, spitting into his palm and passing his ragged shirt-sleeve across his perspiring face.

'Through our Lord Jesus Christ, who shall change our vile body that it may be like unto His glorious body, according to the mighty working, whereby He is able to subdue all things unto Himself . . .' The last spadeful of earth fell on the vile body of Mary Hyatt, and Liff rested on his spade, his shoulder blades still heaving with the effort.

'Lord, have mercy upon us, Christ have mercy upon us, Lord have mercy upon us. . . .'

Mr Miles took the lantern from the old woman's hand and swept its light across the circle of bleared faces. 'Now kneel down, all of you,' he commanded, in a voice of authority that Charity had never heard. She knelt down at the edge of the grave, and the others, stiffly and hesitatingly, got to their knees beside her. Mr Miles knelt, too. 'And now pray with me — you know this prayer,' he said, and he began: 'Our Father which art in Heaven . . .' One or two of the women falteringly took the words up, and when he ended, the lank-haired man flung himself on the neck of the tall youth. 'It was this way,' he said. 'I tole her the night before, I says to her . . .' The reminiscence ended in a sob.

Mr Miles had been getting into his coat again. He came up to Charity, who had remained passively kneeling by the rough mound of earth.

'My child, you must come. It's very late.'

She lifted her eyes to his face: he seemed to speak out of another world.

'I ain't coming: I'm going to stay here.'

'Here? Where? What do you mean?'

'These are my folks. I'm going to stay with them.'

Mr Miles lowered his voice. 'But it's not possible – you don't know what you are doing. You can't stay among these people: you must come with me.'

She shook her head and rose from her knees. The group about the grave had scattered in the darkness, but the old woman with the lantern stood waiting. Her mournful withered face was not unkind, and Charity went up to her.

'Have you got a place where I can lie down for the night?' she asked. Liff came up, leading the buggy out of the night. He looked from one to the other with his feeble smile. 'She's my mother. She'll take you home,' he said; and he added, raising his voice to speak to the old woman: 'It's the girl from lawyer Royall's – Mary's girl . . . you remember. . . .'

The woman nodded and raised her sad old eyes to Charity's. When Mr Miles and Liff clambered into the buggy she went ahead with the lantern to show them the track they were to follow; then she turned back, and in silence she and Charity walked away together through the night.

XVII

Charity lay on the floor on a mattress, as her dead mother's body had lain. The room in which she lay was cold and dark and low-ceilinged, and even poorer and barer than the scene of Mary Hyatt's earthly pilgrimage. On the other side of the fireless stove Liff Hyatt's mother slept on a blanket, with two children – her grandchildren, she said – rolled up against her like sleeping puppies. They had their thin clothes spread over them, having given the only other blanket to their guest.

Through the small square of glass in the opposite wall Charity saw a deep funnel of sky, so black, so remote, so palpitating with frosty stars that her very soul seemed to be sucked up into it. Up there somewhere, she supposed, the God whom Mr Miles had invoked was waiting for Mary Hyatt to appear. What a long flight it was! And what would she have to say when she reached Him?

Charity's bewildered brain laboured with the attempt to picture her mother's past, and to relate it in any way to the designs of a just but merciful God; but it was impossible to imagine any link between them. She herself felt as remote from the poor creature she had seen lowered into her hastily dug grave as if the height of the heavens had divided them. She had seen poverty and misfortune in her life; but in a community where poor thrifty Mrs Hawes and the industrious Ally represented the nearest approach to destitution there was nothing to suggest the savage misery of the Mountain farmers.

As she lay there, half-stunned by her tragic initiation, Charity vainly tried to think herself into the life about her. But she could not even make out what relationship these people bore to each other, or to her dead mother; they seemed to be herded together in a sort of passive promiscuity in which their common misery was the strongest link. She tried to picture to herself what her life would have been if she had grown up on the Mountain, running wild in rags, sleeping on the floor curled up against her mother, like the pale-faced children huddled against old Mrs Hyatt, and turning into a fierce bewildered creature like the girl who had apostrophized her in such strange words. She was frightened by the secret affinity she had felt with this girl, and by the light it threw on her own beginnings. Then she remembered what Mr Royall had said in telling her story to Lucius Harney: 'Yes, there was a mother; but she was glad to have the child go. She'd have given her to anybody. . . .'

Well! after all, was her mother so much to blame? Charity, since that day, had always thought of her as destitute of all human feeling; now she seemed merely pitiful. What mother would not want to save her child from such a life? Charity thought of the future of her own child, and tears welled into her aching eyes, and ran down over her face. If she had been less exhausted, less burdened with his weight, she would have sprung up then and there and fled away. . . .

The grim hours of the night dragged themselves slowly by, and at last the sky paled and dawn threw a cold blue beam into the room. She lay in her corner staring at the dirty floor, the clothes-line hung with decaying rags, the old woman huddled against the cold stove, and the light gradually spreading across the wintry world, and bringing with it a new day in which she would have to live, to choose, to act, to make herself a place among these people – or to go back to the life she had left. A mortal lassitude weighed on her. There were moments when she felt that all she asked was to go on lying there unnoticed; then her mind revolted at the thought of becoming one of the miserable herd from which she sprang, and it seemed as though, to save her child from such a fate, she would find strength to travel any distance, and bear any burden life might put on her.

Vague thoughts of Nettleton flitted through her mind. She said to herself that she would find some quiet place where she could bear her child, and give it to decent people to keep; and then she would go out like Julia Hawes and earn its living and hers. She knew that girls of that kind sometimes made enough to have their children nicely cared for; and every other consideration disappeared in the vision of her baby, cleaned and combed and rosy, and hidden away somewhere where she could run in and kiss it, and bring it pretty things to wear. Anything, anything was better than to add another life to the nest of misery on the Mountain. . . .

The old woman and the children were still sleeping when Charity rose from her mattress. Her body was stiff with cold and fatigue, and she moved slowly lest her heavy steps should rouse them. She was faint with hunger, and had nothing left in her satchel; but on the table she saw the half of a stale loaf. No doubt it was to serve as the breakfast of old Mrs Hyatt and the children; but Charity did not care; she had her own baby to think of. She broke off a piece of the bread and ate it greedily; then her glance fell on the thin faces of the sleeping children, and filled with compunction she rummaged in her satchel for something with which to pay for what she had taken. She found one of the pretty chemises that Ally had made for her, with a blue ribbon run through its edging. It was one of the dainty things on which she had squandered her savings, and as she looked at it the blood rushed to her forehead. She laid the chemise on the table, and stealing across the floor lifted the latch and went out. . . .

The morning was icy cold and a pale sun was just rising above the eastern shoulder of the Mountain. The houses scattered on the hillside lay cold and smokeless under the sun-flecked clouds, and not a human being was in sight. Charity paused on the threshold and tried to discover the road by which she had come the night before. Across the field surrounding Mrs Hyatt's shanty she saw the tumble-down house in which she supposed the funeral service had taken place. The trail ran across the ground between the two houses and disappeared in the pine-wood on the flank of the Mountain; and a little way to the right, under a wind-beaten thorn, a mound of fresh earth made a dark spot on the fawn-coloured stubble. Charity walked across the field to the mound. As she approached it she heard a bird's note in the still air, and looking up she saw a brown song-sparrow perched in an upper branch of the thorn above the grave. She stood a minute listening to his small solitary song; then she rejoined the trail and began to mount the hill to the pine-wood.

Thus far she had been impelled by the blind instinct of flight; but each step seemed to bring her nearer to the realities of which her feverish vigil had given only a shadowy image. Now that she walked again in a daylight world, on the way back to familiar things, her imagination moved more soberly. On one point she was still decided: she could not remain at North Dormer, and the sooner she got away from it the better. But everything beyond was darkness.

As she continued to climb the air grew keener, and when she passed from the shelter of the pines to the open grassy roof of the Mountain the cold wind of the night before sprang out on her. She bent her shoulders and struggled on against it for a while; but presently her breath failed, and she sat down under a ledge of rock overhung by shivering birches. From where she sat she saw the trail wandering across the bleached grass in the direction of Hamblin, and the granite wall of the Mountain falling away to infinite distances. On that side of the ridge the valleys still lay in wintry shadow; but in the plain beyond the sun was touching village roofs and steeples, and gilding the haze of smoke over far-off invisible towns.

Charity felt herself a mere speck in the lonely circle of the sky. The events of the last two days seemed to have divided her forever from her short dream of bliss. Even Harney's image had been blurred by that crushing experience: she thought of him as so remote from her that he seemed hardly more than a memory. In her fagged and floating mind only one sensation had the weight of reality; it was the bodily burden of her child. But for it she would have felt as rootless as the whiffs of thistledown the wind blew past her. Her child was like a load that held her down, and yet like a hand that pulled her to her feet. She said to herself that she must get up and struggle on. . . .

Her eyes turned back to the trail across the top of the Mountain, and in the distance she saw a buggy against the sky. She knew its antique outline, and the gaunt build of the old horse pressing forward with lowered head; and after a moment she recognized the heavy bulk of the man who held the reins. The buggy was following the trail and making straight for the pine-wood through which she had climbed; and she knew at once that the driver was in search of her. Her first impulse was to crouch down under the ledge till he had passed; but the instinct of concealment was overruled by the relief of feeling that someone was near her in the awful emptiness. She stood up and walked toward the buggy.

Mr Royall saw her, and touched the horse with the whip. A minute or two later he was abreast of Charity; their eyes met, and without speaking he leaned over and helped her up into the buggy. She tried to speak, to stammer out some explanation, but no words came to her; and as he drew the cover over her knees he simply said: 'The minister told me he'd left you up here, so I come up for you.'

He turned the horse's head, and they began to jog back toward Hamblin. Charity sat speechless, staring straight ahead of her, and Mr Royall occasionally uttered a word of encouragement to the horse: 'Get along there, Dan. . . . I gave him a rest at Hamblin; but I brought him along pretty quick, and it's a stiff pull up here against the wind.'

As he spoke it occurred to her for the first time that to reach the top of the Mountain so early he must have left North Dormer at the coldest hour of the night, and have travelled steadily but for the halt at Hamblin; and she felt a softness at her heart which no act of his had ever produced since he had brought her the Crimson Rambler because she had given up boarding-school to stay with him.

After an interval he began again: 'It was a day just like this, only spitting snow, when I come up here for you the first time.' Then, as if fearing that she might take his remark as a reminder of past benefits, he added quickly: 'I dunno's you think it was such a good job, either.'

'Yes, I do,' she murmured, looking straight ahead of her.

'Well,' he said, 'I tried —'

He did not finish the sentence, and she could think of nothing more to say.

'Ho, there, Dan, step out,' he muttered, jerking the bridle. 'We ain't home yet. – You cold?' he asked abruptly.

She shook her head, but he drew the cover higher up, and stooped to tuck it in about the ankles. She continued to look straight ahead. Tears of weariness and weakness were dimming her eyes and beginning to run over, but she dared not wipe them away lest he should observe the gesture.

They drove in silence, following the long loops of the descent upon Hamblin, and Mr Royall did not speak again till they reached the outskirts of the village. Then he let the reins droop on the dashboard and drew out his watch.

'Charity,' he said, 'you look fair done up, and North Dormer's a goodish way off. I've figured out that we'd do better to stop here long enough for you to get a mouthful of breakfast and then drive down to Creston and take the train.'

She roused herself from her apathetic musing. 'The train – what train?'

Mr Royall, without answering, let the horse jog on till they reached the door of the first house in the village. 'This is old Mrs Hobart's place,' he said. 'She'll give us something hot to drink.'

Charity, half unconsciously, found herself getting out of the buggy and following him in at the open door. They entered a decent kitchen with a fire crackling in the stove. An old woman with a kindly face was setting out cups and saucers on the table. She looked up and nodded as they came in, and Mr Royall advanced to the stove, clapping his numb hands together.

'Well, Mrs Hobart, you got any breakfast for this young lady? You can see she's cold and hungry.'

Mrs Hobart smiled on Charity and took a tin coffee-pot

from the fire. 'My, you do look pretty mean,' she said compassionately.

Charity reddened, and sat down at the table. A feeling of complete passiveness had once more come over her, and she was conscious only of the pleasant animal sensations of warmth and rest.

Mrs Hobart put bread and milk on the table, and then went out of the house: Charity saw her leading the horse away to the barn across the yard. She did not come back, and Mr Royall and Charity sat alone at the table with the smoking coffee between them. He poured out a cup for her, and put a piece of bread in the saucer, and she began to eat.

As the warmth of the coffee flowed through her veins her thoughts cleared and she began to feel like a living being again; but the return to life was so painful that the food choked in her throat and she sat staring down at the table in silent anguish.

After a while Mr Royall pushed back his chair. 'Now, then,' he said, 'if you're a mind to go along —' She did not move, and he continued: 'We can pick up the noon train for Nettleton if you say so.'

The words sent the blood rushing to her face, and she raised her startled eyes to his. He was standing on the other side of the table looking at her kindly and gravely; and suddenly she understood what he was going to say. She continued to sit motionless, a leaden weight upon her lips.

'You and me have spoke some hard things to each other in our time, Charity; and there's no good that I can see in any more talking now. But I'll never feel any way but one about you; and if you say so we'll drive down in time to catch that train, and go straight to the minister's house; and when you come back home you'll come as Mrs Royall.'

His voice had the grave persuasive accent that had moved his hearers at the Home Week festival; she had a sense of depths of mournful tolerance under that easy tone. Her whole body began to tremble with the dread of her own weakness.

'Oh, I can't —' she burst out desperately.

'Can't what?'

She herself did not know: she was not sure if she was reject-
ing what he offered, or already struggling against the tempta-
tion of taking what she no longer had a right to. She stood up,
shaking and bewildered, and began to speak: 'I know I ain't
been fair to you always; but I want to be now. . . . I want you
to know . . . I want . . .' Her voice failed her and she stopped.

Mr Royall leaned against the wall. He was paler than usual,
but his face was composed and kindly and her agitation did
not appear to perturb him.

'What's all this about wanting?' he said as she paused. 'Do
you know what you really want? I'll tell you. You want to
be took home and took care of. And I guess that's all there is
to say.'

'No . . . it's not all. . . .'

'Ain't it?' He looked at his watch. 'Well, I'll tell you another
thing. All *I* want is to know if you'll marry me. If there was
anything else, I'd tell you so; but there ain't. Come to my age,
a man knows the things that matter and the things that don't;
that's about the only good turn life does us.'

His tone was so strong and resolute that it was like a supporting arm about her. She felt her resistance melting, her strength
slipping away from her as he spoke.

'Don't cry, Charity,' he exclaimed in a shaken voice. She
looked up, startled at his emotion, and their eyes met.

'See here,' he said gently, 'old Dan's come a long distance,
and we've got to let him take it easy the rest of the way. . . .'

He picked up the cloak that had slipped to her chair and
laid it about her shoulders. She followed him out of the house,
and they walked across the yard to the shed, where the horse
was tied. Mr Royall unblanketed him and led him out into the
road. Charity got into the buggy and he drew the cover about
her and shook out the reins with a cluck. When they reached
the end of the village he turned the horse's head toward
Creston.

XVIII

They began to jog down the winding road to the valley at old Dan's languid pace. Charity felt herself sinking into deeper depths of weariness, and as they descended through the bare woods there were moments when she lost the exact sense of things, and seemed to be sitting beside her lover with the leafy arch of summer bending over them. But this illusion was faint and transitory. For the most part she had only a confused sensation of slipping down a smooth irresistible current; and she abandoned herself to the feeling as a refuge from the torment of thought.

Mr Royall seldom spoke, but his silent presence gave her, for the first time, a sense of peace and security. She knew that where he was there would be warmth, rest, silence; and for the moment they were all she wanted. She shut her eyes, and even these things grew dim to her. . . .

In the train, during the short run from Creston to Nettleton, the warmth aroused her, and the consciousness of being under strange eyes gave her a momentary energy. She sat upright, facing Mr Royall, and stared out of the window at the denuded country. Forty-eight hours earlier, when she had last traversed it, many of the trees still held their leaves; but the high wind of the last two nights had stripped them, and the lines of the landscape were as finely pencilled as in December. A few days of autumn cold had wiped out all trace of the rich fields and languid groves through which she had passed on the Fourth of July; and with the fading of the landscape those fervid hours had faded too. She could no longer believe that she was the being who had lived them; she was someone to whom something irreparable and overwhelming had happened, but the traces of the steps leading up to it had almost vanished.

When the train reached Nettleton and she walked out into the square at Mr Royall's side the sense of unreality grew more overpowering. The physical strain of the night and day had left no room in her mind for new sensations and she followed Mr Royall as passively as a tired child. As in a confused dream she presently found herself sitting with him in a pleasant room, at a table with a red and white table-cloth on which hot food and tea were placed. He filled her cup and plate and whenever she lifted her eyes from them she found his resting on her with the same steady tranquil gaze that had reassured and strengthened her when they had faced each other in old Mrs Hobart's kitchen. As everything else in her consciousness grew more and more confused and immaterial, became more and more like the universal shimmer that dissolves the world to failing eyes, Mr Royall's presence began to detach itself with rocky firmness from this elusive background. She had always thought of him – when she thought of him at all – as of someone hateful and obstructive, but whom she could outwit and dominate when she chose to make the effort. Only once, on the day of the Old Home Week celebration, while the stray fragments of his address drifted across her troubled mind, had she caught a glimpse of another being, a being so different from the dull-witted enemy with whom she had supposed herself to be living that even through the burning mist of her own dreams he had stood out with startling distinctness. For a moment, then, what he said – and something in his way of saying it – had made her see why he had always struck her as such a lonely man. But the mist of her dreams had hidden him again, and she had forgotten that fugitive impression.

It came back to her now, as they sat at the table, and gave her, through her own immeasurable desolation, a sudden sense of their nearness to each other. But all these feelings were only brief streaks of light in the grey blur of her physical weakness. Through it she was aware that Mr Royall presently left her sitting by the table in the warm room, and came back after an interval with a carriage from the station – a closed 'hack' with sunburnt blue silk blinds – in which they drove

together to a house covered with creepers and standing next
to a church with a carpet of turf before it. They got out at
this house, and the carriage waited while they walked up the
path and entered a wainscoted hall and then a room full of
books. In this room a clergyman whom Charity had never
seen received them pleasantly, and asked them to be seated
for a few minutes while witnesses were being summoned.

Charity sat down obediently, and Mr Royall, his hands
behind his back, paced slowly up and down the room. As he
turned and faced Charity, she noticed that his lips were twitching a little; but the look in his eyes was grave and calm. Once
he paused before her and said timidly: 'Your hair's got kinder
loose with the wind,' and she lifted her hands and tried to
smooth back the locks that had escaped from her braid. There
was a looking-glass in a carved frame on the wall, but she was
ashamed to look at herself in it, and she sat with her hands
folded on her knee till the clergyman returned. Then they
went out again, along a sort of arcaded passage, and into a low
vaulted room with a cross on an altar, and rows of benches.
The clergyman, who had left them at the door, presently reappeared before the altar in a surplice, and a lady who was
probably his wife, and a man in a blue shirt who had been
raking dead leaves on the lawn, came in and sat on one of the
benches.

The clergyman opened a book and signed to Charity and
Mr Royall to approach. Mr Royall advanced a few steps, and
Charity followed him as she had followed him to the buggy
when they went out of Mrs Hobart's kitchen; she had the
feeling that if she ceased to keep close to him, and do what
he told her to do, the world would slip away from beneath
her feet.

The clergyman began to read, and on her dazed mind there
rose the memory of Mr Miles, standing the night before in the
desolate house of the Mountain, and reading out of the same
book words that had the same dread sound of finality:

'I require and charge you both, as ye will answer at the
dreadful day of judgment when the secrets of all hearts shall

be disclosed, that if either of you know any impediment whereby ye may not be lawfully joined together . . .'

Charity raised her eyes and met Mr Royall's. They were still looking at her kindly and steadily. 'I will!' she heard him say a moment later, after another interval of words that she had failed to catch. She was so busy trying to understand the gestures the clergyman was signalling to her to make that she no longer heard what was being said. After another interval the lady on the bench stood up, and taking her hand put it in Mr Royall's. It lay enclosed in his strong palm and she felt a ring that was too big for her being slipped onto her thin finger. She understood then that she was married. . . .

Late that afternoon Charity sat alone in a bedroom of the fashionable hotel where she and Harney had vainly sought a table on the Fourth of July. She had never before been in so handsomely furnished a room. The mirror above the dressing-table reflected the high head-board and fluted pillow-slips of the double bed, and a bedspread so spotlessly white that she had hesitated to lay her hat and jacket on it. The humming radiator diffused an atmosphere of drowsy warmth, and through a half-open door she saw the glitter of the nickel taps above twin marble basins.

For a while the long turmoil of the night and day had slipped away from her and she sat with closed eyes, surrendering herself to the spell of warmth and silence. But presently this merciful apathy was succeeded by the sudden acuteness of vision with which sick people sometimes wake out of a heavy sleep. As she opened her eyes they rested on the picture that hung above the bed. It was a large engraving with a dazzling white margin enclosed in a wide frame of bird's-eye maple with an inner scroll of gold. The engraving represented a young man in a boat on a lake overhung with trees. He was leaning over to gather water-lilies for the girl in a light dress who lay among the cushions in the stern. The scene was full of a drowsy midsummer radiance, and Charity averted her eyes from it and, rising from her chair, began to wander restlessly about the room.

It was on the fifth floor, and its broad window of plate glass looked over the roofs of the town. Beyond them stretched a wooded landscape in which the last fires of sunset were picking out a steely gleam. Charity gazed at the gleam with startled eyes. Even through the gathering twilight she recognized the contour of the soft hills encircling it, and the way the meadows sloped to its edge. It was Nettleton Lake that she was looking at.

She stood a long time in the window staring out at the fading water. The sight of it had roused her for the first time to a realization of what she had done. Even the feeling of the ring on her hand had not brought her this sharp sense of the irretrievable. For an instant the old impulse of flight swept through her; but it was only the lift of a broken wing. She heard the door open behind her, and Mr Royall came in.

He had gone to the barber's to be shaved, and his shaggy grey hair had been trimmed and smoothed. He moved strongly and quickly, squaring his shoulders and carrying his head high, as if he did not want to pass unnoticed.

'What are you doing in the dark?' he called out in a cheerful voice. Charity made no answer. He went up to the window to draw down the blind, and putting his finger on the wall flooded the room with a blaze of light from the central chandelier. In this unfamiliar illumination husband and wife faced each other awkwardly for a moment; then Mr Royall said: 'We'll step down and have some supper, if you say so.'

The thought of food filled her with repugnance; but not daring to confess it she smoothed her hair and followed him to the lift.

An hour later, coming out of the glare of the dining-room, she waited in the marble-panelled hall while Mr Royall, before the brass lattice of one of the corner counters, selected a cigar and bought an evening paper. Men were lounging in rocking chairs under the blazing chandeliers, travellers coming and going, bells ringing, porters shuffling by with luggage. Over Mr Royall's shoulder, as he leaned against the counter, a girl with her hair puffed high smirked and nodded at a dapper drummer who was getting his key at the desk across the hall.

Charity stood among these cross-currents of life as motion-less and inert as if she had been one of the tables screwed to the marble floor. All her soul was gathered up into one sick sense of coming doom, and she watched Mr Royall in fasci-nated terror while he pinched the cigars in successive boxes and unfolded his evening paper with a steady hand.

Presently he turned and joined her. 'You go right along up to bed – I'm going to sit down here and have my smoke,' he said. He spoke as easily and naturally as if they had been an old couple, long used to each other's ways, and her contracted heart gave a flutter of relief. She followed him to the lift, and he put her in and enjoined the buttoned and braided boy to show her to her room.

She groped her way in through the darkness, forgetting where the electric button was, and not knowing how to mani-pulate it. But a white autumn moon had risen, and the illu-minated sky put a pale light in the room. By it she undressed, and after folding up the ruffled pillow-slips crept timidly under the spotless counterpane. She had never felt such smooth sheets or such light warm blankets; but the softness of the bed did not soothe her. She lay there trembling with a fear that ran through her veins like ice. 'What have I done? Oh, what have I done?' she whispered, shuddering to her pillow; and pressing her face against it to shut out the pale landscape beyond the window she lay in the darkness straining her ears, and shaking at every footstep that approached. . . .

Suddenly she sat up and pressed her hands against her frightened heart. A faint sound had told her that someone was in the room; but she must have slept in the interval, for she had heard no one enter. The moon was setting beyond the opposite roofs, and in the darkness, outlined against the grey square of the window, she saw a figure seated in the rocking-chair. The figure did not move: it was sunk deep in the chair, with bowed head and folded arms, and she saw that it was Mr Royall who sat there. He had not undressed, but had taken the blanket from the foot of the bed and laid it across his knees. Trembling and holding her breath she watched him, fearing that he had been roused by her movement; but he did not stir, and she concluded that he wished her to think he was asleep.

As she continued to watch him ineffable relief stole slowly over her, relaxing her strained nerves and exhausted body. He knew, then . . . he knew . . . it was because he knew that he had married her, and that he sat there in the darkness to show her she was safe with him. A stir of something deeper than she had ever felt in thinking of him flitted through her tired brain, and cautiously, noiselessly, she let her head sink on the pillow. . . .

When she woke the room was full of morning light, and her first glance showed her that she was alone in it. She got up and dressed, and as she was fastening her dress the door opened, and Mr Royall came in. He looked old and tired in the bright daylight, but his face wore the same expression of grave friendliness that had reassured her on the Mountain. It was as if all the dark spirits had gone out of him.

They went downstairs to the dining-room for breakfast, and after breakfast he told her he had some insurance business to attend to. 'I guess while I'm doing it you'd better step out and buy yourself whatever you need.' He smiled, and added with an embarrassed laugh: 'You know I always wanted you to beat all the other girls.' He drew something from his pocket, and pushed it across the table to her; and she saw that he had given her two twenty-dollar bills. 'If it ain't enough there's more where that come from – I want you to beat 'em all hollow,' he repeated.

She flushed and tried to stammer out her thanks, but he had pushed back his chair and was leading the way out of the dining-room. In the hall he paused a minute to say that if it suited her they would take the three o'clock train back to North Dormer; then he took his hat and coat from the rack and went out.

A few minutes later Charity went out too. She had watched to see in what direction he was going, and she took the opposite way and walked quickly down the main street to the brick building on the corner of Lake Avenue. There she paused to look cautiously up and down the thoroughfare, and then climbed the brass-bound stairs to Dr Merkle's door. The same bushy-headed mulatto girl admitted her, and after the same interval of waiting in the red plush parlor she was once more summoned to Dr Merkle's office. The doctor received her without surprise, and led her into the inner plush sanctuary.

'I thought you'd be back, but you've come a mite too soon: I told you to be patient and not fret,' she observed, after a pause of penetrating scrutiny.

Charity drew the money from her breast. 'I've come to get my blue brooch,' she said, flushing.

'Your brooch?' Dr Merkle appeared not to remember. 'My, yes – I get so many things of that kind. Well, my dear, you'll have to wait while I get it out of the safe. I don't leave valuables like that laying round like the noospaper.'

She disappeared for a moment, and returned with a bit of twisted-up tissue paper from which she unwrapped the brooch.

Charity, as she looked at it, felt a stir of warmth at her heart. She held out an eager hand.

'Have you got the change?' she asked a little breathlessly, laying one of the twenty-dollar bills on the table.

'Change? What'd I want to have change for? I only see two twenties there,' Dr Merkle answered brightly.

Charity paused, disconcerted. 'I thought . . . you said it was five dollars a visit. . . .'

'For *you*, as a favour – I did. But how about the responsibility – *and* the insurance? I don't s'pose you ever thought of that? This pin's worth a hundred dollars easy. If it had got lost or stole, where'd I been when you come to claim it?'

Charity remained silent, puzzled and half-convinced by the argument, and Dr Merkle promptly followed up her advantage. 'I didn't ask you for your brooch, my dear. I'd a good deal ruther folks paid me my regular charge than have 'em put me to all this trouble.'

She paused, and Charity, seized with a desperate longing to escape, rose to her feet and held out one of the bills.

'Will you take that?' she asked.

'No, I won't take that, my dear; but I'll take it with its mate, and hand you over a signed receipt if you don't trust me.'

'Oh, but I can't – it's all I've got,' Charity exclaimed.

Dr Merkle looked up at her pleasantly from the plush sofa. 'It seems you got married yesterday, up to the 'Piscopal church; I heard all about the wedding from the minister's chore-man. It would be a pity, wouldn't it, to let Mr Royall know you had an account running here? I just put it to you as your own mother might.'

Anger flamed up in Charity, and for an instant she thought of abandoning the brooch and letting Dr Merkle do her worst. But how could she leave her only treasure with that evil woman? She wanted it for her baby: she meant it, in some mysterious way, to be a link between Harney's child and its unknown father. Trembling and hating herself while she did it, she laid Mr Royall's money on the table, and catching up the brooch fled out of the room and the house. . . .

In the street she stood still, dazed by this last adventure. But the brooch lay in her bosom like a talisman, and she felt a secret lightness of heart. It gave her strength, after a moment, to walk on slowly in the direction of the post office, and go in through the swinging doors. At one of the windows she bought a sheet of letter-paper, an envelope and a stamp; then she sat down at a table and dipped the rusty post office pen in ink. She had come there possessed with a fear which had haunted her ever since she had felt Mr Royall's ring on her finger: the fear that Harney might, after all, free himself and come back to her. It was a possibility which had never occurred to her during the dreadful hours after she had received his letter; only when the decisive step she had taken made longing turn to apprehension did such a contingency seem conceivable. She addressed the envelope, and on the sheet of paper she wrote:

I'm married to Mr Royall. I'll always remember you.

CHARITY.

The last words were not in the least what she had meant to write; they had flowed from her pen irresistibly. She had not had the strength to complete her sacrifice; but, after all, what did it matter? Now that there was no chance of ever seeing Harney again, why should she not tell him the truth?

When she had put the letter in the box she went out into the busy sunlit street and began to walk to the hotel. Behind the plate-glass windows of the department stores she noticed the tempting display of dresses and dress-materials that had fired her imagination on the day when she and Harney had looked in at them together. They reminded her of Mr Royall's injunction to go out and buy all she needed. She looked down at her shabby dress, and wondered what she should say when he saw her coming back empty-handed. As she drew near the hotel she saw him waiting on the doorstep, and her heart began to beat with apprehension.

He nodded and waved his hand at her approach, and they walked through the hall and went upstairs to collect their possessions, so that Mr Royall might give up the key of the room when they went down again for their midday dinner. In the bedroom, while she was thrusting back into the satchel the few things she had brought away with her, she suddenly felt that his eyes were on her and that he was going to speak. She stood still, her half-folded night-gown in her hand, while the blood rushed up to her drawn cheeks.

'Well, did you rig yourself out handsomely? I haven't seen any bundles round,' he said jocosely.

'Oh, I'd rather let Ally Hawes make the few things I want,' she answered.

'That so?' He looked at her thoughtfully for a moment and his eye-brows projected in a scowl. Then his face grew friendly again. 'Well, I wanted you to go back looking stylisher than any of them; but I guess you're right. You're a good girl, Charity.'

Their eyes met, and something rose in his that she had never seen there: a look that made her feel ashamed and yet secure.

'I guess you're good, too,' she said, shyly and quickly. He smiled without answering, and they went out of the room together and dropped down to the hall in the glittering lift.

Late that evening, in the cold autumn moonlight, they drove up to the door of the red house.

BUNNER SISTERS

PART I

I

In the days when New York's traffic moved at the pace of the drooping horse-car, when society applauded Christine Nilsson at the Academy of Music and basked in the sunsets of the Hudson River School on the walls of the National Academy of Design, an inconspicuous shop with a single show-window was intimately and favourably known to the feminine population of the quarter bordering on Stuyvesant Square.

It was a very small shop, in a shabby basement, in a side-street already doomed to decline; and from the miscellaneous display behind the windowpane, and the brevity of the sign surmounting it (merely 'Bunner Sisters' in blotchy gold on a black ground) it would have been difficult for the uninitiated to guess the precise nature of the business carried on within. But that was of little consequence, since its fame was so purely local that the customers on whom its existence depended were almost congenitally aware of the exact range of 'goods' to be found at Bunner Sisters'.

The house of which Bunner Sisters had annexed the base-ment was a private dwelling with a brick front, green shutters on weak hinges, and a dress-maker's sign in the window above the shop. On each side of its modest three stories stood higher buildings, with fronts of brown stone, cracked and blistered, cast-iron balconies and cat-haunted grass-patches behind twisted railings. These houses too had once been private, but now a cheap lunchroom filled the basement of one, while the other announced itself, above the knotty wisteria that clasped its central balcony, as the Mendoza Family Hotel. It was obvi-ous from the chronic cluster of refuse-barrels at its area-gate and the blurred surface of its curtainless windows, that the

273

families frequenting the Mendoza Hotel were not exacting in their tastes; though they doubtless indulged in as much fastidiousness as they could afford to pay for, and rather more than their landlord thought they had a right to express.

These three houses fairly exemplified the general character of the street, which, as it stretched eastward, rapidly fell from shabbiness to squalor, with an increasing frequency of projecting sign-boards, and of swinging doors that softly shut or opened at the touch of red-nosed men and pale little girls with broken jugs. The middle of the street was full of irregular depressions, well adapted to retain the long swirls of dust and straw and twisted paper that the wind drove up and down its sad untended length; and toward the end of the day, when traffic had been active, the fissured pavement formed a mosaic of coloured hand-bills, lids of tomato-cans, old shoes, cigar-stumps and banana skins, cemented together by a layer of mud, or veiled in a powdering of dust, as the state of the weather determined.

The sole refuge offered from the contemplation of this depressing waste was the sight of the Bunner Sisters' window. Its panes were always well-washed, and though their display of artificial flowers, bands of scalloped flannel, wire hat-frames, and jars of home-made preserves, had the indefinable greyish tinge of objects long preserved in the show-case of a museum, the window revealed a background of orderly counters and whitewashed walls in pleasant contrast to the adjoining dinginess.

The Bunner sisters were proud of the neatness of their shop and content with its humble prosperity. It was not what they had once imagined it would be, but though it presented but a shrunken image of their earlier ambitions it enabled them to pay their rent and keep themselves alive and out of debt; and it was long since their hopes had soared higher.

Now and then, however, among their greyer hours there came one not bright enough to be called sunny, but rather of the silvery twilight hue which sometimes ends a day of storm. It was such an hour that Ann Eliza, the elder of the firm, was soberly enjoying as she sat one January evening in the back room which served as bedroom, kitchen and parlour to herself and her sister Evelina. In the shop the blinds had been drawn down, the counters cleared and the wares in the window lightly covered with an old sheet; but the shop-door remained unlocked till Evelina, who had taken a parcel to the dyer's, should come back.

In the back room a kettle bubbled on the stove, and Ann Eliza had laid a cloth over one end of the centre table, and placed near the green-shaded sewing lamp two teacups, two plates, a sugar-bowl and a piece of pie. The rest of the room remained in a greenish shadow which discreetly veiled the outline of an old-fashioned mahogany bedstead surmounted by a chromo of a young lady in a nightgown who clung with eloquently-rolling eyes to a crag described in illuminated letters as the Rock of Ages; and against the unshaded windows two rocking-chairs and a sewing-machine were silhouetted on the dusk.

Ann Eliza, her small and habitually anxious face smoothed to unusual serenity, and the streaks of pale hair on her veined temples shining glossily beneath the lamp, had seated herself at the table, and was tying up, with her usual fumbling deliberation, a knobby object wrapped in paper. Now and then, as she struggled with the string, which was too short, she fancied she heard the click of the shop-door, and paused to listen for her sister; then, as no one came, she straightened her spectacles and entered into renewed conflict with the parcel. In honour of some event of obvious importance, she had put on her double-dyed and triple-turned black silk. Age, while bestowing on this garment a *patine* worthy of a Renaissance bronze, had deprived it of whatever curves the wearer's pre-Raphaelite figure had once been able to impress on it; but this stiffness of outline gave it an air of sacerdotal state which seemed to emphasize the importance of the occasion.

Seen thus, in her sacramental black silk, a wisp of lace turned over the collar and fastened by a mosaic brooch, and her face smoothed into harmony with her apparel, Ann Eliza looked ten years younger than behind the counter, in the heat and burden of the day. It would have been as difficult to guess her approximate age as that of the black silk, for she had the same worn and glossy aspect as her dress; but a faint tinge of pink still lingered on her cheekbones, like the reflection of sunset which sometimes colours the west long after the day is over.

When she had tied the parcel to her satisfaction, and laid it with furtive accuracy just opposite her sister's plate, she sat down, with an air of obviously-assumed indifference, in one of the rocking-chairs near the window; and a moment later the shop-door opened and Evelina entered.

The younger Bunner sister, who was a little taller than her elder, had a more pronounced nose, but a weaker slope of mouth and chin. She still permitted herself the frivolity of waving her pale hair, and its tight little ridges, stiff as the tresses of an Assyrian statue, were flattened under a dotted veil which ended at the tip of her cold-reddened nose. In her scant jacket and skirt of black cashmere she looked singularly nipped and faded; but it seemed possible that under happier conditions she might still warm into relative youth.

'Why, Ann Eliza,' she exclaimed, in a thin voice pitched to chronic fretfulness, 'what in the world you got your best silk on for?'

Ann Eliza had risen with a blush that made her steel-browed spectacles incongruous.

'Why, Evelina, why shouldn't I, I sh'ld like to know? Ain't it your birthday, dear?' She put out her arms with the awkwardness of habitually repressed emotion.

Evelina, without seeming to notice the gesture, threw back the jacket from her narrow shoulders.

'Oh, pshaw,' she said, less peevishly. 'I guess we'd better give up birthdays. Much as we can do to keep Christmas nowadays.'

'You hadn't oughter say that, Evelina. We ain't so badly off as all that. I guess you're cold and tired. Set down while I take the kettle off: it's right on the boil.'

She pushed Evelina toward the table, keeping a sideward eye

on her sister's listless movements, while her own hands were busy with the kettle. A moment later came the exclamation for which she waited.

'Why, Ann Eliza!' Evelina stood transfixed by the sight of the parcel beside her plate.

Ann Eliza, tremulously engaged in filling the teapot, lifted a look of hypocritical surprise.

'Sakes, Evelina! What's the matter?'

The younger sister had rapidly untied the string, and drawn from its wrappings a round nickel clock of the kind to be bought for a dollar-seventy-five.

'Oh, Ann Eliza, how could you?' She set the clock down, and the sisters exchanged agitated glances across the table.

'Well,' the elder retorted, '*ain't* it your birthday?'

'Yes, but –'

'Well, and ain't you had to run round the corner to the Square every morning, rain or shine, to see what time it was, ever since we had to sell mother's watch last July? Ain't you, Evelina?'

'Yes, but –'

'There ain't any buts. We've always wanted a clock and now we've got one: that's all there is about it. Ain't she a beauty, Evelina?' Ann Eliza, putting back the kettle on the stove, leaned over her sister's shoulder to pass an approving hand over the circular rim of the clock. 'Hear how loud she ticks. I was afraid you'd hear her soon as you come in.'

'No. I wasn't thinking,' murmured Evelina.

'Well, ain't you glad now?' Ann Eliza gently reproached her. The rebuke had no acerbity, for she knew that Evelina's seeming indifference was alive with unexpressed scruples.

'I'm real glad, sister; but you hadn't oughter. We could have got on well enough without.'

'Evelina Bunner, just you sit down to your tea. I guess I know what I'd oughter and what I'd hadn't oughter just as well as you do – I'm old enough!'

'You're real good, Ann Eliza; but I know you've given up something you needed to get me this clock.'

'What do I need, I'd like to know? Ain't I got a best black silk?' the elder sister said with a laugh full of nervous pleasure.

She poured out Evelina's tea, adding some condensed milk from the jug, and cutting for her the largest slice of pie; then she drew up her own chair to the table.

The two women ate in silence for a few moments before Evelina began to speak again. 'The clock is perfectly lovely and I don't say it ain't a comfort to have it; but I hate to think what it must have cost you.'

'No, it didn't, neither,' Ann Eliza retorted. 'I got it dirt cheap, if you want to know. And I paid for it out of a little extra work I did the other night on the machine for Mrs Hawkins.'

'The baby-waists?'

'Yes.'

'There, I knew it! You swore to me you'd buy a new pair of shoes with that money.'

'Well, and s'posin' I didn't want 'em – what then? I've patched up the old ones as good as new – and I do declare, Evelina Bunner, if you ask me another question you'll go and spoil all my pleasure.'

'Very well, I won't,' said the younger sister.

They continued to eat without farther words. Evelina yielded to her sister's entreaty that she should finish the pie, and poured out a second cup of tea, into which she put the last lump of sugar; and between them, on the table, the clock kept up its sociable tick.

'Where'd you get it, Ann Eliza?' asked Evelina, fascinated.

'Where'd you s'pose? Why, right round here, over acrost the Square, in the queerest little store you ever laid eyes on. I saw it in the window as I was passing, and I stepped right in and asked how much it was, and the store-keeper he was real pleasant about it. He was just the nicest man. I guess he's a German. I told him I couldn't give much, and he said, well, he knew what hard times was too. His name's Ramy – Herman Ramy: I saw it written up over the store. And he told me he used to work at Tiff'ny's, oh, for years, in the clock-department, and three years ago he took sick with some kinder

fever, and lost his place, and when he got well they'd engaged
somebody else and didn't want him, and so he started this little
store by himself. I guess he's real smart, and he spoke quite like
an educated man – but he looks sick.'

Evelina was listening with absorbed attention. In the narrow
lives of the two sisters such an episode was not to be under-
rated.

'What you say his name was?' she asked as Ann Eliza paused.

'Herman Ramy.'

'How old is he?'

'Well, I couldn't exactly tell you, he looked so sick – but
I don't b'lieve he's much over forty.'

By this time the plates had been cleared and the teapot emptied, and the two sisters rose from the table. Ann Eliza, tying
an apron over her black silk, carefully removed all traces of
the meal; then, after washing the cups and plates, and putting
them away in a cupboard, she drew her rocking-chair to the
lamp and sat down to a heap of mending. Evelina, meanwhile,
had been roaming about the room in search of an abiding-
place for the clock. A rosewood what-not with ornamental
fret-work hung on the wall beside the devout young lady in
dishabille, and after much weighing of alternatives the sisters
decided to dethrone a broken china vase filled with dried
grasses which had long stood on the top shelf, and to put the
clock in its place; the vase, after farther consideration, being
relegated to a small table covered with blue and white bead-
work, which held a Bible and prayer-book, and an illustrated
copy of Longfellow's poems given as a school-prize to their
father.

This change having been made, and the effect studied from
every angle of the room, Evelina languidly put her pinking-
machine on the table, and sat down to the monotonous work
of pinking a heap of black silk flounces. The strips of stuff
slid slowly to the floor at her side, and the clock, from its
commanding altitude, kept time with the dispiriting click of
the instrument under her fingers.

II

The purchase of Evelina's clock had been a more important event in the life of Ann Eliza Bunner than her younger sister could divine. In the first place, there had been the demoralizing satisfaction of finding herself in possession of a sum of money which she need not put into the common fund, but could spend as she chose, without consulting Evelina, and then the excitement of her stealthy trips abroad, undertaken on the rare occasions when she could trump up a pretext for leaving the shop; since, as a rule, it was Evelina who took the bundles to the dyer's, and delivered the purchases of those among their customers who were too genteel to be seen carrying home a bonnet or a bundle of pinking – so that, had it not been for the excuse of having to see Mrs Hawkins's teething baby, Ann Eliza would hardly have known what motive to allege for deserting her usual seat behind the counter.

The infrequency of her walks made them the chief events of her life. The mere act of going out from the monastic quiet of the shop into the tumult of the streets filled her with a subdued excitement which grew too intense for pleasure as she was swallowed by the engulfing roar of Broadway or Third Avenue, and began to do timid battle with their incessant cross-currents of humanity. After a glance or two into the great show-windows she usually allowed herself to be swept back into the shelter of a side-street, and finally regained her own roof in a state of breathless bewilderment and fatigue; but gradually, as her nerves were soothed by the familiar quiet of the little shop, and the click of Evelina's pinking-machine, certain sights and sounds would detach themselves from the torrent along which she had been swept, and she would devote the rest of the day to a mental reconstruction of the different episodes of her walk, till finally it took shape in her thought as a consecutive and highly-coloured experience, from which, for weeks afterwards, she would detach some fragmentary recollection in the course of her long dialogues with her sister.

But when, to the unwonted excitement of going out, was added the intenser interest of looking for a present for Evelina, Ann Eliza's agitation, sharpened by concealment, actually preyed upon her rest; and it was not till the present had been given, and she had unbosomed herself of the experiences connected with its purchase, that she could look back with anything like composure to that stirring moment of her life. From that day forward, however, she began to take a certain tranquil pleasure in thinking of Mr Ramy's small shop, not unlike her own in its countrified obscurity, though the layer of dust which covered its counter and shelves made the comparison only superficially acceptable. Still, she did not judge the state of the shop severely, for Mr Ramy had told her that he was alone in the world, and lone men, she was aware, did not know how to deal with dust. It gave her a good deal of occupation to wonder why he had never married, or if, on the other hand, he were a widower, and had lost all his dear little children; and she scarcely knew which alternative seemed to make him the more interesting. In either case, his life was assuredly a sad one; and she passed many hours in speculating on the manner in which he probably spent his evenings. She knew he lived at the back of his shop, for she had caught, on entering, a glimpse of a dingy room with a tumbled bed; and the pervading smell of cold fry suggested that he probably did his own cooking. She wondered if he did not often make his tea with water that had not boiled, and asked herself, almost jealously, who looked after the shop while he went to market. Then it occurred to her as likely that he bought his provisions at the same market as Evelina; and she was fascinated by the thought that he and her sister might constantly be meeting in total unconsciousness of the link between them. Whenever she reached this stage in her reflections she lifted a furtive glance to the clock, whose loud staccato tick was becoming a part of her inmost being.

The seed sown by these long hours of meditation germinated at last in the secret wish to go to market some morning in Evelina's stead. As this purpose rose to the surface of Ann Eliza's thoughts she shrank back shyly from its contemplation. A plan so steeped in duplicity had never before taken shape in her crystalline soul. How was it possible for her to consider such a step? And, besides, (she did not possess sufficient logic to mark the downward trend of this 'besides'), what excuse could she make that would not excite her sister's curiosity? From this second query it was an easy descent to the third: how soon could she manage to go?

It was Evelina herself, who furnished the necessary pretext by awaking with a sore throat on the day when she usually went to market. It was a Saturday, and as they always had their bit of steak on Sunday the expedition could not be postponed, and it seemed natural that Ann Eliza, as she tied an old stocking around Evelina's throat, should announce her intention of stepping round to the butcher's.

'Oh, Ann Eliza, they'll cheat you so,' her sister wailed.

Ann Eliza brushed aside the imputation with a smile, and a few minutes later, having set the room to rights, and cast a last glance at the shop, she was tying on her bonnet with fumbling haste.

The morning was damp and cold, with a sky full of sulky clouds that would not make room for the sun, but as yet dropped only an occasional snowflake. In the early light the street looked its meanest and most neglected; but to Ann Eliza, never greatly troubled by any untidiness for which she was not responsible, it seemed to wear a singularly friendly aspect.

A few minutes' walk brought her to the market where Evelina made her purchases, and where, if he had any sense of topographical fitness, Mr Ramy must also deal.

Ann Eliza, making her way through the outskirts of potato-barrels and flabby fish, found no one in the shop but the gory-aproned butcher who stood in the background cutting chops.

As she approached him across the tessellation of fish-scales, blood and saw-dust, he laid aside his cleaver and not unsympathetically asked: 'Sister sick?'

'Oh, not very – jest a cold,' she answered, as guiltily as if Evelina's illness had been feigned. 'We want a steak as usual, please – and my sister said you was to be sure to give me jest as good a cut as if it was her,' she added with childlike candour.

'Oh, that's all right.' The butcher picked up his weapon with a grin. 'Your sister knows a cut as well as any of us,' he remarked.

In another moment, Ann Eliza reflected, the steak would be cut and wrapped up, and no choice left her but to turn her disappointed steps toward home. She was too shy to try to delay the butcher by such conversational arts as she possessed, but the approach of a deaf old lady in an antiquated bonnet and mantle gave her her opportunity.

'Wait on her first, please,' Ann Eliza whispered. 'I ain't in any hurry.'

The butcher advanced to his new customer, and Ann Eliza, palpitating in the back of the shop, saw that the old lady's hesitations between liver and pork chops were likely to be in-definitely prolonged. They were still unresolved when she was interrupted by the entrance of a blowsy Irish girl with a basket on her arm. The newcomer caused a momentary diversion, and when she had departed the old lady, who was evidently as intolerant of interruption as a professional storyteller, insisted on returning to the beginning of her complicated order, and weighing anew, with an anxious appeal to the butcher's arbi-tration, the relative advantages of pork and liver. But even her hesitations, and the intrusion on them of two or three other customers, were of no avail, for Mr Ramy was not among those who entered the shop; and at last Ann Eliza, ashamed of staying longer, reluctantly claimed her steak, and walked home through the thickening snow.

Even to her simple judgment the vanity of her hopes was plain, and in the clear light that disappointment turns upon our actions she wondered how she could have been foolish enough to suppose that, even if Mr Ramy *did* go to that particular market, he would hit on the same day and hour as herself.

There followed a colourless week unmarked by farther incident. The old stocking cured Evelina's throat, and Mrs Hawkins dropped in once or twice to talk of her baby's teeth; some new orders for pinking were received, and Evelina sold a bonnet to the lady with puffed sleeves. The lady with puffed sleeves – a resident of 'the Square', whose name they had never learned, because she always carried her own parcels home – was the most distinguished and interesting figure on their horizon. She was youngish, she was elegant (as the title they had given her implied), and she had a sweet sad smile about which they had woven many histories; but even the news of her return to town – it was her first apparition that year – failed to arouse Ann Eliza's interest. All the small daily happenings which had once sufficed to fill the hours now appeared to her in their deadly insignificance; and for the first time in her long years of drudgery she rebelled at the dullness of her life. With Evelina such fits of discontent were habitual and openly proclaimed, and Ann Eliza still excused them as one of the prerogatives of youth. Besides, Evelina had not been intended by Providence to pine in such a narrow life: in the original plan of things, she had been meant to marry and have a baby, to wear silk on Sundays, and take a leading part in a Church circle. Hitherto opportunity had played her false; and for all her superior aspirations and carefully crimped hair she had remained as obscure and unsought as Ann Eliza. But the elder sister, who had long since accepted her own fate, had never accepted Evelina's. Once a pleasant young man who taught in Sunday-school had paid the younger Miss Bunner a few shy visits. That was years since, and he had speedily vanished from their view. Whether he had carried with him any of Evelina's illusions, Ann Eliza had never discovered; but his attentions had clad her sister in a halo of exquisite possibilities.

Ann Eliza, in those days, had never dreamed of allowing herself the luxury of self-pity: it seemed as much a personal right of Evelina's as her elaborately crinkled hair. But now she began to transfer to herself a portion of the sympathy she had so long bestowed on Evelina. She had at last recognized her right to set up some lost opportunities of her own; and once that dangerous precedent established, they began to crowd upon her memory.

It was at this stage of Ann Eliza's transformation that Evelina, looking up one evening from her work, said suddenly: 'My! She's stopped.'

Ann Eliza, raising her eyes from a brown merino seam, followed her sister's glance across the room. It was a Monday, and they always wound the clock on Sundays.

'Are you sure you wound her yesterday, Evelina?'

'Jest as sure as I live. She must be broke. I'll go and see.'

Evelina laid down the hat she was trimming, and took the clock from its shelf.

'There − I knew it! She's wound jest as *tight* − what you suppose's happened to her, Ann Eliza?'

'I dunno, I'm sure,' said the elder sister, wiping her spectacles before proceeding to a close examination of the clock.

With anxiously bent heads the two women shook and turned it, as though they were trying to revive a living thing; but it remained unresponsive to their touch, and at length Evelina laid it down with a sigh.

'Seems like somethin' *dead*, don't it, Ann Eliza? How still the room is!'

'Yes, ain't it?'

'Well, I'll put her back where she belongs,' Evelina continued, in the tone of one about to perform the last offices for the departed. 'And I guess,' she added, 'you'll have to step round to Mr Ramy's tomorrow, and see if he can fix her.'

Ann Eliza's face burned. 'I − yes, I guess I'll have to,' she stammered, stooping to pick up a spool of cotton which had rolled to the floor. A sudden heart-throb stretched the seams of her flat alpaca bosom, and a pulse leapt to life in each of her temples.

That night, long after Evelina slept, Ann Eliza lay awake in the unfamiliar silence, more acutely conscious of the nearness of the crippled clock than when it had volubly told out the minutes. The next morning she woke from a troubled dream of having carried it to Mr Ramy's, and found that he and his shop had vanished; and all through the day's occupations the memory of this dream oppressed her.

It had been agreed that Ann Eliza should take the clock to be repaired as soon as they had dined; but while they were still at table a weak-eyed little girl in a black apron stabbed with innumerable pins burst in on them with the cry: 'Oh, Miss Bunner, for mercy's sake! Miss Mellins has been took again.'

Miss Mellins was the dress-maker upstairs, and the weak-eyed child one of her youthful apprentices.

Ann Eliza started from her seat. 'I'll come at once. Quick, Evelina, the cordial!'

By this euphemistic name the sisters designated a bottle of cherry brandy, the last of a dozen inherited from their grand-mother, which they kept locked in their cupboard against such emergencies. A moment later, cordial in hand, Ann Eliza was hurrying upstairs behind the weak-eyed child.

Miss Mellins's 'turn' was sufficiently serious to detain Ann Eliza for nearly two hours, and dusk had fallen when she took up the depleted bottle of cordial and descended again to the shop. It was empty, as usual, and Evelina sat at her pinking-machine in the back room. Ann Eliza was still agitated by her efforts to restore the dress-maker, but in spite of her preoccu-pation she was struck, as soon as she entered, by the loud tick of the clock, which still stood on the shelf where she had left it.

'Why, she's going!' she gasped, before Evelina could ques-tion her about Miss Mellins. 'Did she start up again by herself?'

'Oh, no; but I couldn't stand not knowing what time it was, I've got so accustomed to having her round; and just after you went upstairs Mrs Hawkins dropped in, so I asked her to tend the store for a minute, and I clapped on my things and ran right round to Mr Ramy's. It turned out there wasn't anything the matter with her – nothin' on'y a speck of dust in the works – and he fixed her for me in a minute and I brought her right back. Ain't it lovely to hear her going again? But tell me about Miss Mellins, quick!'

For a moment Ann Eliza found no words. Not till she learned that she had missed her chance did she understand how many hopes had hung upon it. Even now she did not know why she had wanted so much to see the clock-maker again.

'I s'pose it's because nothing's ever happened to me,' she thought, with a twinge of envy for the fate which gave Evelina every opportunity that came their way. 'She had the Sunday-school teacher too,' Ann Eliza murmured to herself; but she was well-trained in the arts of renunciation, and after a scarcely perceptible pause she plunged into a detailed description of the dress-maker's 'turn'.

Evelina, when her curiosity was roused, was an insatiable questioner, and it was supper-time before she had come to the end of her enquiries about Miss Mellins; but when the two sisters had seated themselves at their evening meal Ann Eliza at last found a chance to say: 'So she on'y had a speck of dust in her.'

Evelina understood at once that the reference was not to Miss Mellins. 'Yes – at least he thinks so,' she answered, helping herself as a matter of course to the first cup of tea.

'On'y to think!' murmured Ann Eliza.

'But he isn't *sure*,' Evelina continued, absently pushing the teapot toward her sister. 'It may be something wrong with the – I forget what he called it. Anyhow, he said he'd call round and see, day after tomorrow, after supper.'

'Who said?' gasped Ann Eliza.

'Why, Mr Ramy, of course. I think he's real nice, Ann Eliza. And I don't believe he's forty; but he *does* look sick. I guess he's pretty lonesome, all by himself in that store. He as much as told me so, and somehow' – Evelina paused and bridled – 'I kinder thought that maybe his saying he'd call round about the clock was on'y just an excuse. He said it just as I was going out of the store. What you think, Ann Eliza?'

'Oh, I don't har'ly know.' To save herself, Ann Eliza could produce nothing warmer.

'Well, I don't pretend to be smarter than other folks,' said Evelina, putting a conscious hand to her hair, 'but I guess Mr Herman Ramy wouldn't be sorry to pass an evening here, 'stead of spending it all alone in that poky little place of his.'

Her self-consciousness irritated Ann Eliza.

'I guess he's got plenty of friends of his own,' she said, almost harshly.

'No, he ain't, either. He's got hardly any.'

'Did he tell you that too?' Even to her own ears there was a faint sneer in the interrogation.

'Yes, he did,' said Evelina, dropping her lids with a smile. 'He seemed to be just crazy to talk to somebody – somebody agreeable, I mean. I think the man's unhappy, Ann Eliza.'

'So do I,' broke from the elder sister.

'He seems such an educated man, too. He was reading the paper when I went in. Ain't it sad to think of his being reduced to that little store, after being years at Tiff'ny's, and one of the head men in their clock-department?'

'He told you all that?'

'Why, yes. I think he'd a' told me everything ever happened to him if I'd had the time to stay and listen. I tell you he's dead lonely, Ann Eliza.'

'Yes,' said Ann Eliza.

III

Two days afterward, Ann Eliza noticed that Evelina, before they sat down to supper, pinned a crimson bow under her collar; and when the meal was finished the younger sister, who seldom concerned herself with the clearing of the table, set about with nervous haste to help Ann Eliza in the removal of the dishes.

'I hate to see food mussing about,' she grumbled. 'Ain't it hateful having to do everything in one room?'

'Oh, Evelina, I've always thought we was so comfortable,' Ann Eliza protested.

'Well, so we are, comfortable enough; but I don't suppose there's any harm in my saying I wisht we had a parlour, is there? Anyway, we might manage to buy a screen to hide the bed.'

Ann Eliza coloured. There was something vaguely embarrassing in Evelina's suggestion.

'I always think if we ask for more what we have may be taken from us,' she ventured.

'Well, whoever took it wouldn't get much,' Evelina retorted with a laugh as she swept up the tablecloth.

A few moments later the back room was in its usual flawless order and the two sisters had seated themselves near the lamp. Ann Eliza had taken up her sewing, and Evelina was preparing to make artificial flowers. The sisters usually relegated this more delicate business to the long leisure of the summer months; but tonight Evelina had brought out the box which lay all winter under the bed, and spread before her a bright array of muslin petals, yellow stamens and green corollas, and a tray of little implements curiously suggestive of the dental art. Ann Eliza made no remark on this unusual proceeding; perhaps she guessed why, for that evening, her sister had chosen a graceful task.

Presently a knock on the outer door made them look up; but Evelina, the first on her feet, said promptly: 'Sit still. I'll see who it is.'

Ann Eliza was glad to sit still: the baby's petticoat that she was stitching shook in her fingers.

'Sister, here's Mr Ramy come to look at the clock,' said Evelina, a moment later, in the high drawl she cultivated before strangers; and a shortish man with a pale bearded face and upturned coat-collar came stiffly into the room.

Ann Eliza let her work fall as she stood up. 'You're very welcome, I'm sure, Mr Ramy. It's real kind of you to call.'

'Nod ad all, ma'am.' A tendency to illustrate Grimm's law in the interchange of his consonants betrayed the clockmaker's nationality, but he was evidently used to speaking English, or at least the particular branch of the vernacular with which the Bunner sisters were familiar. 'I don't like to led any clock go out of my store without being sure it gives satisfaction,' he added.

'Oh – but we were satisfied,' Ann Eliza assured him.

'But I wasn't, you see, ma'am,' said Mr Ramy looking slowly about the room, 'nor I won't be, not till I see that clock's going all right.'

'May I assist you off with your coat, Mr Ramy?' Evelina interposed. She could never trust Ann Eliza to remember these opening ceremonies.

'Thank you, ma'am,' he replied, and taking his threadbare overcoat and shabby hat she laid them on a chair with the gesture she imagined the lady with the puffed sleeves might make use of on similar occasions. Ann Eliza's social sense was roused, and she felt that the next act of hospitality must be hers. 'Won't you suit yourself to a seat?' she suggested. 'My sister will reach down the clock; but I'm sure she's all right again. She's went beautiful ever since you fixed her.'

'Dat's good,' said Mr Ramy. His lips parted in a smile which showed a row of yellowish teeth with one or two gaps in it; but in spite of this disclosure Ann Eliza thought his smile extremely pleasant: there was something wistful and conciliating in it

which agreed with the pathos of his sunken cheeks and prominent eyes. As he took the lamp, the light fell on his bulging
forehead and wide skull thinly covered with greyish hair. His
hands were pale and broad, with knotty joints and square
fingertips rimmed with grime; but his touch was as light as a
woman's.

'Well, ladies, dat clock's all right,' he pronounced.

'I'm sure we're very much obliged to you,' said Evelina,
throwing a glance at her sister.

'Oh,' Ann Eliza murmured, involuntarily answering the
admonition. She selected a key from the bunch that hung at
her waist with her cutting-out scissors, and fitting it into the
lock of the cupboard, brought out the cherry brandy and three
old-fashioned glasses engraved with vine-wreaths.

'It's a very cold night,' she said, 'and maybe you'd like a sip of
this cordial. It was made a great while ago by our grandmother.'

'It looks fine,' said Mr Ramy bowing, and Ann Eliza filled
the glasses. In her own and Evelina's she poured only a few
drops, but she filled their guest's to the brim. 'My sister and
I seldom take wine,' she explained.

With another bow, which included both his hostesses,
Mr Ramy drank off the cherry brandy and pronounced it
excellent.

Evelina meanwhile, with an assumption of industry intended to put their guest at ease, had taken up her instruments
and was twisting a rose-petal into shape.

'You make artificial flowers, I see, ma'am,' said Mr Ramy
with interest. 'It's very pretty work. I had a lady-vriend in
Shermany dat used to make flowers.' He put out a square
fingertip to touch the petal.

Evelina blushed a little. 'You left Germany long ago,
I suppose?'

'Dear me yes, a goot while ago. I was only ninedeen when
I come to the States.'

After this the conversation dragged on intermittently till Mr
Ramy, peering about the room with the short-sighted glance
of his race, said with an air of interest: 'You're pleasantly fixed

here; it looks real cozy.' The note of wistfulness in his voice was obscurely moving to Ann Eliza.

'Oh, we live very plainly,' said Evelina, with an affectation of grandeur deeply impressive to her sister. 'We have very simple tastes.'

'You look real comfortable, anyhow,' said Mr Ramy. His bulging eyes seemed to muster the details of the scene with a gentle envy. 'I wisht I had as good a store; but I guess no blace seems homelike when you're always alone in it.'

For some minutes longer the conversation moved on at this desultory pace, and then Mr Ramy, who had been obviously nerving himself for the difficult act of departure, took his leave with an abruptness which would have startled anyone used to the subtler gradations of intercourse. But to Ann Eliza and her sister there was nothing surprising in his abrupt retreat. The long-drawn agonies of preparing to leave, and the subsequent dumb plunge through the door, were so usual in their circle that they would have been as much embarrassed as Mr Ramy if he had tried to put any fluency into his adieux.

After he had left both sisters remained silent for a while; then Evelina, laying aside her unfinished flower, said: 'I'll go and lock up.'

IV

Intolerably monotonous seemed now to the Bunner sisters the treadmill routine of the shop, colourless and long their evenings about the lamp, aimless their habitual interchange of words to the weary accompaniment of the sewing and pinking machines.

It was perhaps with the idea of relieving the tension of their mood that Evelina, the following Sunday, suggested inviting Miss Mellins to supper. The Bunner sisters were not in a position to be lavish of the humblest hospitality, but two or three times in the year they shared their evening meal with a friend; and Miss Mellins, still flushed with the importance of her 'turn', seemed the most interesting guest they could invite.

As the three women seated themselves at the supper-table, embellished by the unwonted addition of pound cake and sweet pickles, the dress-maker's sharp swarthy person stood out vividly between the neutral-tinted sisters. Miss Mellins was a small woman with a glossy yellow face and a frizz of black hair bristling with imitation tortoise-shell pins. Her sleeves had a fashionable cut, and half a dozen metal bangles rattled on her wrists. Her voice rattled like her bangles as she poured forth a stream of anecdote and ejaculation; and her round black eyes jumped with acrobatic velocity from one face to another. Miss Mellins was always having or hearing of amazing adventures. She had surprised a burglar in her room at midnight (though how he got there, what he robbed her of, and by what means he escaped had never been quite clear to her auditors); she had been warned by anonymous letters that her grocer (a rejected suitor) was putting poison in her tea; she had a customer who was shadowed by detectives, and another (a very wealthy lady) who had been arrested in a department store for kleptomania; she had been present at a spiritualist seance where an old gentleman had died in a fit on seeing a materialization of his mother-in-law; she had escaped from two fires in her nightgown, and at the funeral of her first cousin the horses attached to the hearse had run away and smashed the coffin, precipitating her relative into an open man-hole before the eyes of his distracted family.

A skeptical observer might have explained Miss Mellins's proneness to adventure by the fact that she derived her chief mental nourishment from the *Police Gazette* and the *Fireside Weekly*; but her lot was cast in a circle where such insinuations were not likely to be heard, and where the title-role in blood-curdling drama had long been her recognized right.

'Yes,' she was now saying, her emphatic eyes on Ann Eliza, 'you may not believe it, Miss Bunner, and I don't know's I should myself if anybody else was to tell me, but over a year before ever I was born, my mother she went to see a gypsy fortune-teller that was exhibited in a tent on the Battery with the green-headed lady, though her father warned her not to – and what you s'pose she told her? Why, she told her these very words – says she: "Your next child'll be a girl with jet-black curls, and she'll suffer from spasms."'

'Mercy!' murmured Ann Eliza, a ripple of sympathy running down her spine.

'D'you ever have spasms before, Miss Mellins?' Evelina asked.

'Yes, ma'am,' the dress-maker declared. 'And where'd you suppose I had 'em? Why, at my cousin Emma McIntyre's wedding, her that married the apothecary over in Jersey City, though her mother appeared to her in a dream and told her she'd rue the day she done it, but as Emma said, she got more advice than she wanted from the living, and if she was to listen to spectres too she'd never be sure what she'd ought to do and what she'd oughtn't; but I will say her husband took to drink, and she never was the same woman after her fust baby – well, they had an elegant church wedding, and what you s'pose I saw as I was walkin' up the aisle with the wedding percession?'

'Well?' Ann Eliza whispered, forgetting to thread her needle.

'Why, a coffin, to be sure, right on the top step of the chancel – Emma's folks is 'piscopalians and she would have a church wedding, though *his* mother raised a terrible rumpus over it – well, there it set, right in front of where the minister stood that was going to marry 'em, a coffin covered with a black velvet pall with a gold fringe, and a "Gates Ajar" in white camellias atop of it.'

'Goodness,' said Evelina, starting, 'there's a knock!'

'Who can it be?' shuddered Ann Eliza, still under the spell of Miss Mellins's hallucination.

Evelina rose and lit a candle to guide her through the shop. They heard her turn the key of the outer door, and a gust of night air stirred the close atmosphere of the back room; then there was a sound of vivacious exclamations, and Evelina returned with Mr Ramy.

Ann Eliza's heart rocked like a boat in a heavy sea, and the dress-maker's eyes, distended with curiosity, sprang eagerly from face to face.

'I just thought I'd call in again,' said Mr Ramy, evidently somewhat disconcerted by the presence of Miss Mellins. 'Just to see how the clock's behaving,' he added with his hollow-cheeked smile.

'Oh, she's behaving beautiful,' said Ann Eliza; 'but we're real glad to see you all the same. Miss Mellins, let me make you acquainted with Mr Ramy.'

The dress-maker tossed back her head and dropped her lids in condescending recognition of the stranger's presence; and Mr Ramy responded by an awkward bow. After the first moment of constraint a renewed sense of satisfaction filled the consciousness of the three women. The Bunner sisters were not sorry to let Miss Mellins see that they received an occasional evening visit, and Miss Mellins was clearly enchanted at the opportunity of pouring her latest tale into a new ear. As for Mr Ramy, he adjusted himself to the situation with greater ease than might have been expected, and Evelina, who had been sorry that he should enter the room while the remains of supper still lingered on the table, blushed with pleasure at his good-humoured offer to help her 'glear away'.

The table cleared, Ann Eliza suggested a game of cards; and it was after eleven o'clock when Mr Ramy rose to take leave. His adieux were so much less abrupt than on the occasion of his first visit that Evelina was able to satisfy her sense of etiquette by escorting him, candle in hand, to the outer door; and as the two disappeared into the shop Miss Mellins playfully turned to Ann Eliza.

'Well, well, Miss Bunner,' she murmured, jerking her chin in the direction of the retreating figures, 'I'd no idea your sister was keeping company. On'y to think!'

Ann Eliza, roused from a state of dreamy beatitude, turned her timid eyes on the dress-maker.

'Oh, you're mistaken, Miss Mellins. We don't har'ly know Mr Ramy.'

Miss Mellins smiled incredulously. 'You go 'long, Miss Bunner. I guess there'll be a wedding somewheres round here before spring, and I'll be real offended if I ain't asked to make the dress. I've always seen her in a gored satin with rooshings.'

Ann Eliza made no answer. She had grown very pale, and her eyes lingered searchingly on Evelina as the younger sister reentered the room. Evelina's cheeks were pink, and her blue eyes glittered; but it seemed to Ann Eliza that the coquettish tilt of her head regrettably emphasized the weakness of her receding chin. It was the first time that Ann Eliza had ever seen a flaw in her sister's beauty, and her involuntary criticism startled her like a secret disloyalty.

That night, after the light had been put out, the elder sister knelt longer than usual at her prayers. In the silence of the darkened room she was offering up certain dreams and aspirations whose brief blossoming had lent a transient freshness to her days. She wondered now how she could ever have supposed that Mr Ramy's visits had another cause than the one Miss Mellins suggested. Had not the sight of Evelina first inspired him with a sudden solicitude for the welfare of the clock? And what charms but Evelina's could have induced him to repeat his visit? Grief held up its torch to the frail fabric of Ann Eliza's illusions, and with a firm heart she watched them shrivel into ashes; then, rising from her knees full of the chill joy of renunciation, she laid a kiss on the crimping pins of the sleeping Evelina and crept under the bedspread at her side.

V

During the months that followed, Mr Ramy visited the sisters with increasing frequency. It became his habit to call on them every Sunday evening, and occasionally during the week he would find an excuse for dropping in unannounced as they were settling down to their work beside the lamp. Ann Eliza noticed that Evelina now took the precaution of putting on her crimson bow every evening before supper, and that she had refurbished with a bit of carefully washed lace the black silk which they still called new because it had been bought a year after Ann Eliza's.

Mr Ramy, as he grew more intimate, became less conversational, and after the sisters had blushingly accorded him the privilege of a pipe he began to permit himself long stretches of meditative silence that were not without charm to his hostesses. There was something at once fortifying and pacific in the sense of that tranquil male presence in an atmosphere which had so long quivered with little feminine doubts and distresses; and the sisters fell into the habit of saying to each other, in moments of uncertainty: 'We'll ask Mr Ramy when he comes,' and of accepting his verdict, whatever it might be, with a fatalistic readiness that relieved them of all responsibility.

When Mr Ramy drew the pipe from his mouth and became, in his turn, confidential, the acuteness of their sympathy grew almost painful to the sisters. With passionate participation they listened to the story of his early struggles in Germany, and of the long illness which had been the cause of his recent misfortunes. The name of the Mrs Hochmuller (an old comrade's widow) who had nursed him through his fever was greeted with reverential sighs and an inward pang of envy whenever it recurred in his biographical monologues, and once when the sisters were alone Evelina called a responsive flush to Ann Eliza's brow by saying suddenly, without the mention of any name: 'I wonder what she's like?'

One day toward spring Mr Ramy, who had by this time become as much a part of their lives as the letter-carrier or the milkman, ventured the suggestion that the ladies should accompany him to an exhibition of stereopticon views which was to take place at Chickering Hall on the following evening.

After their first breathless 'Oh!' of pleasure there was a silence of mutual consultation, which Ann Eliza at last broke by saying: 'You better go with Mr Ramy, Evelina. I guess we don't both want to leave the store at night.'

Evelina, with such protests as politeness demanded, acquiesced in this opinion, and spent the next day in trimming a white chip bonnet with forget-me-nots of her own making. Ann Eliza brought out her mosaic brooch, a cashmere scarf of their mother's was taken from its linen cerements, and thus adorned Evelina blushingly departed with Mr Ramy, while the elder sister sat down in her place at the pinking-machine.

It seemed to Ann Eliza that she was alone for hours, and she was surprised, when she heard Evelina tap on the door, to find that the clock marked only half-past ten.

'It must have gone wrong again,' she reflected as she rose to let her sister in.

The evening had been brilliantly interesting, and several striking stereopticon views of Berlin had afforded Mr Ramy the opportunity of enlarging on the marvels of his native city.

'He said he'd love to show it all to me!' Evelina declared as Ann Eliza conned her glowing face. 'Did you ever hear anything so silly? I didn't know which way to look.'

Ann Eliza received this confidence with a sympathetic murmur.

'My bonnet *is* becoming, isn't it?' Evelina went on irrelevantly, smiling at her reflection in the cracked glass above the chest of drawers.

'You're jest lovely,' said Ann Eliza.

Spring was making itself unmistakably known to the dis-
trustful New Yorker by an increased harshness of wind and
prevalence of dust, when one day Evelina entered the back
room at supper-time with a cluster of jonquils in her hand.

'I was just that foolish,' she answered Ann Eliza's wondering glance, 'I couldn't help buyin' 'em. I felt as if I must have
something pretty to look at right away.'

'Oh, sister,' said Ann Eliza, in trembling sympathy. She felt
that special indulgence must be conceded to those in Evelina's
state since she had had her own fleeting vision of such mysterious longings as the words betrayed.

Evelina, meanwhile, had taken the bundle of dried grasses
out of the broken china vase, and was putting the jonquils in
their place with touches that lingered down their smooth stems
and bladelike leaves.

'Ain't they pretty?' she kept repeating as she gathered the
flowers into a starry circle. 'Seems as if spring was really here,
don't it?'

Ann Eliza remembered that it was Mr Ramy's evening.

When he came, the Teutonic eye for anything that blooms
made him turn at once to the jonquils.

'Ain't dey pretty?' he said. 'Seems like as if de spring was
really here.'

'Don't it?' Evelina exclaimed, thrilled by the coincidence
of their thought. 'It's just what I was saying to my sister.'

Ann Eliza got up suddenly and moved away; she remembered that she had not wound the clock the day before. Evelina
was sitting at the table; the jonquils rose slenderly between
herself and Mr Ramy.

'Oh,' she murmured with vague eyes, 'how I'd love to get
away somewheres into the country this very minute – somewheres where it was green and quiet. Seems as if I couldn't
stand the city another day.' But Ann Eliza noticed that she was
looking at Mr Ramy, and not at the flowers.

'I guess we might go to Cendral Park some Sunday,' their
visitor suggested. 'Do you ever go there, Miss Evelina?'

'No, we don't very often; leastways we ain't been for a

good while.' She sparkled at the prospect. 'It would be lovely, wouldn't it, Ann Eliza?'

'Why, yes,' said the elder sister, coming back to her seat.

'Well, why don't we go next Sunday?' Mr Ramy continued. 'And we'll invite Miss Mellins too – that'll make a gozy little party.'

That night when Evelina undressed she took a jonquil from the vase and pressed it with a certain ostentation between the leaves of her prayer-book. Ann Eliza, covertly observing her, felt that Evelina was not sorry to be observed, and that her own acute consciousness of the act was somehow regarded as magnifying its significance.

The following Sunday broke blue and warm. The Bunner sisters were habitual church-goers, but for once they left their prayer-books on the what-not, and ten o'clock found them, gloved and bonneted, awaiting Miss Mellins's knock. Miss Mellins presently appeared in a glitter of jet sequins and spangles, with a tale of having seen a strange man prowling under her windows till he was called off at dawn by a confederate's whistle; and shortly afterward came Mr Ramy, his hair brushed with more than usual care, his broad hands encased in gloves of olive-green kid.

The little party set out for the nearest street-car, and a flutter of mingled gratification and embarrassment stirred Ann Eliza's bosom when it was found that Mr Ramy intended to pay their fares. Nor did he fail to live up to this opening liberality; for after guiding them through the Mall and the Ramble he led the way to a rustic restaurant where, also at his expense, they fared idyllically on milk and lemon-pie.

After this they resumed their walk, strolling on with the slowness of unaccustomed holiday-makers from one path to another – through budding shrubberies, past grass-banks sprinkled with lilac crocuses, and under rocks on which the forsythia lay like sudden sunshine. Everything about her seemed new and miraculously lovely to Ann Eliza; but she kept her feelings to herself, leaving it to Evelina to exclaim at the hepaticas under the shady ledges, and to Miss Mellins, less interested in the vegetable than in the human world, to remark significantly on the probable history of the persons they met. All the alleys were thronged with promenaders and obstructed by perambulators; and Miss Mellins's running commentary threw a glare of lurid possibilities over the placid family groups and their romping progeny.

Ann Eliza was in no mood for such interpretations of life; but, knowing that Miss Mellins had been invited for the sole purpose of keeping her company she continued to cling to the dress-maker's side, letting Mr Ramy lead the way with Evelina. Miss Mellins, stimulated by the excitement of the occasion, grew more and more discursive, and her ceaseless talk, and the kaleidoscopic whirl of the crowd, were unspeakably bewildering to Ann Eliza. Her feet, accustomed to the slippered ease of the shop, ached with the unfamiliar effort of walking, and her ears with the din of the dress-maker's anecdotes; but every nerve in her was aware of Evelina's enjoyment, and she was determined that no weariness of hers should curtail it. Yet even her heroism shrank from the significant glances which Miss Mellins presently began to cast at the couple in front of them: Ann Eliza could bear to connive at Evelina's bliss, but not to acknowledge it to others.

At length Evelina's feet also failed her, and she turned to suggest that they ought to be going home. Her flushed face had grown pale with fatigue, but her eyes were radiant.

The return lived in Ann Eliza's memory with the persistence of an evil dream. The horse-cars were packed with the returning throng, and they had to let a dozen go by before they could push their way into one that was already crowded. Ann Eliza had never before felt so tired. Even Miss Mellins's flow of narrative ran dry, and they sat silent, wedged between a Negro woman and a pock-marked man with a bandaged head, while the car rumbled slowly down a squalid avenue to their corner. Evelina and Mr Ramy sat together in the forward part of the car, and Ann Eliza could catch only an occasional glimpse of the forget-me-not bonnet and the clock-maker's shiny coat-collar; but when the little party got out at their corner the crowd swept them together again, and they walked back in the effortless silence of tired children to the Bunner sisters' basement. As Miss Mellins and Mr Ramy turned to go their various ways Evelina mustered a last display of smiles; but Ann Eliza crossed the threshold in silence, feeling the stillness of the little shop reach out to her like consoling arms.

That night she could not sleep; but as she lay cold and rigid at her sister's side, she suddenly felt the pressure of Evelina's arms, and heard her whisper: 'Oh, Ann Eliza, warn't it heavenly?'

VI

For four days after their Sunday in the Park the Bunner sisters had no news of Mr Ramy. At first neither one betrayed her disappointment and anxiety to the other; but on the fifth morning Evelina, always the first to yield to her feelings, said, as she turned from her untasted tea: 'I thought you'd oughter take that money out by now, Ann Eliza.'

Ann Eliza understood and reddened. The winter had been a fairly prosperous one for the sisters, and their slowly accumulated savings had now reached the handsome sum of two hundred dollars; but the satisfaction they might have felt in this unwonted opulence had been clouded by a suggestion of Miss Mellins's that there were dark rumors concerning the savings bank in which their funds were deposited. They knew Miss Mellins was given to vain alarms; but her words, by the sheer force of repetition, had so shaken Ann Eliza's peace that after long hours of midnight counsel the sisters had decided to advise with Mr Ramy; and on Ann Eliza, as the head of the house, this duty had devolved. Mr Ramy, when consulted, had not only confirmed the dress-maker's report, but had offered to find some safe investment which should give the sisters a higher rate of interest than the suspected savings bank; and Ann Eliza knew that Evelina alluded to the suggested transfer.

'Why, yes, to be sure,' she agreed. 'Mr Ramy said if he was us he wouldn't want to leave his money there any longer'n he could help.'

'It was over a week ago he said it,' Evelina reminded her.

'I know; but he told me to wait till he'd found out for sure about that other investment; and we ain't seen him since then.'

Ann Eliza's words released their secret fear. 'I wonder what's happened to him,' Evelina said. 'You don't suppose he could be sick?'

'I was wondering too,' Ann Eliza rejoined; and the sisters looked down at their plates.

'I should think you'd oughter do something about that money pretty soon,' Evelina began again.

'Well, I know I'd oughter. What would you do if you was me?'

'If I was *you*,' said her sister, with perceptible emphasis and a rising blush, 'I'd go right round and see if Mr Ramy was sick. *You* could.'

The words pierced Ann Eliza like a blade. 'Yes, that's so,' she said.

'It would only seem friendly, if he really *is* sick. If I was you I'd go today,' Evelina continued; and after dinner Ann Eliza went.

On the way she had to leave a parcel at the dyer's, and having performed that errand she turned toward Mr Ramy's shop. Never before had she felt so old, so hopeless and humble. She knew she was bound on a love-errand of Evelina's, and the knowledge seemed to dry the last drop of young blood in her veins. It took from her, too, all her faded virginal shyness; and with a brisk composure she turned the handle of the clock-maker's door.

But as she entered her heart began to tremble, for she saw Mr Ramy, his face hidden in his hands, sitting behind the counter in an attitude of strange dejection. At the click of the latch he looked up slowly, fixing a lustreless stare on Ann Eliza. For a moment she thought he did not know her.

'Oh, you're sick!' she exclaimed; and the sound of her voice seemed to recall his wandering senses.

'Why, if it ain't Miss Bunner!' he said, in a low thick tone; but he made no attempt to move, and she noticed that his face was the colour of yellow ashes.

'You *are* sick,' she persisted, emboldened by his evident need of help. 'Mr Ramy, it was real unfriendly of you not to let us know.'

He continued to look at her with dull eyes. 'I ain't been sick,' he said. 'Leastways not very: only one of my old turns.' He spoke in a slow laboured way, as if he had difficulty in getting his words together.

'Rheumatism?' she ventured, seeing how unwillingly he seemed to move.

'Well – somethin' like, maybe. I couldn't hardly put a name to it.'

'If it *was* anything like rheumatism, my grandmother used to make a tea –' Ann Eliza began: she had forgotten, in the warmth of the moment, that she had only come as Evelina's messenger.

At the mention of tea an expression of uncontrollable repugnance passed over Mr Ramy's face. 'Oh, I guess I'm getting on all right. I've just got a headache today.'

Ann Eliza's courage dropped at the note of refusal in his voice.

'I'm sorry,' she said gently. 'My sister and me'd have been glad to do anything we could for you.'

'Thank you kindly,' said Mr Ramy wearily; then, as she turned to the door, he added with an effort: 'Maybe I'll step round tomorrow.'

'We'll be real glad,' Ann Eliza repeated. Her eyes were fixed on a dusty bronze clock in the window. She was unaware of looking at it at the time, but long afterward she remembered that it represented a Newfoundland dog with his paw on an open book.

When she reached home there was a purchaser in the shop, turning over hooks and eyes under Evelina's absent-minded supervision. Ann Eliza passed hastily into the back room, but in an instant she heard her sister at her side.

'Quick! I told her I was goin' to look for some smaller hooks – how is he?' Evelina gasped.

'He ain't been very well,' said Ann Eliza slowly, her eyes on Evelina's eager face; 'but he says he'll be sure to be round tomorrow night.'

'He will? Are you telling me the truth?'

'Why, Evelina Bunner!'

'Oh, I don't care!' cried the younger recklessly, rushing back into the shop.

Ann Eliza stood burning with the shame of Evelina's self-exposure. She was shocked that, even to her, Evelina should lay bare the nakedness of her emotion; and she tried to turn her thoughts from it as though its recollection made her a sharer in her sister's debasement.

The next evening, Mr Ramy reappeared, still somewhat sallow and red-lidded, but otherwise his usual self. Ann Eliza consulted him about the investment he had recommended, and after it had been settled that he should attend to the matter for her he took up the illustrated volume of Longfellow – for, as the sisters had learned, his culture soared beyond the newspapers – and read aloud, with a fine confusion of consonants, the poem on 'Maidenhood'. Evelina lowered her lids while he read. It was a very beautiful evening, and Ann Eliza thought afterward how different life might have been with a companion who read poetry like Mr Ramy.

VII

During the ensuing weeks Mr Ramy, though his visits were as frequent as ever, did not seem to regain his usual spirits. He complained frequently of headache, but rejected Ann Eliza's tentatively proffered remedies, and seemed to shrink from any prolonged investigation of his symptoms. July had come, with a sudden ardour of heat, and one evening, as the three sat together by the open window in the back room, Evelina said: 'I dunno what I wouldn't give, a night like this, for a breath of real country air.'

'So would I,' said Mr Ramy, knocking the ashes from his pipe. 'I'd like to be setting in an arbour dis very minute.'

'Oh, wouldn't it be lovely?'

'I always think it's real cool here – we'd be heaps hotter up where Miss Mellins is,' said Ann Eliza.

'Oh, I daresay – but we'd be heaps cooler somewhere else,' her sister snapped: she was not infrequently exasperated by Ann Eliza's furtive attempts to mollify Providence.

A few days later Mr Ramy appeared with a suggestion which enchanted Evelina. He had gone the day before to see his friend, Mrs Hochmuller, who lived in the outskirts of Hoboken, and Mrs Hochmuller had proposed that on the following Sunday he should bring the Bunner sisters to spend the day with her.

'She's got a real garden, you know,' Mr Ramy explained, 'wid trees and a real summer-house to set in; and hens and chickens too. And it's an elegant sail over on de ferry-boat.'

The proposal drew no response from Ann Eliza. She was still oppressed by the recollection of her interminable Sunday in the Park; but, obedient to Evelina's imperious glance, she finally faltered out an acceptance.

The Sunday was a very hot one, and once on the ferry-boat Ann Eliza revived at the touch of the salt breeze, and the spectacle of the crowded waters; but when they reached the other shore, and stepped out on the dirty wharf, she began to ache with anticipated weariness. They got into a street-car, and were jolted from one mean street to another, till at length Mr Ramy pulled the conductor's sleeve and they got out again; then they stood in the blazing sun, near the door of a crowded beer-saloon, waiting for another car to come; and that carried them out to a thinly settled district, past vacant lots and narrow brick houses standing in unsupported solitude, till they finally reached an almost rural region of scattered cottages and low wooden buildings that looked like village 'stores'. Here the car finally stopped of its own accord, and they walked along a rutty road, past a stone-cutter's yard with a high fence tapestried with theatrical advertisements, to a little red house with green blinds and a garden paling. Really, Mr Ramy had not deceived them. Clumps of dielytra and day-lilies bloomed behind the paling, and a crooked elm hung romantically over the gable of the house.

At the gate Mrs Hochmuller, a broad woman in brick-brown merino, met them with nods and smiles, while her daughter Linda, a flaxen-haired girl with mottled red cheeks and a sidelong stare, hovered inquisitively behind her. Mrs Hochmuller, leading the way into the house, conducted the Bunner sisters the way to her bedroom. Here they were invited to spread out on a mountainous white featherbed the cashmere mantles under which the solemnity of the occasion had compelled them to swelter, and when they had given their black silks the necessary twitch of readjustment, and Evelina had fluffed out her hair before a looking-glass framed in pink-shell work, their hostess led them to a stuffy parlour smelling of gingerbread. After another ceremonial pause, broken by polite enquiries and shy ejaculations, they were shown into the kitchen, where the table was already spread with strange-looking spice-cakes and stewed fruits, and where they presently found themselves seated between Mrs Hochmuller and Mr Ramy, while the staring Linda bumped back and forth from the stove with steaming dishes.

To Ann Eliza the dinner seemed endless, and the rich fare strangely unappetizing. She was abashed by the easy intimacy of her hostess's voice and eye. With Mr Ramy Mrs Hochmuller was almost flippantly familiar, and it was only when Ann Eliza pictured her generous form bent above his sick-bed that she could forgive her for tersely addressing him as 'Ramy'. During one of the pauses of the meal Mrs Hochmuller laid her knife and fork against the edges of her plate, and, fixing her eyes on the clock-maker's face, said accusingly: 'You hat one of dem turns again, Ramy.'

'I dunno as I had,' he returned evasively.

Evelina glanced from one to the other. 'Mr Ramy *has* been sick,' she said at length, as though to show that she also was in a position to speak with authority. 'He's complained very frequently of headaches.'

'Ho! – I know him,' said Mrs Hochmuller with a laugh, her eyes still on the clock-maker. 'Ain't you ashamed of yourself, Ramy?'

Mr Ramy, who was looking at his plate, said suddenly one word which the sisters could not understand; it sounded to Ann Eliza like 'Shwike'.

Mrs Hochmuller laughed again. 'My, my,' she said, 'wouldn't you think he'd be ashamed to go and be sick and never dell me, me that nursed him troo dat awful fever?'

'Yes, I *should*,' said Evelina, with a spirited glance at Ramy; but he was looking at the sausages that Linda had just put on the table.

When dinner was over Mrs Hochmuller invited her guests to step out of the kitchen-door, and they found themselves in a green enclosure, half garden, half orchard. Grey hens followed by golden broods clucked under the twisted apple-boughs, a cat dozed on the edge of an old well, and from tree to tree ran the network of clothes-line that denoted Mrs Hochmuller's calling. Beyond the apple trees stood a yellow summer-house festooned with scarlet runners; and below it, on the farther side of a rough fence, the land dipped down, holding a bit of woodland in its hollow. It was all strangely sweet and still on that hot Sunday afternoon, and as she moved across the grass under the apple-boughs Ann Eliza thought of quiet afternoons in church, and of the hymns her mother had sung to her when she was a baby.

Evelina was more restless. She wandered from the well to the summer-house and back, she tossed crumbs to the chickens and disturbed the cat with arch caresses; and at last she expressed a desire to go down into the wood.

'I guess you got to go round by the road, then,' said Mrs Hochmuller. 'My Linda she goes troo a hole in de fence, but I guess you'd tear your dress if you was to dry.'

'I'll help you,' said Mr Ramy; and guided by Linda the pair walked along the fence till they reached a narrow gap in its boards. Through this they disappeared, watched curiously in their descent by the grinning Linda, while Mrs Hochmuller and Ann Eliza were left alone in the summer-house.

Mrs Hochmuller looked at her guest with a confidential smile. 'I guess dey'll be gone quite a while,' she remarked, jerking her double chin toward the gap in the fence. 'Folks like dat don't never remember about de dime.' And she drew out her knitting.

Ann Eliza could think of nothing to say.

'Your sister she thinks a great lot of him, don't she?' her hostess continued.

Ann Eliza's cheeks grew hot. 'Ain't you a teeny bit lonesome away out here sometimes?' she asked. 'I should think you'd be scared nights, all alone with your daughter.'

'Oh, no, I ain't,' said Mrs Hochmuller. 'You see I take in washing – dat's my business – and it's a lot cheaper doing it out here dan in de city: where'd I get a drying-ground like dis in Hobucken? And den it's safer for Linda too; it geeps her outer de streets.'

'Oh,' said Ann Eliza, shrinking. She began to feel a distinct aversion for her hostess, and her eyes turned with involuntary annoyance to the square-backed form of Linda, still inquisitively suspended on the fence. It seemed to Ann Eliza that Evelina and her companion would never return from the wood; but they came at length, Mr Ramy's brow pearled with perspiration, Evelina pink and conscious, a drooping bunch of ferns in her hand; and it was clear that, to her at least, the moments had been winged.

'D'you suppose they'll revive?' she asked, holding up the ferns; but Ann Eliza, rising at her approach, said stiffly: 'We'd better be getting home, Evelina.'

'Mercy me! Ain't you going to take your coffee first?' Mrs Hochmuller protested; and Ann Eliza found to her dismay that another long gastronomic ceremony must intervene before politeness permitted them to leave. At length, however, they found themselves again on the ferry-boat. Water and sky were grey, with a dividing gleam of sunset that sent sleek opal waves in the boat's wake. The wind had a cool tarry breath, as though it had travelled over miles of shipping, and the hiss of the water about the paddles was as delicious as though it had been splashed into their tired faces.

Ann Eliza sat apart, looking away from the others. She had made up her mind that Mr Ramy had proposed to Evelina in the wood, and she was silently preparing herself to receive her sister's confidence that evening.

But Evelina was apparently in no mood for confidences. When they reached home she put her faded ferns in water, and after supper, when she had laid aside her silk dress and the forget-me-not bonnet, she remained silently seated in her rocking-chair near the open window. It was long since Ann Eliza had seen her in so uncommunicative a mood.

The following Saturday Ann Eliza was sitting alone in the shop when the door opened and Mr Ramy entered. He had never before called at that hour, and she wondered a little anxiously what had brought him.

'Has anything happened?' she asked, pushing aside the basketful of buttons she had been sorting.

'Not's I know of,' said Mr Ramy tranquilly. 'But I always close up the store at two o'clock Saturdays at this season, so I thought I might as well call round and see you.'

'I'm real glad, I'm sure,' said Ann Eliza; 'but Evelina's out.'

'I know dat,' Mr Ramy answered. 'I met her round de corner. She told me she got to go to dat new dyer's up in Forty-eighth Street. She won't be back for a couple of hours, har'ly, will she?'

Ann Eliza looked at him with rising bewilderment. 'No, I guess not,' she answered; her instinctive hospitality prompting her to add: 'Won't you set down jest the same?'

Mr Ramy sat down on the stool beside the counter, and Ann Eliza returned to her place behind it.

'I can't leave the store,' she explained.

'Well, I guess we're very well here.' Ann Eliza had become suddenly aware that Mr Ramy was looking at her with unusual intentness. Involuntarily her hand strayed to the thin streaks of hair on her temples, and thence descended to straighten the brooch beneath her collar.

'You're looking very well today, Miss Bunner,' said Mr Ramy, following her gesture with a smile.

'Oh,' said Ann Eliza nervously. 'I'm always well in health,' she added.

'I guess you're healthier than your sister, even if you are less sizeable.'

'Oh, I don't know. Evelina's a mite nervous sometimes, but she ain't a bit sickly.'

'She eats heartier than you do; but that don't mean nothing,' said Mr Ramy.

Ann Eliza was silent. She could not follow the trend of his thought, and she did not care to commit herself farther about Evelina before she had ascertained if Mr Ramy considered nervousness interesting or the reverse.

But Mr Ramy spared her all farther indecision.

'Well, Miss Bunner,' he said, drawing his stool closer to the counter, 'I guess I might as well tell you fust as last what I come here for today. I want to get married.'

Ann Eliza, in many a prayerful midnight hour, had sought to strengthen herself for the hearing of this avowal, but now that it had come she felt pitifully frightened and unprepared. Mr Ramy was leaning with both elbows on the counter, and she noticed that his nails were clean and that he had brushed his hat; yet even these signs had not prepared her!

At last she heard herself say, with a dry throat in which her heart was hammering: 'Mercy me, Mr Ramy!'

'I want to get married,' he repeated. 'I'm too lonesome. It ain't good for a man to live all alone, and eat noding but cold meat every day.'

'No,' said Ann Eliza softly.

'And the dust fairly beats me.

'Oh, the dust – I know!'

Mr Ramy stretched one of his blunt-fingered hands toward her. 'I wisht you'd take me.'

Still Ann Eliza did not understand. She rose hesitatingly from her seat, pushing aside the basket of buttons which lay between them; then she perceived that Mr Ramy was trying to take her hand, and as their fingers met a flood of joy swept over her. Never afterward, though every other word of their interview was stamped on her memory beyond all possible forgetting, could she recall what he said while their hands touched; she only knew that she seemed to be floating on a summer sea, and that all its waves were in her ears.

'Me – me?' she gasped.

'I guess so,' said her suitor placidly. 'You suit me right down to the ground, Miss Bunner. Dat's the truth.'

A woman passing along the street paused to look at the shop window, and Ann Eliza half hoped she would come in; but after a desultory inspection she went on.

'Maybe you don't fancy me?' Mr Ramy suggested, discountenanced by Ann Eliza's silence.

A word of assent was on her tongue, but her lips refused it. She must find some other way of telling him.

'I don't say that.'

'Well, I always kinder thought we was suited to one another,'

Mr Ramy continued, eased of his momentary doubt. 'I always liked de quiet style – no fuss and airs, and not afraid of work.' He spoke as though dispassionately cataloguing her charms.

Ann Eliza felt that she must make an end. 'But, Mr Ramy, you don't understand. I've never thought of marrying.'

Mr Ramy looked at her in surprise. 'Why not?'

'Well, I don't know, har'ly.' She moistened her twitching lips. 'The fact is, I ain't as active as I look. Maybe I couldn't stand the care. I ain't as spry as Evelina – nor as young,' she added, with a last great effort.

'But you do most of de work here, anyways,' said her suitor doubtfully.

'Oh, well, that's because Evelina's busy outside; and where there's only two women the work don't amount to much. Besides, I'm the oldest; I have to look after things,' she hastened on, half pained that her simple ruse should so readily deceive him.

'Well, I guess you're active enough for me,' he persisted. His calm determination began to frighten her; she trembled lest her own should be less staunch.

'No, no,' she repeated, feeling the tears on her lashes. 'I couldn't, Mr Ramy, I couldn't marry. I'm so surprised. I always thought it was Evelina – always. And so did everybody else. She's so bright and pretty – it seemed so natural.'

'Well, you was all mistaken,' said Mr Ramy obstinately.

'I'm so sorry.'

He rose, pushing back his chair.

'You'd better think it over,' he said, in the large tone of a man who feels he may safely wait.

'Oh, no, no. It ain't any sorter use, Mr Ramy. I don't never mean to marry. I get tired so easily – I'd be afraid of the work. And I have such awful headaches.' She paused, racking her brain for more convincing infirmities.

'Headaches, do you?' said Mr Ramy, turning back.

'My, yes, awful ones, that I have to give right up to. Evelina has to do everything when I have one of them headaches. She has to bring me my tea in the mornings.'

'Well, I'm sorry to hear it,' said Mr Ramy.

'Thank you kindly all the same,' Ann Eliza murmured. 'And please don't – don't –' She stopped suddenly, looking at him through her tears.

'Oh, that's all right,' he answered. 'Don't you fret, Miss Bunner. Folks have got to suit themselves.' She thought his tone had grown more resigned since she had spoken of her headaches.

For some moments he stood looking at her with a hesitating eye, as though uncertain how to end their conversation; and at length she found courage to say (in the words of a novel she had once read): 'I don't want this should make any difference between us.'

'Oh, my, no,' said Mr Ramy, absently picking up his hat.

'You'll come in just the same?' she continued, nerving herself to the effort. 'We'd miss you awfully if you didn't. Evelina, she –' She paused, torn between her desire to turn his thoughts to Evelina, and the dread of prematurely disclosing her sister's secret.

'Don't Miss Evelina have no headaches?' Mr Ramy suddenly asked.

'My, no, never – well, not to speak of, anyway. She ain't had one for ages, and when Evelina *is* sick she won't never give in to it,' Ann Eliza declared, making some hurried adjustments with her conscience.

'I wouldn't have thought that,' said Mr Ramy.

'I guess you don't know us as well as you thought you did.'

'Well, no, that's so; maybe I don't. I'll wish you good day, Miss Bunner'; and Mr Ramy moved toward the door.

'Good day, Mr Ramy,' Ann Eliza answered.

She felt unutterably thankful to be alone. She knew the crucial moment of her life had passed, and she was glad that she had not fallen below her own ideals. It had been a wonderful experience; and in spite of the tears on her cheeks she was not sorry to have known it. Two facts, however, took the edge from its perfection: that it had happened in the shop, and that she had not had on her black silk.

She passed the next hour in a state of dreamy ecstasy. Something had entered into her life of which no subsequent impoverishment could rob it: she glowed with the same rich sense of possessorship that once, as a little girl, she had felt when her mother had given her a gold locket and she had sat up in bed in the dark to draw it from its hiding place beneath her nightgown.

At length a dread of Evelina's return began to mingle with these musings. How could she meet her younger sister's eye without betraying what had happened? She felt as though a visible glory lay on her, and she was glad that dusk had fallen when Evelina entered. But her fears were superfluous. Evelina, always self-absorbed, had of late lost all interest in the simple happenings of the shop, and Ann Eliza, with mingled mortification and relief, perceived that she was in no danger of being cross-questioned as to the events of the afternoon. She was glad of this; yet there was a touch of humiliation in finding that the portentous secret in her bosom did not visibly shine forth. It struck her as dull, and even slightly absurd, of Evelina not to know at last that they were equals.

PART II

VIII

Mr Ramy, after a decent interval, returned to the shop; and Ann Eliza, when they met, was unable to detect whether the emotions which seethed under her black alpaca found an echo in his bosom. Outwardly he made no sign. He lit his pipe as placidly as ever and seemed to relapse without effort into the unruffled intimacy of old. Yet to Ann Eliza's initiated eye a change became gradually perceptible. She saw that he was beginning to look at her sister as he had looked at her on that momentous afternoon: she even discerned a secret significance in the turn of his talk with Evelina. Once he asked her abruptly if she should like to travel, and Ann Eliza saw that the flush on Evelina's cheek was reflected from the same fire which had scorched her own.

So they drifted on through the sultry weeks of July. At that season the business of the little shop almost ceased, and one Saturday morning Mr Ramy proposed that the sisters should lock up early and go with him for a sail down the bay in one of the Coney Island boats.

Ann Eliza saw the light in Evelina's eye and her resolve was instantly taken.

'I guess I won't go, thank you kindly; but I'm sure my sister will be happy to.'

She was pained by the perfunctory phrase with which Evelina urged her to accompany them; and still more by Mr Ramy's silence.

'No, I guess I won't go,' she repeated, rather in answer to herself than to them. 'It's dreadfully hot and I've got a kinder headache.'

'Oh, well, I wouldn't then,' said her sister hurriedly. 'You'd better jest set here quietly and rest.'

'Yes, I'll rest,' Ann Eliza assented.

At two o'clock Mr Ramy returned, and a moment later he and Evelina left the shop. Evelina had made herself another new bonnet for the occasion, a bonnet, Ann Eliza thought, almost too youthful in shape and colour. It was the first time it had ever occurred to her to criticize Evelina's taste, and she was frightened at the insidious change in her attitude toward her sister.

When Ann Eliza, in later days, looked back on that after-noon she felt that there had been something prophetic in the quality of its solitude; it seemed to distill the triple essence of loneliness in which all her after-life was to be lived. No purchasers came; not a hand fell on the door-latch; and the tick of the clock in the back room ironically emphasized the passing of the empty hours.

Evelina returned late and alone. Ann Eliza felt the coming crisis in the sound of her footstep, which wavered along as if not knowing on what it trod. The elder sister's affection had so passionately projected itself into her junior's fate that at such moments she seemed to be living two lives, her own and Evelina's; and her private longings shrank into silence at the sight of the other's hungry bliss. But it was evident that Evelina, never acutely alive to the emotional atmosphere about her, had no idea that her secret was suspected; and with an assumption of unconcern that would have made Ann Eliza smile if the pang had been less piercing, the younger sister prepared to confess herself.

'What are you so busy about?' she said impatiently, as Ann Eliza, beneath the gas-jet, fumbled for the matches. 'Ain't you even got time to ask me if I'd had a pleasant day?'

Ann Eliza turned with a quiet smile. 'I guess I don't have to. Seems to me it's pretty plain you have.'

'Well, I don't know. I don't know *how* I feel – it's all so queer. I almost think I'd like to scream.'

'I guess you're tired.'

'No, I ain't. It's not that. But it all happened so suddenly, and the boat was so crowded I thought everybody'd hear what he was saying. – Ann Eliza,' she broke out, 'why on earth don't you ask me what I'm talking about?'

Ann Eliza, with a last effort of heroism, feigned a fond incomprehension.

'What *are* you?'

'Why, I'm engaged to be married – so there! Now it's out! And it happened right on the boat; only to think of it! Of course I wasn't exactly surprised – I've known right along he was going to sooner or later – on'y somehow I didn't think of its happening today. I thought he'd never get up his courage. He said he was so 'fraid I'd say no – that's what kep' him so long from asking me. Well, I ain't said yes *yet* – leastways I told him I'd have to think it over; but I guess he knows. Oh, Ann Eliza, I'm so happy!' She hid the blinding brightness of her face.

Ann Eliza, just then, would only let herself feel that she was glad. She drew down Evelina's hands and kissed her, and they held each other. When Evelina regained her voice she had a tale to tell which carried their vigil far into the night. Not a syllable, not a glance or gesture of Ramy's, was the elder sister spared; and with unconscious irony she found herself comparing the details of his proposal to her with those which Evelina was imparting with merciless prolixity.

The next few days were taken up with the embarrassed adjustment of their new relation to Mr Ramy and to each other. Ann Eliza's ardour carried her to new heights of self-effacement, and she invented late duties in the shop in order to leave Evelina and her suitor longer alone in the back room. Later on, when she tried to remember the details of those first days, few came back to her: she knew only that she got up each morning with the sense of having to push the leaden hours up the same long steep of pain.

Mr Ramy came daily now. Every evening he and his betrothed went out for a stroll around the Square, and when Evelina came in her cheeks were always pink. 'He's kissed her under that tree at the corner, away from the lamp-post,' Ann Eliza said to herself, with sudden insight into unconjectured things. On Sundays they usually went for the whole afternoon to the Central Park, and Ann Eliza, from her seat in the mortal hush of the back room, followed step by step their long slow beatific walk.

There had been, as yet, no allusion to their marriage, except that Evelina had once told her sister that Mr Ramy wished them to invite Mrs Hochmuller and Linda to the wedding. The mention of the laundress raised a half-forgotten fear in Ann Eliza, and she said in a tone of tentative appeal: 'I guess if I was you I wouldn't want to be very great friends with Mrs Hochmuller.'

Evelina glanced at her compassionately. 'I guess if you was me you'd want to do everything you could to please the man you loved. It's lucky,' she added with glacial irony, 'that I'm not too grand for Herman's friends.'

'Oh,' Ann Eliza protested, 'that ain't what I mean – and you know it ain't. Only somehow the day we saw her I didn't think she seemed like the kinder person you'd want for a friend.'

'I guess a married woman's the best judge of such matters,' Evelina replied, as though she already walked in the light of her future state.

Ann Eliza, after that, kept her own counsel. She saw that Evelina wanted her sympathy as little as her admonitions, and that already she counted for nothing in her sister's scheme of life. To Ann Eliza's idolatrous acceptance of the cruelties of fate this exclusion seemed both natural and just; but it caused her the most lively pain. She could not divest her love for Evelina of its passionate motherliness; no breath of reason could lower it to the cool temperature of sisterly affection.

She was then passing, as she thought, through the novitiate of her pain; preparing, in a hundred experimental ways, for the solitude awaiting her when Evelina left. It was true that it would be a tempered loneliness. They would not be far apart. Evelina would 'run in' daily from the clock-maker's; they would doubtless take supper with her on Sundays. But already Ann Eliza guessed with what growing perfunctoriness her sister would fulfill these obligations; she even foresaw the day when, to get news of Evelina, she should have to lock the shop at nightfall and go herself to Mr Ramy's door. But on that contingency she would not dwell. 'They can come to me when they want to – they'll always find me here,' she simply said to herself.

One evening Evelina came in flushed and agitated from her stroll around the Square. Ann Eliza saw at once that something had happened; but the new habit of reticence checked her question.

She had not long to wait. 'Oh, Ann Eliza, on'y to think what he says –' (the pronoun stood exclusively for Mr Ramy). 'I declare I'm so upset I thought the people in the Square would notice me. Don't I look queer? He wants to get married right off – this very next week.'

'Next week?'

'Yes. So's we can move out to St Louis right away.'

'Him and you – move out to St Louis?'

'Well, I don't know as it would be natural for him to want to go out there without me,' Evelina simpered. 'But it's all so sudden I don't know what to think. He only got the letter this morning. *Do* I look queer, Ann Eliza?' Her eye was roving for the mirror.

'No, you don't,' said Ann Eliza almost harshly.

'Well, it's a mercy,' Evelina pursued with a tinge of disappointment. 'It's a regular miracle I didn't faint right out there in the Square. Herman's so thoughtless – he just put the letter into my hand without a word. It's from a big firm out there – the Tiff'ny of St Louis, he says it is – offering him a place in their clock-department. Seems they heart of him through a German friend of his that's settled out there. It's a splendid opening, and if he gives satisfaction they'll raise him at the end of the year.'

She paused, flushed with the importance of the situation, which seemed to lift her once for all above the dull level of her former life.

'Then you'll have to go?' came at last from Ann Eliza.

Evelina stared. 'You wouldn't have me interfere with his prospects, would you?'

'No – no. I on'y meant – has it got to be so soon?'

'Right away, I tell you – next week. Ain't it awful?' blushed the bride.

Well, this was what happened to mothers. They bore it, Ann Eliza mused; so why not she? Ah, but they had their own chance first; she had had no chance at all. And now this life which she had made her own was going from her forever; had gone, already, in the inner and deeper sense, and was soon to vanish in even its outward nearness, its surface-communion of voice and eye. At that moment even the thought of Evelina's happiness refused her its consolatory ray; or its light, if she saw it, was too remote to warm her. The thirst for a personal and inalienable tie, for pangs and problems of her own, was parching Ann Eliza's soul: it seemed to her that she could never again gather strength to look her loneliness in the face.

The trivial obligations of the moment came to her aid. Nursed in idleness her grief would have mastered her; but the needs of the shop and the back room, and the preparations for Evelina's marriage, kept the tyrant under.

Miss Mellins, true to her anticipations, had been called on to aid in the making of the wedding dress, and she and Ann Eliza were bending one evening over the breadths of pearl-grey cashmere which in spite of the dress-maker's prophetic vision of gored satin, had been judged most suitable, when Evelina came into the room alone.

Ann Eliza had already had occasion to notice that it was a bad sign when Mr Ramy left his affianced at the door. It generally meant that Evelina had something disturbing to communicate, and Ann Eliza's first glance told her that this time the news was grave.

Miss Mellins, who sat with her back to the door and her head bent over her sewing, started as Evelina came around to the opposite side of the table.

'Mercy, Miss Evelina! I declare I thought you was a ghost, the way you crep' in. I had a customer once up in Forty-ninth Street – a lovely young woman with a thirty-six bust and a waist you could ha' put into her wedding ring – and her husband, he crep' up behind her that way jest for a joke, and frightened her into a fit, and when she come to she was a raving maniac, and had to be taken to Bloomingdale with two doctors and a nurse to hold her in the carriage, and a lovely baby on'y six weeks old – and there she is to this day, poor creature.'

'I didn't mean to startle you,' said Evelina.

She sat down on the nearest chair, and as the lamp-light fell on her face Ann Eliza saw that she had been crying.

'You do look dead-beat,' Miss Mellins resumed, after a pause of soul-probing scrutiny. 'I guess Mr Ramy lugs you round that Square too often. You'll walk your legs off if you ain't careful. Men don't never consider – they're all alike. Why, I had a cousin once that was engaged to a book-agent –'

'Maybe we'd better put away the work for tonight, Miss Mellins,' Ann Eliza interposed. 'I guess what Evelina wants is a good night's rest.'

'That's so,' assented the dress-maker. 'Have you got the back breadths run together, Miss Bunner? Here's the sleeves. I'll pin 'em together.' She drew a cluster of pins from her mouth, in which she seemed to secrete them as squirrels stow away nuts. 'There,' she said, rolling up her work, 'you go right away to bed, Miss Evelina, and we'll set up a little later tomorrow night. I guess you're a mite nervous, ain't you? I know when my turn comes I'll be scared to death.'

With this arch forecast she withdrew, and Ann Eliza, returning to the back room, found Evelina still listlessly seated by the table. True to her new policy of silence, the elder sister set about folding up the bridal dress; but suddenly Evelina said in a harsh unnatural voice: 'There ain't any use in going on with that.'

The folds slipped from Ann Eliza's hands.

'Evelina Bunner – what you mean?'

'Jest what I say. It's put off.'

'Put off – what's put off?'

'Our getting married. He can't take me to St Louis. He ain't got money enough.' She brought the words out in the monotonous tone of a child reciting a lesson.

Ann Eliza picked up another breadth of cashmere and began to smooth it out. 'I don't understand,' she said at length.

'Well, it's plain enough. The journey's fearfully expensive, and we've got to have something left to start with when we get out there. We've counted up, and he ain't got the money to do it – that's all.'

'But I thought he was going right into a splendid place.'

'So he is; but the salary's pretty low the first year, and board's very high in St Louis. He's jest got another letter from his German friend, and he's been figuring it out, and he's afraid to chance it. He'll have to go alone.'

'But there's your money – have you forgotten that? The hundred dollars in the bank.'

Evelina made an impatient movement. 'Of course I ain't forgotten it. On'y it ain't enough. It would all have to go into buying furniture, and if he was took sick and lost his place again we wouldn't have a cent left. He says he's got to lay by another hundred dollars before he'll be willing to take me out there.'

For a while Ann Eliza pondered this surprising statement; then she ventured: 'Seems to me he might have thought of it before.'

In an instant Evelina was aflame. 'I guess he knows what's right as well as you or me. I'd sooner die than be a burden to him.'

Ann Eliza made no answer. The clutch of an unformulated doubt had checked the words on her lips. She had meant, on the day of her sister's marriage, to give Evelina the other half of their common savings; but something warned her not to say so now.

The sisters undressed without farther words. After they had gone to bed, and the light had been put out, the sound of Evelina's weeping came to Ann Eliza in the darkness, but she lay motionless on her own side of the bed, out of contact with her sister's shaken body. Never had she felt so coldly remote from Evelina.

The hours of the night moved slowly, ticked off with wearisome insistence by the clock which had played so prominent a part in their lives. Evelina's sobs still stirred the bed at gradually lengthening intervals, till at length Ann Eliza thought she slept. But with the dawn the eyes of the sisters met, and Ann Eliza's courage failed her as she looked in Evelina's face.

She sat up in bed and put out a pleading hand.

'Don't cry so, dearie. Don't.'

'Oh, I can't bear it, I can't bear it,' Evelina moaned.

Ann Eliza stroked her quivering shoulder. 'Don't, don't,' she repeated. 'If you take the other hundred, won't that be enough? I always meant to give it to you. On'y I didn't want to tell you till your wedding day.'

IX

Evelina's marriage took place on the appointed day. It was celebrated in the evening, in the chantry of the church which the sisters attended, and after it was over the few guests who had been present repaired to the Bunner Sisters' basement, where a wedding supper awaited them. Ann Eliza, aided by Miss Mellins and Mrs Hawkins, and consciously supported by the sentimental interest of the whole street, had expended her utmost energy on the decoration of the shop and the back room. On the table a vase of white chrysanthemums stood between a dish of oranges and bananas and an iced wedding-cake wreathed with orange-blossoms of the bride's own making. Autumn leaves studded with paper roses festooned the what-not and the chromo of the Rock of Ages, and a wreath of yellow immortelles was twined about the clock which Evelina revered as the mysterious agent of her happiness.

At the table sat Miss Mellins, profusely spangled and bangled, her head sewing-girl, a pale young thing who had helped with Evelina's outfit, Mr and Mrs Hawkins, with Johnny, their eldest boy, and Mrs Hochmuller and her daughter.

Mrs Hochmuller's large blonde personality seemed to pervade the room to the effacement of the less amply-proportioned guests. It was rendered more impressive by a dress of crimson poplin that stood out from her in organlike folds; and Linda, whom Ann Eliza had remembered as an uncouth child with a sly look about the eyes, surprised her by a sudden blossoming into feminine grace such as sometimes follows on a gawky girlhood. The Hochmullers, in fact, struck the dominant note in the entertainment. Beside them Evelina, unusually pale in her grey cashmere and white bonnet, looked like a faintly washed sketch beside a brilliant chromo; and

Mr Ramy, doomed to the traditional insignificance of the bridegroom's part, made no attempt to rise above his situation. Even Miss Mellins sparkled and jingled in vain in the shadow of Mrs Hochmuller's crimson bulk; and Ann Eliza, with a sense of vague foreboding, saw that the wedding feast centred about the two guests she had most wished to exclude from it. What was said or done while they all sat about the table she never afterward recalled: the long hours remained in her memory as a whirl of high colours and loud voices, from which the pale presence of Evelina now and then emerged like a drowned face on a sunset-dabbled sea.

The next morning Mr Ramy and his wife started for St Louis, and Ann Eliza was left alone. Outwardly the first strain of parting was tempered by the arrival of Miss Mellins, Mrs Hawkins and Johnny, who dropped in to help in the ungarland-ing and tidying up of the back room. Ann Eliza was duly grate-ful for their kindness, but the 'talking over' on which they had evidently counted was Dead Sea fruit on her lips; and just beyond the familiar warmth of their presences she saw the form of Solitude at her door.

Ann Eliza was but a small person to harbour so great a guest, and a trembling sense of insufficiency possessed her. She had no high musings to offer to the new companion of her hearth. Every one of her thoughts had hitherto turned to Evelina and shaped itself in homely easy words; of the mighty speech of silence she knew not the earliest syllable.

Everything in the back room and the shop, on the second day after Evelina's going, seemed to have grown coldly un-familiar. The whole aspect of the place had changed with the changed conditions of Ann Eliza's life. The first customer who opened the shop-door startled her like a ghost; and all night she lay tossing on her side of the bed, sinking now and then into an uncertain doze from which she would suddenly wake to reach out her hand for Evelina. In the new silence surround-ing her the walls and furniture found voice, frightening her at dusk and midnight with strange sighs and stealthy whispers. Ghostly hands shook the window shutters or rattled at the outer latch, and once she grew cold at the sound of a step like Evelina's stealing through the dark shop to die out on the threshold. In time, of course, she found an explanation for these noises, telling herself that the bedstead was warping, that Miss Mellins trod heavily overhead, or that the thunder of passing beer-wagons shook the door-latch; but the hours leading up to these conclusions were full of the floating terrors that harden into fixed foreboding. Worst of all were the solitary meals, when she absently continued to set aside the largest slice of pie for Evelina, and to let the tea grow cold while she waited for her sister to help herself to the first cup. Miss Mellins, coming in on one of these sad repasts, suggested the acquisition of a cat; but Ann Eliza shook her head. She had never been used to animals, and she felt the vague shrinking of the pious from creatures divided from her by the abyss of soullessness.

At length, after ten empty days, Evelina's first letter came.

'My dear Sister,' she wrote, in her pinched Spencerian hand,

'It seems strange to be in this great City so far from home alone with him I have chosen for life, but marriage has its solemn duties which those who are not can never hope to understand, and happier perhaps for this reason, life for them has only simple tasks and pleasures, but those who must take thought for others must be prepared to do their duty in whatever station it has pleased the Almighty to call them. Not that I have cause to complain, my dear Husband is all love and devotion, but being absent all day at his business how can I help but feel lonesome at times, as the poet says it is hard for they that love to live apart, and I often wonder, my dear Sister, how you are getting along alone in the store, may you never experience the feelings of solitude I have underwent since I came here. We are boarding now, but soon expect to find rooms and change our place of Residence, then I shall have all the care of a household to bear, but such is the fate of those who join their Lot with others, they cannot hope to escape from the burdens of Life, nor would I ask it, I would not live always but while I live would always pray for strength to do my duty. This city is not near as large or handsome as New York, but had my lot been cast in a Wilderness I hope I should not repine, such never was my nature, and they who exchange their independence for the sweet name of Wife must be prepared to find all is not gold that glitters, nor I would not expect like you to drift down the stream of Life unfettered and serene as a Summer cloud, such is not my fate, but come what may will always find in me a resigned and prayerful Spirit, and hoping this finds you as well as it leaves me, I remain, my dear Sister,

'Yours truly,
'Evelina B. Ramy'

Ann Eliza had always secretly admired the oratorical and impersonal tone of Evelina's letters; but the few she had previously read, having been addressed to school-mates or distant relatives, had appeared in the light of literary compositions rather than as records of personal experience. Now she could not but wish that Evelina had laid aside her swelling periods for a style more suited to the chronicling of homely incidents. She read the letter again and again, seeking for a clue to what her sister was really doing and thinking; but after each reading she emerged impressed but unenlightened from the labyrinth of Evelina's eloquence.

During the early winter she received two or three more letters of the same kind, each enclosing in its loose husk of rhetoric a smaller kernel of fact. By dint of patient interlinear study, Ann Eliza gathered from them that Evelina and her husband, after various costly experiments in boarding, had been reduced to a tenement-house flat; that living in St Louis was more expensive than they had supposed, and that Mr Ramy was kept out late at night (why, at a jeweller's, Ann Eliza wondered?) and found his position less satisfactory than he had been led to expect. Toward February the letters fell off, and finally they ceased to come.

At first Ann Eliza wrote, shyly but persistently, entreating for more frequent news; then, as one appeal after another was swallowed up in the mystery of Evelina's protracted silence, vague fears began to assail the elder sister. Perhaps Evelina was ill, and with no one to nurse her but a man who could not even make himself a cup of tea! Ann Eliza recalled the layer of dust in Mr Ramy's shop, and pictures of domestic disorder mingled with the more poignant vision of her sister's illness. But surely if Evelina were ill Mr Ramy would have written. He wrote a small neat hand, and epistolary communication was not an insuperable embarrassment to him. The too probable alternative was that both the unhappy pair had been prostrated by some disease which left them powerless to summon her – for summon her they surely would, Ann Eliza with unconscious cynicism reflected, if she or her small economies could be of use to them! The more she strained her eyes into the mystery, the darker it grew; and her lack of initiative, her inability to imagine what steps might be taken to trace the lost in distant places, left her benumbed and helpless.

At last there floated up from some depth of troubled memory the name of the firm of St Louis jewellers by whom Mr Ramy was employed. After much hesitation, and considerable effort, she addressed to them a timid request for news of her brother-in-law; and sooner than she could have hoped the answer reached her.

'DEAR MADAM,
    'In reply to yours of the 29th ult. we beg to state the party you refer to was discharged from our employ a month ago. We are sorry we are unable to furnish you with his address.
                'Yours Respectfully,
         'LUDWIG AND HAMMERBUSCH'

Ann Eliza read and re-read the curt statement in a stupor of distress. She had lost her last trace of Evelina. All that night she lay awake, revolving the stupendous project of going to

St Louis in search of her sister; but though she pieced together her few financial possibilities with the ingenuity of a brain used to fitting odd scraps into patch-work quilts, she woke to the cold daylight fact that she could not raise the money for her fare. Her wedding gift to Evelina had left her without any resources beyond her daily earnings, and these had steadily dwindled as the winter passed. She had long since renounced her weekly visit to the butcher, and had reduced her other expenses to the narrowest measure; but the most systematic frugality had not enabled her to put by any money. In spite of her dogged efforts to maintain the prosperity of the little shop, her sister's absence had already told on its business. Now that Ann Eliza had to carry the bundles to the dyer's herself, the customers who called in her absence, finding the shop locked, too often went elsewhere. Moreover, after several stern but unavailing efforts, she had had to give up the trimming of bonnets, which in Evelina's hands had been the most lucrative as well as the most interesting part of the business. This change, to the passing female eye, robbed the shop window of its chief attraction; and when painful experience had convinced the regular customers of the Bunner Sisters of Ann Eliza's lack of millinery skill they began to lose faith in her ability to curl a feather or even 'freshen up' a bunch of flowers. The time came when Ann Eliza had almost made up her mind to speak to the lady with puffed sleeves, who had always looked at her so kindly, and had once ordered a hat of Evelina. Perhaps the lady with puffed sleeves would be able to get her a little plain sewing to do; or she might recommend the shop to friends. Ann Eliza, with this possibility in view, rummaged out of a drawer the fly-blown remainder of the business cards which the sisters had ordered in the first flush of their commercial adventure; but when the lady with puffed sleeves finally appeared she was in deep mourning, and wore so sad a look that Ann Eliza dared not speak. She came in to buy some spools of black thread and silk, and in the doorway she turned back to say: 'I am going away tomorrow for a long time. I hope you will have a pleasant winter.' And the door shut on her.

One day not long after this it occurred to Ann Eliza to go to Hoboken in quest of Mrs Hochmuller. Much as she shrank from pouring her distress into that particular ear, her anxiety had carried her beyond such reluctance; but when she began to think the matter over she was faced by a new difficulty. On the occasion of her only visit to Mrs Hochmuller, she and Evelina had suffered themselves to be led there by Mr Ramy; and Ann Eliza now perceived that she did not even know the name of the laundress's suburb, much less that of the street in which she lived. But she must have news of Evelina, and no obstacle was great enough to thwart her.

Though she longed to turn to someone for advice she disliked to expose her situation to Miss Mellins's searching eye, and at first she could think of no other confidant. Then she remembered Mrs Hawkins, or rather her husband, who, though Ann Eliza had always thought him a dull uneducated man, was probably gifted with the mysterious masculine faculty of finding out people's addresses. It went hard with Ann Eliza to trust her secret even to the mild ear of Mrs Hawkins, but at least she was spared the cross-examination to which the dress-maker would have subjected her. The accumulating pressure of domestic cares had so crushed in Mrs Hawkins any curiosity concerning the affairs of others that she received her visitor's confidence with an almost masculine indifference, while she rocked her teething baby on one arm and with the other tried to check the acrobatic impulses of the next in age.

'My, my,' she simply said as Ann Eliza ended. 'Keep still now, Arthur: Miss Bunner don't want you to jump up and down on her foot today. And what are you gaping at, Johnny? Run right off and play,' she added, turning sternly to her eldest, who, because he was the least naughty, usually bore the brunt of her wrath against the others.

'Well, perhaps Mr Hawkins can help you,' Mrs Hawkins continued meditatively, while the children, after scattering at her bidding, returned to their previous pursuits like flies settling down on the spot from which an exasperated hand has swept them. 'I'll send him right round the minute he comes in, and you can tell him the whole story. I wouldn't wonder but what he can find that Mrs Hochmuller's address in the d'rectory. I know they've got one where he works.'

'I'd be real thankful if he could,' Ann Eliza murmured, rising from her seat with the factitious sense of lightness that comes from imparting a long-hidden dread.

X

Mr Hawkins proved himself worthy of his wife's faith in his capacity. He learned from Ann Eliza as much as she could tell him about Mrs Hochmuller and returned the next evening with a scrap of paper bearing her address, beneath which Johnny (the family scribe) had written in a large round hand the names of the streets that led there from the ferry.

Ann Eliza lay awake all that night, repeating over and over again the directions Mr Hawkins had given her. He was a kind man, and she knew he would willingly have gone with her to Hoboken; indeed she read in his timid eye the half-formed intention of offering to accompany her – but on such an errand she preferred to go alone.

The next Sunday, accordingly, she set out early, and without much trouble found her way to the ferry. Nearly a year had passed since her previous visit to Mrs Hochmuller, and a chilly April breeze smote her face as she stepped on the boat. Most of the passengers were huddled together in the cabin, and Ann Eliza shrank into its obscurest corner, shivering under the thin black mantle which had seemed so hot in July. She began to feel a little bewildered as she stepped ashore, but a paternal policeman put her into the right car, and as in a dream she found herself retracing the way to Mrs Hochmuller's door. She had told the conductor the name of the street at which she wished to get out, and presently she stood in the biting wind at the corner near the beer-saloon, where the sun had once beat down on her so fiercely. At length an empty car appeared, its yellow flank emblazoned with the name of Mrs Hochmuller's suburb, and Ann Eliza was presently jolting past the narrow brick houses islanded between vacant lots like giant piles in a desolate lagoon. When the car reached the end of its journey she got out and stood for some time trying to remember which turn Mr Ramy had taken. She had just made up her mind to ask the car-driver when he shook the reins on the backs of his lean horses, and the car, still empty, jogged away toward Hoboken.

Ann Eliza, left alone by the roadside, began to move cautiously forward, looking about for a small red house with a gable overhung by an elm tree; but everything about her seemed unfamiliar and forbidding. One or two surly looking men slouched past with inquisitive glances, and she could not make up her mind to stop and speak to them.

At length a tow-headed boy came out of a swinging door suggestive of illicit conviviality, and to him Ann Eliza ventured to confide her difficulty. The offer of five cents fired him with an instant willingness to lead her to Mrs Hochmuller, and he was soon trotting past the stone-cutter's yard with Ann Eliza in his wake.

Another turn in the road brought them to the little red house, and having rewarded her guide Ann Eliza unlatched the gate and walked up to the door. Her heart was beating violently, and she had to lean against the doorpost to compose her twitching lips: she had not known till that moment how much it was going to hurt her to speak of Evelina to Mrs Hochmuller. As her agitation subsided she began to notice how much the appearance of the house had changed. It was not only that winter had stripped the elm, and blackened the flower-borders: the house itself had a debased and deserted air. The windowpanes were cracked and dirty, and one or two shutters swung dismally on loosened hinges.

She rang several times before the door was opened. At length an Irishwoman with a shawl over her head and a baby in her arms appeared on the threshold, and glancing past her into the narrow passage Ann Eliza saw that Mrs Hochmuller's neat abode had deteriorated as much within as without.

At the mention of the name the woman stared. 'Mrs who, did ye say?'

'Mrs Hochmuller. This is surely her house?'

'No, it ain't neither,' said the woman turning away.

'Oh, but wait, please,' Ann Eliza entreated. 'I can't be mistaken. I mean the Mrs Hochmuller who takes in washing. I came out to see her last June.'

'Oh, the Dutch washerwoman is it — her that used to live here? She's been gone two months and more. It's Mike McNulty lives here now. Whisht!' to the baby, who had squared his mouth for a howl.

Ann Eliza's knees grew weak. 'Mrs Hochmuller gone? But where has she gone? She must be somewhere round here. Can't you tell me?'

'Sure an' I can't,' said the woman. 'She wint away before iver we come.'

'Dalia Geoghegan, will ye bring the choild in out av the cowld?' cried an irate voice from within.

'Please wait – oh, please wait,' Ann Eliza insisted. 'You see I must find Mrs Hochmuller.'

'Why don't ye go and look for her thin?' the woman returned, slamming the door in her face.

She stood motionless on the doorstep, dazed by the immensity of her disappointment, till a burst of loud voices inside the house drove her down the path and out of the gate.

Even then she could not grasp what had happened, and pausing in the road she looked back at the house, half hoping that Mrs Hochmuller's once detested face might appear at one of the grimy windows.

She was roused by an icy wind that seemed to spring up suddenly from the desolate scene, piercing her thin dress like gauze; and turning away she began to retrace her steps. She thought of enquiring for Mrs Hochmuller at some of the neighbouring houses, but their look was so unfriendly that she walked on without making up her mind at which door to ring. When she reached the horse-car terminus a car was just moving off toward Hoboken, and for nearly an hour she had to wait on the corner in the bitter wind. Her hands and feet were stiff with cold when the car at length loomed into sight again, and she thought of stopping somewhere on the way to the ferry for a cup of tea; but before the region of lunch-rooms was reached she had grown so sick and dizzy that the thought of food was repulsive. At length she found herself on the ferry-boat, in the soothing stuffiness of the crowded cabin; then came another interval of shivering on a street-corner, another long jolting journey in a 'cross-town' car that smelt of damp straw and tobacco; and lastly, in the cold spring dusk, she unlocked her door and groped her way through the shop to her fireless bedroom.

The next morning Mrs Hawkins, dropping in to hear the result of the trip, found Ann Eliza sitting behind the counter wrapped in an old shawl.

'Why, Miss Bunner, you're sick! You must have fever – your face is just as red!'

'It's nothing. I guess I caught cold yesterday on the ferry-boat,' Ann Eliza acknowledged.

'And it's jest like a vault in here!' Mrs Hawkins rebuked her. 'Let me feel your hand – it's burning. Now, Miss Bunner, you've got to go right to bed this very minute.'

'Oh, but I can't, Mrs Hawkins.' Ann Eliza attempted a wan smile. 'You forget there ain't nobody but me to tend the store.'

'I guess you won't tend it long neither, if you ain't careful,' Mrs Hawkins grimly rejoined. Beneath her placid exterior she cherished a morbid passion for disease and death, and the sight of Ann Eliza's suffering had roused her from her habitual indifference. 'There ain't so many folks comes to the store anyhow,' she went on with unconscious cruelty, 'and I'll go right up and see if Miss Mellins can't spare one of her girls.'

Ann Eliza, too weary to resist, allowed Mrs Hawkins to put her to bed and make a cup of tea over the stove, while Miss Mellins, always good-naturedly responsive to any appeal for help, sent down the weak-eyed little girl to deal with hypothe-tical customers.

Ann Eliza, having so far abdicated her independence, sank into sudden apathy. As far as she could remember, it was the first time in her life that she had been taken care of instead of taking care, and there was a momentary relief in the surrender.

She swallowed the tea like an obedient child, allowed a poul-
tice to be applied to her aching chest and uttered no protest
when a fire was kindled in the rarely used grate; but as Mrs
Hawkins bent over to 'settle' her pillows she raised herself on
her elbow to whisper: 'Oh, Mrs Hawkins, Mrs Hochmuller
warn't there.' The tears rolled down her cheeks.

'She warn't there? Has she moved?'

'Over two months ago – and they don't know where she's
gone. Oh what'll I do, Mrs Hawkins?'

'There, there, Miss Bunner. You lay still and don't fret. I'll
ask Mr Hawkins soon as ever he comes home.'

Ann Eliza murmured her gratitude, and Mrs Hawkins,
bending down, kissed her on the forehead. 'Don't you fret,'
she repeated, in the voice with which she soothed her children.

For over a week Ann Eliza lay in bed, faithfully nursed by
her two neighbours, while the weak-eyed child, and the pale
sewing girl who had helped to finish Evelina's wedding dress,
took turns in minding the shop. Every morning, when her
friends appeared, Ann Eliza lifted her head to ask: 'Is there a
letter?' and at their gentle negative sank back in silence. Mrs
Hawkins, for several days, spoke no more of her promise to
consult her husband as to the best way of tracing Mrs Hochmuller; and dread of fresh disappointment kept Ann Eliza from
bringing up the subject.

But the following Sunday evening, as she sat for the first
time bolstered up in her rocking-chair near the stove, while
Miss Mellins studied the *Police Gazette* beneath the lamp, there
came a knock on the shop-door and Mr Hawkins entered.

Ann Eliza's first glance at his plain friendly face showed her
he had news to give, but though she no longer attempted to
hide her anxiety from Miss Mellins, her lips trembled too
much to let her speak.

'Good evening, Miss Bunner,' said Mr Hawkins in his
dragging voice. 'I've been over to Hoboken all day looking
round for Mrs Hochmuller.'

'Oh, Mr Hawkins – you *have?*'

'I made a thorough search, but I'm sorry to say it was no

use. She's left Hoboken – moved clear away, and nobody seems to know where.'

'It was real good of you, Mr Hawkins.' Ann Eliza's voice struggled up in a faint whisper through the submerging tide of her disappointment.

Mr Hawkins, in his embarrassed sense of being the bringer of bad news, stood before her uncertainly; then he turned to go. 'No trouble at all,' he paused to assure her from the doorway.

She wanted to speak again, to detain him, to ask him to advise her; but the words caught in her throat and she lay back silent.

The next day she got up early, and dressed and bonneted herself with twitching fingers. She waited till the weak-eyed child appeared, and having laid on her minute instructions as to the care of the shop, she slipped out into the street. It had occurred to her in one of the weary watches of the previous night that she might go to Tiffany's and make enquiries about Ramy's past. Possibly in that way she might obtain some information that would suggest a new way of reaching Evelina. She was guiltily aware that Mrs Hawkins and Miss Mellins would be angry with her for venturing out of doors, but she knew she should never feel any better till she had news of Evelina.

The morning air was sharp, and as she turned to face the wind she felt so weak and unsteady that she wondered if she should ever get as far as Union Square; but by walking very slowly, and standing still now and then when she could do so without being noticed, she found herself at last before the jeweller's great glass doors.

It was still so early that there were no purchasers in the shop, and she felt herself the centre of innumerable unemployed eyes as she moved forward between long lines of show-cases glittering with diamonds and silver.

She was glancing about in the hope of finding the clock-department without having to approach one of the impressive gentlemen who paced the empty aisles, when she attracted the attention of one of the most impressive of the number.

The formidable benevolence with which he enquired what he could do for her made her almost despair of explaining herself, but she finally disentangled from a flurry of wrong beginnings the request to be shown to the clock-department.

The gentleman considered her thoughtfully. 'May I ask what style of clock you are looking for? Would it be for a wedding-present, or – ?'

The irony of the allusion filled Ann Eliza's veins with sudden strength. 'I don't want to buy a clock at all. I want to see the head of the department.'

'Mr Loomis?' His stare still weighed her – then he seemed to brush aside the problem she presented as beneath his notice. 'Oh, certainly. Take the elevator to the second floor. Next aisle to the left.' He waved her down the endless perspective of show-cases.

Ann Eliza followed the line of his lordly gesture, and a swift ascent brought her to a great hall full of the buzzing and booming of thousands of clocks. Whichever way she looked, clocks stretched away from her in glittering interminable vistas: clocks of all sizes and voices, from the bell-throated giant of the hallway to the chirping dressing-table toy; tall clocks of mahogany and brass with cathedral chimes; clocks of bronze, glass, porcelain, of every possible size, voice and configuration; and between their serried ranks, along the polished floor of the aisles, moved the languid forms of other gentlemanly floor-walkers, waiting for their duties to begin.

One of them soon approached, and Ann Eliza repeated her request. He received it affably.

'Mr Loomis? Go right down to the office at the other end.' He pointed to a kind of box of ground glass and highly polished paneling.

As she thanked him he turned to one of his companions and said something in which she caught the name of Mr Loomis, and which was received with an appreciative chuckle. She suspected herself of being the object of the pleasantry, and straightened her thin shoulders under her mantle.

The door of the office stood open, and within sat a grey-bearded man at a desk. He looked up kindly, and again she asked for Mr Loomis.

'I'm Mr Loomis. What can I do for you?'

He was much less portentous than the others, though she guessed him to be above them in authority; and encouraged by his tone she seated herself on the edge of the chair he waved her to.

'I hope you'll excuse my troubling you, sir. I came to ask if you could tell me anything about Mr Herman Ramy. He was employed here in the clock-department two or three years ago.'

Mr Loomis showed no recognition of the name.

'Ramy? When was he discharged?'

'I don't har'ly know. He was very sick, and when he got well his place had been filled. He married my sister last October and they went to St Louis, I ain't had any news of them for over two months, and she's my only sister, and I'm most crazy worrying about her.'

'I see.' Mr Loomis reflected. 'In what capacity was Ramy employed here?' he asked after a moment.

'He – he told us that he was one of the heads of the clock-department,' Ann Eliza stammered, overswept by a sudden doubt.

'That was probably a slight exaggeration. But I can tell you about him by referring to our books. The name again?'

'Ramy – Herman Ramy.'

There ensued a long silence, broken only by the flutter of leaves as Mr Loomis turned over his ledgers. Presently he looked up, keeping his finger between the pages.

'Here it is – Herman Ramy. He was one of our ordinary workmen, and left us three years and a half ago last June.'

'On account of sickness?' Ann Eliza faltered.

Mr Loomis appeared to hesitate; then he said: 'I see no mention of sickness.' Ann Eliza felt his compassionate eyes on her again. 'Perhaps I'd better tell you the truth. He was discharged for drug-taking. A capable workman, but we couldn't keep him straight. I'm sorry to have to tell you this, but it seems fairer, since you say you're anxious about your sister.'

The polished sides of the office vanished from Ann Eliza's sight, and the cackle of the innumerable clocks came to her like the yell of waves in a storm. She tried to speak but could not; tried to get to her feet, but the floor was gone.

'I'm very sorry,' Mr Loomis repeated, closing the ledger. 'I remember the man perfectly now. He used to disappear every now and then, and turn up again in a state that made him useless for days.'

As she listened, Ann Eliza recalled the day when she had come on Mr Ramy sitting in abject dejection behind his counter. She saw again the blurred unrecognizing eyes he had raised to her, the layer of dust over everything in the shop, and the green bronze clock in the window representing a New-foundland dog with his paw on a book. She stood up slowly.

'Thank you. I'm sorry to have troubled you.'

'It was no trouble. You say Ramy married your sister last October?'

'Yes, sir; and they went to St Louis right afterward. I don't know how to find her. I thought maybe somebody here might know about him.'

'Well, possibly some of the workmen might. Leave me your name and I'll send you word if I get on his track.'

He handed her a pencil, and she wrote down her address; then she walked away blindly between the clocks.

XI

Mr Loomis, true to his word, wrote a few days later that he had enquired in vain in the work-shop for any news of Ramy; and as she folded this letter and laid it between the leaves of her Bible, Ann Eliza felt that her last hope was gone. Miss Mellins, of course, had long since suggested the mediation of the police, and cited from her favourite literature convincing instances of the supernatural ability of the Pinkerton detective; but Mr Hawkins, when called in council, dashed this project by remarking that detectives cost something like twenty dollars a day; and a vague fear of the law, some half-formed vision of Evelina in the clutch of a blue-coated 'officer', kept Ann Eliza from invoking the aid of the police.

After the arrival of Mr Loomis's note the weeks followed each other uneventfully. Ann Eliza's cough clung to her till late in the spring, the reflection in her looking-glass grew more bent and meager, and her forehead sloped back farther toward the twist of hair that was fastened above her parting by a comb of black India-rubber.

Towards spring a lady who was expecting a baby took up her abode at the Mendoza Family Hotel, and through the friendly intervention of Miss Mellins the making of some of the baby-clothes was entrusted to Ann Eliza. This eased her of anxiety for the immediate future; but she had to rouse herself to feel any sense of relief. Her personal welfare was what least concerned her. Sometimes she thought of giving up the shop altogether; and only the fear that, if she changed her address, Evelina might not be able to find her, kept her from carrying out this plan.

Since she had lost her last hope of tracing her sister, all the activities of her lonely imagination had been concentrated on

345

the possibility of Evelina's coming back to her. The discovery of Ramy's secret filled her with dreadful fears. In the solitude of the shop and the back room she was tortured by vague pictures of Evelina's sufferings. What horrors might not be hidden beneath her silence? Ann Eliza's great dread was that Miss Mellins should worm out of her what she had learned from Mr Loomis. She was sure Miss Mellins must have abominable things to tell about drug-fiends – things she did not have the strength to hear. 'Drug-fiend' – the very word was Satanic; she could hear Miss Mellins roll it on her tongue. But Ann Eliza's own imagination, left to itself, had begun to people the long hours with evil visions. Sometimes, in the night, she thought she heard herself called: the voice was her sister's, but faint with a nameless terror. Her most peaceful moments were those in which she managed to convince herself that Evelina was dead. She thought of her then, mournfully but more calmly, as thrust away under the neglected mound of some unknown cemetery, where no headstone marked her name, no mourner with flowers for another grave paused in pity to lay a blossom on hers. But this vision did not often give Ann Eliza its negative relief, and always, beneath its hazy lines, lurked the dark conviction that Evelina was alive, in misery and longing for her.

So the summer wore on. Ann Eliza was conscious that Mrs Hawkins and Miss Mellins were watching her with affectionate anxiety, but the knowledge brought no comfort. She no longer cared what they felt or thought about her. Her grief lay far beyond touch of human healing, and after a while she became aware that they knew they could not help her. They still came in as often as their busy lives permitted, but their visits grew shorter, and Mrs Hawkins always brought Arthur or the baby, so that there should be something to talk about, and someone whom she could scold.

The autumn came, and the winter. Business had fallen off again, and but few purchasers came to the little shop in the basement. In January Ann Eliza pawned her mother's cashmere scarf, her mosaic brooch, and the rosewood what-not on which the clock had always stood; she would have sold the bedstead too, but for the persistent vision of Evelina returning weak and weary, and not knowing where to lay her head.

The winter passed in its turn, and March reappeared with its galaxies of yellow jonquils at the windy street corners, reminding Ann Eliza of the spring day when Evelina had come home with a bunch of jonquils in her hand. In spite of the flowers which lent such a premature brightness to the streets the month was fierce and stormy, and Ann Eliza could get no warmth into her bones. Nevertheless, she was insensibly beginning to take up the healing routine of life. Little by little she had grown used to being alone, she had begun to take a languid interest in the one or two new purchasers the season had brought, and though the thought of Evelina was as poignant as ever, it was less persistently in the foreground of her mind.

Late one afternoon she was sitting behind the counter, wrapped in her shawl, and wondering how soon she might draw down the blinds and retreat into the comparative coziness of the back room. She was not thinking of anything in particular, except perhaps in a hazy way of the lady with the puffed sleeves, who after her long eclipse had reappeared the day before in sleeves of a new cut, and bought some tape and needles. The lady still wore mourning, but she was evidently lightening it, and Ann Eliza saw in this the hope of future orders. The lady had left the shop about an hour before, walking away with her graceful step toward Fifth Avenue. She had wished Ann Eliza good day in her usual affable way, and Ann Eliza thought how odd it was that they should have been acquainted so long, and yet that she should not know the lady's name. From this consideration her mind wandered to the cut of the lady's new sleeves, and she was vexed with herself for not having noted it more carefully. She felt Miss Mellins might have liked to know about it. Ann Eliza's powers of observation had never been as keen as Evelina's, when the latter was not too self-absorbed to exert them. As Miss Mellins always said, Evelina could 'take patterns with her eyes': she could have cut that new sleeve out of a folded newspaper in a trice! Musing

on these things, Ann Eliza wished the lady would come back
and give her another look at the sleeve. It was not unlikely that
she might pass that way, for she certainly lived in or about the
Square. Suddenly Ann Eliza remarked a small neat handkerchief on the counter: it must have dropped from the lady's
purse, and she would probably come back to get it. Ann Eliza,
pleased at the idea, sat on behind the counter and watched the
darkening street. She always lit the gas as late as possible, keeping the box of matches at her elbow, so that if anyone came
she could apply a quick flame to the gas-jet. At length through
the deepening dusk she distinguished a slim dark figure coming
down the steps to the shop. With a little warmth of pleasure
about her heart she reached up to light the gas. 'I do believe
I'll ask her name this time,' she thought. She raised the flame
to its full height, and saw her sister standing in the door.

There she was at last, the poor pale shade of Evelina, her
thin face blanched of its faint pink, the stiff ripples gone from
her hair, and a mantle shabbier than Ann Eliza's drawn about
her narrow shoulders. The glare of the gas beat full on her as
she stood and looked at Ann Eliza.

'Sister – oh, Evelina! I knowed you'd come!'

Ann Eliza had caught her close with a long moan of triumph. Vague words poured from her as she laid her cheek
against Evelina's – trivial inarticulate endearments caught from
Mrs Hawkins's long discourses to her baby.

For a while Evelina let herself be passively held; then she
drew back from her sister's clasp and looked about the shop.
'I'm dead tired. Ain't there any fire?' she asked.

'Of course there is!' Ann Eliza, holding her hand fast, drew
her into the back room. She did not want to ask any questions
yet: she simply wanted to feel the emptiness of the room brim-
med full again by the one presence that was warmth and light
to her.

She knelt down before the grate, scraped some bits of coal
and kindling from the bottom of the coal-scuttle, and drew
one of the rocking-chairs up to the weak flame. 'There – that'll
blaze up in a minute,' she said. She pressed Evelina down on

the faded cushions of the rocking-chair, and, kneeling beside her, began to rub her hands.

'You're stone-cold, ain't you? Just sit still and warm yourself while I run and get the kettle. I've got something you always used to fancy for supper.' She laid her hand on Evelina's shoulder. 'Don't talk – oh, don't talk yet!' she implored. She wanted to keep that one frail second of happiness between herself and what she knew must come.

Evelina, without a word, bent over the fire, stretching her thin hands to the blaze and watching Ann Eliza fill the kettle and set the supper table. Her gaze had the dreamy fixity of a half-awakened child's.

Ann Eliza, with a smile of triumph, brought a slice of custard pie from the cupboard and put it by her sister's plate.

'You do like that, don't you? Miss Mellins sent it down to me this morning. She had her aunt from Brooklyn to dinner. Ain't it funny it just so happened?'

'I ain't hungry,' said Evelina, rising to approach the table.

She sat down in her usual place, looked about her with the same wondering stare, and then, as of old, poured herself out the first cup of tea.

'Where's the what-not gone to?' she suddenly asked.

Ann Eliza set down the teapot and rose to get a spoon from the cupboard. With her back to the room she said: 'The what-not? Why, you see, dearie, living here all alone by myself it only made one more thing to dust; so I sold it.'

Evelina's eyes were still travelling about the familiar room. Though it was against all the traditions of the Bunner family to sell any household possession, she showed no surprise at her sister's answer.

'And the clock? The clock's gone too.'

'Oh, I gave that away – I gave it to Mrs Hawkins. She's kep' awake so nights with that last baby.'

'I wish you'd never bought it,' said Evelina harshly.

Ann Eliza's heart grew faint with fear. Without answering, she crossed over to her sister's seat and poured her out a second cup of tea. Then another thought struck her, and she went back to the cupboard and took out the cordial. In Evelina's absence considerable drafts had been drawn from it by invalid neighbours; but a glassful of the precious liquid still remained.

'Here, drink this right off – it'll warm you up quicker than anything,' Ann Eliza said.

Evelina obeyed, and a slight spark of colour came into her cheeks. She turned to the custard pie and began to eat with a silent voracity distressing to watch. She did not even look to see what was left for Ann Eliza.

'I ain't hungry,' she said at last as she laid down her fork. 'I'm only so dead tired – that's the trouble.'

'Then you'd better get right into bed. Here's my old plaid dressing gown – you remember it, don't you?' Ann Eliza laughed, recalling Evelina's ironies on the subject of the anti-quated garment. With trembling fingers she began to undo her sister's cloak. The dress beneath it told a tale of poverty that Ann Eliza dared not pause to note. She drew it gently off, and as it slipped from Evelina's shoulders it revealed a tiny black bag hanging on a ribbon about her neck. Evelina lifted her hand as though to screen the bag from Ann Eliza; and the elder sister, seeing the gesture, continued her task with lowered eyes. She undressed Evelina as quickly as she could, and wrap-ping her in the plaid dressing gown put her to bed, and spread her own shawl and her sister's cloak above the blanket.

'Where's the old red comfortable?' Evelina asked, as she sank down on the pillow.

'The comfortable? Oh, it was so hot and heavy I never used it after you went – so I sold that too. I never could sleep under much clothes.'

She became aware that her sister was looking at her more attentively.

'I guess you've been in trouble too,' Evelina said.

'Me? In trouble? What do you mean, Evelina?'

'You've had to pawn the things, I suppose,' Evelina con-tinued in a weary unmoved tone. 'Well, I've been through worse than that. I've been to hell and back.'

'Oh, Evelina – don't say it, sister!' Ann Eliza implored, shrinking from the unholy word. She knelt down and began to rub her sister's feet beneath the bedclothes.

'I've been to hell and back – if I *am* back,' Evelina repeated. She lifted her head from the pillow and began to talk with a sudden feverish volubility. 'It began right away, less than a month after we were married. I've been in hell all that time, Ann Eliza.' She fixed her eyes with passionate intentness on Ann Eliza's face. 'He took opium. I didn't find it out till long afterward – at first, when he acted so strange, I thought he drank. But it was worse, much worse than drinking.'

'Oh, sister, don't say it – don't say it yet! It's so sweet just to have you here with me again.'

'I must say it,' Evelina insisted, her flushed face burning with a kind of bitter cruelty. 'You don't know what life's like – you don't know anything about it – setting here safe all the while in this peaceful place.'

'Oh, Evelina – why didn't you write and send for me if it was like that?'

'That's why I couldn't write. Didn't you guess I was ashamed?'

'How could you be? Ashamed to write to Ann Eliza?'

Evelina raised herself on her thin elbow, while Ann Eliza, bending over, drew a corner of the shawl about her shoulder.

'Do lay down again. You'll catch your death.'

'My death? That don't frighten me! You don't know what I've been through.' And sitting upright in the old mahogany bed, with flushed cheeks and chattering teeth, and Ann Eliza's trembling arm clasping the shawl about her neck, Evelina poured out her story. It was a tale of misery and humiliation so remote from the elder sister's innocent experiences that much of it was hardly intelligible to her. Evelina's dreadful familiarity with it all, her fluency about things which Ann Eliza half-guessed and quickly shuddered back from, seemed even more alien and terrible than the actual tale she told. It was one thing – and heaven knew it was bad enough! – to learn that one's sister's husband was a drug-fiend; it was another, and much worse thing, to learn from that sister's pallid lips what vileness lay behind the word.

Evelina, unconscious of any distress but her own, sat upright, shivering in Ann Eliza's hold, while she piled up, detail by detail, her dreary narrative.

'The minute we got out there, and he found the job wasn't as good as he expected, he changed. At first I thought he was sick – I used to try to keep him home and nurse him. Then I saw it was something different. He used to go off for hours at a time, and when he came back his eyes kinder had a fog over them. Sometimes he didn't har'ly know me, and when he did he seemed to hate me. Once he hit me here.' She touched her breast. 'Do you remember, Ann Eliza, that time he didn't come to see us for a week – the time after we all went to Central Park together – and you and I thought he must be sick?'

Ann Eliza nodded.

'Well, that was the trouble – he'd been at it then. But nothing like as bad. After we'd been out there about a month he disappeared for a whole week. They took him back at the store, and gave him another chance; but the second time they discharged him, and he drifted round for ever so long before he could get another job. We spent all our money and had to move to a cheaper place. Then he got something to do, but they hardly paid him anything, and he didn't stay there long. When he found out about the baby –'

'The baby?' Ann Eliza faltered.

'It's dead – it only lived a day. When he found out about it, he got mad, and said he hadn't any money to pay doctors' bills, and I'd better write to you to help us. He had an idea you had money hidden away that I didn't know about.' She turned to her sister with remorseful eyes. 'It was him that made me get that hundred dollars out of you.'

'Hush, hush. I always meant it for you anyhow.'

'Yes, but I wouldn't have taken it if he hadn't been at me the whole time. He used to make me do just what he wanted. Well, when I said I wouldn't write to you for more money he said I'd better try and earn some myself. That was when he struck

me. . . . Oh, you don't know what I'm talking about yet! . . .
I tried to get work at a milliner's, but I was so sick I couldn't
stay. I was sick all the time. I wisht I'd ha' died, Ann Eliza.'

'No, no, Evelina.'

'Yes, I do. It kept getting worse and worse. We pawned the
furniture, and they turned us out because we couldn't pay the
rent; and so then we went to board with Mrs Hochmuller.'

Ann Eliza pressed her closer to dissemble her own tremor.
'Mrs Hochmuller?'

'Didn't you know she was out there? She moved out a
month after we did. She wasn't bad to me, and I think she tried
to keep him straight – but Linda –'

'Linda –?'

'Well, when I kep' getting worse, and he was always off, for
days at a time, the doctor had me sent to a hospital.'

'A hospital? Sister – sister!'

'It was better than being with him; and the doctors were
real kind to me. After the baby was born I was very sick and
had to stay there a good while. And one day when I was laying
there Mrs Hochmuller came in as white as a sheet, and told
me him and Linda had gone off together and taken all her
money. That's the last I ever saw of him.' She broke off with
a laugh and began to cough again.

Ann Eliza tried to persuade her to lie down and sleep, but
the rest of her story had to be told before she could be soothed
into consent. After the news of Ramy's flight she had had brain
fever, and had been sent to another hospital where she stayed
a long time – how long she couldn't remember. Dates and days
meant nothing to her in the shapeless ruin of her life. When
she left the hospital she found that Mrs Hochmuller had gone
too. She was penniless, and had no one to turn to. A lady
visitor at the hospital was kind, and found her a place where
she did housework; but she was so weak they couldn't keep
her. Then she got a job as waitress in a down-town lunch-
room, but one day she fainted while she was handing a dish,
and that evening when they paid her they told her she needn't
come again.

'After that I begged in the streets' – (Ann Eliza's grasp again grew tight) – 'and one afternoon last week, when the matinees was coming out, I met a man with a pleasant face, something like Mr Hawkins, and he stopped and asked me what the trouble was. I told him if he'd give me five dollars I'd have money enough to buy a ticket back to New York, and he took a good look at me and said, well, if that was what I wanted he'd go straight to the station with me and give me the five dollars there. So he did – and he bought the ticket, and put me in the cars.'

Evelina sank back, her face a sallow wedge in the white cleft of the pillow. Ann Eliza leaned over her, and for a long time they held each other without speaking.

They were still clasped in this dumb embrace when there was a step in the shop and Ann Eliza, starting up, saw Miss Mellins in the doorway.

'My sakes, Miss Bunner! What in the land are you doing? Miss Evelina – Mrs Ramy – it ain't you?'

Miss Mellins's eyes, bursting from their sockets, sprang from Evelina's pallid face to the disordered supper table and the heap of worn clothes on the floor; then they turned back to Ann Eliza, who had placed herself on the defensive between her sister and the dress-maker.

'My sister Evelina has come back – come back on a visit. she was taken sick in the cars on the way home – I guess she caught cold – so I made her go right to bed as soon as ever she got here.'

Ann Eliza was surprised at the strength and steadiness of her voice. Fortified by its sound she went on, her eyes on Miss Mellins's baffled countenance: 'Mr Ramy has gone west on a trip – a trip connected with his business; and Evelina is going to stay with me till he comes back.'

XII

What measure of belief her explanation of Evelina's return obtained in the small circle of her friends Ann Eliza did not pause to enquire. Though she could not remember ever having told a lie before, she adhered with rigid tenacity to the consequences of her first lapse from truth, and fortified her original statement with additional details whenever a questioner sought to take her unawares.

But other and more serious burdens lay on her startled conscience. For the first time in her life she dimly faced the awful problem of the inutility of self-sacrifice. Hitherto she had never thought of questioning the inherited principles which had guided her life. Self-effacement for the good of others had always seemed to her both natural and necessary; but then she had taken it for granted that it implied the securing of that good. Now she perceived that to refuse the gifts of life does not ensure their transmission to those for whom they have been surrendered; and her familiar heaven was unpeopled. She felt she could no longer trust in the goodness of God, and there was only a black abyss above the roof of Bunner Sisters.

But there was little time to brood upon such problems. The care of Evelina filled Ann Eliza's days and nights. The hastily summoned doctor had pronounced her to be suffering from pneumonia, and under his care the first stress of the disease was relieved. But her recovery was only partial, and long after the doctor's visits had ceased she continued to lie in bed, too weak to move, and seemingly indifferent to everything about her.

At length one evening, about six weeks after her return, she said to her sister: 'I don't feel's if I'd ever get up again.'

Ann Eliza turned from the kettle she was placing on the stove. She was startled by the echo the words woke in her own breast.

'Don't you talk like that, Evelina! I guess you're on'y tired out – and disheartened.'

'Yes, I'm disheartened,' Evelina murmured.

A few months earlier Ann Eliza would have met the confession with a word of pious admonition; now she accepted it in silence.

'Maybe you'll brighten up when your cough gets better,' she suggested.

'Yes – or my cough'll get better when I brighten up,' Evelina retorted with a touch of her old tartness.

'Does your cough keep on hurting you jest as much?'

'I don't see's there's much difference.'

'Well, I guess I'll get the doctor to come round again,' Ann Eliza said, trying for the matter-of-course tone in which one might speak of sending for the plumber or the gas-fitter.

'It ain't any use sending for the doctor – and who's going to pay him?'

'I am,' answered the elder sister. 'Here's your tea, and a mite of toast. Don't that tempt you?'

Already, in the watches of the night, Ann Eliza had been tormented by that same question – who was to pay the doctor? – and a few days before she had temporarily silenced it by borrowing twenty dollars of Miss Mellins. The transaction had cost her one of the bitterest struggles of her life. She had never borrowed a penny of anyone before, and the possibility of having to do so had always been classed in her mind among those shameful extremities to which Providence does not let decent people come. But nowadays she no longer believed in the personal supervision of Providence; and had she been compelled to steal the money instead of borrowing it, she would have felt that her conscience was the only tribunal before which she had to answer. Nevertheless, the actual humiliation of having to ask for the money was no less bitter; and she could hardly hope that Miss Mellins would view the case with the same detachment as herself. Miss Mellins was very kind; but she not unnaturally felt that her kindness should be rewarded by according her the right to ask questions; and bit by bit Ann Eliza saw Evelina's miserable secret slipping into the dress-maker's possession.

When the doctor came she left him alone with Evelina, busying herself in the shop that she might have an opportunity of seeing him alone on his way out. To steady herself she began to sort a trayful of buttons, and when the doctor appeared she was reciting under her breath: 'Twenty-four horn, two and a half cards fancy pearl...' She saw at once that his look was grave.

He sat down on the chair beside the counter, and her mind travelled miles before he spoke.

'Miss Bunner, the best thing you can do is to let me get a bed for your sister at St Luke's.'

'The hospital?'

'Come now, you're above that sort of prejudice, aren't you?' The doctor spoke in the tone of one who coaxes a spoiled child. 'I know how devoted you are – but Mrs Ramy can be much better cared for there than here. You really haven't time to look after her and attend to your business as well. There'll be no expense, you understand –'

Ann Eliza made no answer. 'You think my sister's going to be sick a good while, then?' she asked.

'Well, yes – possibly.'

'You think she's very sick?'

'Well, yes. She's very sick.'

His face had grown still graver; he sat there as though he had never known what it was to hurry.

Ann Eliza continued to separate the pearl and horn buttons. Suddenly she lifted her eyes and looked at him. 'Is she going to die?'

The doctor laid a kindly hand on hers. 'We never say that, Miss Bunner. Human skill works wonders – and at the hospital Mrs Ramy would have every chance.'

'What is it? What's she dying of?'

The doctor hesitated, seeking to substitute a popular phrase for the scientific terminology which rose to his lips.

'I want to know,' Ann Eliza persisted.

'Yes, of course; I understand. Well, your sister has had a hard time lately, and there is a complication of causes, resulting in consumption – rapid consumption. At the hospital –'

'I'll keep her here,' said Ann Eliza quietly.

After the doctor had gone she went on for some time sorting the buttons; then she slipped the tray into its place on a shelf behind the counter and went into the back room. She found Evelina propped upright against the pillows, a flush of agitation on her cheeks. Ann Eliza pulled up the shawl which had slipped from her sister's shoulders.

'How long you've been! What's he been saying?'

'Oh, he went long ago – he on'y stopped to give me a prescription. I was sorting out that tray of buttons. Miss Mellins's girl got them all mixed up.'

She felt Evelina's eyes upon her.

'He must have said something: what was it?'

'Why, he said you'd have to be careful – and stay in bed – and take this new medicine he's given you.'

'Did he say I was going to get well?'

'Why, Evelina!'

'What's the use, Ann Eliza? You can't deceive me. I've just been up to look at myself in the glass; and I saw plenty of 'em in the hospital that looked like me. They didn't get well, and I ain't going to.' Her head dropped back. 'It don't much matter – I'm about tired. On'y there's one thing – Ann Eliza –'

The elder sister drew near to the bed.

'There's one thing I ain't told you. I didn't want to tell you yet because I was afraid you might be sorry – but if he says I'm going to die I've got to say it.' She stopped to cough, and to Ann Eliza it now seemed as though every cough struck a minute from the hours remaining to her.

'Don't talk now – you're tired.'

'I'll be tireder tomorrow, I guess. And I want you should know. Sit down close to me – there.'

Ann Eliza sat down in silence, stroking her shrunken hand.

'I'm a Roman Catholic, Ann Eliza.'

'Evelina – oh, Evelina Bunner! A Roman Catholic – *you?* Oh, Evelina, did *he* make you?'

Evelina shook her head. 'I guess he didn't have no religion; he never spoke of it. But you see Mrs Hochmuller was a Catholic, and so when I was sick she got the doctor to send me to a Roman Catholic hospital, and the sisters was so good to me there – and the priest used to come and talk to me; and the things he said kep' me from going crazy. He seemed to make everything easier.'

'Oh, sister, how could you?' Ann Eliza wailed. She knew little of the Catholic religion except that 'Papists' believed in it – in itself a sufficient indictment. Her spiritual rebellion had not freed her from the formal part of her religious belief, and apostasy had always seemed to her one of the sins from which the pure in mind avert their thoughts.

'And then when the baby was born,' Evelina continued, 'he christened it right away, so it could go to heaven; and after that, you see, I had to be a Catholic.'

'I don't see –'

'Don't I have to be where the baby is? I couldn't ever ha' gone there if I hadn't been made a Catholic. Don't you understand that?'

Ann Eliza sat speechless, drawing her hand away. Once more she found herself shut out of Evelina's heart, an exile from her closest affections.

'I've got to go where the baby is,' Evelina feverishly insisted.

Ann Eliza could think of nothing to say; she could only feel that Evelina was dying, and dying as a stranger in her arms. Ramy and the day-old baby had parted her forever from her sister.

Evelina began again. 'If I get worse I want you to send for a priest. Miss Mellins'll know where to send – she's got an aunt that's a Catholic. Promise me faithful you will.'

'I promise,' said Ann Eliza.

After that they spoke no more of the matter; but Ann Eliza

now understood that the little black bag about her sister's neck, which she had innocently taken for a memento of Ramy, was some kind of sacrilegious amulet, and her fingers shrank from its contact when she bathed and dressed Evelina. It seemed to her the diabolical instrument of their estrangement.

XIII

Spring had really come at last. There were leaves on the ailanthus tree that Evelina could see from her bed, gentle clouds floated over it in the blue, and now and then the cry of a flower-seller sounded from the street.

One day there was a shy knock on the back-room door, and Johnny Hawkins came in with two yellow jonquils in his fist. He was getting bigger and squarer, and his round freckled face was growing into a smaller copy of his father's. He walked up to Evelina and held out the flowers.

'They blew off the cart and the fellow said I could keep 'em. But you can have 'em,' he announced.

Ann Eliza rose from her seat at the sewing-machine and tried to take the flowers from him.

'They ain't for you; they're for her,' he sturdily objected; and Evelina held out her hand for the jonquils.

After Johnny had gone she lay and looked at them without speaking. Ann Eliza, who had gone back to the machine, bent her head over the seam she was stitching; the click, click, click of the machine sounded in her ear like the tick of Ramy's clock, and it seemed to her that life had gone backward, and that Evelina, radiant and foolish, had just come into the room with the yellow flowers in her hand.

When at last she ventured to look up, she saw that her sister's head had drooped against the pillow, and that she was sleeping quietly. Her relaxed hand still held the jonquils, but it was evident that they had awakened no memories; she had dozed off almost as soon as Johnny had given them to her. The discovery gave Ann Eliza a startled sense of the ruins that must be piled upon her past. 'I don't believe I could have forgotten that day, though,' she said to herself. But she was glad that Evelina had forgotten.

Evelina's disease moved on along the usual course, now lifting her on a brief wave of elation, now sinking her to new depths of weakness. There was little to be done, and the doctor came only at lengthening intervals. On his way out he always repeated his first friendly suggestion about sending Evelina to the hospital; and Ann Eliza always answered: 'I guess we can manage.'

The hours passed for her with the fierce rapidity that great joy or anguish lends them. She went through the days with a sternly smiling precision, but she hardly knew what was happening, and when night-fall released her from the shop, and she could carry her work to Evelina's bedside, the same sense of unreality accompanied her, and she still seemed to be accomplishing a task whose object had escaped her memory.

Once, when Evelina felt better, she expressed a desire to make some artificial flowers, and Ann Eliza, deluded by this awakening interest, got out the faded bundles of stems and petals and the little tools and spools of wire. But after a few minutes the work dropped from Evelina's hands and she said: 'I'll wait until tomorrow.'

She never again spoke of the flower-making, but one day, after watching Ann Eliza's laboured attempt to trim a spring hat for Mrs Hawkins, she demanded impatiently that the hat should be brought to her, and in a trice had galvanized the lifeless bow and given the brim the twist it needed.

These were rare gleams; and more frequent were the days of speechless lassitude, when she lay for hours silently staring at the window, shaken only by the hard incessant cough that sounded to Ann Eliza like the hammering of nails into a coffin.

At length one morning Ann Eliza, starting up from the mattress at the foot of the bed, hastily called Miss Mellins down, and ran through the smoky dawn for the doctor. He came back with her and did what he could to give Evelina momentary relief, then he went away, promising to look in again before night. Miss Mellins, her head still covered with curl-papers, disappeared in his wake, and when the sisters were alone Evelina beckoned to Ann Eliza.

'You promised,' she whispered, grasping her sister's arm; and Ann Eliza understood. She had not yet dared to tell Miss Mellins of Evelina's change of faith; it had seemed even more difficult than borrowing the money; but now it had to be done. She ran upstairs after the dress-maker and detained her on the landing.

'Miss Mellins, can you tell me where to send for a priest – a Roman Catholic priest?'

'A priest, Miss Bunner?'

'Yes. My sister became a Roman Catholic while she was away. They were kind to her in her sickness – and now she wants a priest.' Ann Eliza faced Miss Mellins with unflinching eyes.

'My aunt Dugan'll know. I'll run right round to her the minute I get my papers off,' the dress-maker promised; and Ann Eliza thanked her.

An hour or two later the priest appeared. Ann Eliza, who was watching, saw him coming down the steps to the shop-door and went to meet him. His expression was kind, but she shrank from his peculiar dress, and from his pale face with its bluish chin and enigmatic smile. Ann Eliza remained in the shop. Miss Mellins's girl had mixed the buttons again and she set herself to sort them. The priest stayed a long time with Evelina. When he again carried his enigmatic smile past the counter, and Ann Eliza rejoined her sister, Evelina was smiling with something of the same mystery; but she did not tell her secret.

After that it seemed to Ann Eliza that the shop and the back room no longer belonged to her. It was as though she were there on sufferance, indulgently tolerated by the unseen power which hovered over Evelina even in the absence of its minister. The priest came almost daily; and at last a day arrived when he was called to administer some rite of which Ann Eliza but dimly grasped the sacramental meaning. All she knew was that it meant that Evelina was going, and going, under this alien guid-ance, even farther from her than to the dark places of death.

When the priest came, with something covered in his hands,

she crept into the shop, closing the door of the back room to leave him alone with Evelina.

It was a warm afternoon in May, and the crooked ailanthus tree rooted in a fissure of the opposite pavement was a fountain of tender green. Women in light dresses passed with the languid step of spring; and presently there came a man with a hand-cart full of pansy and geranium plants who stopped outside the window, signaling to Ann Eliza to buy.

An hour went by before the door of the back room opened and the priest reappeared with that mysterious covered something in his hands. Ann Eliza had risen, drawing back as he passed. He had doubtless divined her antipathy, for he had hitherto only bowed in going in and out; but to day he paused and looked at her compassionately.

'I have left your sister in a very beautiful state of mind, he said in a low voice like a woman's. 'She is full of spiritual consolation.'

Ann Eliza was silent, and he bowed and went out. She hastened back to Evelina's bed, and knelt down beside it. Evelina's eyes were very large and bright; she turned them on Ann Eliza with a look of inner illumination.

'I shall see the baby,' she said; then her eyelids fell and she dozed.

The doctor came again at nightfall, administering some last palliatives; and after he had gone Ann Eliza, refusing to have her vigil shared by Miss Mellins or Mrs Hawkins, sat down to keep watch alone.

It was a very quiet night. Evelina never spoke or opened her eyes, but in the still hour before dawn Ann Eliza saw that the restless hand outside the bed-clothes had stopped its twitching. She stooped over and felt no breath on her sister's lips.

The funeral took place three days later. Evelina was buried in Calvary Cemetery, the priest assuming the whole care of the necessary arrangements, while Ann Eliza, a passive spectator, beheld with stony indifference this last negation of her past.

A week afterward she stood in her bonnet and mantle in the doorway of the little shop. Its whole aspect had changed.

Counter and shelves were bare, the window was stripped of its familiar miscellany of artificial flowers, note-paper, wire hat-frames, and limp garments from the dyer's; and against the glass pane of the doorway hung a sign: 'This store to let'.

Ann Eliza turned her eyes from the sign as she went out and locked the door behind her. Evelina's funeral had been very expensive, and Ann Eliza, having sold her stock-in-trade and the few articles of furniture that remained to her, was leaving the shop for the last time. She had not been able to buy any mourning, but Miss Mellins had sewed some crape on her old black mantle and bonnet, and having no gloves she slipped her bare hands under the folds of the mantle.

It was a beautiful morning, and the air was full of a warm sunshine that had coaxed open nearly every window in the street, and summoned to the windowsills the sickly plants nurtured indoors in winter. Ann Eliza's way lay westward, toward Broadway; but at the corner she paused and looked back down the familiar length of the street. Her eyes rested a moment on the blotched 'Bunner Sisters' above the empty window of the shop; then they travelled on to the overflowing foliage of the Square, above which was the church tower with the dial that had marked the hours for the sisters before Ann Eliza had bought the nickel clock. She looked at it all as though it had been the scene of some unknown life, of which the vague report had reached her: she felt for herself the only remote pity that busy people accord to the misfortunes which come to them by hearsay.

She walked to Broadway and down to the office of the house-agent to whom she had entrusted the sub-letting of the shop. She left the key with one of his clerks, who took it from her as if it had been anyone of a thousand others, and remarked that the weather looked as if spring was really coming; then she turned and began to move up the great thorough-fare, which was just beginning to wake to its multitudinous activities.

She walked less rapidly now, studying each shop window as she passed, but not with the desultory eye of enjoyment:

the watchful fixity of her gaze overlooked everything but the object of its quest. At length she stopped before a small window wedged between two mammoth buildings, and displaying, behind its shining plate-glass festooned with muslin, a varied assortment of sofa-cushions, tea-cloths, pen-wipers, painted calendars and other specimens of feminine industry. In a corner of the window she had read, on a slip of paper pasted against the pane: 'Wanted, a Saleslady', and after studying the display of fancy articles beneath it, she gave her mantle a twitch, straightened her shoulders and went in.

Behind a counter crowded with pincushions, watch-holders and other needlework trifles, a plump young woman with smooth hair sat sewing bows of ribbon on a scrap basket. The little shop was about the size of the one on which Ann Eliza had just closed the door; and it looked as fresh and gay and thriving as she and Evelina had once dreamed of making Bunner Sisters. The friendly air of the place made her pluck up courage to speak.

'Saleslady? Yes, we do want one. Have you anyone to recommend?' the young woman asked, not unkindly.

Ann Eliza hesitated, disconcerted by the unexpected question; and the other, cocking her head on one side to study the effect of the bow she had just sewed on the basket, continued: 'We can't afford more than thirty dollars a month, but the work is light. She would be expected to do a little fancy sewing between times. We want a bright girl: stylish, and pleasant manners. You know what I mean. Not over thirty, anyhow; and nice-looking. Will you write down the name?'

Ann Eliza looked at her confusedly. She opened her lips to explain, and then, without speaking, turned toward the crisply-curtained door.

'Ain't you going to leave the *ad*-dress?' the young woman called out after her. Ann Eliza went out into the thronged street. The great city, under the fair spring sky, seemed to throb with the stir of innumerable beginnings. She walked on, looking for another shop window with a sign in it.

TITLES IN EVERYMAN'S LIBRARY

R. K. NARAYAN
Swami and Friends
The Bachelor of Arts
The Dark Room
The English Teacher
(in 1 vol.)
Mr Sampath – The Printer of
Malgudi
The Financial Expert
Waiting for the Mahatma
(in 1 vol.)

IRÈNE NÉMIROVSKY
David Golder
The Ball
Snow in Autumn
The Courilof Affair
(in 1 vol.)

FLANN O'BRIEN
The Complete Novels

GEORGE ORWELL
Animal Farm
Nineteen Eighty-Four
Essays

THOMAS PAINE
Rights of Man
and Common Sense

BORIS PASTERNAK
Doctor Zhivago

SYLVIA PLATH
The Bell Jar (US only)

PLATO
The Republic
Symposium and Phaedrus

EDGAR ALLAN POE
The Complete Stories

MARCEL PROUST
In Search of Lost Time
(in 4 vols, UK only)

ALEXANDER PUSHKIN
The Collected Stories

FRANÇOIS RABELAIS
Gargantua and Pantagruel

JOSEPH ROTH
The Radetzky March

JEAN-JACQUES
ROUSSEAU
Confessions
The Social Contract and
the Discourses

SALMAN RUSHDIE
Midnight's Children

JOHN RUSKIN
Praeterita and Dilecta

PAUL SCOTT
The Raj Quartet (2 vols)

WALTER SCOTT
Rob Roy

WILLIAM SHAKESPEARE
Comedies Vols 1 and 2
Histories Vols 1 and 2
Romances
Sonnets and Narrative Poems
Tragedies Vols 1 and 2

MARY SHELLEY
Frankenstein

ADAM SMITH
The Wealth of Nations

ALEXANDER SOLZHENITSYN
One Day in the Life of
Ivan Denisovich

SOPHOCLES
The Theban Plays

MURIEL SPARK
The Prime of Miss Jean Brodie,
The Girls of Slender Means, The
Driver's Seat, The Only Problem
(in 1 vol.)

CHRISTINA STEAD
The Man Who Loved Children

JOHN STEINBECK
The Grapes of Wrath

STENDHAL
The Charterhouse of Parma
Scarlet and Black

LAURENCE STERNE
Tristram Shandy

ROBERT LOUIS STEVENSON
The Master of Ballantrae and
Weir of Hermiston
Dr Jekyll and Mr Hyde
and Other Stories

HARRIET BEECHER STOWE
Uncle Tom's Cabin

ITALO SVEVO
Zeno's Conscience

This book is set in BEMBO which was cut
by the punch-cutter Francesco Griffo
for the Venetian printer-publisher
Aldus Manutius in early 1495
and first used in a pamphlet
by a young scholar
named Pietro
Bembo.